THE HOUSE OF LOVE AND DREAMS

LAUREN WESTWOOD

Boldwood

First published in 2018 as *Finding Dreams*. This edition published in Great Britain in 2025 by Boldwood Books Ltd.

Copyright © Lauren Westwood, 2018

Cover Design by Emma Graves Design

Cover Images: Shutterstock and iStock

The moral right of Lauren Westwood to be identified as the author of this work has been asserted in accordance with the Copyright, Designs and Patents Act 1988.

All rights reserved. No part of this book may be reproduced in any form or by any electronic or mechanical means, including information storage and retrieval systems, without written permission from the author, except for the use of brief quotations in a book review. This book is a work of fiction and, except in the case of historical fact, any resemblance to actual persons, living or dead, is purely coincidental.

Every effort has been made to obtain the necessary permissions with reference to copyright material, both illustrative and quoted. We apologise for any omissions in this respect and will be pleased to make the appropriate acknowledgements in any future edition.

A CIP catalogue record for this book is available from the British Library.

Paperback ISBN 978-1-83678-017-5

Large Print ISBN 978-1-83678-018-2

Hardback ISBN 978-1-83678-016-8

Ebook ISBN 978-1-83678-019-9

Kindle ISBN 978-1-83678-020-5

Audio CD ISBN 978-1-83678-011-3

MP3 CD ISBN 978-1-83678-012-0

Digital audio download ISBN 978-1-83678-015-1

This book is printed on certified sustainable paper. Boldwood Books is dedicated to putting sustainability at the heart of our business. For more information please visit https://www.boldwoodbooks.com/about-us/sustainability/

Boldwood Books Ltd, 23 Bowerdean Street, London, SW6 3TN

www.boldwoodbooks.com

For Eve, Rose and Grace, with love

I've dreamt in my life dreams that have stayed with me ever after, and changed my ideas: they've gone through and through me, like wine through water, and altered the colour of my mind.

— EMILY BRONTË, *WUTHERING HEIGHTS*

PROLOGUE
MARCH

When Death came to Tanglewild, I was at the supermarket. I'd just dropped Katie off at ballet and had fifteen minutes before I was due to pick up Jack from Little Kickers. Just enough time to nip into Tesco and grab some loo roll, night pull-ups, a tin of dog food, and a bottle of Rioja, and dig through my handbag for my Clubcard while the checkout assistant scanned my items.

My mobile rang – 'Dave', my husband's name, flashed on screen.

'Hi,' I said, answering breathlessly, slinging up my bag-for-life to start packing.

'Mrs Greene?'

Instantly, my stomach clenched. Not Dave, but Allison, Dave's new PA. Blonde, young, a body untrammelled by pregnancies, time on her hands to meet friends after work without having to help with homework or drive Mum's Taxi. In other words, I hate her.

'Hi there, Allison,' I said. 'Why are you calling from Dave's phone?'

'Oh, Lizzie... I don't know how to say this...'

I picked up the bottle of Rioja, checking to make sure it was at least 13 per cent. An awful little fantasy popped into my head. Allison and Dave at the airport running away together, leaving me with two young kids, a fat old dog, and a big mortgage. But no... I laughed at my own groundless worries. Dave would never do that. He's a good husband and a good father. And besides, Dave lacks... imagination.

So why is she calling from his phone?

'What is it, Allison?'

'It's Dave. I'm afraid he's... um... God, I'm so sorry.'

My life flashed before my eyes. Working day and night in my twenties to build a career as a lawyer. Meeting Dave, getting married, moving out of London, giving up said career to become a mum. And it was totally worth it. There have been so many good times: holidays abroad, birthday parties, cycling to the pub, winter evenings by the fire. Dave and I have things in common. We're focused on the family and each other, and we both love our quirky old house, Tanglewild. We're living the dream...

OK, admittedly we've been going through a rough patch lately. Me always complaining about the kids and dithering about whether I should go back to work. Him working all hours at the law firm, or else sitting idle, worrying about his billables target for the year. My halcyon twenties slipped away long ago, and now, at thirty-seven, I'm on a collision course with my forties like a hurtling fast train. The house is a mess, our sex life non-existent, our days chaotic. Sometimes I don't recognise the people we've become. But still – we're happy.

'We're happy,' I heard myself saying to the checkout woman, brandishing the bottle for emphasis. Her bored look morphed into one of 'possible looney in the shop'; she glanced sideways at the security guard near the self-checkout.

'Look,' I said to Allison, 'put Dave on the phone. Whatever he has to say, he can say it to my face. I'm not letting him off that easily.'

'I can't put him on the phone,' Allison said.

'Why the hell not!' From the corner of my eye, I spotted a manager on his way towards me.

'I found him slumped over his desk. I checked his pulse and called the paramedic. But it was too late.'

It was like I'd slammed into a wall – an unstoppable force hitting an immovable object. 'What?' The word gurgled out of my throat. 'You mean... he's—'

But I didn't hear her reply. I held the phone away from my ear. My hand opened and the wine bottle crashed to the floor, shattering into a million pieces.

And as the manager arrived with the in-store cleaner, I collapsed against my bag-for-life and my whole body began to shake. With the shock of my life as I knew it coming to an end, and the sheering of my heart as it cracked in two.

PART I

Et in Arcadia ego

PART I

Et in Arcadia ego.

1

PROLOGUE, THE LADY'S SECRET BY PHILLIPA KING

West Sussex 1790

The river shimmered green in the sunlight, the remains of the picnic cast aside. She leaned back on her elbows and looked up at the spreading branches of the willow tree above and the place on the trunk where Tom had carved their initials with the apple knife. Her eyelids grew heavy from the wine and the summer heat.

Beside her, Tom knelt down and picked a long-stemmed daisy, twining the stem into a knot. 'Won't be long now, my sweet. Next week I come of age and we can be married straight away. But until then, accept this as a token of my feelings.' He reached for her hand and slipped the daisy ring onto her finger. 'Till death do us part.'

Victoria laughed merrily. 'Oh, go on then – one kiss. As an early birthday present.'

'One kiss?' He leaned over her, his breath hot on her face. 'That's not what you promised.'

She laughed again, then kissed her finger and planted it on his cheek. 'I was joking. We can't. And besides, it's only a week.'

'Then it won't matter, will it?' His hand crept up under her skirt and touched the bare flesh above her stocking as he swung on top of her.

She gasped as a thousand emotions flooded her mind – desire... yes. But surely it was wrong not to wait.

'Tom,' she said, 'I think we should...'

'Shh,' he said, silencing her words with a kiss and a lopsided smile. 'You did promise, my love.'

2

JANUARY – TEN MONTHS LATER

On the scale of human tragedies, 'Sussex mum loses husband' is a drop in the ocean. It's not like I've been forced to leave the country due to war or disease or famine. I don't have to live with the guilt of suicide or the drain of terminal illness. I haven't even suffered the shame of having my husband run off with a toned and tanned 'other woman' many years my junior to start a new life. Dave was a good husband and a good father, but he lacked imagination. He had a weak heart that gave out suddenly and unexpectedly. Ashes to ashes, dust to dust...

Even now, I can hear the voice of the priest intoning these futile words as the coffin was lowered into the earth. They screamed in my head like fingernails scratching across a blackboard, and I felt like they might pull me down with him. Why hadn't Dave given instructions to be cremated? Why would he want to be buried in a wooden box in the ground? That little detail became the hook, the outlet for my grief. It seemed so pointless – so bloody cold – to lie there forever in the dank darkness, all alone except for the bugs and worms. It seemed *so* bloody Dave.

A light coating of frost covers the ground as I pull into the car park of Westbury Junior School. The sky is heavy and overcast, and spring feels very far away. The heater in the car is going full tilt, but I can't stop shivering. Not with the cold, but with the decision I made last night, lying in bed sleepless and alone. I can't put off any longer the thing I've been dreading. I have to do it today.

As I look round for a space, I practise deep breathing like the grief books say to do – trying to find a moment of stillness and inner peace. Life has definitely thrown me lemons, but when that happens, aren't you supposed to 'make lemonade'?

Jamming on the brakes, I narrowly miss being mown down by a Range Rover reversing into a compact car space.

'Jeez, Mum,' Katie grumbles. 'You're such a bad driver.'

'Thanks.' I swallow back what I really feel like saying to my nine-going-on-nineteen-year-old daughter. She's having a hard time right now with having lost her dad and the pressures of Year 4, but for some reason, I've become the focus of her issues. Most of the time, she acts like I'm Colonel Mustard in the library with the lead pipe, solely responsible for how bad she's feeling. Though I try my best to shield the kids from my own worries, they aren't stupid. Once or twice, Katie's found me crying my eyes out. I want her to believe that I'm upset only because I miss her dad – her loveable, squeezable, just-a-little-dull dad – rather than the *real* reason.

I find a space in the far corner of the car park. Katie unloads her rucksack; when I try to hand her her coat, she looks at me like I'm an alien life force. With a sigh, I get out of the car and go round to unbuckle Jack from his car seat.

'Luv you, Mummy,' he says, smearing a sticky hand on my jumper.

'Me too, pumpkin.' I lift him out. His trousers are soaking wet. While my love for him in no way diminishes, it blurs right out of focus. 'Jack!' I say. 'You went to the potty before we left!'

His plump little face screws up and all of a sudden he starts to howl.

Katie rolls her eyes. 'I'm going in, Mum,' she says. 'This is just *so* embarrassing.' She pokes Jack in the arm. 'You're a BIG FAT CRY BABY!'

'Am not!' he cries.

'Katie!' I yell, but she's already run off, weaving her way between two SUVs that are poised like bellowing bulls waiting for a parking space. I lay Jack down in the driver's seat and pull off his welly boots, his wee-soaked socks, trousers and Disney *Cars* so-called absorbent pants, noting that somehow, he's also managed to get wee on his T-shirt and coat. I strip him down, my jaw clenched as he kicks at me and yells, 'Katie's mean.'

'You're a big boy,' I say, the lie tripping easily off my tongue. 'Three years old! So just ignore her. Now, let's get dressed and go to nursery.'

I manage to wriggle him into a set of spare clothing, clean everything off with a baby wipe, and bundle him into his coat and woolly hat. When I lead him across the car park by the hand, he screams for a 'cuggle'. I give in and pick him up. Ten months on from Dave's death, and I'm surviving by taking the path of least resistance. Besides, if I carry him, he'll serve as a kind of human shield from some rogue mum who might try and ask me how I'm doing.

For the first few weeks after Dave died, everyone was sympathetic and helpful. I'd pull into the car park in my dirty blue Passat Estate, with my rumpled, tear-streaked children, and be bombarded with kindness as I walked them to the gate. The hands on the arm, the 'I'm *so* sorry for your loss's, the smothering hugs from people whose names I didn't know. The worried looks from the teachers, the offers of lifts for the kids and extra after-school playdates. While all of it was thoughtful and well meant, if anything, it made the grief even more overwhelming.

I couldn't sleep or eat. Familiar things became wicked little pins scratching and pricking at my heart. Telling the kids had been the hardest. Jack's understanding was limited: he wanted to know why Daddy wasn't around to kick a ball round the garden and put on a DVD. Katie shut herself away in her own airless, impenetrable shell, and I couldn't begin to reach her.

In those early days, I tried to go on as normal – shopping online, cooking the kids' favourite meals, tidying up, throwing the ball for Jammie Dodger, our aged Siberian Husky. But nothing cut through the smothering, stifling sense of loss. I was living one of those nightmares where you're running for your life but every step is like wading through quicksand, and try as you might, you can't escape.

Dave was buried; his older brother organised a memorial service. I was present and accounted for. My mum came for the service and to help with the kids, but she'd never liked Dave and it felt like she was blaming him for departing. In truth, it was a relief when she went home to her retirement community in Spain and the rest of the mourners trickled away. By then, the quicksand was over my head and I'd stopped struggling; I let it seep into my lungs and prepared to suffocate.

But something happened that yanked me out of the quicksand for good. Just after the funeral, I got a call from Dave's solicitor inviting me in for a meeting. I was mildly surprised that Dave even had a solicitor – we'd had someone do the conveyancing on the house and made a will when the children were born, but that was about it.

It felt very Dickensian to enter the lawyer's office in the nearby town, housed in a three-storey Georgian townhouse. The solicitor, Mr Keswick, was a balding man in his early sixties, well-groomed in a smart pinstriped suit. He was joined by an equally fastidious PA, a hawk-nosed woman in her fifties wearing a neat cashmere twin set. The pair made me hyperconscious of the dog hair on my jumper and the mud on the cuffs of my jeans. They sat at opposite ends of the table, making it impossible for me to look at both of them at once.

'Mrs Greene, I'm very sorry for your loss.' The lawyer's voice was grave and sympathetic, but there was something in the way he kept twisting the cap on his fountain pen that made me ill at ease. 'These things are never easy, and it's all well and good what they say – that time heals. It does, but it takes... time, doesn't it?'

I looked at him, unsure whether he had just tried to make a joke.

The PA nodded, scribbling away on a notepad in an incoherent cipher. (Was she actually transcribing the chit-chat?)

'And in the meantime, there are so many things to sort out. It's the little things that are difficult, I'm told. Things that seemed so easy before.' He set down his pen and steepled his fingers. 'Never mind the big things.'

'I guess so.' I could feel the numbness start to creep in.

'Which is why I hate to be the bearer of even more bad news.'

'What was that?' I sat forward, alert.

'Mrs Greene, I'll cut to the chase. There are some *issues* with your husband's estate. If you'd like to retain your own counsel, I'm more than happy to go over the details with him... or her. But as you're a lawyer too, I wanted to give you the overview in person.'

'The overview of what? Dave and I are married. We own the house together. We have a joint account. We...' I felt a strong urge to explain our marriage to this man. The good times, the bad times. The things that were part of day-to-day life and now were no more. 'We're normal,' was all I could manage.

'Your husband had some other assets and liabilities that you may not have been aware of. We received a box of papers from his place of work. Unfortunately, it appears that his overall financial situation was... shall we say... precarious.'

'Precarious?' I'd assumed my being here was a formality. Signing papers to close out the estate, or appoint the firm as executor. I may have been a lawyer once, but I did corporate work, not family law. I knew nothing about this sort of thing.

'Here.' He slid a spreadsheet across the table to me. 'Let me talk you through it.'

Two hours later, I was still sitting there. My wall of grief was riddled with holes, cracked through and broken down for good. The man's voice droned in my head. Telling me that my loveable, squeezable, just-a-little-dull Dave wasn't what he seemed. He'd had a bolthole flat in London; he'd put a second mortgage on our house. Run up debts at casinos and sordid little clubs on those nights when he was supposedly 'working late'. The PA brought a box of things from Dave's office. Receipts for expensive dinners and gifts for lady 'friends'; unpaid bills... Every object, every word, a knife blade in my stomach.

The details washed over me. Dave had let his life insurance lapse; he hadn't bothered with mortgage insurance. Dave had maxed out six credit cards. Dave had siphoned all the money out of our retirement account. Dave had left his family destitute.

Eventually, the solicitor stopped talking. The PA stopped scribbling and looked up at me. 'Cup of tea?'

I stood up and ran from the room. I felt dirty, violated. The place inside where the grief had lived only hours before was now flooded by a tide of searing-hot rage. Dave was dead – I'd never have the chance to confront him, accuse him, hold him accountable. He'd ruined my present with his death, my future with his shenanigans, and worst of all, he'd utterly destroyed my happy memories of the past.

In the months that followed, my rage vented itself like tiny blasts of steam from a geyser. Honking other vehicles in the car park, not bothering to check Katie's homework, letting Jack writhe in a tantrum on the floor of the supermarket. The sympathetic looks at the school gates turned wary; whispered conversations stopped when I came into view. Somehow, I was dropped from the class email lists – no one felt they could remind me to pay £30 towards the teachers' end-of-year gifts or volunteer for a slot to run a stall at the summer fete. Even Jammie, with her greying muzzle and deep, all-knowing eyes, started keeping her distance from me.

When I was called in to see the headmaster because Katie had quit book club and choir, and Jack had regressed in his potty training, I told him point blank that it was his job to sort it. I felt like a recalcitrant suspect in a dark and sordid police investigation – I had a duty to confess my problems and reassure the school that I was coping. Instead, I was determined to keep silent and hoard the anger and betrayal to myself. The school promised to help, but I left that meeting feeling ashamed of myself. I might not have known my husband, but I hated this person I'd become.

Finally, my friend Hannah took me aside. She's the grandma of Flora, one of Katie's school friends, and we sometimes alternated doing school pickups. One afternoon, when I dropped Flora off at her house, she put on a DVD for the kids and frogmarched me into her kitchen. She put a cup of sweet tea and a plate of lemon cake in front of me and told me to start talking.

The cup rattled on the saucer as everything came out in a torrent. The debts, the shag pad, the women. I watched her reaction mirror my own: shock, then anger, and finally, that thing that was so unbearable – sympathy. I told her not to say 'sorry' – that weak, futile word. I told her not to ask me if I was doing 'OK'. I wasn't – so please don't ask.

Ever.

Finally, I burst into tears.

'Lizzie,' Hannah had said, 'it's all just awful. But you need to hang on for the kids' sake. Take things one day at a time.'

'I know,' I'd said. 'I just feel so betrayed. I keep asking myself whether deep down I *knew* what was going on. When I got the call from Dave's PA, my mind had leapt dangerously close to the truth. But I dismissed the possibility that my husband was anything other than what he seemed. Because that's how I needed him to be.'

'The thing is, Lizzie,' she said, 'none of that really matters now. He's gone, and it's the future you need to focus on.'

'The future?' I half-choked on a bite of lemon cake (third slice). The concept sounded so alien, so distant. So utterly frightening.

'Things have a way of working out the way they're meant to,' she said. 'You have to give it time. You've got two lovely children, and you want the best for them. If you don't want them to give up, then you can't either.'

I cried some more; she'd given me a hug. Opening up to her *had* helped a little. I was still sinking in a black, bottomless pool. But for the first time since that fateful night at Tesco, I felt a little twinge of muscle memory – like someday, I might remember how to swim.

* * *

Today, ten months on from Dave's death, Jack the Human Shield successfully fends off any would-be well-wishers. I take him to the nursery (relieved that his potty problems are now *their* problem for a few hours). He screams and clings to my leg, throws his hat on the floor, and refuses to take off his coat. I feel the familiar guilt seep into my heart and the little voice in my head crooning 'Bad mum, bad mum...'

On my way out, I say a passing hello to a few other mums, almost wishing that someone would stop and chat. Anything to delay what I've decided to do this morning. I was hoping to see Hannah and beg her to talk me out of it. Tell me again that these things take time; that I should give it a little more time...

Time. I add another day to my mental checklist. Ten months since Dave's death, nine and a half months since the funeral, eight months since the meeting with the lawyer. Six months since the longest summer of my life, one month since the unmerriest Christmas ever, and two months to go until the anniversary of Dave's death. So many seconds, minutes, hours passing, and yet each day when I wake up, the nightmare begins all over again. I never know which emotion will rise to the surface, just that most of them are painful and ugly. And underneath everything, the anger flows like an underground river. Maybe that's the thing that's kept me going day after day. On the scale of human tragedies, 'Sussex mum discovers her whole life was a lie' may be infinitesimal.

But damn it, it's *my* tragedy.

I've learned to put on a brave face. I cry behind closed doors and curse into an empty closet. I make up dialogues about what I'd like to say to Dave and play them out in front of the dog. I smile even though it hurts. I try to be there for the kids and go through the motions of being the loving mother they deserve. I've lied and told them that I'm fine – that everything will be fine for us.

All in all, I've hung on by my fingernails, bleeding and bruised, but I've managed to keep hanging on...

Setting my mouth in a thin line, I get in the car and join the queue to leave the car park. Instead of turning towards home, I go down the hill towards the village high street. As much as I never hoped this day would come, I have to accept the fact that I've hung on long enough.

Now, it's time to start letting go.

3

'So, it's a semi, is that right?'

I swallow hard. Am I speaking Martian? Because this man – with his pinstriped suit and stick-up gelled hair – is not understanding what I'm saying. Around me, three other estate agents are at their desks talking on the phone, and a nervous-looking couple is sitting in a small waiting area flanked by potted palms. The office is so clean; so white. I suppose most people who come here are looking for a blank canvas. A new start. I'd like a new start too, but I just wish it could be in my own home. Tanglewild: the quirky old house I fell in love with when I first viewed it with Dave eight years ago. I knew immediately that I wanted to raise my kids in that house, and I was amazed that we could afford to buy it. Now, I'm going to lose it.

'No, it's not...' I try again. 'The original Tudor manor house was built in 1602. But in 1908, the old servants' annex was partitioned off into a separate residence. The other house has its own drive and is completely separate.'

'So your house shares a wall with another house?'

'Yes, but...'

SEMI. He writes the word in capital letters on the form.

'OK.' I sigh.

'And how many acres are there?'

'Twelve. But two acres are the lake. And two acres are in the middle of the land that belongs to the other house. So there's no access. It's complicated.'

'Lake,' he repeats. 'No access.' He makes another note on the pad: *Problem Property?*

I can't bear it. The facts and figures don't tell the whole story – or even close. They can't convey the beauty of Tanglewild: its original features, the things it's seen, the things it's survived. Nor do they tell the story of the people who've lived there over the years – people like me and my family. In the last ten months, I've clung to the hope that I wouldn't have to uproot my children from the only home they've ever known. I should have known, however, that in the absence of a miracle, this day would come.

'So when can you come and do the valuation?' I say. 'I need to get it on the market as soon as possible.'

'Overstretched yourself on the mortgage, did you?' My estate agent smiles, white-toothed and wolfish.

'Actually, it was my husband.' I decide to wipe the smarmy grin off his face. 'Dave had debts, a bolthole in London, credit card bills up to here.' I tap my forehead. 'All those nights "working late".' I wiggle exaggerated air quotes. 'Getting up to what men *do*. And then he died.'

The word echoes off the white walls and smooth, polished floor. I feel a tiny stab of satisfaction when my estate agent starts to splutter that he's 'sorry for my loss', then asks me instead if I'm 'doing OK'. The other agents pause in their conversations; the nervous couple look ready to stand up and bolt.

'I'm not sorry, and I'm not OK.' I address everyone. 'I can't keep up with the mortgage payments, I can't find a job, and I have two kids to support. And as you've already noted' – I point to the paper in front of my agent – 'my home is a *problem property* and might take a while to sell. I need to sell it; there's no other choice. So when can you come round and do the valuation?'

'Um, how about on Friday?'

'See you then.'

The sense of relief is palpable as I get up from the chair and walk to the door. I'm out of there so fast that I almost convince myself that this is just another part of the nightmare, and any second now I'm going to wake up.

* * *

Back on the high street, I collapse against the wall of the family butcher and try to keep from hyperventilating. I must 'keep calm and carry on' – words that look good on a mug or a tote bag but are tosh in real life. I did what I had to do, end of story.

On my way home, I drive to the big supermarket at the edge of the village and stock up on baked beans, tuna, potatoes, soup, and the mini chocolates that make good homework bribes. In the pet food aisle, I blanch at the cost of the senior dog food tins – Jammie's favourite brand is never on special. I put a few tins in the trolley and take out the bottle of bubble bath I'd put in as a treat to myself, planning to leave it there among the kibble (but then feel guilty and go all the way back across the store to put it back on the proper shelf). In the old days, I used to fill up an entire jumbo-sized trolley every week without worrying about credit card balances or e-vouchers. Those days are gone, and maybe that's a good thing. Life was too soft then, and it might be too hard now, but there must be a happy medium somewhere. I have to keep looking.

* * *

The traffic has subsided by the time I drive back through the village. Just past the train station, there's a gravel road that twists on for a quarter mile, past two barn conversions and the entrance to the old servants' annex. At the end of the road, I drive through a pair of large wrought-iron gates, the paint flecked and flaking off the twists of metal. The gateway to Tanglewild. My home.

Through the gates, there's a carport with a wonky tiled roof that was once part of the old stables. I squeeze the car in between an overflowing pile of firewood and a pile of old junk and tools. Outside, I breathe in the smell of old wood, damp soil, and decaying leaves. It smells homely and familiar. As I'm unloading my shopping, Jammie ambles up to the arched gate in the high stone wall that surrounds the house and the front garden, her tail wagging slowly.

'Hi, girl,' I say. 'I've brought breakfast.'

I carry the bags inside the gate and set them down, kneeling next to the dog and burying my face in her thick silver-grey fur. Aching with regret, I look at the house, trying to take in every detail like I'm seeing it for the first time – or the last.

The oldest part of the house is Elizabethan, red brick on the bottom and wattle and daub on the top. Three twisted brick chimneys rise from the roof, and the windows have hundreds of diamond-shaped panes. A high stone wall separates our house from the servants' annex, and from the front you'd never know that the building shares a wall with another residence. I suppose the fact that it's a 'problem property' on paper is the only reason Dave and I could afford to buy it.

Although the frost is gone from the lawn, the tile roof is white with a thin coat of ice. I can only afford to heat the house for two hours a day – at breakfast and teatime. The windows are single glazed, and the house is cold even in the height of summer.

'You're lucky to have such lovely warm fur,' I say, shivering. Jammie thumps her tail. Dave never used to allow the dog in the house, but since the onset of winter, I've let her come inside – I love it when she lies on my feet and keeps them warm.

I pick up the bags to go inside. I'm expecting Jammie to follow, but instead she goes off towards the left side of the house where there's another gate in the stone wall, and beyond that, the old kitchen garden, a rose garden, and then the lake. Her gait is awkward and arthritic. As I watch her go, I catch sight of the peaked roof of the old dovecote, which sits at the far tip of the lake. The little building might have been quaint at one time, but now it's fallen to ruin. When we moved in, the estate agent told us that years ago someone drowned in the lake. I don't know the details, but the place gives me the creeps. Dave and I had vague plans to fix it up to use as a studio or an office, but it never happened. He did, however, put a brand new lock on the door so that the kids couldn't go there exploring and end up getting hurt.

Soon, the whole thing will be someone else's problem. Some other family will buy Tanglewild. They'll get used to the house's quirks and rough edges, the bone-chilling cold and the fickle plumbing. They'll arrive with their own things and make their own memories here. Our memories will be little more than names on a deed of sale and clutter thrown haphazardly into a removals lorry. Sad little cardboard crates to be unpacked in another house somewhere, where my family will start our own new life...

Tears sting my eyes as I open the front door, trying to memorise every detail. The door is made of ancient oak timbers that came from old ships. When the house was built, the lake was actually a wide bend in an unnamed tributary of the River Arun and regularly navigated by boats. Now, though, the flow of the river is only a trickle in and out of the lake through a small weir.

Inside, the house is silent and freezing. There's a small alcove where we keep our coats and shoes and beyond that the so-called great hall. Small but perfectly formed, the room is two stories high, the walls covered halfway up with dark oak panelling, the ceiling an intricate pattern of ribbed plaster in the Jacobean style. At the centre of one wall is a huge brick fireplace almost as tall as I am. Opposite the fireplace, a carved wooden staircase goes up to a small minstrel's gallery and the two wings on either side that make up the first floor. When we bought the house, Dave and I lacked the money and wherewithal to update the décor, so it's just as well that the previous owners left behind their heavy damask curtains, now dusty and moth-eaten, but our best defence against the cold.

When I step into the room, there's a snap underfoot. The plastic Power Ranger Dino Supercharge action figure is apparently strong enough to face intergalactic monsters and save the world – but not strong enough to withstand an air assault from my trainer. His arm is snapped off, and I toss him onto the old sofa by the window, his fall broken by a pile of laundry and some of Katie's music books scattered next to the piano.

Maybe I've stopped appreciating the house. It's hard to see past the kids' clutter, the muddy shoes, the dog hair, the untidy toys. Over time, I've forgotten to look at the beauty and craftsmanship, the sheer age of everything around me. I have a pet theory that the house's original features have survived intact because it's always been a family home: inhabited by stressed-out mums, hard-working dads, and messy kids, with everyone too busy to notice the décor. Now, though, I wish I'd tried a *lot* harder.

I take the shopping to the kitchen and put the kettle on. The kitchen is a vast open space with dark wood panelling, a long oak refectory table, and a row of tired units along one side. When Katie first started at the junior school, I went along to a couple of coffee mornings hosted by other mums. I remember gaping at the pristine units, shiny work surfaces, comfortably warm Agas, and the *de rigueur* island breakfast bars, and feeling like a jealous, green-eyed monster. At the time, I could have killed for new appliances, underfloor heating, and a double-wide refrigerator. Back then, those things mattered to me.

I'm ashamed of how entitled and materialistic I was in those days. Now I'm grateful for the roof over our heads and the kitchen that, for the most part, functions. I'm glad that, for however short a time, we still have this special old house. It may be cluttered and shabby and a money pit. It may be a 'problem property' in the eyes of some slick estate agent. But Tanglewild is my home and I don't want to lose it.

I sit in front of the cold fireplace with a cup of tea. Even if I get the house on the market this week, the estate agent told me not to expect a quick sale. Secretly, I'm glad of it. There's still time to save my home. Still time for a miracle to happen.

4

It's a miracle that the printer in the study even works. It groans and wheezes the paper out line by line, streaked with toner from the nearly empty cartridge:

> Lizzie Greene
> British; Age 37
>
> Position sought: A challenging part-time role as a company solicitor in the West Sussex or London area, with good opportunities for advancement.
>
> Summary of experience: Seven years as a corporate solicitor at a top London City firm, followed by a career break.

I reread the words that are the job-market equivalent of a death warrant: *part-time; career break*. Words that don't convey the person I want to be. I glance up at the family photos on the wall behind the desk. I've kept the photos of Dave up for the kids' sake, but also to remind me of the dangers of giving away my heart to another person – not something I'm planning to do again. In the last family photo, taken by my mum in Spain,

Dave has a cocky grin on his face, Jack is sticking out his tongue, and Katie is doing her serious model face. I look flustered, my blonde hair blown every which way by the wind. But I look happy – and I was. (We'd just had a nice lunch with a big pitcher of sangria, I recall.)

A cloud goes across the sun and the room grows darker; I can see my own hazy reflection in the glass frame. On the surface, I haven't changed that much. My hair needs a trim, my face looks a bit paler and thinner – wiser. I'm still intelligent, driven, and determined to do the best I can. But I don't recognise the expression in my eyes. There's no trace of the me who used to laugh a lot, used to have friends, used to enjoy life. Is she gone forever, or simply hibernating?

I read through the rest of the CV to make sure I've captured the positives. If Dave were here, he would tell me to 'sell my strengths' and 'downplay the negatives'. He would have told me to 'make yourself look good on paper', and 'save the bad stuff for the interview'. Probably, he would just advise me to lie. But I can't do that. It's one thing making my kids happy by telling them that Santa Claus is real, Daddy's an angel looking down on them from heaven, and of course they won't have to move house. But it's against everything I believe in to lie on a CV, and I'm sure people would see right through it.

I email the CV off in response to three new job adverts in *The Lawyer*. Tomorrow, I'll bite the bullet and phone some recruiters. Listen to their platitudes: 'I'm so sorry for your loss. You've been through a lot. Unfortunately, it's not a good market for lawyers in your field right now. We don't have anything on our books that seems quite right for you. But of course, we'll keep you on file. No, you don't have to call again. We'll call you.'

I've been applying for jobs for two months now, and although I've had two interviews, I've been passed over in favour of candidates with 'more recent experience'. When Dave was alive and I talked about going back to work, he'd convinced me that I didn't need the stress, the childcare issues, the commute. Now, I realise that it was easier for him to lead his double life if I was at home in the suburbs with the kids.

Despite the logistics, I focus on how much I'd welcome the mental stimulation and conversations about something other than Huggies vs Pampers, gymnastic classes, drama exams, and quantities of wine consumed on weekday nights. I'd welcome the confidence I'd regain from being a valued member of society again. (Rightly or wrongly, an unemployed mum of two does not rank high on the scale of social utility.) Confidence I lost the moment I learned that the man I married turned out to be a liar, a cheat, and a profligate.

Most of all, though, I need the money. At the far corner of the desk, there's a stack of unopened bills that have been accumulating from just after Christmas. Each day, the pile gets a little bigger, and I sink a little deeper into the hole.

It's been that way ever since the meeting at the lawyer's office. The bottom line is this: while I wasn't responsible to pay the credit card debts, or the lease on the London flat, I'm responsible for the mortgage repayments on the house. In the months after Dave's death, I phoned every creditor, had regular visits with the bank manager, contacted debt consolidators, begged free advice off lawyer acquaintances. I liquidated my pension, borrowed money from my mum to buy the kids a few gifts for their birthdays and Christmas. But despite my efforts, it wasn't enough. At this point, no amount of paying instalments, paying half of a bill, conveniently 'losing' a bill on my desk, or anything else is making any difference.

I pick up the stack of unopened mail and flip through it. At the bottom of the pile is a plain envelope without a postmark addressed 'to the resident' – probably some kind of political circular that someone dropped off in person at the house. I'm about to put it in the bin unopened when a notice from eBay flashes up on my screen with a little bell sound. 'You've sold your Phase Eight striped jersey dress size ten.' I toss the envelope aside and jiggle the mouse to wake up the computer. I may be broke and on the cusp of losing our family home, but my eBay empire has provided a welcome trickle of funds. I started out by flogging all of Dave's suits, along with his golf clubs, his skis, his books, his shoes, his cufflinks (and even a lacy women's nightdress I found in his briefcase). Dave's stuff made a few hundred quid, so when that was gone, I listed all my clothes from my lawyer days – suits and dresses, cashmere cardigans, high-heeled shoes – anything associated with the woman I had once been.

Clicking on the link, I open the listing. The dress that I once paid eighty-five quid for has sold for eight pounds plus shipping. It's barely worth the trip to the post office, and yet it all adds up. As I write down the buyer's address on the tag, I calculate that I've now got enough to buy the 'worn once' Hermione costume that Katie wants for World Book Day. Small victories.

'Mummy!' a high voice cries from outside the door. The dog howls and whines in excitement. I've lost track of time; Katie and Jack are home from school already. I shut the lid of the laptop and go to greet them. *Small victories*. I've almost made it through another day.

* * *

'Mummy!' When I open the door, Jack bursts into tears.

I scoop him into my arms. 'How's my big boy?' I say.

'Katie hit me!' He sticks out his tongue at his sister. Katie is standing at the doorway with her arms crossed and *that* look on her face. The one that means it's going to be a long, difficult evening chivvying her to do her homework, practise her piano, and eat beans on toast for supper because they've had tuna fish for the last three nights. She glares at me in passing before running upstairs with Jammie bounding after her.

'I'm sure Katie's had a tiring day, pumpkin.' I try to put him down but immediately his little face scrunches up again.

'Up cuggle!' he demands.

I lift him up again. Hannah comes to the door carrying the school bags. Sometimes I think I might go crazy (*crazier?*) if I didn't have her to talk to for a few minutes at the end of the day. I feel guilty that Hannah does more than her fair share of the afternoon school runs, even though she works part-time at the local farm shop and I don't have a job. She never complains about it though – Hannah's one of those 'water off a duck's back' kind of people. I wish I could be more like her.

'I hope Katie wasn't too awful,' I say.

'Nope, they were perfect little angels in the car.'

'Thanks, Hannah.' I'm sure she's lying, but I read somewhere that it's a good sign that Katie's doing most of her acting out at home rather than elsewhere. Lucky me. 'Do you have time for a cuppa?' I say.

'Not today. I'm going out with the girls from work after Flora has her tea.'

'OK.' I've been meaning to ask her to get me a job application, but somehow I've never got round to it. It's not that I think I'm too good to work at a shop – far from it. It's just that right now, I've put my eggs in the basket of trying to return to the legal profession. A basket that seems to have a hole in the bottom. 'Another time, then.'

'Sure. Maybe next week.' Hannah lingers for a moment, seeming to grasp that I'm not OK.

'If you need me to do a few extra days, just let me know. I'm sure Flora would love having Katie over for tea.'

'Thanks, Hannah. I'm the one who should be offering. But I might be busy in the next few weeks.' I take a breath. 'I'm putting the house on the market.'

I'm hoping she'll act shocked – tell me that I shouldn't do it. Give me another speech about time and hanging on. But she nods with sympathy rather than surprise. 'That's hard, Lizzie. I know how much you love this place.'

'Yes, but I've got no choice. Unless I find hidden treasure in the garden or something.'

She laughs. 'I hope you do.'

As I'm walking Hannah to the door, Katie skulks past me. I feel a tremor of panic. I thought Katie was in her room, but what if she overheard me telling Hannah about selling the house? Of course, she'll find out eventually, but it would have been better if I'd sat her down, woman to woman, and told her the truth.

'Say sorry!' Jack shouts after her.

'I hate you!' Katie yells back in what has lately become her mantra and final word on everything. She runs out of the house without shutting the door. I watch her as she goes and climbs up into her old playhouse in the corner of the front garden next to the trampoline and a fenced-off area with the doghouse. Right now, I don't even blame her for how she feels.

Jammie pads downstairs, and I have the urge to squeeze her like a soft toy and cry, but I resist it. Instead, I put her outside with Katie and send Jack upstairs to put on his Spiderman onesie. I go back into the study and sink down in the chair with my head in my hands. Will I ever stop feeling like everything is my fault?

My eye snags on the plain envelope with no postmark that I'd tossed aside earlier. *To the resident.* I pick it up and tear it open, if only to stall for a minute or two before facing teatime.

Inside the envelope is a single piece of paper. I skim over the words, my hand moving automatically to throw it in the bin. And then I stop, the air backing up in my lungs.

'Oh God, no!' The unopened letter is dated 3 January – more than three weeks ago. Talk about my ship coming in while I was at the airport (or probably the post office, mailing off clothing and shoes bought for a fiver).

Quickly, I turn on the computer and compose a new email. Outside the study door, I can hear Jack rustling a pack of mini cheddars, looking for me. 'Just a minute, love,' I say. 'Mummy's working.'

'Open!' he calls out, banging on the door.

My fingers fly like lightning over the keys.

I received your note in the letterbox. I'd be very interested in your project. Please give me a call at your earliest convenience.

'Mummy!'

I hit send just as Jack bursts into the room, his face smeared with tears and salt. 'Come here, darling.' I open my arms to scoop him up again and twirl him around in the desk chair – which he loves. As we twirl, I keep eyeing the screen, willing a response to pop up instantaneously. It doesn't. Of course not. I'm too late. Three weeks is an eternity for some things.

We're spinning so fast that the air current knocks the letter to the floor and the wheels crunch over it. I pray to the god of junk mail, swearing that if only this can work out I'll never leave another envelope unopened or an email not responded to (even if it's titled 'OMG I'm so sorry for your loss!').

If only—

My phone number. We stop spinning and I whack myself on the head, making Jack laugh. In my email, I told the man, Theo Weston, to phone me, but I forgot to include my phone number.

'I'm such an idiot!' I say.

'What's an id'jet?'

I look down at Jack's round, earnest little face. I have the urge to squeeze it, kiss it, and send it packing all at the same time.

'Nothing. It means I'm a nice mummy.' I open up another new message and type in *Sorry – Ha! Forgot to include my phone number*. I add the number and press send.

'Can I have a sweetie?' Jack says, pushing his luck. He knows he's only allowed one after dinner. 'Some Haribos?'

'Yeah, sure,' I say, caving in. 'Go to the kitchen.'

He waddles off; I read the letter again. I feel a rush of panic that I'm too late, but also the kindling of a tiny flame of hope.

Dear resident,

We have determined that your house may have the potential to feature as a key location in an upcoming film entitled The Lady's Secret, based on the bestselling novel by Phillipa King. The filming schedule will commence in March and complete in June. A generous location fee will be payable. If you are interested in this opportunity, please contact me at your earliest convenience.

Yours truly,

Theo Weston, Assistant Location Scout

Rabbit-N-Hat Locations

5

THE LADY'S SECRET BY PHILLIPA KING

The rose petals were curled and wilted underfoot as she walked through the silent church. Had it only been a month ago that she had stood here, glowing with happiness, as the priest spoke the words 'man and wife'? And where was Tom now? He was already drunk when he went out last night after supper, and hadn't been home since. She twisted the thin gold band on her finger hard enough to hurt. Ever since she'd told Tom her good news, he hadn't wanted to touch her. But wasn't this what marriage was for? She put her hand on her still flat belly. He'd come around to the idea – he'd have to.

She walked out of the church and round the back to the path along the river. She had little desire to go home – until she and Tom could find their own house, she was living with his family. But walking since dawn had made her tired and she wanted to lie down and sleep.

Tom's mother and sisters were out for their morning social calls. From the first, they'd been cold and aloof to her and hadn't invited her to go with them. She sighed. So far, nothing was at all what she'd expected. Had her father been right to oppose the match?

No, she couldn't even consider that possibility.

She walked up the stairs to the room at the end of the hall that she shared with her husband. The door was closed, but she heard a noise coming from inside – *a woman's cry? It must be the new maid laying the fire. She turned the knob and opened the door. And gasped in shock and horror.*

'Tom!' She clapped her hand to her mouth.

Naked and covered in a sheen of sweat, he tried to pull up the covers. But it was too late – beneath him, the servant girl began to giggle and laugh.

6

It's meant to be... I can feel it. Yet there's no message. I keep my mobile in my pocket on ring *and* vibrate so there's no chance of missing a message from Theo Weston.

Theo... The name is like a long-forgotten melody in my ears. This man is going to save Tanglewild. This man – I check my phone again. It's been forty-eight hours and still nothing – is a complete bastard.

I clear away the plates from the kids' tea, scraping the uneaten bread crusts and half-chewed carrots into the recycling bin. I'm a fool even to get my hopes up. To me, Tanglewild is a special place, but surely there are hundreds of houses in Britain that are better preserved, larger, less *lived-in* than my house. It would be much more sensible to make the film at a National Trust property, or a private house that's already open to the public. A house with a budget to preserve and maintain it. A house with a name and status that would look impressive in the closing credits.

And yet the letter was put in *my* letter box. A scout must have come down the lane, seen the house and decided that it had potential. I have to believe that things happen for a reason, and if there's even the slightest chance that—

My thoughts are interrupted by the scraping of gravel and the squeal of brakes coming from the front of the house. Across the lawn, through the tiny arch in the stone wall, I see a huge silver vehicle backing up, away from my carport. 'No!' I cry. This can't be happening. Not now of all times.

A rainbow stripe passes the arch, confirming my worst fears. It's Constance Greene McKenzie, better known as 'Yo Connie' in the family once drink has been taken. Dave's mum, my ex-mother-in-law, arriving unscheduled in her carriage, or, in this case, a large caravan pulled by an ancient Land Rover Defender. Two years ago, she married an Irishman named Simon McKenzie who's at least ten years her junior. Since the wedding (somewhere on a cliff in County Clare – we weren't invited), they've been on an extended honeymoon, travelling around Europe and America doing odd jobs like two overgrown kids on a gap year.

When Dave passed away, they were somewhere in Eastern Europe. Connie sent a wreath, a crate of whisky, and a note to be read out at the funeral. The note basically said that she was sorry to lose him, but she knew he wouldn't want her to cut short her trip on account of his ill timing, and to please raise a glass on her behalf at the wake. Dave's older brother read out the missive as requested, and more than one glass was raised down the pub. My mum thought it tragic that Dave's own mother hadn't attended his funeral, but in hindsight, I suspect Connie knew her son's character better than the rest of us. If I'd known then what I know now, I would have given the whole thing a miss.

As the caravan pulls into my drive, I reflect on the reasons I haven't had much contact with Connie. First, from the moment we met, she disliked me. (Dave assured me that she disliked most people on sight, and vice versa.) Second, because Constance Greene is absolutely terrifying. She's six-foot two, weighs well over seventeen stone, and her face looks like an angry bulldog. But, as I'm always telling Katie, looks don't matter and shouldn't shape our opinion of people. What does shape my opinion of her is her brusque, overbearing manner, and the fact that her conversational niceties have mostly been honed by her long career as a policewoman, dressing down criminals, suspects, witnesses, and male colleagues. Before her retirement, she headed up a specialist firearms unit, fully trained to use a range of conventional and semi-automatic weapons. Which, according to her, they gleefully did on a number of occasions.

'Mum!' Jack yells from the trampoline.

I don't like to provide ammunition (no pun intended) for Connie's negative opinion of me, but there's no time to make myself presentable. I go outside as Jack continues to bounce (it strikes me that he won't even remember Gran Connie at all). Katie – sitting in her treehouse writing her diary – hasn't made a move.

Jammie runs to the gate like a young pup as Simon enters the garden; she jumps on him and licks his face. Simon's hair is longer than I remember from when they came round at the start of their honeymoon, about eighteen months ago. Now, he seems thinner, ganglier, and, if anything, younger. The one weird thing about Simon is that he never seems to quite make eye contact. 'Uh, hi, Lizzie,' he says, his eyes wandering towards the fig tree. 'I'm afraid I had a little bump with the carport.'

I smile through my teeth, wondering how *little*. 'I'm sure it will be fine,' I say. 'It's great to see you.' I walk across the expanse of lawn and give him a light hug, worrying that anything more energetic might crush him. The old nursery rhyme pops into my mind: 'Jack Sprat could eat no fat; his wife could eat no lean. But between the two of them, they licked the platter clean.' It could have been written for Connie and Simon.

'Lizzie.'

The croaky, cigarette-phlegmy voice startles me even though I know it well.

'You'd better come here. I think your carport is about to come down.'

I run then, almost glad for the excuse to skip the niceties. Connie is standing next to the caravan holding a cigarette, only a few feet away from the dry wood store. In front of her, there's a crack in the main pillar, and the roof looks wonkier than before. I sigh. Another thing that needs fixing, and never will be.

'He's never got used to the sightlines of the vehicle,' Connie says. She ashes the cigarette into the gravel. 'Bloody man.'

'Oh well.' I wave my hand. 'At least it's still standing.' Barely, I don't add.

'I knew you'd be a sport. You always were.' She gives a throaty laugh. 'I mean, who else could have put up with Dave for so long?'

I look at her in surprise. It's one thing to miss the funeral of her son, but to slag him off too? I open my mouth to come to his defence, but no words come to mind.

'I always thought you deserved better than the likes of him,' she growls. 'He was difficult to toilet train. That's always a sign right there. Still wetting the bed at age—'

Simon clears his throat as Jack comes running out the gate. Instead of going to his grandma, he grabs my leg and cowers behind me.

'This is your Grandma Connie, Jack,' I say. 'It's been a while since you've seen her.'

'Grandma?' Jack comes slowly out from behind me. 'Is that your silver bus?'

'Yes, it is,' Connie says. 'And what a big boy for knowing your colours. How old are you now? Five?'

'I'm three and one quarter,' Jack announces proudly.

'Are you now?' She looks down at the edge of the pull-up sticking out of his elastic-waist jeans and gives it a little tug. 'Following after your daddy, I see. And where's that sister of yours?'

'Katie!' I call through the gate. 'Your grandma's here.'

There's no answer from the tree house.

'She's, um... going through a stage,' I say apologetically.

'Don't worry. I'll shake her out of it.' Connie guffaws. 'Come on, Jack. Let's go see your sister.'

She waddles through the gate, pulling Jack along by the hand, the dog following at a discreet distance. I stare at the back of her, wondering why they're here and what they plan on doing. Connie's had a special oven fitted in the caravan and she does things like baking and jam making, but somehow I doubt that it keeps her fully occupied. If I didn't know her better, I'd suspect her of something nefarious, like Walter White and Jessie cooking meth in their camper van out in the desert. But I *do* know her, and it certainly isn't that.

'Would you like a cup of tea?' I ask Simon. Since they're here, I may as well be hospitable.

He glances at me sheepishly beneath his ginger eyelashes. 'Do you have any beer?'

I smile conspiratorially. 'Let's go see.'

* * *

Being a man of few words, Simon doesn't assault me with a barrage of questions, or use the word 'sorry' in a sentence directed at me. I appreciate that about him, and the fact that he reveres Connie, who has more than enough to say for the both of them. In the kitchen, I unearth two dusty bottles of beer and pass one to him.

He clinks his bottle against mine. 'How are things, Lizzie?' he says.

'I'm hanging in there. How were your travels?'

'Fine.' He gestures with his bottle. 'We've been on the road pretty steadily for the last few months. It's good to be home.'

The way he says 'home' gives me a little flash of terror, but since they've just arrived, it would be rude to ask how long they plan on staying.

'Sorry we missed the funeral,' he says. 'Heard it went well, though.'

'It was' – my throat tightens – 'a good send-off.'

He downs the rest of his beer. 'I guess that's all anyone can hope for.'

I get him another beer and he takes it solemnly. 'Connie *is* upset, you know,' he says. 'Don't be fooled.'

'I won't. She must be devastated to lose her son. For a mother, it's the worst thing in the world.'

'Yes. But Connie's all about getting on with things, and it's you she's worried about now.' He lowers his voice. 'We heard about the other... things.'

'What things?' Connie enters the room, her voice booming in the open space. She immediately goes over to the corner cupboard and has a look inside. 'Got any Scotch?'

'Um, no,' I say. 'There might be some brandy all the way in the back.'

Connie manages to find a bottle of brandy left over from the Christmas pudding. She takes one of the BPA-free child beakers from the cabinet and fills it halfway. I make the snap decision that I'm going to have a drink too. I've got a few bottles of cheap red wine bought at weak moments that I save for emergencies – like unannounced visits from relatives.

'So what exactly did that son of mine get you into?' Connie levels me a weighty stare.

'Oh, the usual thing.' I pour myself a glass of wine, deciding not to spare anyone's blushes. 'Lady friends, shag pad in London, credit card debts, second mortgage on the house...'

'What a scumbag,' Connie roars. 'And how come you didn't have a clue what was going on? I didn't have you down as the wifey-wifey type.'

My brain flits between the primitive limbic response of throwing her out of my house and the more 'wifey-wifey' response of not. I settle on pouring her another brandy.

It's a question I've asked myself a hundred times. How could I not have known what Dave was up to? Was he so discreet? Such a good liar? So seasoned and practiced at deception that I had no reason to suspect him of anything? One day in a parallel future, would I have been doing laundry and discovered a condom wrapper in his pocket, an acrylic nail in his underwear? Would I have happened upon a strange receipt in his study for an expensive gift I never received; a torn bit of paper with his London address? Maybe. Or would I have continued on as before, not knowing because I didn't want to look beneath the surface? Ignorant of the truth because it was easier that way?

'I don't know, Connie,' I say calmly. 'I guess I was a complete idiot.'

Simon looks a little embarrassed; Connie's response is both unexpected and unsettling. 'Come here, you,' she says, opening her arms. I have no choice but to step into them. I pretend I'm being squeezed by Katie's pink faux suede beanbag chair, turning my face to the side to avoid any well-meant maternal kisses. 'His father was a shit too, you know.'

'Really?' I use my ignorance as an excuse to pull away. 'I thought Dave worshiped his dad.'

'You know what they say,' Connie says. 'The apple never falls far from the tree.'

I take a generous sip of wine, mulling this over. I know that Dave's dad was a civil servant who did something hush-hush for the foreign office, which is where he met Connie, who was with the police. As far as I knew, Connie wore the trousers in the family, leaving her husband at home with the kids. But I've learned by experience that looks can be dangerously deceiving.

'When he left, I had four kids,' she elaborates. 'Ran off to Thailand with a Greenpeace lobbyist. As you do.' She gestures expansively. 'I won't bore you with the details, but the point is, you're not the only pebble on the beach. You'll get through it. And some day, when you're out the other end, you'll be better for it.'

She smiles at Simon and he smiles back. As inconceivable as it is, I feel a little flash of jealousy at what they have.

'Anyway,' she says, turning back to me, 'what are your plans now?'

The glass trembles in my hand. Right now, whatever Dave did or didn't do pales in comparison with the terror this question evokes in me. One thing's for sure – I'm not going to tell her about the letter in the post box and the potential opportunity that, by omission, I've managed to cock up. Have Rabbit-N-Hat Locations already conjured another house to feature in the film? My insides ooze with jealousy at the thought.

'I'm going to sell the house,' I say. 'I've got an estate agent coming round to do the valuation.'

I stare my mother-in-law squarely in the face, as if daring her to blink first. She doesn't.

'Well, you gotta do what you gotta do.' She picks up the glass as if she's going to drain it. Instead, she sets it back down and pushes it away. 'Dave was Dave, but I always suspected you were made of sterner stuff. You'll do what it takes. But are things really all that bad?'

'Bad enough. I can't find a job.'

'Have you thought of turning the place into a B&B? It's an idyllic little spot – away from it all, and yet near the train and the airport. You could make a good go of it, and Simon and I would be happy to help out for a bit.' She looks at her husband. Without quite meeting her eyes, he nods.

Oddly, now that they're here, the idea of Connie and Simon staying for 'a bit' doesn't fill me with the horror I'd have expected.

'I hadn't thought of that,' I say. 'But it's an interesting idea.'

'That's assuming you *do* want to keep the house, right?'

'More than anything.' I swallow back a rogue tear. 'The kids love it here, and I don't want to uproot them. Tanglewild is our home.'

Connie crosses her arms. 'Then there must be options, Lizzie. Think outside the box.'

'You're right.' I finish the wine in my glass, feeling a little like something has shifted inside me. Maybe it's the fact that Connie and Simon are here and I've opened up to them. Or maybe it's the letter, safely tucked away under my laptop in the study. 'What I need to do now is find a way to pull a rabbit from a hat.'

7

THE LADY'S SECRET BY PHILLIPA KING

Shame burned in her stomach as she ran down the forest path. How had it come to this? She had been happy, blissful even. She had done everything right: she'd fallen in love, got married — and now she had a child growing inside her. But her life had been turned upside down.

The cottage was hidden in a coppice of birch and oak trees. Stingers lashed her bare ankles as she lifted her skirts to go faster. Eventually, she broke through to the clearing. Old Hester was outside, stirring a foul-smelling concoction in a black cast-iron pot over an open fire. The smoke and ash stung Victoria's eyes, turning her tears to runny black lines.

The old woman leaned a gnarled hand on her stick and stared at Victoria with red-rimmed eyes. 'Got yourself in trouble, girl?' She cackled almost gleefully.

'No... I...' Victoria put a protective hand over her belly. She didn't want to do this. But the memory of Tom, the girl's laughter... She leaned over onto the path to be sick. Perhaps she didn't need the old woman's vile herbs after all.

The old woman's laugh grew louder. 'You got money?'

'Money?' The word died on her tongue. How could she be so stupid? She'd run here directly without a thought for anything but her pain and humiliation. But of course Old Hester would want money.

'I have this.' She twisted her wedding ring off her finger and held it out. She

had no idea what it was worth, but it was gold. She'd be glad to get rid of the thing. The daisy ring Tom had given her that day by the river had meant so much more – at the time, at least. Now, that day felt like a dream that she longed to return to but was just beyond her reach. In the coldness of reality, only nightmares awaited.

The woman took the ring and bit it between her teeth. She then spat on the ground and shook her head. 'That's enough for the herbs, but you'll need more than that to get shot of him. He'll come after you, you know.'

'But how? Where can I go? I have no money.'

The old woman curled her lips back in a smile. 'Then you'll have to get some. Go downriver to Idyllwild Hall. Go round to the kitchens and ask for Susan.'

'A servant – you're saying I should become a servant?' The shock was like a physical blow. She'd already fallen so low. Defied her father, married 'beneath' her. Traded a spoiled, if empty, life for one of loveless humiliation.

'Better that than a slave. And he won't think to look for you there, will he?'

'No.' Victoria hung her head. 'No, he won't find me there.'

8

Alone in my room that night, I try to enjoy the fact that I don't have to fight anyone for the duvet, wear earplugs to drown out snoring, or wait for someone to finish the sudoku before I can start on the crossword. I try not to listen to the creaking of the wood and the lonely keening of a fox in the woods. Try not to feel the solitude pressing on me like a stone slab – after all, it's not like I'm alone in the house. Jack is asleep in his room and Katie is still up reading a book, the dog sprawled out at the end of her bed like a fuzzy silver rug. No matter what's gone wrong in my life, I have two lovely children, and for that I am eternally grateful. And if I were still lacking company, outside in the drive is a large silver caravan inhabited by Connie and Simon.

I'd invited them to stay at the house, of course. But Connie had declined. 'Can't live without my ultra firm mattress and my heating pad,' she'd said. 'The little home comforts.' Then she'd winked at Simon. 'Besides, wouldn't want to keep the kids up with any hanky-panky in the guest room.'

Which was just too much information.

'Fine,' I'd agreed breezily. 'See you in the morning.'

To my surprise, Connie had handed me a package. 'Bought this for you on the Navajo Reservation in Arizona.'

'What is it?' While in the past I'd dutifully tried to buy Connie little presents at Christmas (bath salts, which were disdained; chocolates, which were grudgingly accepted; and finally settling on an annual bottle of Glenfiddich) she'd never given me anything.

'Well, open it,' she'd said.

I tore off the tissue paper and opened the box. Inside was a bundle of beads and delicate silver wires woven into a circular spider web pattern about the size and width of my palm. Long leather thongs dangled down from the circle, with feathers attached to the ends. The craftsmanship was superb, but I had no idea what it was. So I took a punt. 'What a lovely thing,' I said. 'It will look great on the Christmas tree next year.'

'It's not an ornament,' Connie said. 'It's a dreamcatcher.'

'A dreamcatcher?' I'd once seen something similar – in a Disney video maybe? Like *Pocahontas*? In the last few years, the sum total of my cultural experiences seemed to derive from Disney films.

'It clears the fuzz from your mind. Catches it while you're asleep. That way, you'll remember your dreams. Protects you from bad dreams too.'

'Does it work?'

She shrugged. 'Look, I know you like jewellery and whatnots. So suck it and see.'

I hook the dreamcatcher over the reading lamp above my bed. The beads shimmer in the light, the feathers whispering from the slightest current of air.

Though I'm tired from a day of worries, and the disappointment of *not* hearing from Rabbit-N-Hat Locations, I know it will be some time before I drop off to sleep. In bed, I pick up the e-reader that I bought myself two Christmases ago and let the kids give me as a gift. Most of the books on it are unread. In the days *Anno Dave Morte* I liked romantic comedies and historic dramas. Nowadays, gritty crime dramas have become my thing. It's a guilty pleasure to read about people who have more problems than I do.

Tonight, though, I'm doing research. I browse the online store for *The Lady's Secret* by Phillipa King.

I find it easily. Apparently it really *is* an international bestseller (though I'd never heard of it before the letter came). The cover is cringeworthy: an auburn-haired beauty in a pink silk gown passing through a wrought-iron gate towards a dark, forbidding-looking house. I focus on the house: Elizabethan in style, with twisted Tudor chimneys silhouetted against a bruised purple sky. Chimneys like the ones Tanglewild has in spades! A tremor of anticipation shoots down my backbone as I read through the testimonials and the blurb:

'Historical romance at its best.' *The Daily Mirror*

'Achingly romantic; chillingly suspenseful.' *The Lady*

'Perfect for fans of Daphne du Maurier and Barbara Cartland.' *The Sun*

As the 18th century draws to a close, young and beautiful Victoria Easterbrook seeks escape from her doomed marriage and goes to work as a servant at Idyllwild Hall, home of disgraced nobleman and notorious smuggler, William Clarke. Caught in a web of jealousy and deceit, Victoria is haunted by secrets from her old life and her new. But most haunting of all is her new employer and the way he looks at her with those dark, mysterious eyes. Can Victoria rise above the dangers clouding around her to experience a powerful new love?

'Dark, mysterious eyes'. 'Powerful new love'. Rubbish. It sounds like a garden-variety-mystery-cum-bodice-ripper – definitely not my usual fare. But as I purchase and download the text, I feel a little giddy at the prospect of reading it. *It's research*, I remind myself as I move my finger across the screen to scroll to the first page.

* * *

Guilty pleasure or no, Victoria Easterbrook's story is a page-turner. The opening scene is ambiguous – was Victoria a willing participant in Tom's 'amorous advances', or was she in fact raped? We find out soon enough that, either way, she's made a life-changing mistake. She marries Tom against the wishes of her father, who cuts her out of his will. This pleases her new husband not at all. Then she tells Tom the 'good news' that she's pregnant. He goes right off her and she finds him in bed with a servant girl.

I find myself squirming in uncomfortable sympathy for poor Victoria. She's clearly been a bit of a dupe, but what other options did she have? Marry or don't marry – that's about it. And if Victoria, married for less than a month, is a dupe, then where does that leave me?

In the third chapter, Victoria visits a so-called wise woman in the forest to take care of her 'problem'. The woman gives her purgative herbs and also a name – Idyllwild Hall – where they're looking for servants. Victoria is shocked at the suggestion, but when her father refuses to protect her from Tom, she makes the choice to leave her marriage and cast herself adrift into the unknown.

She waits until late at night when her father is passed out drunk. Then, she goes to his study, spills ink on his papers, jimmies the drawer with a lizard-shaped paperknife, and steals money from his desk drawer to run away. As I read the words, the father's study morphs into Dave's office in the Square Mile, looking eastwards towards the towers of Canary Wharf. The spilled ink becomes a keyboard. He slumps forwards, his forehead typing an endless row of characters until his PA finds him and…

I close the cover on the e-reader, my eyes strained and bleary from the words on the screen. The clock on the bedside table shows that it's after midnight. No wonder *The Lady's Secret* is a bestseller.

Above my head, the dark blue draperies of the canopy are meant to look like the night sky. When the previous owners left Tanglewild, the huge, carved oak bed wouldn't fit down the stairs, so it stayed put. Would I have stayed put if Dave had lived? Or, if (when?) his financial and amorous shenanigans came to light, would I have had the courage to leave all this and start again? I'd like to think that I would. I'd uproot myself and my children, and bear the consequences. I'd reinvent myself and start again, living to fight another day. Just like I'm doing now. I know she's just a soppy heroine in a soppy romance novel, but I feel for Victoria – more than I'd like to.

I'm a little disappointed that the early part of *The Lady's Secret* hasn't evoked any visions of my own house. But maybe that's a good thing. The real *star* of the book must be Idyllwild Hall.

I try to read on, but my eyes won't cooperate. The last thing I see as I turn out the light is the dreamcatcher, its beads sparkling in their silver web, waiting to come alive just as I drift off to sleep.

9

In the middle of the night, I wake up breathless, tangled in the sheets. Feeling panicky, I sit up and turn on the light. Dust motes rise up from the sudden movement, and the feathers of the dreamcatcher move ever so slightly.

In my dream, I was running down the corridor on the first floor that runs the length of the house. Moonlight was streaming in through the diamond panes of glass. I rushed into one of the rooms – Katie's room? – and went to the window. Light from tiny lanterns twinkled as a boat floated past the house on a strong current. I was wearing a thin white nightgown and my hair was long and done up in a thick plait. I pushed open the casement and peered out. I was looking for someone. On the boat? On the bank? My heart was pounding so hard I thought it might explode from my chest. Where was he? Why hadn't he come?

And who the heck was *he*?

With a little laugh, I lie back down. Obviously, I'd stayed up too late reading *The Lady's Secret*, which, in the words of Louisa May Alcott, has 'addled my brain'. I remember that according to Freud, dreams are some kind of wish fulfilment relating to sex or death. I put my hand to my chest, feeling my still-elevated heartbeat. My dream definitely wasn't about death...

I put out the light and pull the duvet up to my chin. But sleep won't come. At first light, the ducks and geese wake up and start quacking and squabbling. I get out of bed, bundle up in two jumpers, fleece trousers and a pair of wool socks and go downstairs to make some coffee. As I wait for it to brew, there's an electronic ping. I take my phone from my pocket, expecting a push notice from eBay or an electronic reminder about an overdue bill.

But when I see a new email from T_rex@rabbitNhat.com, my hand starts to shake; my stomach feels like it's at the top of a roller-coaster ready to plummet straight downwards. I read the words on the screen.

> Dear Lizzie, Thanks for your email. If it's convenient, my boss and I would like to come round and take some photos of the house this afternoon. The director is looking to make a decision on the location this week. I look forward to meeting you – and your house.
> Regards,
> Theo Weston, Rabbit-N-Hat Locations

'Oh my God!' I feel like I'm a can of fizzy drink that someone's just shaken up, ready to burst with excitement.

'Mum?'

I turn to find Katie standing in the doorway. She's wearing an old nightie that used to be long but now barely passes her knees, and clutching her old, battered teddy bear. Even though I tuck her in every night, I didn't realise she was still sleeping with it. She holds Teddy tightly, her jaw clenched like she's terrified and trying to be brave. Jammie pokes her head warily out from behind Katie.

'Oh Katie! Darling.' I rush over to her and engulf her in my arms.

She stays for a moment longer than usual before pushing me away. 'What's up, Mum? What's happened?'

'What's—' I look at her again. She's crying. 'Oh, darling,' I say. 'Nothing bad has happened.' I risk hugging her again. This time, she stays in my arms. 'I'm sorry if you were scared. But things are looking up.'

'I heard you telling Hannah and Grandma that we have to move house. Because of Dad. You said it was his fault.'

I tighten my arms around her. For so long, Katie's been shut away in her own grief and pain, that maybe this is a positive sign. She's been angry at me for her dad's death and my blaming him for our current situation. I should have sat down with her and explained everything – the grown-up version, rather than just the sugar-coated kid version. But with everything so bleak, I'd kept putting it off. Now, though, I'm determined to try.

'Your dad loved you,' I say. 'And it's OK if you miss him. But it's also true that he did some bad things. Things that are making it difficult for us now, after he's gone.'

'I know that, Mum. But I just want to stay here. If we move house, I might… I don't know… forget him.'

'I understand, Katie. And I know it's really hard for you. I'm sorry I can't take the pain away.' I stroke her hair. 'But just so you know, I don't want to move house either. Please believe that I'm doing everything I can to make sure we can stay here.'

'I know, Mum.'

'And there's actually been some good news – just now. Some people are coming here to look at the house as a possible film location.'

'Huh? Like using it for a cinema?'

'No.' I laugh. 'They might want to film a movie here.'

'Really?' She pulls back, frowning. 'Why?'

'Because it's a lovely old house, and the film has a lovely old house in it.'

'Can I get a drink of water?' She squirms away and goes over to the cupboard, pulling up a chair to stand on. Normally, I just let her do it, but today, I jump up, get her a glass, and fill it with water. I'm bubbling with new-found energy. Although… it's not like we've been chosen.

Yet!

I smile at my daughter, my lips and facial muscles feeling like they've been liberated from a corset. I open a tin of dog food for Jammie, and she ambles over to her bowl, her tail wagging.

'Now, what would you like for breakfast?' I say, turning back to Katie. 'Weetabix, or… I could make eggs. Or even pancakes.'

'Pancakes?' My daughter looks at me like I've grown a second head. I *never* offer to make pancakes on a school day. Or, come to think of it, on any other day. Not for a very long time.

'Yes, we're celebrating.' I grin.

When she smiles back – something I haven't seen *her* do for a very long time – I'm fizzy with joy. 'OK, Mum,' she says. 'I'll have pancakes with butter and jam.'

* * *

I feel like Superwoman as I whip up the pancakes, bring up a jar of blueberry jam from the cellar, drink a cup of coffee, and send two emails. The first is to Theo Weston confirming our meeting; the second is to the estate agent cancelling the valuation. A little voice niggles in my head that I'm being too hasty, but I ignore it. Seeing the words whoosh off into the ether makes me feel like dancing a jig.

My buoyant mood survives Katie not being able to find her homework or her trainers, and Jack having wet the bed *and* doing a poo in his pants when we're already late for school. 'Don't you give up, Jack,' I say as I dump the 'business' in the toilet and try to decide whether to wash the trousers or put them in a plastic bag and chuck them in the bin.

As I herd them both out the door, I start panicking that Theo and his boss might turn up while I'm on the school run. *But that's silly*, I tell myself. Most likely, he'll have to come all the way down from London. I very much doubt that he'll turn up any time before noon. If he turns up at all. My stomach twists. Surely he will...?

By the time I've dropped off the kids at school and returned home, the worries are running rampant in my mind. The caravan parked outside the sagging carport, the toys and clutter inside the house, the overgrown state of the garden. To an outsider, it might look like I'm the kind of person who lies in bed all day eating crisps and watching TV. I suppose some people in my place might have taken out their frustrations by cleaning behind the fridge, going round the skirting board with a toothbrush, or hoovering up in the attic. Whereas I've barely even noticed the state of the house since Dave's death. Now, though, I'm seeing everything with new eyes. Theo Weston will probably take one look inside and realise that he'll have to wipe his feet on the way out.

'Think outside the box, Lizzie,' I mutter to myself.

I go to the caravan and knock on the door. 'Um, hi!' I say. 'Wake up. I need help.'

There's no response so I knock louder.

'It's kind of urgent.'

The door opens a crack. Connie's sleepy face bulges out. 'What time is it?' She rubs her eyes crossly.

'Time to get up,' I say. 'I need you and Simon over at the main house.' For once, my fear of my mother-in-law is eclipsed by my fear of what will happen if this opportunity slips away. 'And if you happen to have a roll of bin bags, well, bring those too.'

10

I put Simon and Connie to work – or more accurately, Simon and I work, while Connie stands at the open window overlooking the lake chewing gum and listening with great suspicion as I explain about the letter, the email, and the opportunity.

Connie chucks her chewing gum into the wisteria and barks an order to Simon about some missed Lego and a stray pen without a lid. Then she expounds on what a terrible idea this whole thing is.

'Have you thought about what a hassle it will be? We saw some filming when we were in America. It's not just cameras, you know, but trailers and dressing rooms, and' – she wrinkles her nose – 'actors.'

'I think she's right to give it a go,' Simon says. I'm surprised at how gallant and brave he is voicing an opinion contrary to his wife's. 'I don't suppose these opportunities come along very often.'

'And are they even legit?' Connie says.

'I googled the location company,' I say, feeling defensive. 'They scout for the BBC and some big-name Hollywood production companies. And' – I pause for effect – 'according to what I found on the web, the going rate for a private home being used for a film set can be upwards of a thousand pounds per day.' The words sound miraculous. 'A thousand pounds – a day!'

'Are you sure that's not just smoke and mirrors?' Connie sniffs. 'Hollywood movie magic?'

'Look, I don't know. But surely I've got nothing to lose by showing Theo round today. It's not like I've got anything else to do.'

Connie eyes me like a hawk on steroids. 'Oh, so it's Theo now, is it? If you ask me, sounds like you're counting your chickens before the egg is even laid.'

'But I didn't ask you,' I say.

We glower at each other; the doorbell rings. I look around the room in horror. If anything, it looks even worse than when we started. I may only have read the first few chapters of *The Lady's Secret* and not yet encountered Idyllwild Hall, but I'm guessing that heaping bin bags and headless Barbie dolls don't form the overriding impression for the reader.

'Maybe it's the postman,' I say optimistically. I flick my hand to Simon to indicate that he should put the bin bags out the door to the garden. He nods. Thank God for someone sensible in the family.

The house seems to grow in size as I rush to the door. There's a part of me that wants to usher in the winds of change with courage and fortitude. But most of me – the part that deals with the unpaid bills, the grieving children, the dashed hopes, and the fractured dreams – is just plain shit-scared.

There's another knock on the door, less certain this time. I swallow hard, fiddle with the latch, and open the door...

I'm an educated woman. I don't believe in two-penny romances, or Cinderella moments, or living happily ever after. I don't believe in blind luck, or the alignment of the spheres, or, for that matter, dreamcatchers and their so-called powers. But when I see the man standing outside on my doorstep, next to a petite Asian woman, I almost wish I did.

It's not that Theo Weston is amazingly attractive. He's tall, but not overly, fit, but not fanatically. His hair is light auburn (which, let's be honest, is only one step removed from ginger). He's wearing jeans, a button-down shirt with no tie, and a blue jacket. His face is pleasant and friendly.

'Mrs Greene, right?' I detect a hint of an American accent.

I catch myself gawking. 'Hi, Theo... I mean, Mr Weston. Please... call me Lizzie.' I ramble like a fool as we shake hands. I've built up this whole thing in my mind, and I want it to go well. I want him to like the house – to like me. I want him to choose *us*.

'Theo, please. And this is my boss, Michelle Kim.'

'Hello, Lizzie.' The woman smiles pleasantly, but I sense she's clocked how flustered I am.

I stand aside so they can enter. Shoved as I am against the coats hung on the wall, there really isn't enough room in the hallway for two people to pass without brushing against each other. Theo comes inside and immediately stops to examine the door. I pin myself closer to the wall.

'Wow, this looks ancient,' he says.

'The timbers are from an old ship.' I wriggle to the side to get past him, knocking off a coat in the process.

'Really?' Theo moves past me and goes into the main hall. He makes the right noises – oohs and ahhs. Michelle Kim follows behind him; I sense that of the two of them, it's her I need to impress.

I stand to the side as they look around. It's as if I'm seeing the room for the first time too, but all I can focus on are the cobwebs on the woodwork, the trail of muddy dog prints leading into the kitchen, and Katie's mountain bike parked in the corner. It's now obvious to me that we should have started Operation Bin Bag in this room instead of the drawing room, but it's too late.

'Um, please ignore the mess,' I say, addressing Michelle. 'I've got two kids and a Siberian Husky. It's... you know... a family home.'

'If the house is chosen, a crew will be sent in to clear it out,' Michelle says.

'Oh. Of course.'

'It's a lovely old place,' Theo says. 'I think it's nice that it's lived in.' He gives me a warm smile, which I return gratefully. Maybe it's his role to be the good cop, but even so, I'm glad of his enthusiasm.

'Do you mind if we take some photos to show the director?' Michelle says.

'Not at all.' I flip on the light switch. Only two bulbs on the cast-iron chandelier actually light up.

Theo takes a camera out of his satchel and screws on an enormous lens. Whatever he photographs is going to come out warts and all. I sigh. I wish I could explain to them the things that the camera won't capture. The image of Katie zipping around the hall in her roller skates, being chased by Jack in his red and yellow Cozy Coupe. One year, when it rained on Katie's birthday, we managed to fit an entire bouncy castle in here. The kids bounced almost high enough to swing from the chandelier. I can still hear the echoes of their screams and laughter. On the door frame to the kitchen, there are strips of masking tape stuck to the wood. Their heights and the date are scribbled in biro: red for Katie, blue for Jack. The highest one – Katie's, of course – is almost up to my chest. When did she grow so much? And when did I stop measuring?

A part of me fervently tries to make a bargain with the universe. If Tanglewild gets chosen, then I'll start measuring again. Start *appreciating...*

How can I make these people understand that this room, with its dark panelled walls, elegantly carved woodwork, and heavy atmosphere of *age* is more than the sum of its dimensions, décor, and original features? It's a happy house – or it can be again – and one with an old soul. A house with texture and depth, rough edges, corners worn smooth with age and use. A house that has endured, and will continue to do so. I want them to understand; I want them to share it with the world. And, on a much grubbier note, I want a thousand pounds a day so we don't have to leave.

I try not to listen as Michelle and Theo confer together in low voices. But of course I can't help but glean that there are some issues: the house is too small, there are visible radiators and wires, the windows are set at the wrong height, the electrics are antiquated.

'If you ask me...' Theo is saying to Michelle as they move to the kitchen, 'it seems to fit the brief.'

It fits! I feel like punching the air in triumph. I smile broadly, sensing Connie and Simon huddled inside the drawing room, listening to everything that's going on.

'It's old,' he continues, 'it has a lot of character, and it's slightly down at heel...'

'Yes,' I answer without realising I've spoken aloud. 'I mean... oh...' I close my mouth as it sinks in what he's said. The house is shabby, rundown. A *problem property*. My cheeks flame with embarrassment, and something else... Anger. How dare this man come here and insult my house? And, by implication, me?

Michelle turns to me. 'We'll recommend that Luke Thornton come and see it,' she says. 'He's the director – I'm sure you've heard of him.'

I feel like my life has suddenly turned into a badly dubbed foreign film where my mind is moving slower than my mouth, or maybe vice versa. 'You're going to recommend it? To... what was his name...?'

'Luke Thornton.' Absently, she checks her phone. 'Theo,' she says, 'take a few more photos and meet me at the car. I've got a call with the Americans. It was nice to meet you, Lizzie.'

'Yes...' I say, but she's already turned and is walking to the door.

Left alone with Theo, I feel suddenly awkward. In my mind, I've set him up to be the one person who can help me, and maybe that's why I felt drawn to him from the minute he appeared at the door. He, however, seems completely oblivious of his role in my pantomime. Besides which, he's not even the decision maker.

'Do you think there's a chance it might be chosen?' I ask.

'It's possible,' Theo says. 'I mean, it's the right—'

'How much are you paying?' The throaty voice startles us both. For a second, Theo looks like a deer in the headlights as we both turn towards the door of the drawing room, filled by Connie's bulk. 'Sure, it sounds like fun to have the house in a film and all that. But at the end of the day, there's got to be something in it for Lizzie—'

'Connie, please!' I turn back to Theo. 'Um, this is my mother-in-law, Connie. She's visiting at the minute.'

'Nice to meet you.' Theo holds out his hand. Connie looks at it, then cautiously shakes it. Theo does well to hide a grimace – I know from experience that Connie's handshakes are more vice-like than firm.

'The location fee is usually a daily rate,' Theo explains, sounding rehearsed. 'It's determined by the length of the shoot, the hours involved, and, of course, the budget. Rest assured, though, if the house is chosen, there will be *ample* compensation.'

Ample compensation. The words should fill me with glee and relief. But instead, I feel a stab of something more akin to despair. Instead of doing the adult thing and facing up to my demons and vanquishing them, I take up the time-honoured alternative of having a go at my mother-in-law.

'Connie,' I say, my voice low and frigid, 'I can handle this.'

She turns her cobra stare to me. I refuse to turn away; refuse to flinch. Because I've suddenly realised that I don't just want this for the money and the chance to call off the estate agents for good. This special project, this opportunity that's dropped into my post box from out of the blue, is something that I want for myself. Call it a distraction; call it a new focus. Maybe even call it fate. But whatever it is, I don't want to lose it by quibbling over money. If they take over the house with their cameras and trailers, lights and microphones, then so be it. I can deal with those things. What I can't deal with is going on another day in the sad state of torpor that's been my life for the last ten months, wondering if the best moments are behind me. I *need* this...

Maybe Connie senses my despair, or maybe she's just bored of the whole thing. 'Suit yourself.' With a shrug, she turns and waddles back into the drawing room, punctuating her exit with a slammed door.

'Sorry about that.' I rake the hair back from my face, surprised at my own forcefulness.

'That's OK,' Theo says. 'And actually, she's quite right. If your house is chosen, it will be a big disruption to your lives.'

'I can handle that,' I say. 'Because the whole thing sounds very exciting. I mean, since my husband died, we haven't had much in the way of... um...' I trail off. If I didn't already have 'desperate' written on my forehead, I do now.

'I'm sorry for your loss,' Theo says. The words that usually sound like fingernails on a blackboard are almost like a balm coming from him. Heat rises to my face even in the freezing cold hall.

'Thanks.' I look down at the stalwart planks of the floor. 'It was very sudden.'

Without warning, my eyes blur with tears – for everything that's been lost. And for how thin and fragile the thread is that I'm clinging to.

'Gosh, that's tough.' He comes over and puts a hand on my arm. Normally, such a thing would make me flinch. But right now, it feels genuinely comforting.

'Sorry, I'm fine. It's just been quite hard.'

'I'm sure,' he says. 'I lost my mum two years ago. Cancer. I know it's not the same as losing a husband, but it was really hard.'

'Losing a mum is probably even worse,' I say. 'I'm not close to mine, but still, I like to know she's there.'

'I guess it's hard with anyone you love. But life goes on, doesn't it?'

There's something loaded in that question. His hand is still on my arm, warm and solid. I suddenly feel awkward, and I pull away under the pretence of digging in my pocket for a tissue. I don't want to feel any kind of spark for a man ever again. There be dragons. And yet, I find myself looking down at his hands. No wedding ring. Not that that means much these days.

'Can I show you the rest of the house?' I say, a little flustered. 'We have a lovely panelled library, and the drawing room designed by Bailey Scott. He was an important architect round here in the 1900s. And then we have—'

'Actually,' he says, 'I think I've seen enough.'

'Oh.' It's like he's body-slammed my heart to the ground. All my foolish – stupid – musings about hope and fate vanish into the air like tendrils of smoke.

'But I was wondering if I might see that little building by the lake shore – I caught a glimpse of it on the way in?'

'The dovecote?' I say, caught off guard.

'Is that what it is?'

'It's quite rundown,' I say, trying to dissuade him from the idea. 'We never use it. The floor joists are rotting, and there's an old balcony that overhangs the lake. It's not safe.' I stop before I can blurt out that the place gives me the shivers.

'Sounds atmospheric,' he says. 'And I think Michelle will be a while on her call.'

'OK.' I shrug. 'If you really want to see it, I'll get the key.'

* * *

My enthusiasm wanes as I lead him out of the house into the garden. I'd locked Jammie in her dog run in the morning before the scouts arrived, and she whines as we go by, clearly wanting to come along.

'Beautiful dog,' Theo says as we pass. 'What's his name?'

'Her. She's called Jammie Dodger. Named after the biscuit – the ones with the jam heart in the middle?' I blush a little. 'Do they have those... I mean, you're American, right?'

'Born and raised in Boston. Go Red Sox. I'm sure we do have them. We'd call them cookies, though.'

'Right.' I laugh, feeling a little more relaxed. 'Anyway, it's around here.'

I lead him through the gate round the side of the house. In spring, the beds will be beautiful and colourful – full of delphiniums, dahlias, tulips, and peonies. Now, though, everything is brown and dead. Add thousands of mouldering leaves into the mix, plus half a dozen bin bags piled up next to the house, and you get shabby, unkempt, and 'down at heel'. Long ago, Dave and I used to spend autumn afternoons outside clearing leaves while the kids played on the trampoline or in the playhouse. This year, though, I haven't even got the rake out of the shed.

Maybe I should *sell-up*. The thought comes from nowhere, the idea kindling in my head like a flame. Maybe it is all too much, and I should turn it over to someone with the will – and the money – to look after it properly. My shoulders droop. I can't give up that easily. I just can't.

At the end of the garden is an archway cut into the yew hedge. Theo turns back for the view of the house. 'Stunning,' he says, snapping it with his camera.

'Um, the gardens are at their best in spring and summer... just about any other time of year than right now.' I hate the way I keep apologising. The house has stood here for generations, centuries even. It's witnessed worse crises than mine, weathered them, and remained stalwart. It doesn't need me to justify its existence.

When he's done taking photos of the garden, I lead Theo through the gate into the unkempt paddock that's pockmarked with mole hills. The grass is long and wet, and I can feel my feet getting soaked through my shoes. On the other side of the field, the steeply gabled roof of the dove- cote rises over the top of a copse of birch trees. Though the roof is visible from the house, due to the way the lake curves in a crescent, it's actually a fair walk to get to it.

As we enter the copse and the trees close around us, I feel an odd sense of disquiet. It's the fact that someone died here – drowned in the lake. The estate agent who sold us the house didn't have any details. Maybe if I had more information I'd be OK, but as it is, I feel anxious and unsettled out here. But I need to keep my eye on the prize – getting Tanglewild chosen for the film.

'What an idyllic spot,' Theo says as the building comes into view.

The dovecote is a half-timbered building that's roughly hexagonal. It stands two stories high with a bottom layer of red bricks, and an upper storey of wattle and daub. The roof has a little cupola on top with hundreds of small holes, once occupied by roosting doves. The building is covered with a tangle of ivy and wisteria vines. Around the door is the skeleton of a climbing rose. The dead plants reveal the dilapidation – the crumbling daub, the bricks in need of repointing. The door is small, barely tall enough for me to enter without ducking down. The keyhole is below an iron door-pull in the shape of a lion's head with a ring in its mouth.

Looking at it through a stranger's eyes, though, I realise that it has a certain charm. It's a little like the house of the seven dwarfs – before Snow White came on the scene with a broom and mop. Maybe the film people could use it as the forest cottage of the wise woman who sold herbs to young women 'in trouble'. In letting the place go, maybe I've done myself a favour.

Theo snaps a few photos of the outside as I try to get the door open. The lock is stiff and the key won't turn. I twist with all my might and jiggle it, trying it every which way.

'Here, let me try.' Theo's fingers brush mine, sending a spark down my backbone. He turns the key and the lock clicks open. I feel foolish and relieved in equal measure.

Inside, the place is in a bad state. The stone floor is speckled with dead greenfly, wasps, and mouse and bird droppings. The walls are mottled with black and green mould.

'I'm sorry...' is all I can think to say.

'Hey, no worries.' Theo seems completely unperturbed by the state of the place. He climbs the stairs that spiral round the edge of the space to the second level. Reluctantly, I follow him. Along the stairs are little gaps in the bricks where a bevy of doves once roosted. The former owners of the house put votive lights in some of the holes; I have no idea why.

'It's a very cool place,' Theo says. 'I bet your kids love it.'

'They're not allowed here. Not until I can... um... make repairs.'

We reach the upper level. The wooden floorboards fan out from the centre in a starburst shape, but a number of the boards are loose or missing. Above, the bare beams crisscross the ceiling at jagged angles and the underside of the roof is stained with damp. I sigh. I'd need to win the lottery to be able to afford repairs out here.

Theo begins to walk across the rickety floor to the other side. My breath catches. 'Be careful,' I call out. 'The floor's not safe.'

'Oh, I'll be fine.'

I stand rooted to the spot as he ignores my warning and keeps going, the wood creaking under his feet. He makes it across to the French doors, beyond which is a balcony. He opens the door and steps out, peering over the rickety railing to the deep water underneath.

I close my eyes, envisioning the stone cracking under his feet and him hurtling headlong into the murky green void below. 'So you own the lake too?' he says.

'Yes.' My breathing is shallow as he comes back inside and closes the window. 'It was once a river – a tributary of the River Arun.'

To my relief, we make it back to the entrance in one piece. Only when the door is shut behind us do I notice how hard my heart has been pounding. This place... Eventually I'm going to have to do something with it. Like pull it down.

We return to the gardens; hesitantly, I ask Theo if he'd like a cup of tea.

'Love to,' he says. 'But I'm afraid we've got another appointment.'

'Of course.' I feel a flash of envious panic. Are they going to visit other properties? Is there anything else I can do to make sure Tanglewild gets chosen? And after he leaves, what am I going to do with the rest of the day? The rest of my life? 'Thanks for coming round.' I shake his hand – his grip is firm as it holds mine.

'My pleasure, Lizzie,' he says. 'It was nice to meet you.'

I ponder the finality of this statement as I walk with him up to the gate. I stand there as he gets into the driver's seat of a Black VW Golf. Michelle, still on the phone in the passenger seat, gives me a brief wave. Theo starts the car and does a three-point turn in the drive. When the car disappears from sight down the tree-lined lane, I walk back to the house. I know that it's utter madness to pin my hopes and dreams on the success of this one, extraordinary event.

But that's exactly what I've done.

11

I can't bring myself to read more of *The Lady's Secret*. I don't want to get excited about something that probably won't happen. Instead, as I lie in bed that night, I plough through a police procedural that I can't keep my mind on. In my peripheral vision, the leather and bead tendrils of the dreamcatcher move ever so slightly on a current of air that must be caused by my breathing.

Should I have done something differently when Theo and Michelle were here? Appeared more desperate? Less? Acted like the Lady of the Manor? That's something I've never been able to do with any conviction. I grew up in a semi in North London; Dad was a postman and Mum taught at the local primary school. When I went off to uni, they moved to a little bungalow in Somerset. Dad died when I was nineteen, and Mum sold the bungalow and moved to Spain. I funded my university studies through loans and working weekends at the campus ice cream shop. I never had a lot of money, and I didn't miss what I didn't have.

When I graduated and became a trainee at a City law firm, not much changed for me financially. I didn't earn a huge amount the first two years, and what I did earn went on rent and student loans. Eventually, when I qualified as a solicitor, my salary was bumped up. It was a lifestyle of long hours in the office, drinks with colleagues, night buses and short, casual flings. I was put on a contentious acquisition of a power plant, and found myself in heated negotiations with a particularly obstinate fourth-year associate called David Greene. I wouldn't say it was love at first sight, but by the time we met at the closing, we'd spent enough hours arguing that we were almost like an old married couple. It seemed only natural that we fell in love, moved in together, and got married in a small civil ceremony.

In the first year of our marriage, there were a series of bubbles and crashes in the London property market. It somehow created a perfect storm that worked to our advantage. Dave sold his flat at a high, and we managed to cobble together enough money to buy a house in Twickenham at a low. Dave made partner, I was still working, and by the time Katie came along, we'd managed to pay off the mortgage.

When Katie arrived, we were eager to move even further out of London. It was fun looking at properties within an hour's commute of the city, and Dave and I both wanted something old and quirky. Dave had grown up in an old farmhouse in Hertfordshire, so he appreciated things like that. On paper, Tanglewild didn't look very promising. It was too far from London, it was oddly partitioned, and the lake was not a bonus for a family with a small child. But those things worked in our favour. We viewed the house on an overcast February day. For me, it was love at first sight. The fact that it was a 'problem property' had put other people off viewing it, and ours was the only offer. Fate had dealt us a winning hand – for a short time, at least.

I close my eyes, trying to clear my mind of all thoughts and feelings. Tanglewild will be chosen for the film – or not – based on what the director and the film company envision for the setting. It has little or nothing to do with me. I feel the familiar dizzying sensation of things careering out of control around me. In receiving the letter and meeting Theo, I've allowed myself to get my hopes up. That, clearly, was a mistake.

* * *

I must have fallen asleep, because when I open my eyes, the room is dark, the blackness thick and cloying. The pillow is damp and my heart is beating wildly. In the dream, I'd been leaning out the window looking for... *him*. Some tall, handsome figment of my imagination. But instead, I'd seen a dark figure; a pair of sharp malevolent eyes looking for me—

'Mummy!' The scream cuts through the darkness. The dream flits away into the hidden crevices of my memory.

Jack. I sit up, wide awake. He used to be a good sleeper, but since losing his dad, he's been sporadic at best.

'Mummy!' he screams again.

I swing out of bed and go to his room, turning on the light. He's sitting up in his cot bed, sucking the arm of his plush Spiderman.

'Hey, pumpkin, you OK?' I go over and ruffle his hair.

'I was following the ducks to Snow White's house. Then I fell into the water.'

'Snow White's house?' My heart screeches to a halt. Could he be talking about the dovecote? I used to walk him there with the dog when he was a baby, strapped into the carrier on my chest. But other than that, I've no idea how he even knows it's there. 'It was just a dream, honey,' I say. 'And Mummy's here now.'

'Can I come in with you, Mummy?'

'Of course, love.' I open my arms and he climbs into them for an up-cuggle. I carry him back to my room and lay him down in the centre of the big canopy bed. Whatever terrors the night and the future may hold, for now, at least, they aren't going to touch us.

* * *

The next few days are torture. There's no message from Theo, but there are more bills, along with two rejections from recruiters. I know I should reschedule with the estate agent, but I fail to do so. What's taking the film people so long? What if they don't bother to get back to me at all?

I google the director to see what I'm up against. When the search engine results come up, it's blindingly obvious that I don't get out much. I haven't seen any of the films that Luke Thornton has directed, but most of them were big Hollywood earners with a constellation of well-known stars. He was nominated for a best director Golden Globe for a hard-hitting psychological drama that went on to win best film. His fame bodes poorly for Tanglewild, I think.

I also find a series of articles on his private life. Apparently, he's originally from Yorkshire, though for most of his career he's lived in Hollywood. The tabloids set out the grim details of his seismic divorce from an up-and-coming American starlet. Once said starlet had 'come up', she had a well-publicised affair with an up-and-coming co-star.

There are numerous photos of the starlet ex-wife – a tall, lithesome blonde with crystal-blue eyes – but few of him. In the last article, however, the paparazzi have caught him on camera on the steps of a sunny Los Angeles divorce court. His sunglasses are pushed up into his hair, and he's glaring accusingly at the camera.

I close down the webpage. The world of Hollywood film types is one I don't understand. Maybe Connie's right after all. If Tanglewild isn't chosen, it will be a blessing in disguise. But as I'm shutting down my computer, my phone beeps. My heart jumps – is it from Theo?

No. It's from a partner called Harry Reynolds at my old law firm. I never liked him, but I recall sending him my CV at a low moment. He was one of those partners who married a junior associate, had a kid, divorced, married another junior associate, and there were rumours of his exploits in the disabled toilet after hours with the trainees. I never worked with him directly, but a few times at group drinks, he'd made it known to me that he would be available for a little extra 'mentoring' should I happen to be interested. I wasn't. To me, he was a smarmy scumbag who took advantage of circumstances – like the fact that his wife and family lived in Hertfordshire and he had carte blanche to 'work late' at the office. I'd been so high-minded and smug back then, thinking that nothing like that could ever happen to me.

Seeing his name, the old feelings of shame, betrayal, and violation crash over me like a rogue wave. But I'm way too old for him to bother with, so I read through his email inviting me to call him if I'm still looking for work.

Against my better judgement, I call right away. The phone rings and is answered; small talk is made; the chase is cut to. Hearing Harry's voice sets my teeth on edge, but I try not to question whether I ought to be rewinding my life by ten years, returning to the same firm where once upon a time I was a different person. I don't think about the long hours, juggling the school run and the commute to London. I don't think about having to prove myself all over again. I focus on the fact that this job could be real – much more real than a letter in the post box or 'Hollywood smoke and mirrors'. I can call off the estate agents, catch up on the mortgage payments, buy a netball kit for Katie, throw Jack a proper birthday party. I'll be back in the saddle, prospecting for my long-lost self-esteem, and who knows – maybe I'll even strike it rich.

And fifteen minutes later, when it's all agreed (I'll start the following week, part-time to begin with) I can't help but feel elated, jubilant even. I cross my fingers and pray that maybe my run of bad luck has turned around at last.

* * *

'Guess what?' I say.

Connie sticks her head out of the caravan. I can smell baking, and there's a tray of chocolate chip biscuits set out on a wire rack next to the oven. Connie throws one to Jammie, who leaps up and swallows it down like the fox that ate the gingerbread man. Connie does not, however, offer me one. She's been bent out of shape ever since Simon volunteered to help me spring-clean the house. Having him there, a silent, steady force, has really helped motivate me to get on with the job. Together we've blitzed the downstairs, sorted the toys, and carted a lot of them up to the attic. Having things out of sight is making me feel a lot better about the house. If the film team ever comes here – and with each passing day, it seems increasingly unlikely – I'll be ready.

'What?' Connie says. 'You've sold another job lot of boys' three to six months sleepsuits on eBay for a fiver?'

My eBay empire, which has been so important to me over the last few months, seems to provide Connie with an endless source of amusement. Though, from my daily trips to the post office, to my up and down moods depending on whether an item has sold or not, I can't say I blame her.

'No,' I say. 'I'm not going to have time for eBay now. I've got a *job*.'

'The film thing?' She purses her lips. 'Or did you take my advice and decide to look into the B&B idea?'

'Neither.' I tell her about my new job, keeping to myself the misgivings about my boss-to-be. Then I casually let drop the reason I braved knocking on her door in the first place. 'I was hoping that maybe you or Simon could do the school run on the days I'm working in London. I'll pay you, of course,' I add quickly.

She crosses her arms without speaking, forcing me to ramble on.

'I mean, that's assuming you were planning on sticking around for a little while. Which I hope you are. Not just because Simon's helping me, but because it's actually... um... nice to have you here.' Now that I'm saying it, I realise that it's true.

'Hmmf,' Connie says. 'You know Simon's applied for a part-time job at the fruit farm?'

'He didn't mention it. But that sounds really good.'

'So you can work it out with him. I'm busy here.'

'Oh? That's good. With your baking?'

For a moment, she seems to hesitate. Her eyes flick involuntarily to the table where a laptop computer is set up. 'I've got a few things on,' she says. 'Tax returns and that sort.'

I decide not to press it. Since arriving here, Connie has been acting oddly evasive (my mind keeps wandering back to the *Breaking Bad* hypothesis). She seems to like spending a good portion of the day in her own space, and she and Simon live off her police pension and occasional work. But other than that, I know little of how she spends her time.

'But in principle,' she says, 'we can help out until you get sorted. Though I don't see how you're going to manage with a London job – to me the B&B sounds like a no-brainer. But to each his own.'

'OK, thanks for that.'

'Don't mention it.' She closes the door, ending the conversation.

'To each his own,' I mutter. Connie's brusqueness, while not unusual, has taken the wind out of my sails. But I force myself to focus on the positives. I've now got a job *and* temporary childcare. Today is a *much* better day than yesterday.

I go back to the house and inventory my closet. In my zealous attempt to make money, I've flogged most of my office clothing. Nearly every suit, every pair of heels, every blouse and nice top has gone (in most cases for a fraction of what I paid). I've kept a few jumpers and cardigans which are practical for a house with a medieval heating system and two out-of-fashion skirts that didn't sell.

Until I'm earning money again, I'll have to make do. Once I'm back on my feet, I can objectively consider my options. Commit to a career in the City or 'think outside the box' about an alternative like the B&B.

I close the closet door and sit down on the edge of the bed, letting my mind wander over the possibilities. Once upon a time, I used to like meeting new people. Dave and I liked to take weekend breaks to country inns and B&Bs. We stayed at some lovely little places – some very twee and toile, others with the upscale 'boutique' look. It's only now that I'm starting to realise that Tanglewild could be a perfect retreat for busy Londoners. I could convert the dovecote into a gym or spa and get some canoes for the lake. I could provide walking maps and cycling guides, and build a tennis court in the paddock.

I stand up and walk through the upstairs of the house. In addition to Jack and Katie's rooms, there are two decent-sized bedrooms in this part of the house, plus two guest bedrooms in the wing above the kitchen. Four rooms would be manageable, and if I did the painting myself and bought some old furniture off eBay then I might be able to—

My phone vibrates in my pocket with a new email. As soon as Theo's name comes up on screen, my visions of a B&B evaporate, along with all my back-to-work hopes and fears...

> Dear Lizzie, thank you for showing me round your lovely house. Unfortunately, the director has chosen another location. Sorry about that, and all the best. Theo Weston

My eyes blur with tears as I delete the message and hurl the phone across the room. It lands with a thud on the carpet. The screen goes dark.

PART II

All we see or seem is but a dream within a dream.

— EDGAR ALLEN POE

12

FEBRUARY

I feel like someone's died. It's ridiculous, I know. But just when the mists had finally parted and I'd had a glimpse of a magical world, the doorway closed again. Now, the real world seems drained of energy and colour.

I try to hide my disappointment, but Connie sees through it immediately.

'Come on, Lizzie,' she says, 'don't look so down in the mouth. It was always going to be a long shot.' It's Sunday night and she's agreed to make the kids their tea so I can finish the laundry and ironing for tomorrow – the first day of the rest of my life. Getting up at 5.45 to catch the 6.39 into London Bridge, then the Tube to Bank, then walking fifteen minutes to Broadgate Circus where the office is located. According to Google Maps, it's one hour forty-three minutes door-to-door – on a good day. I'll work a nine-hour day, before doing it all again in reverse. By the time I get home, I'll be lucky to catch Katie before she drifts off to sleep. Jack will long be in dreamland; I'll stroke the hair back from his soft, sleeping face and cry silent tears. Tears that I've missed this day of his precious little life, and tears that I'm glad he's asleep because I'm way too exhausted to deal with reading him a book, or finding his toothbrush, or filling his sippy cup.

Even though I haven't done it yet, I know exactly how it's going to be.

'You're right.' I wrench a smile onto my face for Katie's benefit. She's sitting at the table staring at her maths homework, her face a frown of concentration. I press the button and the iron bellows out steam. But the creases in the linen skirt I'm hoping to wear tomorrow just won't come out. 'I did everything I could, but it didn't work out,' I say. 'But I'll get over it. I mean, it would have been exciting, but a disruption too.' I glance at Connie. 'I'm sure we're better off.'

'I'm not so sure.' Connie chuckles. 'Did you know that Dominic Kennedy is the star? I wouldn't kick him out of bed for leaving crumbs.'

'Connie!' I say, rolling my eyes in Katie's direction.

My daughter sets down her pencil and looks at Connie. 'Who's he?'

'A gorgeous film star,' Connie says.

I pause in my ironing and stare out the window at the dull line of trees and grey sky on the other side of the lake. Even I've heard of Dominic Kennedy: an ex-Shakespearean actor turned forty-something heartthrob. Famous for playing the costume-drama rogue, such as Mr Wickham, Willoughby, Alec d'Urberville and their ilk – and especially noted for any role that requires him to remove his shirt. His six-pack is almost as notorious as his reputation for deflowering young British starlets.

'How do you know that?' I say.

'I googled it,' Connie replies.

I shake my head – it's just as well he's not coming here. I've never aspired to be the talk of the school gates. Having Dominic Kennedy at the house would have catapulted me from recluse to minor celebrity.

'It seems your little project would have had its perks after all.' She winks.

'Maybe.' I look out the window towards the lake and think not of Dominic Kennedy, but of Theo. He seemed nice; attractive too. But dreamcatchers and romance novels will have to do for me. At least I'll never have to see the blasted film that they'll shoot somewhere other than at my house—

My thoughts are shattered by the shriek of the smoke alarm. Jack comes scooting into the kitchen in his Cozy Coupe and Katie looks at me, startled.

'Mum!' she yells.

'Shit!' I shout.

'Mum said a bad lang-wage,' Jack chants in a sing-songy voice.

Only Connie has the presence of mind to actually do something. She gets up from her chair, lumbers over, and lifts up the iron – which has burned a neat hole right through my linen skirt.

* * *

Somehow, I get through my whole first week of work. Being back is stressful and difficult. Among all the young, bright-eyed, bushy-tailed, child-free lawyers, I feel like a fish out of water. Or maybe a fish in water – a perilous sea of sharks. It's not that the people aren't perfectly nice and polite. But underneath, it's a dog-eat-dog world of jockeying for the best transactions and keeping a constant eye on billable hours. I keep my head down, work hard, and pray that Jack's runny nose doesn't win him a trip to the school nurse and a forty-eight-hour exclusion.

At the end of each day, I rediscover the difference between my mental scenario and reality. By the time I'm on the train home, I'm hoping that Katie will be asleep as well as Jack, because I'm too exhausted to do anything other than drink a big glass of red wine, take a hot bath, and tumble into bed. Although I'm only part-time (three days in the office and one day working at home) I also have work to do at the weekend, and by Sunday night, I'm dreading doing it all over again for another week.

The Monday night train journey home morphs and stretches itself out into years. Years of being alone, raising my kids as a single mum. Moving to full-time when Jack starts school, getting a nanny so that I can leave earlier for work and stay later. Having Katie grow up hating me, thinking that I'm 'pathetic', like she called me this morning because I was stressing over a ladder in my stockings. How can I do that to her? To Jack? To myself?

On the other hand, at least we'll still have our home—

My phone vibrates with a new message. I've been out of the office for less than an hour and already I've received twenty new emails relating to work and sundry, including two new documents to draft tomorrow. It's not a bad thing – after all, a busy lawyer is an employed lawyer. I should get a jump on things... but would it really hurt if just this once I turned off the phone?

I look around at my fellow passengers. Almost everyone else has their eyes glued to their phone, tablet, or a rumpled copy of the *Evening Standard*. A noisy group of teenagers are eating smelly food from Burger King. Life on a home-bound commuter train... My life.

With I sigh, I check the new message. Suddenly, I'm sitting bolt upright. It's from Theo Weston!

My hand judders as I open the message with no idea what to expect.

> Hi Lizzie, the other location for The Lady's Secret fell through. As the schedule is tight, the director and the production team would like to visit Tanglewild on Wednesday to make a final decision.
> Best wishes,
> Theo Weston, Rabbit-N-Hat Locations

If I wanted to be offended – by the tone that takes my interest as given and the fact that another location was chosen over my house – I could find ample cause. But my heart is doing star jumps and all offence goes right out the window. I've been given a second chance. I'm not going to throw it away due to some misplaced sense of pride.

I draft a quick message back.

> Brilliant. Wednesday OK. See you then, Lizzie

The train slows and the guard announces my stop. I get to my feet, collect my belongings, and jump off. I stand on the platform as the doors close.

I press send.

The train rumbles off.

For the first time all day, a smile creeps onto my face.

13

The next few days are chaos as I try to get things sorted for the film crew's visit. I make a list of tasks – from replacing light bulbs, to polishing the woodwork, to moving the kids' trampoline out of the sight line of the house. Things that might improve the film team's first impression. I add 'move caravan' to the list but scribble it out again. By helping out with the kids and the list of odd jobs, Connie and Simon are helping me save my home. I'm not going to make them move theirs. The good thing about the visit is that it's scheduled for a Wednesday, which is my day off. So at least I don't have to skive off work.

On the morning of the visit, Connie takes the kids to school. (To their delight, the caravan is hooked up to get some air in the tyres, so although they can't ride in the back, it gets to come along). Simon uses my car to haul some old junk to the tip. I spend the morning dusting cobwebs, hoovering up dog hair, and doing a final tidy-up. We may succeed or we may fail, but we've tried our best.

Theo texts to say that the crew will arrive at two o'clock. At half one, I turn the heating on; at ten minutes to two, I put the dog in her run. At a quarter past two, there's still no sign of them. I pace the floor of the hall that I mopped earlier and which now smells of lemon. I could make a cup of tea, clean something else, try to calm down…

A text pings on my phone. This is it then. My heart sinks. They're cancelling... I bite my lip and force myself to open the message. It is indeed from Theo – telling me the crew is delayed because they stopped off at a pub for lunch.

I text back that it's no problem, then feel ashamed of myself for being so available. I guess because they're in the film industry, they think the rest of us will dance to their tune. And in this case, they're right. Stressed by their lateness, I tidy the kitchen for the fifth time, but only manage to kill fifteen minutes. I go upstairs to Katie's room, which does nothing to improve my mood. I blitz the room, picking up knickers, socks, pens, books, crisp packets and pieces of balled-up paper that make her room look like the cage of a bored zoo animal. I gather up the laundry and next tackle Jack's room, finding that he *knows* the difference between wet and dry, at least to the extent it takes to put a pair of wee-soaked pants under his pillow. I heft the laundry basket and move on to my own room. The film people may have time for a nice long boozy pub lunch, but some of us have things to do. I've wasted my whole day off preparing for them, and they can't even show up on time?

I throw my laundry in with the rest: shapeless mum bras and high-waisted pants. It's not like anyone cares if I'm dressed for comfort or run around wearing nothing at all. I used to have fancy matching bras and knickers back in the day. I should find them and flog them on eBay.

The basket is overflowing as I go down the stairs. The aged washer-dryer does little more than wash and spin round the wet clothes, so this lot will probably take—

The doorbell rings. My thoughts fly away. I stagger over to the door, trying to free a hand. This is it, my one big chance...

I manage to pull the door open. Standing there in front of me is Luke Thornton, big-shot Hollywood director.

'Oh, hi,' I say, completely flustered. A mum bra and pair of pants fall off the top of the laundry pile and land at his feet. He looks down. I look down. Then he looks up at me. I wish the floor would open up and swallow me.

'Sorry we're late.' Theo steps forward like a knight-in-shiny-Puffa-jacket and skilfully clears the bra and pants with his shoe. I'm so grateful (and glad that he's here) that I feel like hugging him. Behind him and Luke there are four other people standing at my door.

'Uhh... no problem.' I try to bend over to get the errant laundry. The whole top of the pile falls to the floor, wee-soaked pants and all. 'No problem at all.'

Theo steps past me and the laundry. Luke Thornton is next, his nose twitching like there's a bad smell. He's taller and thinner than Theo, wearing jeans and a dark blue button-down shirt and a suede jacket. He rakes a hand through his dark blond hair and takes no further notice of me as he walks into my house.

For some irrational reason, I feel little bubbles of anger form in my chest. I know from Theo's first message that Luke Thornton was the one who rejected my house and wanted to make his precious film elsewhere. I guess he's used to people swanning around, kowtowing to his every whim. How disappointing this must be for him.

The others trip in behind. There's a middle-aged woman with big orange hair, and a petite blonde woman in a thick woolly scarf. There's a bearded man in a bobble hat and sandals with socks. The last man is bald with pasty slug-like skin. He's wearing small wire-rimmed glasses and a black turtle-neck and jeans. If Lord Voldemort worked in the film industry, this could be him.

When they're all inside, Theo makes some introductions. Voldemort is Richard Silverman, the producer, Bobble Hat is John C, the location manager. The two women are Claire and Phoebe in charge of properties and set design, or maybe the other way around. The names exit my brain as quickly as they arrive, and I feel intimidated and powerless over their decision. Luke and Theo wander into the kitchen, and the two women and Bobble Hat chat amongst each other convivially in the great hall. It doesn't take long to get the gist – the house is way too small for their setup and totally unsuitable. Voldemort aka Richard Silverman, standing apart from the others, glares at me like it's my fault and he's about to invoke *cruciatus*.

I pick up the laundry and stand awkwardly in the corner of the hall. Then, Bobble Hat asks to see the drawing room on the lake side. I point him in the right direction, thrilled to finally be of use.

He even rewards me with a 'nice house', mumbled under his breath.

I stay in the room after he leaves, where eventually, Theo finds me again. 'I tried to fight your corner,' he says. His accent is homely and comforting. 'I think the house is perfect. And you seemed to really want this.'

'Thanks. It sounds like such a fun project.'

'It should be. But the schedule is getting tight now. It will be good to get the details sorted.'

'What happened with the other location?' I'm almost afraid to ask.

'Well...' Theo hesitates as Luke Thornton comes into the room. Maybe he's stressed about the schedule, or maybe he's still pissed off about the other location falling through. Either way, it's as if an icy wind has found its way in through a crack in the walls.

'I need to go now, Theo.' He lifts his arm and glances down at an expensive gold watch. 'The Tate Modern reception is tonight.'

'Of course.' Theo's tone is reverent, like he's addressing a deity.

Anger rises inside me again as Luke's eyes rest on me for a second, darkening like I'm a piece of furniture that doesn't belong in the room. Then he turns and walks out.

'Sorry.' Theo sounds a little embarrassed. 'It looks like we're going.'

'But you just got here,' I protest. 'Don't they want to see the rest of the house, or the dovecote? I can get the key right now.'

'I guess not. Sorry.'

My breath shortens in panic. This is not going to plan, and I have no idea why. I've spent days preparing for this visit, riding a roller coaster of hope and disappointment. And now, it's all slipping away. I can't let that happen.

Leaving Theo to follow me, I go out of the drawing room back to the hall where the group is still assembled. I stand at the edge of the group and try to feign an air of confidence. 'Thank you for coming to my home,' I say, keeping my voice even.

A few of them turn, looking startled, like I'm a rusty suit of armour that's suddenly come to life.

'I'd be very happy to welcome you here for your project.' I stare at Luke Thornton. 'Provided we can come to adequate arrangements.' I walk across the huge expanse of floor towards the front door, pausing only to turn briefly to Theo. 'I look forward to hearing from you in due course.'

Theo gives me a surreptitious little thumbs up like I've done the right thing in asserting myself – showing Luke that I'm no doormat. I turn the heavy iron latch and hold the front door open for them. As the visitors file past me one by one, the ice seems to have melted a little.

'Thank you for showing us your home,' the orange-haired woman says.

'Yes,' the blonde woman echoes. 'It seems like a very special place – good energy.'

Bobble Hat gives me a pleasant 'cheerio'; Voldemort doesn't speak, but his lips curl back in a rictus smile and he inclines his head as he passes me.

The last to leave is Luke Thornton. As I'm about to shut the door, he stops and turns to me, his brow creased in a frown. 'The author is quite taken with your house,' he says, a hint of northern accent coming through.

'The author?' I gape at him. 'Phillipa King saw the photos?'

'She's been... involved,' he says coolly. 'Which is usually a recipe for disaster. But for now, at least, it looks like you've got friends in high places.'

As I'm trying to process this new information that's come completely out of the blue, he turns and walks up the stone path to the gate. I close the door and lean against it, emotions churning inside me. I'm annoyed with the way I've been taken for granted, and yet delighted that whatever this lot thinks may not matter. Because, totally unbeknownst to me, I've acquired a new ally. Phillipa King, international bestselling author. Who on earth would have thought?

14

> Dear Lizzie, I'm delighted to let you know that your house has been chosen to feature as Idyllwild Hall in The Lady's Secret. I'll be in touch about the schedule and the arrangements, but the plan is to start in early March, getting everything ready for a late spring shoot. All the best, and talk soon – Theo

I'm in! It's happening! The kids have finished their tea and are watching *Descendants* when the text comes in from Theo.

'Woohoo!' I yell, rushing in to smother Katie and Jack in a hug.

'Shh,' Katie says, pulling away so she can see the TV. 'Maleficent is about turn up at the coronation.'

'Just think!' I say, ignoring her. 'Our house is going to be on that screen. And a much bigger one too – in a real cinema.'

'Will it have a superhero?' Jack asks, beaming proudly. I'm glad that he's excited, because we probably will have to make some changes to our lifestyle to accommodate the film. I remember what Michelle said about bringing in removal people to clear out our things.

'I'm sure there will be,' I lie. 'I mean, I haven't read the whole story yet, but Superman must at least have a cameo.'

'Look, can you two please be quiet?' Katie ups the already overpowering volume with the remote. Her eyes are glued to the screen as Maleficent tries to steal the Fairy Godmother's magic wand. Fleetingly, I wonder again about my fairy godmother – Phillipa King. The woman who's saved my bacon and allowed me to keep my house – for now, at least. Obviously, I still need the key details – like the amount of the location fee. I'll have to make sure it's enough to give me some breathing space on the mortgage. And who knows? If this works out, maybe I will follow through with some other outside-the-box idea like turning the house into a B&B.

Because right now, I feel like anything's possible.

Leaving the kids to their DVD, I go to the cellar and dig out a bottle of champagne that I was given as a Christmas present years ago. I take the bottle outside to Connie's caravan and bang on the door.

'Connie!' I holler. 'Simon?'

There's a shuffling sound inside and, eventually, Simon opens the door. 'Lizzie,' he says, looking surprised. 'What is it? Is something wrong?'

'No!' I gush. 'We got it!' I hoist up the bottle. 'They've chosen Tanglewild!'

The caravan begins to gently rock and Connie appears, framing Simon in the doorway on either side. 'So it's official?' she says.

'Yes.' I can't stop grinning. 'I mean, I haven't seen the contract yet, but yes – I want to do it.'

'Well, I hope it's the right thing.' Connie's tone is disapproving, but then she gives me a little wink. 'I think it is.'

'Great.' I'm quite relieved that she's on board. 'So can I tempt you?' I hold up the bottle.

'Yes, we'll take that.' She reaches out and takes the bottle from me. 'But I think you should get yourself to the mums' drinks.'

'The what?' I look at her, horrified.

She crosses her arms, the bottle still in her hand. 'Katie's year is having mums' drinks tonight. At the Lamb and Star. Hannah and I think you should go.'

'Hannah and you?' I practically choke. 'You've been talking to Hannah?'

'Of course. We both agree that you're too isolated. It would do you good to get out.'

My stomach gives a vestigial clench at the thought of going to drinks with the other mums – and at the fact that Connie has been talking to my friend behind my back. Of course, technically, they're both grandmas and technically, I have been shirking my social responsibilities, but surely they understand...

'Come on, Lizzie,' Connie chivvies. 'I can understand how it was before, but now you've really got no excuse. Things are looking up. You've got a job, you've got the film, and you've got Simon and me to babysit tonight. So make an effort. Get changed – you look scruffy – and get going.' She waves the bottle at me. 'We'll save you a glass.'

'Well...' Though my natural inclination is to argue, on this occasion I let myself be persuaded. I'm opening my house up to a film crew. I'll have to renounce my solitude sooner rather than later.

And damn it, I've been through hell. I deserve a night out.

'Yes, OK.' Before I can give it any more thought, I turn and go back to the house to give the kids a goodnight kiss and grab my handbag.

* * *

Twenty minutes later, I enter the Lamb and Star feeling like a bug in search of a rock to crawl under. In this case I would settle for Hannah, but she's nowhere in sight. The pub is tasteful, the bar done in mellow oak – not that I can see much of it through the forest of skinny jeans, knee-high boots, and shearling gilets that together say 'mums' night out'. I'm wearing yoga pants and a baggy hoodie as a snub to Connie who said I should make an effort. But right now, she and Simon are no doubt happily drinking champagne while the kids are finishing the video, and I'm wishing I hadn't been quite so stubborn.

'Lizzie?' I'm aware of a surprised whisper passing along the bar. 'Is that Lizzie Greene?'

'Hi,' I say, smiling weakly as I walk over to them. Everyone is staring at me now. I expect to hear undertones of 'Are you OK?' and 'Sorry for your loss', but instead a woman I recognise as Parker, the PTA rep from Katie's year, asks me if I want white or red.

'Red please,' I croak. I'm instantly handed a large globe filled halfway up with dark, blood-coloured wine. 'Thanks,' I say, taking a big sip.

'Now, Lizzie, do you know everyone?' Parker asks. I look where she indicates. Most of the other mums are familiar from the school run and from the old days when I attended events and get-togethers like a normal parent. But I've been avoiding people for so long that I draw a blank on most of the names. I know there's a Susan, and at least two Emilys, and maybe a Tracy?

Parker decides that perhaps everyone needs a little refresher. She introduces a couple of mums of new girls – Cherie, mother of Isla; and Erin-Joan, mother of Arabella-Joan.

'Lovely to meet you,' I say, not worrying if, in fact, I'm saying it to people I'm supposed to know already. Having drunk most of the first glass fairly quickly, my inhibitions are slipping away.

'And how is Katie coping with Year 4?' Tracy or Emily asks.

I know the proper response is 'fine, she loves it'. But having risked coming here, I also decide to risk the truth. 'Not too well, to be honest,' I say. 'She's still struggling with the loss of her dad, and I've gone back to work in London now. It's long hours, so I'm not around very much.'

'My daughter is in awe of Katie when the caravan comes to school,' Cherie says.

I glance at her narrowly to see if she's taking the piss – but I don't get the sense that she is. A few people nod. It's clearly a Topic of Conversation at the school gates.

'Yes.' I smile. 'I'm very lucky that my mother-in-law showed up when she did. Did you know she used to be in the police?'

I surprise myself by talking about Connie and Simon and how helpful they've been since arriving in my drive. Someone refills my glass and, as much as I've almost forgotten the feeling, I start to enjoy myself. Everyone is being so nice. I suspect it's because they feel sorry for me, but who cares? Right now, it's good to be around people.

The conversation deflects from me to the usual things – secondary schools, clubs and activities, homework, time allowed on tablets. I'm interested to hear that Katie isn't the only nine-year-old who's acting up. 'It's a difficult age,' Susan says. 'Not quite a child, not quite a teenager.'

'It sure is,' I agree. 'And I've no idea how Katie will react when Dominic Kennedy and the others come to our house.' The words are out before my brain can catch up.

All conversations stop.

'Dominic Kennedy?' Parker says.

'Yes. I mean, it's not official yet...' I pause, praying that by letting the cat out of the bag, I'm not jinxing anything. Though in truth, I was only brave enough to come at all because now there's something to celebrate.

I tell them about the letter, the film scouts, the tense moments I had waiting for responses to texts and emails. I don't tell them that Tanglewild was initially rejected, or that the director, Luke Thornton, seems unpleasant and full of himself. I also keep silent on the fact that even though I've sworn off men, I feel ridiculously glad that I'll be seeing Theo again.

'And, of course, I don't know the whole cast yet,' I say. 'But Connie googled it and said that Dominic Kennedy is rumoured to be the star.'

'OMG! That is fantastic!' Cherie says. 'You are so lucky.'

Parker nudges Cherie in the skinny, aerobicised arm. I realise that because Cherie's new, she's probably forgotten the coaching from the others to not upset me. I give her a reassuring smile.

'You know what?' I say. 'You're absolutely right.'

* * *

In another move orchestrated by Connie, Hannah turns up an hour later to give me a ride home. By then I'm tipsy from the wine, and though I've enjoyed (actually enjoyed!) myself, I'm ready to leave. As we're walking to the car, I have the urge to give her a piece of my mind for colluding with Connie on my behalf. Instead, all I can say is, 'Thank you, Hannah. For helping me. I... don't know what I would have done without you.'

'You seem different,' she says as we get in the car. 'I guess having a job suits you.'

'Maybe.' I don't tell her that I'm not enjoying the work as much as I expected to. I thought I would like the intellectual challenge, but it's all the other stuff – the commute, the office, the stress – that is dominating everything. 'I guess you and Connie are right. I do need to get out more. I feel like maybe it's time. And with the film and all...'

'That's so exciting, Lizzie,' Hannah gushes. 'I'm glad it's happening – it will be just the thing.'

'I hope so. I just want it to go well. Then between that and working, I'll be out of the hole. And who knows, maybe I will think about this crazy B&B thing.'

We chat the rest of the way home about her daughter, and the children, and about the refurbishment going on at the farm shop where she works. It feels normal, even good. When she drops me off, I give her a big hug. As I go through the squeaky gate and walk towards the dark silhouette of the house, I know that whatever happens, I've taken a big step forward, and there's no going back.

15

THE LADY'S SECRET BY PHILLIPA KING

The coachman cast Victoria's trunk off the roof, whipped the horses, and sped off. She was left standing outside a pair of vast gates, twisted and forbidding, the tendrils of iron seeming ready to snatch the full moon from the sky. Beyond was a stone wall, above which she could just glimpse the jagged line of a roof. Bats dived between the soaring chimneys, cold and smokeless despite the icy chill. Victoria forced herself to take a few steps nearer to the narrow arch in the wall that led to a tangled, overgrown garden. The gate shrieked as she pushed it open. Before her, the house was a dark monolith. Not a single candle was burning inside the hundreds of mullioned windows. There was no sign of any habitation, and certainly none of any welcome.

She thought of the rumours she had heard before leaving. The master's wife had disappeared, and some said he had murdered her because she'd been unfaithful with another man. Others spoke of smugglers on the river, their night boats laden down with the spoils of the East, and desperate men stowing their cargo in hidden tunnels under the ground. But all she could think of was that no one would know her. She would change her name and become someone else. Despite her doubts, she had to see this through.

Idyllwild Manor. Her new home. Shivering with dread, Victoria walked up the crooked stone path to the door.

16

MARCH

I jump as the buzz of an incoming text message jars me from the scene I've been reading. As I set down my e-reader, I find that I can't catch my breath. Everything about it seemed so real. Like I was – *am* – there.

The message is from Theo. My heart goes into fight or flight mode, worried that something's gone wrong; everything's off, all my hopes dashed. So far, though, things have gone relatively smoothly. I've negotiated the contract with the production company, and I expect to receive it any day now. The filming will start in a month's time and go on for about three months. Theo's been acting as a general go-between (tonight he's texting to confirm a time later in the week for the set-building team to come by for a final recce). But it's the last line of his message that I read and reread: 'PS – I look forward to seeing you again soon.'

It could mean nothing. Or he could be flirting with me. The idea feels oddly electrifying. I'm not kidding myself that there could be something between us – nor do I want there to be anything, I remind myself.

To get my mind off Theo, I return to *The Lady's Secret*. I was sorry to have abandoned poor Victoria and her plight when I thought the project was off, and am glad to return to her story. I'm reading it slowly to keep up the suspense and anticipation. In the last scene I'd read, she'd stolen money from her drunken father to board the coach for Idyllwild Hall.

Idyllwild. Tanglewild. *My house.* Just thinking about it gives me a surge of adrenaline. I reread with a critical eye the passage where Victoria arrives at the house, trying not to allow my imagination or emotions to intervene.

The similarities are immediately apparent. The stone wall with the arch, the jagged roofline, the mullioned windows. I'm sure lots of old houses in England have those things, but to me, the book describes what I see each time I come home.

In the pages that follow, Victoria is let into the house by a kitchen maid. There is work to be had at the house, as two of the servants had recently quit. She learns that the master of the house, William Clarke, is away, but his elderly mother lives at the house. His sister-in-law, Belle, who lives in the village, is a frequent visitor. The maid shows her to the servants' quarters for the night. Victoria is led through the dark and freezing ground floor and up the back stairs to a tiny room at the top of the house. The room is stuffy and airless, and Victoria goes to the window to breathe the outside air. The moon sparkles on water – the river behind the house. On the opposite bank, a huge copper beech tree stands sentinel, flanked on either side by a dense woodland of oak, willow, and giant rhododendron. At the point where the river bends out of view, Victoria can just make out the silhouette of a little house with a peaked roof, a weathervane on top.

The words niggle at me as I read them. All the descriptions in the book are pretty over the top, lavishing on the adjectives and adverbs. But it's all so clear in my head. It's so... familiar.

Switching on the overhead light, I get out of bed and go downstairs, through the great hall to the kitchen. From there, a corridor leads to a flight of stairs used for accessing the guest rooms above – the only rooms with a view of the dovecote.

The moon is a bright crescent of silver above the horizon. I stare across the dark water of the lake at the silhouettes of the trees. A monumental copper beech tree dominates the opposite shore, its branches spreading to dwarf the oak, willow, and giant rhododendron, and forcing them to lean and twist almost to the water's edge. I open the window and crane my neck to see the outline of the dovecote, hunkered down in the trees. Only the roof is visible, jutting up above the top branches. I'm not sure I ever noticed it before, but now, I see the rusty arrow of a weather-vane at the apex of the roof.

The little details are so similar – it's almost as if Phillipa King is describing the view from *this* window.

Returning to my bedroom, the house suddenly feels alien to me. Even a little creepy. What was it that Luke Thornton said? *You've got friends in high places.* Could he have been referring to a woman I've never met – a bestselling novelist?

For the rest of the night, sleep won't come. My mind tosses and turns, seeking in vain the answer to a new question: *Does Phillipa King have a connection to my house?*

* * *

In the light of day, I'm certain that last night I was mistaken. I open the curtains to a cold but sunny day. The lake is greenish brown, with a shimmering of white sunlight on the surface. Two ducks float near the opposite bank, where the trees are still grey and skeletal, and spring feels a long way off. The lake is just a lake; the trees are just trees.

Aren't they?

I dress for work and go downstairs. Jack and Katie are still asleep, but Connie arrives with a plate of freshly baked scones. She takes one look at me and frowns.

'Didn't you sleep?' she says. 'You look like hell.'

'Thanks, Connie.'

She offers me a scone and I bite into it eagerly. 'Actually, I was up late reading *The Lady's Secret*.'

She snorts. 'You must be the only woman in the world who hasn't read it before now.'

'You mean you have?' I look at her in surprise. Connie's the last person I'd expect to read a historical romance novel. But, on the other hand, maybe she's exactly the target market.

She rolls her eyes and sticks her head into the stairwell. 'Come on, you layabouts!' she hollers. 'Time to get up. If you make Grandma come up the stairs, they'll be no scones for breakfast.'

There's a scrambling noise, and the sound of footsteps. When I ask the kids – especially Katie – to do something, it's like I'm addressing a particularly unresponsive stone wall. Other than five inches in height, a few stone, and occasional freshly baked goods, what does Connie have that I don't?

'The descriptions in the book are pretty similar to this house, don't you think?'

Connie eyes me sidelong. 'To be honest, I wasn't really focusing on that kind of stuff. Haven't you got to the sex bit yet?'

'No,' I admit. 'It's just, some of it is a little uncanny. It's like Phillipa King was writing about this house.'

She frowns. 'Look, Lizzie, you got the film contract. You need to stop overanalysing things. The book has an old house in it that's similar to this one.'

'Yes, but I'm just wondering about Phillipa King.'

'You're going to miss your train if you don't hurry,' Connie says. 'And don't forget, on Friday morning you've got coffee with the nursery mums.'

'I do?'

Jack comes running down the stairs, his pull-up hanging low like a gangsta rapper. 'Mummy!' he cries. 'Don't go, Mummy. Please!'

I feel the familiar ripping sensation inside. As I'm about to scoop him up, Connie sets down the tray, grabs him, turns him upside down, and gives him a swing and a tickle. He convulses with giggles and laughter, and I use the distraction to take another scone and slip out the door. 'Bye,' I say, knowing that no one is listening.

* * *

That night, I return home from work exhausted, and, due to a signal failure at East Croydon, over an hour late. The night is freezing as I walk home from the station along the tree-lined gravel road. The moon is still only a sliver, but it's enough to illuminate the diamond dusting of frost on the grass.

I imagine Victoria Easterbrook, her nose pressed to the window of the coach, her eyes peering through the darkness to catch a glimpse of the house where she hopes to start a new life. The lane curves between the trees, and I stop near the old stone gateposts, just where Victoria would have been dropped off. But unlike her, I don't stare at the roofline of the house just visible over the top of the high stone wall. Nor do I give a second glance to the silver caravan parked in front of the carport, rounded and globular like some kind of amoebic life form. Instead, I focus on the sleek black Porsche that I've never seen before and which is now parked in the drive.

Just inside the wall, there's the sound of voices.

'A widow, you say?' The voice is deep and sonorous. 'How very *séduisant*.'

'Come off it, Dom.' Another male voice. 'She's too old for you.'

'Well, if she owns this house, I might be willing to make an—'

The gate screeches open and a pencil-thin light blinds me. I raise an arm to shield my eyes.

'Oh,' the second man says in alarm. He lowers the torch beam. 'I didn't know you were there.'

'This is my home,' I assert. 'I have a right to be here.' My eyes adjust to the darkness. Luke Thornton's eyes shine green, almost like a cat's.

'Of course.' Luke shrugs.

The fabled Dominic Kennedy steps forward, his hand outstretched. The face that launched a million middle-aged crushes shines on me like a second moon. And, I must say, the photos and film clips don't do him justice. Not by a long way.

'"Ill-met by moonlight, proud Titania,"' he quotes.

I know the proper response is something about Oberon, but all I can think about is how, after a fourteen-hour day, I must look like a right dog's dinner. As I go to shake hands, he lifts my hand to his lips and kisses it.

At least it's dark enough that, hopefully, neither of them can make out that I'm blushing.

'I'm Lizzie Greene.' My hand tingles as I withdraw it. 'The aged widow.' I glance at Luke long enough to take in the look of embarrassment on his face, before turning back to Dominic. 'So I take it the rumours are true? You're the star?'

'William Clarke, at your service.' He gives me a mock bow.

'Come on, Dom, let's go.' Luke sounds irritated – with what, I'm not sure. Maybe it's because until the contract is signed he's got no right to be here, and I've caught him trespassing. But he's staring at me like *I'm* the interloper.

There's a grating sound and a window slides open on the caravan. 'Everything OK?' Simon says from inside.

'Yes, fine,' I reply.

'We knocked on the door earlier,' Luke says, as if following my train of thought. 'Your mother-in-law gave us permission to have a look round. As you may know, quite a few of the scenes take place at twilight or full darkness.'

'No, I don't know,' I say sharply. 'And she doesn't own the house. It's *my* permission you need.'

'Of course!' Dominic cuts in. 'Terribly sorry. Won't happen again. Now, can I tempt you to come along with us for a drink down the pub?'

'No thanks,' I say automatically. 'I've been at work all day and I need to see my kids. Sorry.'

'I understand completely.' Dominic Kennedy walks over to the driver's door and beeps the lock. 'In that case, I'll say goodnight, my lovely Lizzie. It's been a pleasure to meet you.'

'Yes, a pleasure.' All of a sudden I realise what I've done – I've turned down a chance to have a drink with Dominic Kennedy! Involuntarily, I smooth my hair, almost tempted to change my answer. But then I catch a glimpse of Luke's face. Somewhere between him rejecting my house originally, his cool disinterest when he came round with the crew, and now the 'too old' comment to Dominic Kennedy, he's really starting to annoy me. And I have the strong feeling that it's mutual.

'Goodnight.' Ignoring Luke, I address Dominic. 'Have fun.'

With a little salute, Dominic gets in the car and turns on the engine. Luke goes round to the passenger side and gets in.

'They're sending the contract round tomorrow,' he says. 'Then it will all be official.'

He closes the door before I can respond.
'Fine.' I glare in his direction until the car has sped off out of sight.

17

'Dominic Kennedy!'

The mum sitting in the deep leather chair next to me grabs my arm so quickly that I almost drop my coffee cup. The others look up from their muesli and lattes and look in my direction. I've humoured Connie by going to a coffee morning with the mums from Jack's nursery class, and despite my crippling inability to remember the names, I'm actually starting to get into the groove of it.

'He's so hot!' Mary, one of the new mums, comes over and takes the empty chair beside me. 'I can't believe he's going to be at your house for... How long did you say again?'

'About three months.' I smile and decide to skip the bit where I turned down his invitation to the pub. Instead, I regale them with the other members of the cast that I know about through Connie's online subscription to *Tatler*. Victoria Easterbrook will be played by an up-and-coming starlet called Natasha Blythe. Sambrooke, the master's servant, will be played by a young stage actor called Will Fairfax. I spout off a few more names that clearly mean more to them than they do to me. The group is suitably awed.

'It all sounds fabulous,' Mary says. 'I'd love to see your home. Maybe you can give us a tour when it's all over.'

For a long second, I sense that no one is daring to breathe. It's like the elephant in the room has plopped down on its haunches, squishing the air from the room. But as Mary smiles unsuspectingly, I have a sudden urge to get everything out in the open.

'I think that's a good idea,' I say. 'When the crew is gone, I'll have you all over for coffee.' I direct my smile at the group. 'I owe you all that much for how supportive you've been of me.'

Mary looks blank.

'I lost my husband, you see. Almost a year ago now.'

Even underneath her make-up and her tan, her face grows pale.

'It was very sudden, and things have been difficult.' I give her a brief overview – how I've been on the cusp of losing everything, but now have drawn back, ever so slightly, from the brink.

Another woman, Daisy, I think, puts a stealthy hand on my arm. I can feel the floodgates loosening, and I blink hard to keep the tears at bay. It's not so much pride as practice that makes me hold everything inside, afraid of getting any sympathy. Afraid that once a crack opens up, there'll be no end to what comes out. But as I look around at each of them, my fears begin to subside. Despite their shiny SUVs, low-carb figures, and well-adjusted children, I know that beneath the surface, they have their own problems.

And as someone hands me a tissue to wipe my eyes, and someone else hands me a fresh cup of coffee with extra sugar, I do let everything come out. And for once, the 'sorry's and the 'you're so brave's and the 'keep your chins up's don't feel like needles to my skin. Instead, they feel well-meant and sincere. Because, at the end of the day, if they'd been through what I have, I'd want to reach out too with comfort and compassion. These women are no different.

I take a sip of the coffee, enjoying the sharp feeling as it burns my throat. Somehow, I've turned another corner. While part of my life has ended, another part is being pulled forward into the future. It's not so much time but the growing distance between those two parts of myself that is making things easier.

'Thank you,' I say, wiping my eyes. 'Thank you so much for being kind.'

* * *

What a difference a day makes, I think as I leave the coffee shop and walk up the high street. A new day, a new opportunity, and the glacial coming to terms with my new reality. I know I still have a lot of ground to make up, and the upcoming anniversary of Dave's death will be a real test of my fortitude. But having come out of my shell, I've no intention of holing up again.

Out on the high street, I stop to peer in the window of the local estate agents. There are placards advertising country cottages, semis, and the new flats that are going up across from Waitrose. I smile, not at what I see, but at what I don't. My house, my Tanglewild. I've managed to chase the wolves from the door.

I walk to the nearest post box, take the large brown envelope from my bag and drop it in. It's official. *The Lady's Secret* is coming to Tanglewild.

Instead of going directly home, I take a detour to the local museum further up the high street. I'm not really sure what I'm looking for, but it strikes me that with the film crew coming, I ought to know more than I do about the local area.

Inside, the main room is long and narrow, with a low ceiling laced with tarred black beams. Display cases line the two long walls, containing odd Victorian-looking curiosities. In the centre of the room is a fire-station bell and an unexploded (but hopefully defused) bomb. The far wall is devoted to wartime casualties, and local school children have made giant poppies from paper plates for Armistice Day.

A grey-haired man in a suit jacket with a military medal pinned to the lapel is seated at a desk, surrounded by leaflets and postcards for sale. He greets me, looking a little surprised to have a visitor. I don't have any cash for the entrance fee, but he allows me in anyway. 'Free for you,' he says. 'As you're my first visitor.'

'Thanks.'

I browse the display cabinets. Most are wartime exhibits with old photographs and letters, and there's a special exhibit on the fire-station bell.

The old man gets up from his chair and hobbles towards me leaning on a cane.

'You local then?' he asks me.

'Not exactly.' I explain my North London origins. 'We moved here a few years ago. My family and I, that is.'

He nods. 'I've been here over seventy-five years. Born and bred Sussex lad.'

'Impressive,' I say, feeling a little like an interloper. But it also means that he's most likely a font of local knowledge, and, from the looks of things, largely untapped.

'I was hoping to find out some information about my house,' I say. 'It's called Tanglewild.'

'Oh aye.' His eyes narrow. 'I know it.' He points a gnarled finger over to a case at the far end near the war wall.

Intrigued, I go to the case. The central exhibit is an old photograph of Tanglewild – the whole manor before it was divided up. The captions document local smuggling along the River Arun and the Wey-Arun Canal.

'Smuggling?' I look at the old man in disbelief.

'It was the rumour, yes,' he says. 'A lot of the old houses along the river were perfect places to stow away a bit skimmed off the top to avoid the taxman. And Zachary Jones was rumoured to be the ringleader.'

'Zachary Jones?'

He points to a small handwritten notecard at the bottom of the display. Apparently, Zachary Jones owned Tanglewild back in the late 1700s. He lost the family fortunes in the American Revolution and took to making 'a little on the side' in the rum smuggling trade. Next to the notecard is a miniature portrait of a severe-faced woman in a white lace cap.

'That's his wife, Veronica,' he says. 'She disappeared under mysterious circumstances. Her body was never found, but Zachary was investigated for her murder. Zachary spared himself the hangman's noose by departing of natural causes.'

'How fascinating,' I say. It's also a bit unsettling that something like that might have happened at my house, even if it was hundreds of years ago.

'We've got archives in the back room,' he says. 'If you'd like to see them.'

'Maybe another day,' I say. While I am interested in seeing the archives, I have a sneaking suspicion that someone has beaten me to it. Someone who must have seen this display and researched the story of a local smuggler who did in his wife. Someone who then chopped and changed it beyond all recognition, making it into a bestselling romance novel.

Phillipa King. It has to be.

'*The Lady's Secret,*' I say, thinking aloud. 'I think Phillipa King based her book on the story of Zachary and Veronica. She even set it at Tanglewild. She describes the house so vividly.'

He scratches his balding head. 'Well, she would, wouldn't she? She spent the summer there back then.'

'Did she?'

I feel like I'm chasing shadows in broad daylight. Of course Phillipa King could have visited the house before we owned it. Dave and I never met the vendor, and I know nothing about the former residents. Maybe I should have taken more of an interest in the history of my house – *the* house. Because Tanglewild will be standing long after I'm gone. I'm just a passing denizen, like Zachary Jones, Veronica, and all the others.

'I don't know anything about that business, mind.' The old man hobbles backwards a step, as if to avoid the conversation. 'She came here to look at some old plans and documents. That's all I know.'

I get the feeling that he's holding something back. He twists the end of his cane into a groove on the floor and seems to be debating with himself – historian, custodian, local busybody. But I never know which one wins out, because just then, the door opens with a disagreeable screech. An elderly woman comes inside peering into the room over half-moon trifocals.

'I'm sorry, miss,' the old man says to me. 'Mrs Carter-Smith is here for the bell.' He taps the tip of his cane on the old fire bell in the centre of the room. It makes a tinny, hollow sound that in no way befits its brave history. 'It's going on special exhibition over at the Guildhall. I'm closing up now to get it sorted.'

Taking the hint, I take a photo of the display case with my phone. Though, I'm less interested in eighteenth-century smugglers at Tanglewild than in what the old man knows – and is clearly reluctant to tell me – about the house's more recent history, and the connection with Phillipa King.

'Thank you,' I say as I make my way out. 'It's been enlightening.'

'Happy to oblige.'

'I may come back again to look at those archives, if that's OK.'

'You do that,' he replies. But I sense a coolness in his voice as he flips the sign on the door from open to closed. I leave the museum with the distinct impression that the elderly curator has been saved by the bell.

18

THE LADY'S SECRET BY PHILLIPA KING

Victoria's hands turned hard and rough. She'd given her name as 'Tilly' on that first grey morning, and had been put to work before dawn carrying wood up and down the stairs for fires that were never lit, washing the linen with lye soap, and scrubbing the kitchen floors and the pantry clean of mice droppings. Within a week, her spirit was bowed from exhaustion, her body weak from the bone-chilling cold and the thin soup not fit for pigs. Within a fortnight, she packed her trunk in the middle of the night, her hands shaking from tiredness. Anything, anywhere, had to be better than this. Would Tom take her back after she'd run away? Her father after she'd stolen his money?

Victoria hung her head. In her heart, she knew the best solution, and the only option left. The master of the house – a man she hadn't seen since her arrival but who was described by the other servants as brooding and cruel – would surely have to pay for her burial service. Tom and her father would never know that she'd been here at all, and that she'd taken the ultimate step to escape from a life that was unendurable.

She left her mother's locket in the trunk at the foot of the bed. Where she was going, she wouldn't be needing it. Putting a dressing gown over her thin night-gown, she crept down the back stairs and through the door at the back. The house was silent and tomb-like as she walked across the lawn that sloped gently down to the river's edge. The cold lacerated her skin, her bare feet wet from the *frost-covered grass. Unconsciously, she put her hand on her belly. Where a life had once taken hold and started to grow, now there was only a sharp ache and emptiness. But soon it wouldn't matter any more. Soon, she would feel nothing...*

Her body trembled as she stepped into the shallow water at the bank, the mud oozing between her toes. In the distance, an owl hooted, and a splash stunned the night silence. She turned to look upstream. A faint light glowed on the water at the bend in the river. The splashes grew rhythmic. Oars – a boat. Someone was coming.

She took a few tentative steps further into the river until she could feel the current sweeping against her legs. If she didn't act soon, it would be too late. She willed herself to keep walking as her body screamed from the cold and her heart raced on, desperate to keep beating. The boat was coming closer now, drifting in her direction. She had to act... She had to...

Victoria jumped. The dark freezing water covered her head like a shroud.

19

When I return home from the museum, there are three cars in the drive and the house is a flurry of activity. There are two men and a woman in the great hall, surveying, discussing, and measuring up, all overseen by the monolithic presence of Connie, who's sitting on the sofa (Simon is next to her, folding the laundry). Jammie is with them, looking distinctly wary with all the strangers in her house. Theo's already let me know that for health and safety reasons, she'll have to stay locked up in her dog run while the filming is going on. So far, however, the crew members I've met seem to like having her around.

'Hi.' I greet them all, feeling excited that it's really happening. I pat Jammie reassuringly on the head.

'Hello, Mrs Greene,' one of the men says to me. 'Lovely house.'

'Thanks.' I grin. 'And you can call me Lizzie.'

'When's the last time you had the washer looked at?' Connie grunts in my direction. 'It's on its last legs.'

'Is it?' I don't even let this bother me. The washing machine is old and pernickety, just like the house. But if Connie's bothered, then she can take their laundry to the cleaners. I walk past her to the kitchen and practically bump into Theo, who's carrying a tray of steaming mugs full of tea.

'Oh, hi, Lizzie,' he says, looking a tiny bit embarrassed. For a second, I worry that he's having second thoughts about his message: *PS – I look forward to seeing you again soon.* 'Hope it's OK, but I used your kettle.'

'It's fine.' I don't point out that he's also using my tray, mugs and teabags. The contract gives the film crew access to the entire premises, but the use of personal property is strictly by arrangement. But until the bulk of the crew arrives with their food tents and trailers, I've stocked up on tea, Sainsbury's Basics mugs, and chocolate digestive biscuits. I'm pleased to see that my efforts are contributing to the project in some small way. 'Help yourself.'

'Great.' He grins as his eyes brush mine. 'Let me hand these out and I'll make you one too.'

'Black with one sugar, please.' It's been a long time since a man other than Simon has offered to make me tea or anything else, and I feel the same frisson of pleasure as I did the other night. I find Theo quite attractive, in a low-key, unassuming way. I know nothing about him (or the Red Sox, which I think is a baseball team), but I *feel* something when I'm around him. An awareness of another person – of a man – that I didn't think I'd ever be willing or able to feel again.

I tidy up the kitchen, listening to snippets of conversation in the adjacent hall: Connie talking about Dominic Kennedy; Simon conferring with the crew about removing the radiators and modern light fittings. It's all so alien and fascinating. The crew all seem focused and professional, but there's a buzz too, of people genuinely excited about doing their bit on the film. It's a very different environment from a law firm.

Theo returns to the kitchen with the empty tray. 'It's a full-time job keeping up with the teas and coffees,' he says.

'I'm happy to help out,' I say.

His smile wavers for a second, and I worry that I've overstepped the mark. Once things get going, the kids and I will need to stay out of the way. We're supposed to move to the two guest bedrooms above the kitchen, accessible by the back stairs. For us it will be like staying in a hotel, without the cleaning service, of course.

'I mean, just until things ramp up,' I clarify. 'Then we'll try not to get underfoot.'

'That might be difficult.' Theo refills the kettle and boils it, making two more mugs of tea. 'It will be very chaotic. There's no avoiding it.'

'I understand.'

'It's great that you're so keen on the project, Lizzie. That really helps.' He brings our mugs to the table.

'And what about you?' I say as soon as he's seated. 'Now that you've found the location, are you off to the next thing?' I try not to sound too invested in his answer. The film project will go on for several months. It would be nice if Theo was around to keep me company while I'm staying out of the way. And then, who knows...

'Actually, I have some exciting news.' He leans forward. 'I've got a new role working with Phillipa when she's here on set.'

'Phillipa King? Really?'

'Yeah. I met her when the project first came to Rabbit-N-Hat. She wrote the screenplay herself, which is unusual these days. But it means that she'll be here once the filming begins. She needed an assistant, and she chose me.'

'That sounds... good.' I'm chuffed that Theo will be here on set, but a little alarmed that Phillipa King will be here too. It's one thing to have 'friends in high places' – quite another to meet them.

'For me, it's perfect. She really is a first-rate writer.'

'Yes, she is.' I feel like a ventriloquist's dummy allowing him to put words in my mouth. I'm enjoying *The Lady's Secret*, but I'm not quite sure I'd classify Phillipa King as a 'first-rate' writer.

Theo continues to wax lyrical about Phillipa King. My tea suddenly tastes too sweet, and I wish I'd had milk instead of sugar. I stand up and take my mug to the sink.

'I understand she has a connection with the house,' I say when he stops for a breath. 'She spent a summer here, or something?'

'I'm not sure,' he says. 'I think someone mentioned this area to Michelle when we first started the location search. But I don't know the details.'

'The house in the book does bear a remarkable similarity, don't you think? I went to the local museum and learned some of the history. Apparently there was a smuggler, Zachary Jones, who lived here in 1790.

His wife, Veronica, disappeared under mysterious circumstances. I assume their story was one of her inspirations for the book?'

'Phillipa has many influences,' he says. He proceeds to give me a long litany of them – from a pub in Dorking with smuggling tunnels underneath, to the novels of Daphne du Maurier, to the TV series of *Poldark*.

'How interesting,' I say.

He catches the tone in my voice. 'Sorry,' he says, a little flushed. 'Didn't mean to go on like that. It's just exciting to be working with a famous writer. But what about you? Your mother-in-law says that you've got a new job?'

'Oh, that.' I wave a hand dismissively. 'I'm a lawyer. I took a few years out, and now I'm trying to get back into it. Clients, conference calls, commuting…' I close my mouth. These things can't possibly be interesting to someone who works in the glamourous film industry.

'What kind of law do you do?' Theo asks.

'Mostly corporate. Mergers, acquisitions, asset sales, that sort of thing.'

'Sounds interesting.'

I look at him closely, trying to decide whether he's sincere or just making conversation. I decide that if I'm going to compete with Phillipa King, I'll need to put my best foot forward. 'It can be,' I say. 'It's quite fast paced, and some of the companies do interesting things. Plus, it's an intellectual challenge.'

'It must be. I've a lot of respect for people who do that kind of work.'

'Well,' I say, pleasantly surprised, 'it pays the bills. Things were really hard after Dave died.' He listens with interest as I tell him about the posthumous mess left behind by my errant husband. 'That's why this project is a godsend, really—'

'Theo?' The set designer pokes her head into the kitchen. 'We're leaving in five.'

'Sure.' Theo looks at me apologetically and, for a second, I think he's going to put a hand on my arm. 'Sorry, Lizzie, but we need to get back to London – we're hoping to beat the traffic.'

'Yes, of course.' Having told him my story, I feel a little let down. I go to the sink to do the washing up.

'But maybe one of these evenings we can grab dinner at a pub.'

I turn to look at him. His face gives nothing away and I'm not sure if I should read anything into the invitation. Except, a part of me – the lion's share – *wants* to read something into it.

'I'd like that,' I say.

'OK, I've got your number. And thanks for the tea.' At the last second, he leans in conspiratorially. 'Though just between you and me, I prefer coffee.'

'Just between you and me, I do too,' I say, laughing. 'I'll stock up on some for next time.'

'Great.'

When Theo is gone, I look around my kitchen, taking in the familiar chaos and disorder that exists in counterpoint to the simplicity of the stone floor, dark panelling, and carved fireplace. I feel a strange lightness inside me, like I'm a butterfly that's been trapped inside a jar, and someone has taken the lid off and shaken me out into the world again. Just for a moment, I experience that magical something I thought I'd never be capable of feeling again.

I feel happy.

20

THE LADY'S SECRET BY PHILLIPA KING

Her hair felt like it was being ripped from her scalp as the hand grabbed it and pulled her upwards.

'What the hell are you doing?' The deep male voice rumbled in her stomach like thunder. She blinked the icy water from her eyes. She knew she should struggle away and continue on with her fatal quest. But as the strong arms lifted her waterlogged body into the boat, she lacked the energy to struggle.

'Please...' she sputtered. Surely it was a trick of the pale moon shining on the water, but the man's eyes almost seemed to glow a deep sapphire as he stared into hers, hard and accusing.

'We must make haste, William,' another voice said from the stern of the boat. 'They were only minutes behind us.'

Victoria tried to look towards the second voice, but the man's dark hooded cloak made him fade into the blackness beyond. Only the whites of his eyes caught the dim light.

'No,' said the deep voice of the man called William. 'We must get her to shore. The cold will kill her otherwise.'

'That must have been her intent,' the second man reasoned.

'No. Get to shore and tie up the boat. Signal to the others. It's all off for tonight.'

'But—'

'Damn it, Sambrooke, do as I say.'

The second man didn't respond, but the boat began to creep towards the shore.

Victoria drifted in and out of consciousness until at last, strong arms lifted her and carried her up towards the place she had been so eager to escape. Idyllwild Manor.

The Master, it seemed, had returned.

21

I jolt awake, my forehead damp with sweat. Above my head, the beads of the dreamcatcher dance and twinkle in the sliver of moonlight piercing through the gap in the curtains. I throw off the duvet and jump to my feet. Before I went to sleep, I'd been reading the scene where Victoria Easterbrook tries to kill herself by walking into the river and is pulled out by the master, William Clarke. But that wasn't what I had dreamed about...

The silence seems almost unnatural. I get up and check on Jack; his breathing whuffles in deep sleep as he sucks the arm of his Spiderman. Seeing him makes me feel instantly calmer. In her room down the hall, Katie is snoring loudly, gripping her old teddy. The dog is sprawled at the end of the bed, snoring too. My heart aches thinking of my daughter's internal struggle between remaining a child and becoming a young woman. I have a strong urge to lie down beside her and hold her in my arms. But sleep is the best thing for her right now.

I return to my room and climb back into bed, rewinding the earlier dream. Reliving the heart-palpitating part where I was lying in bed – this bed – with an unknown man. I feel a sharp stab of pleasure radiate down my body. Whoever he was, he'd managed to *awaken* me from a deep hibernation (one that began somewhere around the time I became pregnant with Katie, and lasted until my husband's untimely demise).

I close my eyes, hoping to conjure the face of the dream man in my mind's eye. I can't do it. He's not real, and it's definitely better that way.

Minutes later, or maybe it's hours, I wake up to the beeping of the alarm. My stomach dives at the thought of another day commuting into London, missing the excitement and chaos here. As I shower and dress, I think of Theo and his invitation to the pub. In the light of day, the whole thing strikes me as absurd. It's been almost a year since Dave's death, and though I've realised that my marriage was over long before that, the idea of opening myself up and trusting someone again is an alien concept. Dreams are one thing. But in reality, Theo and I would never work.

On the other hand, there is no 'Theo and I' that needs to 'work'. It's a night down the pub for Christ's sake, not a one-knee two-carat diamond proposal. A few drinks, a nice chat, no strings attached. I've been out with the other mums, welcomed Connie and Simon into my drive, and let a whole crew of strangers into my house. This seems a logical next step. I might (God forbid!) even enjoy it like I have those other things. Besides which, it's research. I need to find out more about Phillipa King. My trip to the museum has confirmed that she has a connection to the house, but I don't know much more than that. It's a little unnerving that she once came to this house and possibly used it as a setting for her book. At the very least, I'd like to know when she's due to come on set.

I down a cup of coffee and bowl of cereal and chuck my dishes in the dishwasher. On my way out of the house, I stop by the caravan and knock on the door.

'I'm coming,' Connie groans sleepily from inside. 'Go on – don't miss your train.'

'Have a good day.' I continue walking up the lane to the station, determined to get my mind on work and the day ahead. Meetings, calls, billable hours, stress. But the thoughts fly out of my head as I near the top of the road and a silver Audi turns in suddenly so that I have to jump out of the way. 'Hey!' I yell as the car slows down just past me. The window rolls down.

'I didn't see you,' the driver says. And I don't want to feel those green eyes on me, or look at that face. I don't want to acknowledge him at all.

'You should drive slower,' I say to Luke Thornton. I turn and walk as quickly as I can up the road.

* * *

Maybe it's my restless night, or maybe the fact that it's all happening at my house, while I'm stuck in an airless conference room, but whatever it is, I have trouble focusing on work. I keep wondering about what's going on at Tanglewild.

Around midday, Theo texts me and clears up that particular mystery. There are risk managers and insurers, electricians, and set builders due on site. While the producer, Richard Silverman, is responsible for finance and logistics, it's Luke Thornton who's overseeing all the creative aspects. I guess that's why, unfortunately, he's on site at all hours.

In the late afternoon, I wait alone in the conference room for the signatories to turn up so I can close my renewable financing deal. I stand by the huge window and stare out at the vertiginous panorama of East London. A skyline of cranes, punctuated at ground level by shops, housing terraces, rail lines, and in the hazy distance, the towers of Canary Wharf. A world-class view, but it strikes me how much I'd rather be home doing something homey and simple like working in the garden, watching the children play, or having a chat with Hannah or Connie—

'Oh!' I cry out as I feel a hand placed on the small of my back. I whirl around; the hand belongs to Harry Reynolds, my boss. 'Sorry,' I say, flustered. 'I didn't hear you come in.'

'No worries, Lizzie.' He smiles at me, the tips of his teeth pointy and vulpine beneath his fleshy lips. 'I just came in to see how you're doing.'

I pace a few steps away and update him on the deal. Everything is done and dusted and we're just waiting for signatures.

'Good work,' he says, moving towards me again. 'But I knew you'd have everything in hand.'

'Thanks.' I resist a strong urge to step back. Harry's leaning in so close that I can smell mint on his breath, masking an undernote of stale cigarette.

'You've settled in here so well, Lizzie,' he purrs. 'And you're looking well too. Much more like your old self.'

My skin crawls as his eyes wander over me. I feel that same dirty, violated feeling as I did the moment I learned the truth about Dave. He reaches up and brushes a strand of hair behind my ears. I want to flinch – or better yet, slap him. But I need this job; I step back with an embarrassed laugh. 'Thanks, Harry.' I force myself to smile. 'Cuppa tea?'

His fleshy face morphs for a nanosecond into cuckolded boss, but he recovers quickly. 'No thanks. But maybe after the signing we could go out for a drink. You deserve a reward for all your hard work.'

The invitation is as unmistakable as the irony. It's been barely twenty-four hours since Theo asked me out (admittedly with much less of a display of romantic intent), and now Harry has thrown his hat into the ring. He helped me out in my darkest hour, but not, it seems, out of the goodness of his heart. I suppose I should be flattered: Harry usually goes for the bright-eyed, bushy-tailed, twenty-something ingénue type. I found such things repulsive then, and I'm even more disgusted now.

'I'm afraid I can't.' I move to the other side of the conference table. 'It's so difficult making last-minute childcare arrangements.'

'Of course.' He frowns. Outside the glass wall of the conference room, a receptionist is leading a quintet of men in suits in our direction. Thank God.

'Another time then,' he grumbles.

I let out a relieved breath as the men enter the room and the receptionist offers teas and coffees all round. Harry does the obligatory greetings and handshakes, then, thankfully, leaves the room. My voice sounds unnaturally high-pitched as I address the newcomers. 'I'm Elizabeth Greene,' I say. 'Now, let's get these documents signed, and I'll have you out of here and down the pub in no time.'

22

'It's a "thing", you know, for some men.'

'What is?' I pour Connie a slug from the bottle of Scotch I bought at the station. As I didn't manage to get home from the signing until half nine, I figured I owed her a stiff one.

'Fresh widow,' Connie says. 'They can sniff it out.'

'You're joking.' I pour myself a glass of Zinfandel and plop down in a chair to drink it. I hadn't planned on telling Connie what happened with Harry, or with Theo. Even though she's here all the time and knows the details of my life, she's also Dave's mother, and it seemed a bit gauche. And, quite frankly, in replaying what happened with Harry, I feel disgusted by my own behaviour. Instead of acting like Victoria Easterbrook – simpering and people-pleasing –I should have been a strong, modern woman and told him where to go.

But actually it was Connie who 'sniffed it out' herself, saying that I had an unusual amount of colour in my cheeks.

'No, I'm not joking.' Connie shakes her head. 'I think you'll find, Lizzie, that once you're "back out there", so to speak, you won't lack for attention.'

'Don't be ridiculous. I'm well the wrong side of thirty-five and I've got two kids. As someone pointed out recently, I'm much too old for any shenanigans.' I bristle at the memory of being 'ill met by moonlight' by Luke Thornton and Dominic Kennedy.

Connie laughs. 'Do you really need *me* to reassure you? What do I need to say – that you're beautiful? Tick. That you're clever and dedicated? Tick. Do you want me to identify areas of improvement? Because there's one big one. You need to lighten up and enjoy life a bit.'

'Christ, Connie. So you're saying I should have stuck around and shagged my cheating boss?'

'Hell no, you should have kicked him where it counts. But there will be other opportunities that come your way. Don't be a martyr just because your marriage wasn't everything you thought. I mean, you let yourself be duped before, but that's all water under the bridge. This time, hold out for something better. You'll find it.' She lowers her voice. 'And take it from me. The second time around is twice as nice.'

I think of Simon, and my uncharitable image of Jack Sprat. I didn't know Dave's dad, but Connie makes him sound like a prototype for Dave. There are no perfect marriages, of course. But Simon and Connie seem to have that odd thing going where they actually like each other and have a lasting (if incomprehensible) physical spark.

'I'll have to take your word for it,' I say. 'And in fact, I am considering "other opportunities". Like I said, Theo's invited me to dinner.'

'The scout.' Connie pours herself another glass. 'He seems... young.'

'Maybe. But you've got a few years on Simon.'

'Sure.' Her face lights up at the mention of her husband. 'But it's not so much years that matter as experience. Simon has lived a lot. He's had a hard life, and he's all the better for it. That's important, I think.'

'I guess I tick that box too. As for Theo, all I know is that he's nice. I like him, and I want to get to know him better.'

'Nice.' Her tone is dismissive.

'Simon's nice too,' I assert.

'Oh, yes, he's nice. Among other things.' She actually winks.

I finish my wine and put my glass in the dishwasher before I'm tempted to have another. While I'm glad they're a happy couple, I really don't need any details.

'Speaking of Simon, how's the dreamcatcher?' Connie says out of the blue. 'It was his idea. He's not religious, but he's very spiritual.'

'It's fine.' Like an idiot, I blush. Maybe it's *The Lady's Secret* or maybe it is the dreamcatcher and the power of suggestion. Either way, the profane masculine presence (and there's nothing sacred or spiritual about it) in my dreams can't be denied.

'Ah.' Connie annoys me further by not letting it pass. 'Maybe your subconscious is trying to tell you something. That you're too young to throw in the towel completely.'

'Maybe my subconscious is making a play for Dominic Kennedy.' I hope she knows I'm joking.

Her smile is enigmatic. 'Perhaps. Or the other one.'

'The other one?'

'Luke Thornton, of course.' She makes it sounds like it's the most obvious thing in the world.

'Luke?' I laugh out loud.

'He's something, isn't he? Brooding, untameable...'

'Come on, Connie, you've been reading too much romantic drivel.' I make an instant decision to get another glass from the cupboard and pour myself a second drink that I don't need or want. 'Luke Thornton rejected my house,' I say. '"Moody" and "unpleasant" are the words I would use – if we're going literary. "Irritating bastard" if we're not.'

'I didn't know you had such strong feelings for him.' Connie chuckles.

I've had enough. At the end of the day, my love life, or lack thereof, is none of Connie's business. I shove aside the new glass of wine.

'Whatever,' I say, using Katie's classic put-down line. 'I'm going to bed. Thanks for staying tonight.'

'We had a nice chat earlier on,' Connie says, giving me an infuriatingly smug look. 'We talked about the project, and the cast, and about his film *The Lost People* that won the Golden Globe. Did you see it?'

'No.' I start walking out.

'You should. It was very dark and, actually, quite philosophical.'

'I'm sure.' I roll my eyes.

'I gather he'll be here almost every day from now on. Just so you know.'

'I'm sure he'll appreciate having you as a member of his fan club,' I say. 'As for me, I'm afraid I'll be at *work*.'

Connie downs the last of her drink and screws the top onto the bottle. 'And miss the excitement here?'

'I'll leave that for you and the tabloids.'

23

THE LADY'S SECRET BY PHILLIPA KING

When Victoria opened her eyes, she thought she'd been damned to eternal hellfire. Her body was covered in sweat, but still, she was shivering. The room was bathed in an unfamiliar orange glow: a fire burned in the grate. The housekeeper came in the room and placed a tray of tea on the table, frowned in disapproval and left quickly. She grabbed the mug of tea and drank greedily, the hot liquid burning her throat. It was only then that the room came fully into focus. That he came into focus.

He was a solid man, tall and broad-shouldered. He still wore his breeches and boots, his shirt open at the neck. His hair was dark and unruly, tied back at his nape. All this she took in in an instant. What drew her gaze and held it fast was his eyes. A deep, crystalline blue, the colour of a cloudless summer sky. But these eyes were not cloudless. Something dark and dangerous flickered underneath. Something that made her want to run — but whether towards him or away, she wasn't quite sure. She was suddenly aware that her clothing had been changed; she was no longer wearing the soaked nightgown. Instead, she was wearing a billowing man's shirt, and she could feel her nakedness underneath. Victoria put her hands to her face to hide her shame, but his eyes burned through her body like dark stars.

She was aware of him moving in his chair, reaching to the side to pour two *glasses of amber liquid. He held one out to her. Refusing to look at him, she removed her hands from her face, took the glass, and gulped it down.*

'So you wanted to die, is that right?' His voice shot straight to the centre of her abdomen.

Victoria nodded slowly.

'Why? The servants tell me you work here now. That your name is Tilly. Is your life such a misery?'

The last few months of her life came back to her in a rush of images, colours, and pain. Tom carving their initials in the tree; discovering him with the servant; the foul herbs she'd swallowed that made her insides explode with blood and agony; her father at his desk, asleep as she jimmied the lock with the lizard paperknife and took the money; the endless coach journey into the unknown – nearly all of it forgotten and eclipsed by the weeks of drudgery and deprivation.

She looked up suddenly, allowing herself to yield to the gravitational pull of those sapphire eyes. And it was then that she knew – with all her heart, body, and soul – that more than anything, she wanted to live.

24

I put down the e-reader and roll my eyes, feeling like I might drown in a sea of bad prose. It's been such an awful day though that reading a few pages of *The Lady's Secret* at home in bed feels like a guilty escape from reality (and I wouldn't be caught dead reading it on the train). The kids are asleep, and the dreamcatcher sparkles above my head. I'm exhausted, but at least I'm not due in the office tomorrow. I read on, turning back to the illuminated page.

William Clarke, having caught on to the fact that Victoria was a bit higher class than your garden variety kitchen maid (not to mention, more beautiful), reassigns her to work as a companion to his elderly mother. The days become even more tedious dealing with a spiteful old lady who loves gossip and playing patience, and who takes an instant dislike to Tilly/Victoria. The only visitor is a woman called Belle, the master's sister-in-law, whose presence brings to the surface one of the dark secrets of Idyllwild Hall – the fact that the master's wife, Charity, disappeared under mysterious circumstances. Some rumours say that she ran away with a lover; others, that the master did away with her.

Reading the words, I can picture every room in the house that Victoria inhabits. The great hall, the library, the drawing room. The little similarities: a woman's face carved on a mantelpiece, crests made of coloured glass set high into the windows that look out over the river, the great studded door made from timbers of a ship. I also recall the photo of Veronica Jones that I took at the museum. As far as I know, her mystery remains unsolved. Did *she* run away with a lover or did her husband, Zachary, 'do away' with her? At some point, I'll go back to the museum and find more information. Information that Phillipa King has already used in her bestselling novel. She may have set her book at my house, but at least it's still my house.

I finish the chapter. Victoria hears a noise in the night. She goes downstairs and outside wearing a diaphanous nightgown and thin flannel dressing gown, her auburn hair flowing around her shoulders (of course). She hides in the hedge as the smuggling boats arrive, their lanterns flickering like fireflies against the blackness of the trees. And overseeing the unloading of the cargo is the master, William Clarke. He's a tall, dark, and handsome hero – nothing new there. But it's his intensity – the smouldering masculinity that might be anger and cruelty, *or* might be wild, untameable passion – that keeps readers like me turning the pages.

Did Dave and I ever have that kind of passion? If we did, it's so long buried in the past that I can't remember. In the early months I'd be working late at the office and he'd invite me out to a club in Soho. We'd share a bottle of wine, then take a taxi back to his flat in Battersea. When we woke up in the morning, we'd go for breakfast and a long walk along the Embankment. I remember the little pub we went to behind the Tate Modern with the dark little booths. I was flattered that he'd chosen me, and the fact that I sometimes didn't hear from him for days kept things on edge.

Over time, things changed. Marriage, children, moving out of London. When I think of him now, I see him as a loving but absent father; a companionable but disinterested partner. In the years after the children came along, I suppose I kept thinking that things would change – when Jack went to nursery/when Katie could go to afterschool club/when I went back to work/when Dave finished this deal or that deal and finally started making more time for the family. We'd eventually start having 'date nights' again and rekindle whatever spark we once had. *Eventually. Someday. In the future...*

In hindsight, it was never going to happen. Dave did manage to rekindle a spark – with women who were not me. He never gave up that illicit London lifestyle at all. A part of me doesn't even blame him. I'm not one of those women that finds motherhood easy and fulfilling in and of itself. I cringe at the memory of my own voice: complaining, nagging, feeling secure and complacent in my right to do so. I stopped seeing our marriage as something important, something that needed nurturing just like the children did. My hope that things would change in the future was just one more illusion. Although I still struggle with the finality of Dave's death, it did provide a much-needed catalyst for change.

I pull the duvet up to my chin and sigh, feeling guilty for viewing Dave's death as a good thing. But nothing is going to bring him back, and I can't keep using guilt as an excuse to avoid getting on with my life. Connie says it's better 'the second time around'. It's only in the last few days and weeks that I've been able to imagine a possible second time around. Am I mad to want a new relationship – a new love – at some point in the future?

Eventually, I drift off to sleep under the watchful eye of the dream-catcher. My dreams are chaotic and indistinct, all except for the strong sense of a masculine presence. Watching me from the shadows, wanting me in a way that I've never been wanted before. But as I twist and turn through the labyrinth of the dream world, try as I might, I can't catch a glimpse of his face.

25

I was prepared for excitement; prepared for chaos and disruption. Prepared for the huge upheaval that people like Connie said would happen but that I chose to brush off and sweep under the carpet. But none of my so-called preparation comes close to reality once the film crew moves in.

The house clearance team arrives in mid-March. Luckily, Jack and Katie are at school because, otherwise, I'm sure there would be tears and sit-in protests. They attack all of our worldly possessions on the ground floor with bubble wrap, shove them into boxes, and cart them away. All the toys, all the photos, all the books and DVDs – even the TV has to go. Clearly, I should have done more sorting and packing myself. Our things will be sent away to storage for three whole months – we might as well be moving to America or Australia rather than into the two spare bedrooms in the wing above the kitchen.

When Jack and Katie do finally arrive home, the ground floor is almost completely bare, except for the kitchen (I had the old piano moved in there so that Katie could keep practising for her Grade II exam) and one sofa in the drawing room. Katie immediately dons her roller blades and spends two hours careering round the empty floors. Jack has a good howl when he discovers that his Cozy Coupe is gone, but he persuades

Simon to bring his tricycle in from the shed, and he and Katie chase each other on their wheels. Jammie goes berserk, nipping at their heels like a young pup. Of course, it all ends in tears when they collide like errant atoms, and Katie sprawls onto her face, bloodying her lip, on top of the yelping dog, and Jack goes down with them like a wiggly domino. He proceeds to scream for England.

I expected to feel sad, or at least nostalgic, at seeing the house so bare. The opposite is true. As I walk through the ground floor while the kids are having their tea, it's like looking at an oil painting that's been cleaned of the layers of old varnish and grime and suddenly regains its colours. I notice the grain of the wood panelling, the cracks and tool marks in the carvings, mineral veins in the stones of the hearth, the irregularities in panes of glass that have survived for hundreds of years. The old curtains are gone (and I gave firm instructions that they were not to be brought back), and there's dust and dog hair in all the nooks and crannies. But the rooms themselves are elegant and spacious. I feel, if anything, a little excited. Having a blank canvas in my own home is just the thing I've needed.

And true to my bargain with the universe, when Katie and Jack are finished eating, I find a pencil and call them over to the door to the hall.

'What's up, Mum?' Katie looks wary.

'Stand against the door frame,' I say. 'Back straight, chin up.'

She rolls her eyes as I mark her height and the date. I feel a little bit teary as I see how much she's grown. I then measure Jack, and then (because they insist) the dog. And when I'm done, I pull them to me, and we all have a big hug. For once, even Katie doesn't protest.

***

After supper, I move our things upstairs to the spare bedrooms, lugging clothing and laundry up the back stairs. I've warned Katie that she needs to pack, and for once, she actually listens. She hauls in practically everything she owns: books, journals, colouring pens, clothing, toys she hasn't played with in ages, and her precious Kindle Fire tablet. Although Jack's room isn't being used for the filming, I move him in with us too. As I drag the Pack-N-Play travel cot down from the attic for him to sleep in, I feel the familiar prickles of guilt. What kind of mum uproots her son from his cosy room with the Winnie the Pooh wall stickers, superhero mobile, and everything that's familiar to him since he was a baby? On the other hand, it's this project that's allowing him to keep his room at all.

When it's packed full of stuff and the kids are asleep, I return to my own room to spend a last night in my own bed. It feels even more final because tomorrow's the one-year anniversary of Dave's death. I've arranged with Connie and Hannah to take the children to the grave and put flowers there.

I lay in bed staring up at the dark blue canopy over my head. I've moved the dreamcatcher to my new room, and I miss its now-familiar presence. Katie wasn't conceived in this bed, but Jack was. How long ago that seems. And now, it will be used for a simulated love scene between Victoria and William, played by Natasha Blythe and Dominic Kennedy. I feel a pang of guilt, but talk myself out of it. It wasn't me who 'violated the sanctity of the marital bed', but rather, my husband. I've spent way too much time in anger, turmoil, and fear. Now I'm becoming a different person, and I'm not going to feel guilty for it.

I open my e-reader. After Victoria watches the smugglers unload their cargo, she sneaks back to the house:

> She closed the door silently behind her, letting out a relieved breath. No one had seen her, and if anyone asked, she had seen nothing. But as she made her way silently across the hard stones of the kitchen floor, she heard a sound behind her. The door opened and slammed shut. Hard footsteps came towards her. She willed herself to run, but instead, her legs froze uselessly beneath her.
>
> His eyes were wild as he came to where she stood, rooted to the spot.
>
> 'What did you see?' he asked her, his voice dark and menacing.
>
> 'I won't tell anyone. I promise. And I'll leave in the morning. It's better that way.'
>
> 'It's better this way,' he growled. And in an instant, his hands were circling her waist, pulling her to him, his mouth hot and wet as he

found hers. She felt like she was teetering on a ledge, defying gravity only by his iron grip and the sheer force of his desire. He pushed her against the wall, struggling more with himself than with her.

But then, just as suddenly, he removed his hands from her, stepping back, pushing her away. She slid to the floor, her heart exploding in her chest, unable to remember what it ever was to breathe. His spurs clicked on the stones as he stalked across the kitchen and went back outside into the night...

The upshot is that Victoria is left panting, terrified, and wanting more.

As am I, and no doubt, millions of other readers as well. I turn out the light, feeling a little ashamed of what this says about me and my fellow womenkind. But surely we're as entitled to our guilty pleasures as men. Since the dawn of time, Adam and Eve have a lot to answer for.

* * *

Where guilty pleasures are concerned, it's like speaking of the devil. The next morning, the Master himself arrives at Tanglewild – Dominic Kennedy. It's the worst possible moment: the house is a flurry of removals and deliveries, I'm flustered getting the kids ready for school, and Jammie doesn't want to be locked in her run.

Dominic pulls up in his low black sports car, rolls down the window, and speaks to the security guard, a man called Danny, who's been posted at the gate to keep out paparazzi and onlookers. The guard waves him in and he parks next to the stone wall just as I'm trying to wrestle Jack into his car seat, out of breath for having run back to the house to retrieve a forgotten Spiderman. As I'm about to drive off, Dominic gets out of the car and I suffer a momentary paralysis. My God – he's hot.

Like the rest of the world, I've seen him in a few mini-series on TV. He usually plays the dashing rogue – tall, dark-haired, perfectly turned-out in period costume. In real life, he's a little shorter and older than the screen makes him out to be. He's wearing a grey T-shirt, just tight enough to hint at the chest that launched a thousand hot flashes, and well-fitting jeans. If anything, he's even more handsome than his on-screen alter egos.

'Mum, we need to go,' Katie calls out.

'Um... yeah.' I do nothing.

'Elizabeth.' He walks towards me. 'So what do you think, Miss Bennet?' he quotes in a deep, Shakespearean voice. 'Will you come to Pemberley?'

The cheesiness of the quote almost puts me off him. Almost. He immediately senses my reaction and drops the bad Derek Jacobi impression.

'Sorry, Lizzie.' He leans casually against the wooden post of the garage. 'Couldn't resist.'

'I'm sure, uh... Dominic.'

His beams his smile upon me, his lips full, eyes rakish. He may be too handsome for anyone's own good, but there's a warmth about him too. I find myself wanting to like him.

'Call me Dom,' he says. 'I've just seen the call sheet. It's pretty full-on. I think we're all going to be getting rather cosy around here.' He laughs, and I join in. Whatever chaos is in store, there are worse things than having Dominic Kennedy on the premises.

'Are they starting already?' I say. 'I didn't expect the cast to be here until after they finished the set. But then, this whole thing is completely new to me.'

'No, you're spot on,' he says. 'The rest of the cast won't be here yet.' His smile fades and I detect an undernote of something unexpected... Vulnerability. 'I like to get on location before anyone else, if possible. The truth is, I get stage fright. How lame does that sound?'

'Not at all,' I say. 'I mean, I can't even imagine...' I trail off as the scene I read last night pops into my head – William Clarke entering the house wild-eyed and sweaty, teeming with testosterone. Demonstrating his feelings for (or, not to split hairs, forcibly accosting) Victoria Easterbrook, leaving her a quivering mass of heaving bosom. This man. In my house. And though I haven't got there in the book yet, the final outcome is clear...

He'll be in bed with her.

My bed.

He studies me with half-closed eyes; his eyelashes are long and black. For a moment, I'm sure he can read my thoughts.

'Mum!' Katie calls out.

'Yes,' he says, 'some parts of the job are harder than others. For me, it's that first bit – getting into character. Once I'm there though...' This time, there's no mistaking the spark in those melting brown eyes.

I flush to the roots of my hair. My kids are in the car and we're late. I don't have time to let him practise 'getting into character' on me.

As delicious as that sounds.

'Well, knock yourself out,' I say. 'Under the terms of the contract, we're all at your disposal.'

* * *

'I think he likes you.' The incredulity in Katie's voice jars me from my thoughts as we're forced to stop at the level crossing, already late for school.

'He's an actor,' I say. 'He's paid to be like that.'

It strikes me that Dominic Kennedy is a sort of con man. Not the kind who perpetrates a scam by making his victims trust him, but rather one who dupes his victims by pretending that *he's* the one who's trusting them. If he is playing a role and pretending to suffer from stage fright, he's well-practiced and convincing. I'm certainly won over. Or, maybe he's just a nice guy who, thanks to an accident of birth, scored a perfect ten in the genes department and became an unwitting sex symbol. If there is such a thing.

'Is he going to be our new dad?' Jack says, the words muffled by the thumb in his mouth.

'No, silly,' Katie cuts in. 'Not him.'

The barrier goes up but I stay put, drawing a honk from a Range Rover behind me. Why are we even having this conversation? What the hell has Connie been saying?

'Now just hold on,' I say, driving on. 'You don't have to worry about getting a new dad. We have each other – we're a family.'

Katie sniffs. It's like she was anticipating my response and is disappointed, as usual.

'What?' I glare into the rear-view mirror. 'Are you saying you *want* a new dad?'

'Yeah!' Jack says. 'I wanna play football!'

'I don't know.' Katie chews on the end of her ponytail and stares out the window.

I repeat the lecture I've given them time and time again. 'Your dad loved you very much,' I say. 'And no one will ever replace him. But you've both got a wonderful life ahead of you, and your dad will be with you in spirit. We'll go later today and put flowers on his grave.'

'Why bother?' Katie's reply is as sharp and hurt as ever. 'Dad was a shit. I've heard you say it.'

'Katie!' I yell. 'Don't you ever use that word.'

'What's a shit?' Jack says.

'I'm just saying, you deserve better, Mum.' Katie glances at me in the mirror. I can't quite decide if she's being sincere.

'What's a shit?' Jack repeats.

'It's a poo poo,' Katie says, a glimmer of a smile on her face.

'It's a word we don't say,' I growl. 'It's "a bad language".'

'I just want you to be happy, Mum,' Katie says.

'Do you?'

She nods and I almost believe her, though it's the first I've heard her say anything like that. Connie again? I didn't know that Katie wanted anything except her own pain to go away. Which is fair enough – I want that too for her. Emotion wells up in my chest. Jack is so little; he won't end up with many memories of Dave, if any at all. He'll look at the photos and believe whatever he's told about the dad that didn't live to see his third birthday. Katie will remember him though, and I want her to remember the good things, not the bad. There were good times: family dinners, holidays, trips to the seaside, laughs. To me, it all seems fuzzy and remote, but I want them to be real for her.

'Shit, shit, shit,' Jack parrots proudly.

I sigh. 'Thanks, Katie. I want you to be happy too. I want it for all of us, and I'm getting there – slowly. But I don't need a new man for that. Happiness comes from within, not from another person. Remember that, OK?'

'Yeah, Mum. Whatever.'

'Shit, shitty shit.' Jack grins from ear to ear. Katie starts to giggle.

'Jack, stop that.' I know it's futile, and in truth, I'm fighting the urge to giggle too. I pull into the school car park, anticipating a future trip to see the headmaster because my son is using 'a bad language'. We're so late that there are actually plenty of spaces, and only a few mums left in the queue to leave the car park. I herd Jack and Katie through the gate and run into Parker coming out, along with another woman who I think is called Melissa. Both are dressed in galaxy print yoga pants.

'Hi,' I say as I pass them.

'Lizzie!' Parker says. 'How are you? We heard that the film project is all systems go!'

'It is,' I say. 'And guess who arrived this morning?' I lean in, lowering my voice. 'Dominic Kennedy. That's why we're a little late.'

'OH MY GOD!' Melissa cries. 'Did you speak to him? Is he as hot in real life as he is on screen?'

'Even more so!' Since we're having an exclamation mark kind of conversation, I almost feel like telling them everything – from the stage fright to the 'getting into character'. It's nice to be something other than the grieving widow and to have something worth talking about at the school yard gates. But in the end, I decide to keep my cards close to my chest. I don't want my hot leading man to see his words in a tabloid and end up giving me the cold shoulder.

'You must have us over,' Parker says. 'Is that allowed?'

'I don't know. I can ask when the filming starts.' I make a mental note to do just that.

'Dominic Kennedy,' Melissa repeats, shaking her head.

'He seems very nice,' I say, giving her a bemused smile. 'Though, I'm still getting used to the idea that he'll be filming a love scene in my bed.'

* * *

On the way home, I think about Jack and Katie, and how there will always be a part of them that misses having a dad. I want Katie to believe what I told her. That happiness doesn't come from a man, or a house, or even having children. It has to come from within rather than the *things* around you. Before Dave died, I was the kind of person who was always whinging about today and worrying about tomorrow. The kind of person who never had a clue how to enjoy the here and now. But I'm changing, I realise. I'm beginning to see that it's the little moments that matter.

When I reach the gates, I have to turn back and park along the road. The drive is completely packed with removal and delivery lorries and people unloading a giant marquee to be constructed on the front lawn. Dominic Kennedy's black sports car is still there, as is another car I recognise – a silver Audi.

I dodge out of the way of three men bringing in a load of scaffolding rods and some painting supplies. The entire entryway to the house and the great hall has been taken over by workers and tools. I make a beeline for the kitchen. But just outside the door, I hear raised voices.

'But if I had my way we wouldn't be here, would we? So don't you dare lay that on me too, Richard.'

My hackles rise. If Luke Thornton doesn't want to be here, then why the hell is he here?

I don't hear Richard's reply, but Luke continues. 'No! That's not right. I didn't put it in my contract because you gave me your word.'

'Come on, Luke,' Richard says. 'Don't be this way. You'll make it work, I know you will. And… you have to.'

I steel myself to enter the kitchen, which is the only access to our temporary bedrooms.

'She'll be the end of this project. It won't come to any good—'

As I'm about to fling open the door, a hand grabs my arm. I whirl around, startled, then weak in the knees.

'Sorry, Lizzie,' Dominic Kennedy says. 'It's just, you might want to give them a minute.' He leans in conspiratorially. 'I'm afraid Luke's in a right old mood.'

Anger boils up in my chest. 'Of all the directors that might have been hired for this project, why do I get stuck with the one who's an unpleasant arse?'

Dominic laughs, and I realise I've spoken aloud. He steers me through the obstacle course of the great hall to the drawing room. Once we're there, he digs in a rucksack that he obviously left there earlier and tosses me a can of beer.

'Sometimes it's good to bring one's own provisions,' he says. 'Just in case.'

'Thanks.' Though it's only 9 a.m. and I hate beer, I crack it open anyway and take a swig. My stomach protests, which feels good in my present mood. I walk over to the window and stare out at the lake. The sun is just beginning to come out, and the water is a dark mirror, perfectly reflecting the trees on the other side.

Dominic too stares out at the view. 'Don't let him bother you,' he says. 'Luke's a good guy. He can just be a little intense sometimes.' He takes a long swig of his beer. 'And just between us, something about this project has put a real bee in his bonnet. I'm not really sure what's up with him, to be honest.'

'Maybe it's because he doesn't want to be here.' I gesture at the landscape with the can. 'He's been against using Tanglewild from the start.'

'It seems like the perfect setting if you ask me.'

'Why did he even take the job?' I lament. 'Surely he must have tonnes of offers for work. He can't need the money.'

Dominic laughs; a low, deep rumbling sound that vibrates in my lower abdomen. 'No, he doesn't need the money, or the work. But it's a great project, and it's got quite a bit of media hype surrounding it. It's not Luke's usual thing, but I know he's the man for the job. He has a way of drawing out the emotion in a script and getting the cast to really feel, really *become* the characters. And he's taken a risk and decided to go with Natasha Blythe in the lead role even though she's a relative unknown. He's a champion of young talent.'

'I'm sure you're all "champions" of young female talent, aren't you?' I say sarcastically. Maybe Luke Thornton's taken on the project because he's hoping to replace one starlet wife with another.

'I suppose that's one way to look at it.' He does that lowered eyelid thing again that gets my pulse beating faster. 'Though, frankly, some of us prefer a more *seasoned* cast.'

'Yeah, right.' I can't help but laugh.

There's a commotion in the front hall as something heavy gets dropped and someone swears at the top of their voice. I can only be thankful that Jack isn't here – this time.

'The problem is,' I say, 'I need to go through the kitchen to get up to my room. I wish they'd fight their battles somewhere else.'

He laughs. 'It's your house, so show him who's boss.'

'I will.' As I turn to leave, I notice the pages of his script spread out on a side table. 'By the way, how's the rehearsing going?'

'Oh, fine,' he says. 'And actually, I've found a lovely lady to help me run my lines—'

'Knock, knock. You ready, Dom?'

'Ah, in fact, here she is.' His smile turns wicked as we both turn towards the person standing in the door frame, taking up the entire space. 'Come in, my lovely Victoria.'

I've never imagined that Connie – all six-foot two, seventeen stone of her – might actually seem to float as she enters a room. But there's a first for everything. I roll my eyes and give her a little smirk, but she only has eyes for one person in the room. And it sure as heck isn't me.

* * *

I leave them to it. Connie deserves her fun after everything she's done for me. In the great hall, two men are manoeuvring a huge ladder into place next to the chandelier, and two others are picking up paint cans and tools that dropped out of the bottom of a carton – the commotion I heard. I stop and help them stack the paint cans. The argument in the kitchen seems to have quietened down, but I don't know if anyone's still in there. I chat for a minute with the workmen about protecting the floor, lingering for longer than I need to. Eventually, I decide it's stupid to feel unwelcome in my own house. Taking a breath, I head to the kitchen.

The back door is open. I immediately see Luke Thornton – he's outside pacing back and forth on the lawn near the edge of the lake. (Unkindly, I hope he'll ruin his expensive leather shoes stepping in goose poo.) The light catches the top of his dark blond hair and strong profile. Though he lacks Dominic Kennedy's devastating looks, I can't deny that he's objectively attractive. Too bad he's such a total arse—

'Mrs Greene? Is everything all right?'

I turn quickly; it's the man I've dubbed Voldemort, though I recall his name is Richard Silverman, the producer. Despite the morning chill, his bald pate is beaded with sweat, probably from the heated argument with Luke. He's wearing a black rollneck, black jeans, and black biker boots. The name 'Charles' is tattooed on his left hand with a heart around it.

'Um, yes, fine,' I say. 'Hi, I'm Lizzie.'

He reintroduces himself and we shake hands. I'm not sure who has more clout, he or Luke, but either way, I feel like I'm a lowly wolf cub intruding on a territorial dispute between two alpha males.

'I don't want to disturb you,' I say, 'but the only access to our rooms is up the back stairs.' I point to the short corridor at the back of the kitchen.

'No worries. In fact, I'm off now. Luke has things well in hand.' If he's being sardonic, there's no sign.

'Why doesn't he like the house?' I ask before my courage wanes. 'I heard the two of you arguing.'

Richard shrugs. 'He's been here before.'

'What?' I look at him, stunned.

'You'll have to ask him.' He pulls up his sleeve and checks his watch. 'Sorry, but I have to dash.'

As he leaves the room, I catch sight of Luke walking back up the lawn towards the house. I make a beeline for the corridor and up the kitchen stairs. It's only when the door to the guest room is closed behind me and I've turned the key in the lock that I realise quite how quickly my pulse is racing. I lean against the wall until I can catch my breath.

26

Luke sodding Thornton. A man with a plan – that failed. Richard Silverman's little snippet explains everything. Tanglewild was initially rejected for *The Lady's Secret* not because of the location itself – which, by all accounts is not only perfect, but was the exact setting used in the book – but because Luke Thornton had some kind of personal objection to using it. An objection that arose due to a personal connection, just like Phillipa King apparently has. Either it's the world's most improbable coincidence, or it's not a coincidence at all. The two things must be related. But how?

I sit down at the dressing table by the window, turn on my laptop, and try to chivvy the weak Wi-Fi signal on this side of the house. I do a few searches and confirm that in film-world hierarchy, Richard is Luke's boss. I also search for variations on 'Luke Thornton', 'Tanglewild', 'Sussex', but nothing comes up. My sleuthing having drawn a blank, the mystery remains unsolved.

I check my work emails and take care of a few things that have come up. The problem with being a part-time lawyer is that I'm always on call, even on my non-work days. And, if I'm honest, my enthusiasm about the job has waned considerably after encountering Harry in the conference room. Since then, I've managed to avoid him, or at least keep a safe distance. But I'm still angry with myself for not setting clear boundaries so that he'll leave me alone.

As I'm shutting down the computer, a text comes from Theo. I open it with the usual mix of hope and trepidation and find that he's inviting me to the pub tomorrow night. I reread the message several times, especially the x after his name. I've been in such a kerfuffle about meeting Dominic Kennedy and feeling affronted by Luke Thornton that I've barely thought about Theo all day. But now I sit back and enjoy the fact that an attractive man – a man who's fought my corner from the get-go – has invited me out on a real date. I close my eyes and conjure up his image in my mind. Reddish hair, a smattering of freckles. Tall, but not too tall. A face that's warm and open; he seems a lovely guy all round, and I'm looking forward to getting to know him better. And to see what happens from there…

I respond briefly and to the point, telling him that it 'sounds perfect'. I press send before I can ruminate over adding a return 'x' or not. As soon as the message is gone, I worry about what on earth I'm going to wear. Jeans? A dress (do I even have one)? I tidy up the room, putting mine and Katie's things in the chest of drawers, hoping that something suitable will materialise. It doesn't.

Feeling a little breathless, I open the window to get some air. The lake is dark brown and placid, the sun now high enough that the trees are no longer reflected. On the other side, the beech tree towers over the other trees, its branches twisted and gnarled like aged hands. I look further on to the crooked weathervane on the roof of the dovecote, which is just visible if I crane my neck. A huge black shadow suddenly takes to the sky – a murder of crows. The sight of them makes me shiver. Then another a flash of movement catches my eye. Someone's walking out on the path that goes around the lake just behind the trees.

It's Luke Thornton. I slam shut the window. I know he's the director and probably out there to think about camera angles and 'drawing out the emotion in the script', but I also know that I won't rest easy until I know how he's connected to this house. Sooner or later, I'm going to have to ask him.

* * *

A while later, I go down to the kitchen. At the front of the house, the workmen are having their lunch on the lawn, and there's no sign of Luke, Dominic, or Connie. The great hall is still in disarray and now smells of paint – they've begun working on repainting the white plaster ceiling. That alone is worth taking on the film project as I'd never be able to afford to do it myself.

I make a tray of tea for the workmen and take it out to them. Then, Jammie and I go out to the paddock to gather daffodils to put on Dave's grave. I try to reflect on the good times we shared, and to my surprise I find that my anger is starting to dissipate. But my mind strays back to the present: Theo, the pub, the fact that I have nothing to wear. I take the flowers back to the house and get my handbag so I can go to the supermarket and buy some new make-up; maybe even find a top or a skirt that I can wear tomorrow tonight. It may be sacrilegious, but I'm sure Dave, of all people, would understand.

When I go out to the car, the door of the caravan is open. Connie's sitting at her table, frowning at the screen of her laptop. When she looks up and sees me, she closes the lid.

'Good "rehearsal"?' I say with a smirk.

She gives me a pained look. 'Just because I'm fat, old and married doesn't mean I can't enjoy the company of a handsome man, does it?'

'I'm not judging you. Knock yourself out.'

'Good, because Dom is quite a fragile man – very sensitive.'

I sputter with laughter. 'Fragile and sensitive?'

'Just because he's gorgeous, doesn't mean he can't be insecure.'

'And how do you know all this?'

'He's been round here a few times while you've been at work. We got to chatting, as you do.'

'As you do.'

'I think he might be dyslexic. That's why he struggles to learn his lines.'

'Really?' I suppose Connie's right – just because Dominic Kennedy makes things look easy and natural on-screen doesn't mean they are. I guess that's why he's rated as an actor, not just a heartthrob.

'Yes, and for that, that repetition is key. That's what I'm helping him with.'

'And what about the getting into character part?' I can't resist adding. 'Are you helping him with that too?'

'Do I detect a hint of jealousy?'

'No. Because as it happens, I've got a date myself. Tomorrow night. That is,' I add a bit sheepishly, 'if you're OK to watch the kids...'

I tell her about Theo's text. She nods, not quite approvingly, but confirms that she'll babysit. Then I tell her that I'm off to Sainsbury's and ask her if she needs anything. She grabs a sticky to make a list, and while she's writing, I feel a strong pang of guilt. Here I am talking to Dave's mum on the anniversary of his death about going out with another man. Here I am going to the supermarket to buy make-up and clothing. I should be... I don't know... reflecting? Grieving?

Connie stops writing and hands me the list.

'I'm so sorry,' I say. 'I've been very insensitive. I mean, about Dave, and the cemetery and the anniversary.'

For a second, her deep-set eyes go dark. 'Don't be silly,' she says. 'Dave's gone. We're all very sad about that, but it's not going to bring him back. You know my views on the subject, which is that you need to move on.'

'Yes, I know.' I'm grateful for her stoicism, given her own loss.

'Which brings me to another point,' she says. 'While you're out and about, you should consider ditching the mum bras and pants.'

'How do you know about my pants?' I say, horrified.

'There are no secrets when you're sharing a washer-dryer.' She gives me a knowing smile. 'You're young and attractive, Lizzie. Theo and the rest of them are in the film industry. You can afford to be a little glamourous. Try to look the part.'

'Thanks... I think.'

'OK, now off with you. I'll see you later.' She closes the door and I shove her list into my pocket. I get in the car, my face flushed and my stomach churning.

* * *

In the end, I feel shamed enough drive to the big M&S in Horsham. There, a fitting room attendant called Susan takes me under her wing. I suppose it's because the first round of bras I bring in to try on are all of the plain cotton T-shirt variety, with the only thing racy being that one has a racer back and hooks in front.

'I think we should measure you,' she says, checking the sizes. 'I think you're a C cup at least.'

I'm not sure whether to feel flattered or panicky. I've always been a 34B (or so I thought), so that's what I've been trying on. Susan measures me, then takes it upon herself to pull me an assortment of 36Cs in different colours, and some including lace or polka dots, and little bows in the middle.

'These are the nicest ones this season,' she says before I can make an objection. 'They're comfortable and... pretty too.'

I frown. Had she said 'sexy' I would have sent back the lot. As it is, when I try the first one on, I realise she's right that I've been wearing the wrong bra size. What else have I been holding on to that's wrong?

'I'll take the lot,' I say when I've tried them on.

'Great,' Susan says. 'And I've got you the matching pants.'

'Thanks,' I say through my teeth.

I almost make it to the till incognito with my loot. Almost. But as I'm nearly through the queue, I spot two of the mums from Jack's class. Mary and Daisy, I think. I try to avert my face, but Mary sees me and comes over.

'Lizzie!' she says. 'Are you well?'

'Yes,' I sputter. 'You?'

'Oh fine, just checking out the spring collection.' She looks down at my armful of lacy pants. 'I see you're doing the same.'

The other woman, Daisy, gives me a knowing little smile. I recall my tearful interlude at the mums' coffee morning about how difficult it's been to lose my husband. I try to smile nonchalantly, but it's like there's an unspoken triangle of understanding between us. There's a thin line between a grieving widow and a merry one.

'Till number five,' the loudspeaker announces. I exhale, relieved that I'm at the front of the queue.

'Nice to see you both,' I say breezily.
'Have fun,' the woman called Daisy has the nerve to say.

* * *

It irritates me that Daisy would think that I'm only buying nice underwear for a man, rather than for myself. (Though, if I'm being honest, it was Theo's invitation and Connie's naming and shaming that prompted my purchases.) It strikes me that I should have done this a long time ago – I've got a job now, and surely I deserve a few nice things after what I've been through. It's more than time for an upgrade.

I browse the rest of the shop and end up splurging on a cashmere tunic dress in a dusty rose colour, and I also buy some new make-up. I begin to regret the whole shopping trip even before I reach my car and question this *thing* with Theo all over again. Why can't I just 'lighten up' and go with the flow? Is Dave and the spectre of what he did going to haunt me forever? He took away my security, my self-esteem, my self-worth as a woman and a human being. Am I so weak that I'm going to let him win even now?

No.

I drive back to the village, collect the kids from school, and take them to the cemetery. It's a sunny afternoon and it's a nice quiet spot. The trees are budding with green shoots, and there are crocuses and primroses amid the grass. Connie and Simon are there already – they've brought the flowers and the dog – and Hannah and Flora arrive just after we do. I divide up the daffodils and let the kids put them on the grave. Jack acts like a little man, taking the responsibility very seriously. In the car, Katie was unusually quiet, but when she goes to lay her flowers down, she ends up in a fit of giggles. She and Flora run off to find more flowers, and Jack and Jammie chase each other amongst the headstones. The rest of us stand in silence, until Hannah unveils a bottle of champagne. The four of us raise a glass to Dave, and another glass to life – the ones that must go on without him. Then, by tacit agreement, it's time to go.

As I walk back to the car, I feel strangely uplifted. One year on. And tomorrow's another day.

***

But I'm wondering how much I really have changed when I return home from work the next day with butterflies battering my stomach. I've spent the whole day worrying about whether I would be able to get away from work on time to meet Theo, and then stressing about the fact that I *did* get away on time. 'Lighten up,' I tell myself for the thousandth time.

At home, the kids are jumping on the trampoline and Connie is making dinner. Jack tags along with me upstairs, and the thought of leaving him to go out for the evening makes me a little sick. He plays Lego in the corner while I change into a silky lace bra in black and matching pants, put the rose-coloured dress over my head, and dab on some of my new make-up.

'Mummy's pretty,' he says.

I fight a rogue tear. My beloved son – he loves me no matter what. I hold my arms open and he rushes into them for a 'cuggle'. I hold him up, looking at the two of us in the mirror. He sucks his thumb and then slobbers it onto the shoulder of my dress. I hold him tighter, breathing in the smell of his warm skin and soft, wispy hair. 'I love you so much,' I say.

He starts to wriggle and I set him down. I stare at myself in the mirror, surprised at what I see. I look softer and curvier than before, and my honey-blonde hair, now grown past my shoulders, is thick and wavy. Sure, I've seen myself in the mirror over the last year, but I never really wanted to look. The changes, though, seem to suit me.

Downstairs, I can hear Connie's voice as she chivvies Katie to do her homework before tea. I check my watch; it's now almost six. Is Theo even here?

'Can I play the monkey game on your phone?' Jack asks.

'No, darling, not now,' I say.

His little face screws up. 'Wanna play monkey. Now!' he yells.

I sigh. 'Let's go downstairs and see Grandma. Mummy's going out, OK?'

'Monkey game!' His initial outburst explodes into a full-blown tantrum. I stick him in the travel cot so he'll be safe and leave him to scream it out. I go downstairs, feeling stressed, eager to be out of the house, and guilty for being so eager.

In the kitchen, Katie is sitting at the table, pouting over her maths homework. Simon is back from his job at the farm shop and is helping Connie make a fish pie. When I come into the kitchen, I can see the surprise on their faces.

'Mum?' Katie says worriedly. 'Where are you going?'

'I told you yesterday. I'm going to the pub with a friend.'

'But you're wearing lipstick. And you look—'

'Lovely,' Connie says, cutting her off. I can feel her eyes gravitate to my new 36C bust beneath the snug-fitting dress. The insecure part of me wonders if there's not a glimmer of judgement in them. If I hadn't let myself go, maybe her son wouldn't have been such a shit to his family. But she shakes her head imperceptibly and I know she only wishes me the best. 'And not before time,' she adds.

'That colour really suits you,' Simon says.

'Thanks,' I say. 'It was a splurge, but I needed something to boost my courage.'

'Absolutely,' Connie agrees. 'Now, off with you. I think your chap's outside in the garden.'

'Oh.' I feel another lurch of anxiety. 'I'd better go say goodnight to Jack.'

I run back upstairs, half of me wanting to lock myself away in my room and forget the whole thing. Jack's stopped screaming and is sucking on his Spiderman, looking wide-eyed and moist-faced. I pick him up again and hug him tight.

'I'm taking you down to Grandma now,' I say. 'She's going to look after you.'

For a second I think he's going to wail again. Gripping his Spiderman in one hand, he puts his other arm around my neck and wraps his legs around me like a baby koala. He nuzzles his face (including his snotty nose) into my hair and I carry him downstairs.

'Night, night,' I say. I try to hand him off to Connie, but he clings to me.

Simon comes to the rescue. 'Hey, fella, Spidey wants to go play football.'

'Football!' Jack says. I know then that he's sorted. Sometimes, I realise, it is useful to have a man about the place.

When I try to kiss Katie, she pulls away as usual, then surprises me by clinging on to me and trying to plant a kiss on my cheek. 'When are you going to be home, Mum?' she asks.

'I don't know, honey. I probably won't be too late.'

'I'll wait up for you.'

I laugh, feeling a rush of love. 'OK, sweetheart. I'll see you later.'

As I walk to the door, Connie comes along behind, and I worry that she's going to give me some kind of embarrassing lecture.

'Stay out as long as you like,' she says in a low voice. 'We've got everything covered here.'

I turn then to say thank you, but all of a sudden I'm overcome with emotion. If it wasn't for her being here, camped in my drive, able to step in at a moment's notice to watch the kids, I wouldn't be able to make any of it work. I throw my arms around her neck and hold her tight.

'Thank you for everything.' The tears rise up again. Is the mascara I bought waterproof? Stupid me if it isn't.

She gently pushes me away, ending my sloppy display of affection. 'Save that for him, OK?' She winks. 'Now, off with you.'

27

I'm giddy with nerves as I dodge the obstacle course of paint equipment and rolls of flooring in the great hall, put on my coat and go out the door. Half of the front garden is now covered with a vast white marquee which will serve as a kind of green room for the cast to hang out in between scenes – with food tables, make-up stations, and Wi-Fi – because the house isn't big enough to accommodate the fifty or more people who will be on set each day.

There's no sign of Theo out front, but the gate that leads to the side garden is open. Part of the film is going to be shot in the woods near the lake, so there's been a fair amount of coming and going between the house and the spot they've chosen. As I go through the gate and around the hedge, I practically collide with a man. 'Oh!' I cry, stumbling backwards. It's not Theo, but Luke Thornton.

He grabs my arm to steady me, his grip hard. He gives me an odd look, like I'm a stranger he doesn't recognise. His eyes remind me of the photo I saw: Luke on the steps of the divorce court. A wild, wounded creature ready to lash out at anything near it.

I pull away from him.

'Going out?' There's an edge to his voice. He doesn't know anything about me. So why does he look so angry?

'Oh, hi, Lizzie, sorry – we were tied up on something.' Theo appears from the gap in the hedge that leads to the rose garden and walks towards me, smiling. 'Wow,' he says, 'you look great.'

'Thanks,' I say, blushing.

Theo hasn't made the special effort that I have, but he's wearing a nice pair of jeans and a plaid button-down shirt. I force myself to smile at him, but I'm all too aware of Luke Thornton looking from Theo to me and back again. Under his scrutiny I feel flustered and uncomfortable.

'No rush,' I say. 'Just let me know when you're ready to go.' I focus on Theo, avoiding Luke and his judgemental stare.

'Sorry,' Luke says to Theo. 'I didn't know you two were —'

'We're going for dinner at the pub,' Theo clarifies. 'Do you want to come along?'

There's a long pause. My heart sinks like a block of cement. Have I got this all wrong? Is this really just a trip down the pub between two might-be friends, when I was thinking it might be more than that?

'No, thanks,' Luke says. 'I wouldn't be welcome.'

Obviously that's my cue to protest. Say that of course it's fine. We'll all go together like three mates. But I am *done* being polite. The last thing in the world that I want is for Luke Thornton to come with us. I address Theo. 'Shall I meet you at the car?'

'Sure. I'll just be a minute.'

I turn and walk off in a hurry. But not before I hear Luke say to Theo in a voice that's obviously meant for me to hear, 'You know the main bedroom is part of the set now. So it's strictly off limits.'

My knuckles twitch with the urge to go back and punch him in the face. I go out to Theo's car regretting my outfit, the date, the film project, and ever having met Luke Thornton.

* * *

'Sorry about that,' Theo says. When he comes to the car, he acts the perfect gentleman by opening the passenger door for me. In the meantime, I've been pacing the drive kicking stones and scuffing the toes of my shoes.

'It's fine.'

To his credit, Theo seems to sense that it's not fine – at all. 'Just for the record, Lizzie, I only invited Luke along because I didn't want to be awkward.' He gets into the driver's seat. 'And because I knew he'd say no.'

'I'm glad he did,' I say. 'He's so unpleasant.'

Theo laughs as we pull out of the drive. 'I know he can come across that way. It's a shame because he's actually a good guy once you get to know him. He can really inspire a team and coax the best performances out of everyone. This isn't really his kind of project, but he had a pretty bad time a few years back. You've probably seen the tabloids.'

'I've seen the articles. And people keep telling me what a good guy he is. But I've seen no sign of it myself.'

Theo glances over at me. 'I hope you're not regretting taking on the project and meeting all of us.'

I look at him and smile. His profile is steady and solid as we drive along the narrow, tree-lined lanes towards civilisation. Now that we're away from the house, I'm starting to feel a lot more relaxed. 'Well, maybe not *all* of you.'

* * *

Like most of the pubs in the area, the one he takes me to is posh. It's called The White Swan and is in a refurbished mill with a stream running underneath it. Part of the wooden floor has been replaced with glass so that the waterwheel is visible, along with the occasional tame swan floating along the stream below. I'm prepared to sit in the bar area near the cosy log fire, but Theo surprises me by having booked a table.

Companionably, we order drinks: red for me, white for him. I like the way he's polite and solicitous; I like his reddish-brown hair and deep-set brown eyes. Overall, he makes a good impression: open, friendly, and appealing, but not drop-dead gorgeous. Which is just as well. The memory of Luke Thornton's angry glare comes slamming back like a physical force. It takes me a moment to wrestle him from my mind.

'It's a nice pub,' Theo says, looking around him. 'I like the little touches. To be honest, I've always been a city boy. But I'm definitely starting to appreciate the charms of the countryside.' The way he says it... that hint of a smile... I blush warmly. We talk about the local area and how Dave and I came to find the house. Our wine arrives. He sniffs his and swirls his glass by the stem before drinking. I wonder if I ought to do the same, but instead just take a big gulp. He's easy to talk to, and I'm liking him more and more. The brief mention of Dave brings on a pang of guilt, especially given the recent anniversary. But I push it aside. Dave is gone, and I'm getting on with my life.

Inevitably, however, the conversation steers to a different topic – Phillipa King. 'I asked her about Tanglewild,' he says, 'after we spoke.'

'Oh?'

'Her stepmum owned it, apparently. That's why Phillipa was there. She went to boarding school during term time, but she stayed there in the summer. I suppose, years later, when she was writing the book, the place stuck in her mind.'

'That makes sense.' I'm relieved to have finally got to the bottom of Phillipa's connection with the house. 'But what about Luke Thornton?'

'Luke?'

'Apparently he knows the house too. It can't be a coincidence.'

'Well, they know each other, of course. She's doing the screenplay, and naturally, he's involved with that. And Phillipa has many friends and contacts. She's always travelling around doing book tours and signings. And now, the film. She's at the top of her game.' His face grows a little flushed as he talks about her.

'I'm sure,' I say flatly. 'Though, I admit, I'm not a huge fan of bodice-ripping romance novels.'

'But the book is more than that, don't you think?' he asserts. 'It's got hidden depths. At the end of the day, it's a social commentary on the plight of women. Victoria is trapped by her time and situation, but she manages to break free. I'm helping Phillipa revise the screenplay. It's given me a whole new insight into just how complex the book really is.'

'To be honest, I haven't finished it yet.'

'That makes sense. You know what they say about judging a book by its cover.'

'I'll keep that in mind.'

It's a relief when the waitress finally comes and takes our order. When she's gone, I deliberately change the subject.

'So, Theo,' I say, 'I'd love to know more about you.'

'There's not much to tell,' he says with a little laugh.

'Try me.'

I sip my wine as he tells me about his childhood growing up in a suburb of Boston. Two sisters and a brother, typical middle-class Irish-Catholic upbringing. The family went to the movie theatre every Saturday afternoon (and twice a year to see the Red Sox), and he grew to love films. When his grandmother died, the family inherited some money. Theo was able to live his dream of going to California and doing a postgraduate degree at UCLA film school. He stayed in LA, got a job at a studio, and worked his way up the totem pole. He had a long-time relationship with a girl who worked as an extra in films. They talked about getting married, moving out to the suburbs; having a house, kids. But she wasn't ready to give up her Hollywood lifestyle. Eventually, they split and the production company transferred him to London. He's into rock climbing, golf, and though he'd never heard of cricket in his life before coming across the pond, he's now the star batsman on his local team.

It's interesting to hear about his life, but other than the film, we seem to have little in common. Since I haven't been on a date in years, I don't know how much that matters. I suppose Dave and I had a few things in common at the start. We shared a profession and a common set of stresses. We were both into travel and London culture. We both liked history, and old houses. Bringing Dave to mind inevitably pokes a hole in my mood. Theo seems to sense that the conversation is starting to flag.

'There is one other thing about me – but it's kind of a secret,' he says. 'I don't really tell many people, because it's a little embarrassing.'

'Oh?' I lean forward. 'Do tell.'

'When I first came to London, I was at a bit of a crossroads. I ended up taking a night class in creative writing,' he says. 'Now, I'm working on a novel.'

'A novel? Why is that embarrassing? It sounds great.'

He takes a sip of his drink. 'It's great, in theory. But when you say you're a writer, most people ask you what you've published, whether you're famous, and why haven't they heard of you. When you tell them that you're working on your first novel, they glaze over. So normally, I just keep it to myself.'

'I think it sounds very exciting. What sort of novel is it?'

'It's a crime novel,' he says. 'A dead girl, a jaded police detective, everyone with different motives to lie.'

'Interesting,' I say. 'That's the kind of book I like to read.'

'Really?' Theo looks a little relieved.

'Yes, really.' In truth, the novel thing has definitely given Theo a few more points in my book. I've never aspired to be a writer, but I do love to read.

'Phillipa is helping me with the structure and pacing,' he says. 'Hiding clues in the text, red herrings and misdirection, that sort of thing.'

'Does she have aspirations to be the next Robert Galbraith?' I joke. 'I wouldn't think there'd be much call for that sort of thing in romance novels.'

'Well, she has such a clever mind…'

I give him a look.

'Sorry,' he says. 'I do go on a bit, don't I?'

We both laugh; our food arrives, and all of a sudden I feel quite hungry. We have a little flirtation over him giving me a bite of his crab cakes and me giving him a taste of my steak and ale pie. I have a second glass of wine and he has a beer. We discuss books and films. He tells me a little more about his location scouting job, and some of the more interesting scenes he's had to set – from Victorian brothels to tower block crack houses. The conversation turns to the finer points of *The Lady's Secret*, including which room is going to be used for which seduction scene, and how much rehearsal time will be needed in the bed. It's all very jokey and light. And when at one point he reaches out his hand and lightly brushes my fingers, curled around the stem of my glass, I feel pleasantly warm but not pressured.

'Would you like another drink?' he says as our empty plates are cleared away.

'Oh no,' I say. 'I've had enough.' I smile decadently, allowing myself a moment's fantasy of where the evening might lead.

'Maybe some hot chocolate, then?' he suggests. 'When Phillipa and I came here, she said the hot chocolate was amazing. Dark, Belgian, frothy—'

The words slam into me, and all of a sudden, I'm completely sober. 'You came here with Phillipa?'

'Yes.' Theo smiles. 'When she interviewed me for the job as her assistant.'

I feel a crawling sense of jealousy – which I know is ridiculous. Theo knew a good restaurant in the area and took me there on our date. But the insecure part of me – the part that fears I'll never be able to compete with his bestselling novelist mentor – feels like second-hand goods.

'Oh, well, she has good taste in restaurants,' I say blandly. 'I'll pass on the hot chocolate though.'

As if on cue, the waitress comes by and asks if we'd like anything else. Theo glances at me and I ask for the bill. I offer to pay half, but he insists it's his treat. As we're leaving, I try to recapture the anticipation I felt for the remainder of the evening. But it seems to have fizzled out.

'Are you OK, Lizzie?' Theo says when we're outside.

'I'm fine, really.' I put my hand lightly on his arm. 'It's been such a lovely evening. Thank you.'

'My pleasure.' He puts his hand on mine.

Above our heads, the night sky is clear and full of stars. We pause for a moment, looking up. The moment feels nice – romantic...

'Of course, you can always ask Phillipa yourself about restaurant recommendations.' He opens the door for me as we reach the car. 'She'll be on set tomorrow.'

'Tomorrow?'

'Yes. She'll be around quite a bit from now on. It's her first screenplay, and mine too. It's quite exciting. But there's a lot of work involved.'

'I'm sure.'

He drives me home down the dark road, talking about the different versions of the screenplay that are required for the technical and artistic functions. But all I can think about is Phillipa King. Even though I've already become acquainted with big names like Luke Thornton and Dominic Kennedy, I feel daunted by the prospect of meeting her. It's not just the fact that she's an internationally bestselling author – though that's part of it, surely. Maybe it's the fact that her book, with its main character that I've come to empathise with, has made me feel like a stranger in my own home. It's almost like there's a ghost walking the rooms and corridors of Tanglewild with her own thoughts, worries and feelings, while my children and I are getting on with our lives in a parallel universe. And tomorrow, I'll meet the ghost's creator. Though I'm sure she'll have more important things to do than have a coffee and a chit-chat with me.

When we reach the house, there's a single light on in the wing above the kitchen. Katie must have tried to wait up for me. I feel an overwhelming surge of love for her. My buzz from the wine is completely gone, and in its place is a thick lump in my throat.

'Here we are,' Theo says. His voice is low and husky. I realise that I've been sitting in the car for almost a minute, not getting out. He's looking over at me, as if unsure what to do next.

'Um, would you like to come in?' I blurt out nervously.

'Would you like me to?'

'Of course. It's just…'

Two little words… It's just that my mother-in-law is in the house, along with my kids. It's just that the main bedroom is part of the film set and 'strictly off limits'. It's just that Phillipa King is coming tomorrow. The temporary bond that Theo and I shared seems overstretched and fragile. There are too many '*it's just*'s.

'I understand,' he says, before I elaborate. 'And there's no rush, Lizzie. I want you to know that.'

'Thanks,' I stammer, tears perilously close to the surface. He comes round as I get out of the car. I appreciate him all the more now that he's leaving…

He takes my hand and pulls me slowly but steadily to him. I offer no resistance. This is what I want. Romance, a nice dinner, a nice man. It's an unfamiliar feeling as his lips touch mine. It's been so long since Dave and I… I push Dave from my mind. I make a conscious decision to respond. But despite his assurance of 'there's no rush', the kiss starts to get a little heated and for a second I worry that he's after a Victoria Easterbrook/William Clarke moment. My body starts to recoil at the idea of being touched, and I break my lips free from his.

'I... can't...' I say.

'Of course.' His voice is cool as he holds up his hands and steps back. 'No worries. I should be going anyway. Big day tomorrow.' He gets back in the car.

'Yes,' I say, but he's already closed the door and turned on the engine.

'Big day,' I whisper to the red taillights as they disappear down the drive.

PART III

Or when the moon was overhead
Came two young lovers lately wed;
'I am half sick of shadows,' said
The Lady of Shalott.

— ALFRED LORD TENNYSON, 'THE LADY OF SHALOTT'

PART III

28

THE LADY'S SECRET BY PHILLIPA KING

Gone. But of course he would be gone. Victoria had spent a sleepless night feeling the phantom touch of his hands on her body, seeing his bold eyes as he possessed her, if only for a moment. She'd come downstairs to begin the day's tedious duties: looking after the sour-faced old woman, finding a deck of cards for a promised visit from Belle, all the while feeling a strange sense of anticipation tinged with dread. She'd learned from the kitchen maid that the master had ridden off at dawn.

'He's got a woman up in London, they say,' the toothless girl had said, smiling lasciviously. 'Much as Belle wishes him for herself.'

'Surely not,' Victoria said flatly. The lustre had gone out of the day. There would be no chance encounter in the rose garden, no repeat of the heart-pounding sensations of the previous night. And the mention of other women suddenly reminded her of Tom. Lately, she'd felt a strange crawling sensation, like someone was watching her when she pushed the old woman in her bath chair through the tangled gardens. She remembered the daisy ring and the words he'd spoken, 'Till death do us part,' and the words of Old Hester that seemed a lifetime ago: 'He'll never let you go.' And she'd laughed and Victoria had felt sick and strange and had known that she would never be free. Until the moment when she met the master and felt that with his strength, his love, anything might be possible.

The servant girl laughed. 'Don't tell me you're jealous, miss.'

Victoria grabbed a crust of bread from the basket and walked away from the cursed girl without answering. Jealous, yes – she supposed that much was obvious. She took a bite of the bread, tasted mould, and spat it out. But at that moment, what she felt more than anything was scared.

29

When I go inside the house, I find Connie and Simon snuggled up on the sofa in the lounge with the lights off. They're watching Queen on *Top of the Pops* on Connie's laptop.

'Hi, Lizzie,' Connie says, not bothering to budge. Simon, I realise, is asleep. 'Where's your bloke?'

'On his way home.' It sounds lame and futile.

Connie shrugs. 'It was a good start. For when the right one comes along. You mind if we finish the show?'

'Go ahead.' I'm not sure whether to feel annoyed over her smug assuredness that Theo is not 'the right one', or relieved to have escaped a lecture about how I need to move on. I make myself a cup of tea and go upstairs to check on the kids. In a world where I feel uncertain about the future – and myself – I'm grateful that at least I have my children.

Jack is fast asleep in the cot with Spiderman's arm in his mouth. When I stroke the hair off his face, he makes a sucking motion with his cheeks, like he did when he was a baby. A few feet away, Katie is asleep in the guest bed. Her brown hair is spread out on the pillow like a fairy-tale princess, and the book she was reading has slid down beside her. Jammie, sprawled across the foot of her bed, lifts her head when I come in and gives a single thump of her tail, before going back to doggy dreamland. I lean over Katie and kiss her on the forehead, my eyes swimming with tears. As I switch off the reading light, she groans.

'Mum, leave it on.'

I do as she says. 'Go back to sleep, darling. I love you.'

'Did you have a good night?'

I smile. 'It was nice, and I appreciate you "waiting up" for me.'

'Umm.' Her brown eyes flutter and close, and she drifts back to sleep.

I go into the bathroom and look in the mirror. My lips have been kissed bare and my mascara has smeared a little, making my eyes look dark and sultry. I wash it off my face, wondering if I made the right decision in sending Theo on his way. The two futures present themselves in my mind – the one where I'm carried upstairs and ravaged in my bed, and damn the set rules and the morning after; and the one I've chosen – kissing my children goodnight, taking off my rose-coloured dress and putting on a long T-shirt, and crawling into bed alone with the light on.

As I sip my cup of tea, I stare at the unfamiliar room: the heavy wooden beams on the ceiling, the brass wall lights, a miniature wattle-and-daub house that I made with Katie when she was studying the Great Fire of London in Year 2. The bed is smaller than the one in the master bedroom, but for some reason, it feels cavernous. The dreamcatcher is a few feet away from me, tied to one of the light fittings.

I open my e-reader and switch off the light. I read about Victoria Easterbrook feeling awkward and guilty the next morning after her so-called romantic encounter with William Clarke, and her disappointment tinged with relief when she discovers that he rode off on his horse at the crack of dawn. She's told that he's gone to London, and that he's courting a rich society woman there.

Typical. I'm reminded of Edward Rochester courting Blanche Ingram after leading on Jane Eyre, and, more recently, of Dave entertaining women in his London flat, and my boss Harry hitting on his subordinates. Phillipa King's plot isn't very original, but it is universal.

I read on. With William Clarke now gone to London, the plot shifts to something bordering on suspense. Victoria worries that her secret may be revealed, and that Tom or one of his servants will seek her out and bring her home to a loveless marriage. Most of all, she senses a dark, malevolent presence watching her:

> There was no moon. The water was black and dead far below beneath the window. A perfect night for the boats, and yet she knew that tonight there would be no boats. He was gone. Her body ached with the cold, her heart with loneliness.
>
> As she was about to close the window, the gravel crunched beneath it. She leaned out, her hair tumbling over the sill. Was it possible that he had returned? Her soul leapt with hope. She waited, but the sound was not repeated. She leaned out further. Could it have been an animal? She caught a flash of something by the lake shore. A figure emerged from behind the giant plane tree. Swathed in a cloak of black, all she could make out were a pair of glittering eyes. Eyes that searched for hers and burned into her flesh, angry and accusing. She drew back and slammed the window shut, her heart galloping in her chest. The watcher slipped away into the shadows by the water's edge.

The *watcher*. A chill overtakes me despite the warmth of the duvet. What must it be like for Phillipa King who has to keep dreaming up bad things happening to her heroine? Part of me wishes that Victoria and William would just get on with the inevitable – their big love scene and their happily ever after. But I guess it would be a pretty boring story if they didn't encounter a few bumps in the road along the way. What was it Shakespeare said? 'The course of true love never does run smooth'? How – unfortunately – true.

I close the e-reader and turn off the light. As I'm trying to coax myself into sleep, I think of Theo and the moments we shared; the kiss we shared. But try as I might, my mind keeps wandering. To the earlier encounter in the garden, and a pair of green eyes that are judgemental and accusing.

* * *

'Mum? Mum?'

Katie's voice jars me out of sleep. Beside me, the alarm is beeping. My daughter is standing next to the bed with Jack beside her, sucking his thumb.

I sit up and check the clock, horrified to see that it's already half-seven. Today's a 'big day', and I can't even manage to wake up. For a second I close my eyes, longing to sink back into the shifting pool of images just below consciousness. Walking along a moonlit corridor. Knocking on the door... Would he open it? And who the heck is *he*?

'Mummy.' Jack's thumb has popped out of his mouth. 'Cuggle?'

'Of course, darling.' The dream sinks away to nothingness. I scoop him up, expecting to feel him wet with wee. But to my surprise, he's all dry, and I calculate that it's actually been at least a week since he last had an accident. Maybe with all the excitement going on, he's turned a corner.

'I'm so proud of you,' I say, giving him a kiss on the forehead. I hold my other arm out to Katie. To my surprise, she comes over and lets me hug her. Her body feels thin and fragile in my arms – so vulnerable...

'No. *My* mummy!' Jack gives Katie a push to get her off my lap.

'Come on Jack,' I say, 'I love both of you.'

'Mine.' He scrambles off my lap and hits Katie. Thus begins five minutes of 'playful' mayhem – Katie and Jack wrestling with each other, the dog leaping on top of them, me trying to send one or both kids to time-out, all of them totally ignoring me, and me finally giving up as they collapse in a heap on the bed laughing, with Jammie licking their faces.

Eventually, I get them dressed and downstairs. We're late for school as usual, but seeing the kids laughing and happy, I don't really mind. I give them their breakfast and put on a pot of coffee for the crew. The first members of the set-building team have already arrived. The location manager's name is John C (aka 'Bobble Hat'), and there are at least two other Johns. I'm not good with names, so I'm planning to call them all John.

John C tells me that they'll start 'dressing the set' – bringing in and putting in place all the furniture and props that they'll need for the shoot. The electrical equipment will arrive the following day. They're also going to construct a dock at the lake shore behind the house where the smuggling boats will moor up. It's all heating up. But despite everything that's going on, all I can think about is Phillipa King coming to Tanglewild.

I drop the kids off at school and return home. It's my day to work at home, so I'm planning to closet myself upstairs and stay out of the way. Maybe I'll be able to avoid seeing Luke Thornton entirely. And Phillipa King. I've built her up in my mind so much that I'm now quite nervous about meeting her.

When I reach the house, the site workers are trying to manoeuvre two huge trailers of Portaloos through the gates and round the side of the garage to the field beyond. I join the queue of cars and vans waiting for them to finish so they can park. Immediately in front of me is a silver Audi. I feel a surge of annoyance as Luke Thornton gets out of the car and goes up to the man in charge of the lorries. There's some gesturing and discussion. Luke shakes his head. I can just imagine that the narrow gates and small access road are more strikes against Tanglewild, and – by implication – me.

While they're talking, I crane my neck to see if there's anyone else in the car with Luke. He and Phillipa both have a past history here. They must at least be acquaintances. Maybe they're more than that – who knows? But I can't see anyone in the passenger seat. She'll probably be coming down with Theo later. I wait for the stab of jealousy that doesn't come.

The men finally get the Portaloo trailer through the bottleneck, and the cars in front of Luke move on. He walks back towards his car, tall and self-assured, wearing jeans and a blue button-down shirt. He rakes his dark blond hair back from his face and, instead of going to his own car, comes up to me. If he wasn't blocking me, I'd drive around him, but the road is too narrow. With a sigh, I put the window down.

'Sorry,' he says. 'They're trying not to damage the garage – it's quite narrow.'

I stare at him with distaste. Maybe he's making an effort to be polite, but somehow, he still manages to sound critical.

'John C will speak to you later, but they may need to take down the fence to the orchard. There's an even bigger lorry due tomorrow.'

'I'll speak to John C, then – no need to trouble yourself.' I put the window up, ending the conversation. He looks at me for a long moment as the pane of glass comes up between us. There's something I can't quite read in those green eyes of his, but I get the sense that he can see right through me.

30

THE LADY'S SECRET BY PHILLIPA KING

The master had returned. He invaded Victoria's thoughts as she lay awake staring at the shadows of the tree branches moving across the ceiling. She tried to recall his touch, the brief moment when his lips had possessed hers. But he had been gone many weeks, and in that time she had felt such a strong sense of fear and despair. And try as she might, she couldn't block out the whispers of the servants, and Belle, who was so fond of gossip. Wondering what had become of the master's wife, and when he would be called to answer for the crime.

Did he do it? Like a hanging judge, tall and stern behind an imposing wooden bench, her mind asked the same question over and over. Did he kill his wife? She pulled the blanket up to her chin as the spectre of his sapphire eyes, his wild hair, his strong body, invaded her thoughts, pushing aside everything else. Forcing her to listen to another voice, small and fragile, and yet rising in strength. The voice of her heart whispering its own unanswerable question: Do I care?

Victoria threw off the tangled bedcovers and gave up trying to sleep. The candle had long burned down to a shapeless stump, but she managed to free the wick enough to light it with a taper from the last embers of the fire. Her heart was pounding so hard that she was sure it would wake the whole house. She slipped silently out of her room and walked down the corridor to the long gallery. The silver light shimmered against the diamond panes of glass, and she scarcely needed the candle to light the way. She had walked this journey in her dreams so many times. And yet, now that it was real, her mind itched with the question: what on earth am I doing?

When the master had arrived home earlier in the night, his horse heaving and lathered, he closeted himself in his study to take supper. How foolish she was to think that she might be sent for. How foolish to stay here at all when his absence had offered her a chance of escape. And yet, the memory of his hands, his mouth on hers, beckoned her onwards like a dangerous will-o'-the-wisp. She continued to another corridor, the one that led to his room. She stood outside the door, the candle raised before her like it might ward off the evil spirit that was about to make her do this shameful thing. But it failed. The wood was hard against the skin of her knuckles as she knocked softly on the door...

31

When I finally manage to park the car, there's no sign of Luke. I go into the marquee where tables have been set up with food and drink for the crew: plates of croissants and fruit, sandwiches, biscuits, juice, bottled water, hot water for coffee and tea. There are a few people inside chatting and working on laptop computers. I recognise Annie, one of the assistant producers, and Ruby, an assistant set manager who works on logistics. I say a quick hello, make myself a cup of coffee, and go into the house and upstairs to work.

I open my laptop; as new emails ping onto the screen, my mind escapes to a fantasy B&B. I'd decorate this room with white curtains and matelassé linen to accent the cherry wood furniture, and put a posy of fresh flowers in a vase on the dresser. I'd have goose-down pillows and extra fluffy towels for each room, and locally made bath salts and toiletries. Mismatched china teacups and saucers on a tray, a complimentary bottle of sparkling water, and a tin of posh biscuits and chocolates on the pillow. It would be a delightful mix of boutique and homely. I know I could make it work.

There are more than fifty new emails. The B&B is a nice fantasy, but unfortunately, work is reality. I read through the messages, mechanically accepting meeting requests and conference calls. My day sorted. Eventually, I take a break to drink my coffee and stare out the window. The lake is a turbid mix of brown and grey, a pale sun just breaking through the clouds. A few of the trees have sprouted their leaves, and a family of ducks are pruning themselves on the shore near the house.

Just then I see a flash of blue on the other side of the lake moving towards the dovecote. Luke? It must be. Why does he keep snooping around out there? They aren't using the dovecote for the filming – not even the wise woman's cottage. They are, however, planning to install some kind of camera zip wire from the new dock to the far shore. Of course, Luke's the director, and I know he's got free rein to be out and about, searching for the perfect shot. That in itself is unnerving, because unless I stay closeted in this room for two months, I'll never know when I might run into him and have that top-of-a-roller-coaster lurch in my stomach. But seeing him there has got me alarmed. I'll have to talk to Theo – or maybe one of the Johns – about making the dovecote off limits. The place is derelict and dangerous, and everyone needs to be kept away.

I give up on work and go downstairs for more coffee. The scuffling sounds of the workmen have gone oddly quiet, and as I enter the kitchen, I discover why. A circle of men – Theo, Richard, and two of the Johns – are standing around a central, pivotal figure.

Phillipa King.

I'm not quite sure what I was expecting. I've googled her author photo, of course – a side profile shot of a woman sitting at a desk, her tousled hair piled in a bun, with a pair of small wire-framed glasses on a chain. Early fifties, prim and proper, a cross between Joanna Trollope and a young Camilla Parker-Bowles. But this woman... I cock my head and squint. Have I made a mistake?

The woman sitting at the table is youthful and beautiful.

My mind processes her image like camera film. Tiny wrinkles around her eyes, the skin on her neck just starting to crease. Not young – probably mid-forties – five or ten years older than me. Her hair is blonde and straight, pulled back into a ponytail with a few stray wisps around her face. She's wearing a blue cashmere jumper and white skinny jeans tucked into brown riding boots. Her fingers sparkle with rings made from semi-precious stones. She looks part Sloane Ranger, part horsey set, and all self-assurance and vivacity as she laughs at something one of the Johns says.

When she looks up and sees me, she immediately stands up. The circle parts and in two strides, she's over to me.

'Hello!' she says, stretching the syllables. 'Are you Mrs Greene?'

She holds out her hand, and I shake it, feeling the rings hard beneath my fingers.

'Please, call me Lizzie.'

'And you must call me Phillipa,' she says. 'I'm so pleased to meet you. Thank you so much for allowing us to use your lovely home – what a special place!'

'Thanks, I mean, you're welcome.' Her friendly manner has put me distinctly on the back foot. 'I'm just happy we were chosen. I mean, the book is really great and all.' I close my mouth, realising that I sound like a fangirl.

'How kind.' She waves a bejewelled hand, laughing a little. 'It pays the bills until I can win the Booker Prize.'

I don't quite know what to say so I fall back on the time-honoured convention of offering her a cup of tea.

'Let me make *you* a cup of tea,' she says. 'Theo's been telling me all about how hospitable you've been to the team. Do sit down – put your feet up.'

'I'll get it.' Theo springs to life like a knight in service to his lady – Phillipa, not me. My mind flashes back to the previous evening. Despite the aborted kiss, things had seemed promising. Now, however, I get the distinct impression that in the glow of his mentor, he's barely registered my presence. Before Phillipa can move, he takes charge of the kettle like he's worried that she might somehow soil her hands, rendering herself unable to type her next bonk buster. Or lift a red pen to provide comments on his draft manuscript. But I'm probably just being unfair.

'Really, I can get it myself...' I start to say.

Just then, Luke enters the kitchen from the great hall. His eyes land on mine and for a second I catch a glimpse of the wounded animal, cornered and desperate. But then he turns to Phillipa, and for the first time since I've encountered him, he smiles.

'Phillipa. Lovely to see you.' His face transforms from moody and unpleasant to something... quite different. He walks up to her and gives her a kiss on each cheek, his lips lingering against her skin.

'Luke,' she practically purrs. 'You *are* looking well.'

'It's the climate,' he says jokingly, 'you know California never really suited me.'

'Of course not. You're a northern boy.' She laughs. She lifts her hand and brushes her fingers across his cheek.

The display between them makes me feel completely awkward, and I'm not the only one. Theo bangs two mugs down on the counter. 'You want some tea, Luke?' His voice sounds unusually strained.

'No thanks.' Luke moves away from Phillipa, going over to the windows that look out over the lake. Though it's cold in the room, he opens one of the casement windows and gulps in the fresh air.

Phillipa sits back down at the table, her eyes never leaving Luke. Theo sets the mug in front of her. 'Thank you,' she says absently.

Theo must have forgotten that I was the one who was supposed to have the tea in the first place, because he leaves the second mug on the countertop. I go over and spoon in my own sugar. Seeing Theo behave like a star-struck groupie – or maybe an overprotective puppy – has soured me towards him. Why did he invite me out? And then there's Luke. Seeing *him* so changed in Phillipa's presence is even more disconcerting. For once I'm grateful that I've got work to do so I don't have to hang about down here drowning in testosterone. (Though I'd be very upset if they ruin the oak panelling by marking their territory like dogs.)

Phillipa turns to me. 'Do you know, Lizzie, I was so lucky to get Luke to agree to take on this project,' she says. 'He's the best.'

'Don't, Pippa,' Luke says under his breath. He slams the window shut hard enough to make it rattle. I frown – both for the window and the nickname.

'Well, you are.' She smiles at me. 'He's also too modest.'

'That's one word for it,' I can't help saying.

'But even better was your agreeing to let us use the house,' she says. 'I have such vivid memories of coming to Tanglewild as a girl.'

Her overt admission fills me with surprise and relief. There's no sinister motive here. She had good memories of the place and decided it would be the perfect location to set her book. Mystery (if there ever was one) solved.

'Has the place changed much?' I ask.

'No!' She looks delighted at the question. 'It's exactly the same. Right, Luke?'

He turns away from the window towards her, and I see a flash again of something on his face. Pain? That can't be right; and anyway, it's gone in a split second. He glances in my direction, and once again I feel like an interloper. Obviously I don't belong here in his vision of his precious film set – or the house of his memories. I frown at him, and he looks away. 'Yes, Pippa,' he says. 'It's just the same.' Then he gives her *that* smile again, like they're the only two people in the universe. Anger churns in my stomach. In all this time he's never bothered to acknowledge his connection to the house, but now that *she's* here, it's as if none of the rest of us even exist. 'Now, if you'll excuse me,' he says, 'I need to be getting on. Filming starts soon. There's a lot to do.' As he goes out the door, it's like the air has been sucked from the room.

As I'm about to leave too, Phillipa turns to me. 'I'm so glad to see things in good hands. Luke is so dedicated to his work.'

'I'm sure.' I can't keep the sarcastic edge from my voice.

'Do you know how he got his big break?'

I shake my head.

'When he was a film student, he did a documentary on teenage runaways in LA. He lived on the streets for almost three months trying to figure out what made them tick. He wasn't doing it for fame, or money, or even the respect of those he revered in the industry. He just wanted to do his work – to make the film he envisioned. It won him a prestigious award and got the attention of the powers that be. Every time someone took a chance on him, he delivered. And he did it without compromising his principles or his vision. That's something I've always admired about him.'

To me, the last statement doesn't ring true. Luke *has* compromised his principles and vision in using Tanglewild as a set. It continues to beg the question: *why?* It's on the tip of my tongue to ask her when Theo comes up.

'Would you like more tea, Phillipa?' His face is guarded, and all the talk about Luke has clearly taken the wind from his sails.

'No thanks.' She smiles upwards at Theo. 'Sorry, I have been going on a bit, haven't I?' I have the distinct impression that she knows how far she's pushed him and is now reining him back on side. 'And, in fact, I'm just dying to get outside and have a look round. Can I tempt you to join me, Lizzie?'

Before I can respond, my phone vibrates in my pocket. I take it out and check the screen. 'Sorry,' I say, 'but I'm afraid duty calls. Maybe another time?'

'Of course,' she says. 'And once again, thanks for having us.'

'I'd be happy to join you, Phillipa,' Theo says.

I'm sure, I think as I leave the room. I'm almost glad to take the phone call from 'Harry – work' and have an excuse to get away.

* * *

Luke and Phillipa. The kiss, the smiles. The way she fawned over him; the way he acted like an overproud tom-cat – not wanting to let on how much he's enjoying being stroked.

Phillipa and Luke.

I dial in to the conference call I'd totally forgotten about until Harry reminded me. As I'm listening to the introductions, I speculate on their relationship. Perhaps they were childhood friends – or more than friends. They drifted apart and each married someone else. According to Wikipedia, Phillipa is twice married and twice divorced. Both of them became successful and famous in their own professions. Both are now single. Both are (as much as it pains me to admit it about Luke) attractive. Perhaps they once shared a Victoria Easterbrook/William Clarke moment together, and Phillipa chose to memorialise it in her novel. And now, like two magnetic poles drawn together, the two of them are converging on the scene where it all kicked off. Somehow, I doubt the fact that the huge canopy bed is part of the set and off limits will put off Luke Thornton. The idea of the two of them together makes my stomach turn—

'Lizzie, are you there?'

Harry sounds rattled and annoyed – understandably, since I'm supposed to be leading the call and I'm a million miles away. I click onto autopilot and go through the comments I've made on a loan agreement, arguing points, conceding points, doing my job by rote. Only weeks ago I was desperate for this job, and I was doing well. Then Harry's conduct made me realise that I wasn't hired for my razor-sharp legal brain, which made me doubt myself all over again. And the film project is disruptive, but exciting too. It's opened my mind to new ideas – like the B&B – and out-of-the-box thinking—

'Lizzie – are there any final points?'

I jolt back to reality once again. 'No,' I say. 'That's it.'

'Good, so can you turn the draft this afternoon, Lizzie?'

'Yes,' I say. 'I'll do it right now.'

One by one, the phone lines blip off. Alone in the guest room staring out at the lake, I look towards the dovecote. This time, there's no one out there.

32

THE LADY'S SECRET BY PHILLIPA KING

Victoria waited for an eternity, but there was no answer. Had she steeled her courage for nothing? She tried the handle, the brass knob cold against her skin. The door swung open.

The room was empty, and she was spurred on by fascination to go inside. The smell was familiar – leather, tobacco smoke, warm skin. Him. She breathed in deeply, heat spreading through every inch of her body. She shouldn't have been there – that she knew. But surely this was fate.

The bed was dark and huge in the middle of the room. She was drawn to it instinctively, like a moth to a light. But she toyed with avoiding it, going instead over to the bureau and flipping through the open books on top of it. A book of love poetry, she noted. She opened the small silver snuffbox, and then one of the drawers. Inside were his shirts – snow white and whisper soft. She picked one up and held it to her nose, breathing in. But it only smelled of clean linen, not of him. She put it back in the drawer, unable to bear it any longer. She moved to the bed and pulled back the thick green damask cover, her heart galloping in her chest. Casting off her dressing gown onto the floor, she slipped naked under the sheet. Her auburn hair tangled beneath her as she nuzzled the pillow, still indented from where his head had lain. And inside, she felt a spark ignite and begin to burn, sweeping through her, leaving an unquenchable thirst.

The minutes went by, her heart refusing to slow. Her head was flooded by a *thousand reasons why this was wrong, why she should get up right now and run – out the door, down the stairs, and away from here, forever. But her muscles refused to obey, languishing, sinking into the soft warmth of the bed and a gossamer mist of anticipation.*

A moment later, the blissful pleasure darted away, frightened into the shadows. Footsteps outside the door. His boots, the spurs jangling metallic against the wood of the corridor. And then he stopped. The door, left slightly ajar, swung inward with a heavy creak.

She pulled the covers up to her chin and squeezed her eyes closed. She couldn't bear to look; couldn't bear to see his face. Couldn't bear to see shock, or worse, distaste. Most especially, she couldn't bear to see the desire that she knew burned hot behind the crystal blue of his eyes.

Her eyes were still tightly shut as the footsteps came closer. She could hear him breathing, feel the change in the current of air. She pinched her nails to the palm of her hand. Too late... too late...

And when his hand brushed the strand of hair off her face, his skin lingering against hers, agonisingly slow and impossibly gentle, she couldn't bear it any longer. She opened her eyes to face up to what she'd set in motion.

33

I revise the draft agreement, feeling completely wiped out. The commuting, the kids, the long hours of work – surely no one would mind, or even notice, if I sloped off for an hour. I don't like to admit it, but seeing Phillipa and Luke's clear bond has made me feel uncomfortable – even a bit jealous. Not *of* either of them, mind, but jealous of that spark of sexual tension that existed between them – and between Phillipa and every other man in the room. Even Richard acted differently around her, and I'm pretty sure he's gay. I haven't spoken to Theo, and I'm not sure what there is to say. I can't deign to compete when Phillipa is around.

Abandoning my work, I turn back to *The Lady's Secret*. It doesn't take me many pages before I'm there – at the seduction scene. Victoria has spent several weeks in a state of high alarm, worried about the mysterious watcher. When the master finally returns home, she knows it's now or never. She goes to his bedroom, slips naked into his bed, and waits for him there. Seduction by candlelight – even more over the top than the rest of the book.

I toss the e-reader aside. The events of the morning have soured Victoria's story for me. Was Phillipa King thinking of herself when she wrote that scene, putting herself in the mind and body of Victoria? When the others look at her, is that who they see? Is that who Theo sees? Luke?

I return to my work, determined not to waste any more time on such drivel. A new email has come in inviting me to a legal awards reception, and as a show of good faith, I decide to accept. It's tomorrow night, and the dress code is listed as semi-formal. I sigh. I've certainly nothing in the spare room fitting that description, so I decide to brave the construction work downstairs and the possibility of running into Luke/Phillipa/Theo and check my bedroom closet.

My bedroom looks different than before. All the knickknacks and trappings of modern life are gone. Along one wall, a table has been set up with props: candles, old books, vases, a heavy wooden coffer chest, bedding, a pile of shirts – all quite authentic-looking. The bed still has my old duvet on it, and someone's tossed a dog-eared script on the pillow.

I go to the window and look out at the lake. The crew is erecting a giant piece of scaffolding near the house, and Phillipa and Theo are on the back lawn chatting. He laughs at something she says; I feel deflated and resigned.

My closet has little to offer in the semi-formal category. I find the black dress that I wore to Dave's funeral and take it off the hanger, holding it to my nose. It smells faintly of cedar and sweat. I hate the idea of wearing it again, but I've no other option.

I flop onto the bed and stare up at the canopy. I've not been sleeping in the guest room for long, but this room now feels strange and impersonal. Certainly there's little or no sense of the time I spent here with Dave. I'm not quite sure how that makes me feel.

I listen for a minute to the sounds from outside the windows: hammering, voices, and birdsong. Rolling over, I grab a copy of the script. There's a bookmark in the middle – a torn page that's marked and underlined with a red pen. I lie back and read the passage from the book:

> The room was aglow with candlelight. She stretched out her body in pleasure and breathed in the scent of beeswax, sweat and skin. Beside her, he breathed hard, spent and satisfied. She pushed the damp hair back from her face and traced with her finger the long contours of muscle along his shoulder blades, the hills and valleys of his spine, and the sleek smooth skin of the hollow in his lower back just where the

edge of the sheet covered him. Once again, he groaned in pleasure, and her body waited, anticipating him rolling back to her, his hands continuing their exploration.

'There's something I have to tell you.'

Those words, spoken in the darkness, curdled her blood. Her body pressed against his, she tried to move closer, smother the need for him to say any more. But deep down, she knew that it was futile. Whatever he was, whatever he had to say, he was part of her now.

'What is it, my love?'

'I know you've heard the rumours. About my wife. Charity.'

'Please,' she said. 'Don't.'

'No.' He moved away from her, sitting upright in the bed. 'You have to know the truth. I didn't kill her, but what happened was my fault.'

She expected the words to chill her blood. But instead, something shifted inside her, spreading its wings, suddenly taking flight.

'It doesn't matter,' she whispered. She ducked her head under the covers and made sure he couldn't reply.

I stop reading; my heart is beating rapidly. *The Lady's Secret* has definitely addled my brain. What am I doing in the middle of the day, with my house full of people... lying here... reading this—

There's a footstep outside the door. Dominic Kennedy takes in my presence, the bed, the script in my hand. Except for his T-shirt and jeans, he could have stepped straight out of the pages of the book. And he knows it too. A slow smile comes over his face. I blush to the roots of my hair.

'Ah, Lizzie, I see you found my script. I've been looking for it.'

'Um... yeah.' I swing up into a sitting position.

He enters the room and sits down beside me on the bed, his hip touching mine. He smells faintly of cigarette smoke, sweat, and a dark, musky cologne. He takes the pages from my hand, frowning down at them. 'I'm struggling with the dialogue in the love scene,' he says. 'It just sounds so fake. I wanted to go through it once though, in situ, before I speak to Phillipa about changing it.'

'I guess it is a little over the top.'

He turns to me and takes my hand in his. 'I was watching you, Lizzie. I hope you don't mind. You looked so beautiful just lying there. You are beautiful – do you know that?'

'Um...'

He traces the veins on my hand. 'I heard about what happened with your husband. It must have been so hard for you. I lost someone I loved, too. When he died, I felt I'd be alone forever. I felt ugly and unlovable. It was all I could do not to get out a bottle of vodka and some pills and try to follow.'

'He?' I say, a little surprised.

He gestures expansively with his free hand. 'I'm not gay. I just like beautiful things. Beautiful people. I'm only saying it because I know you won't tell anyone. You're a real person, not like the people in the industry. Some of them would sell their mother to leak a juicy story about me to the paps.'

'You're right – I would never do that.'

He lets out a deep sigh. 'It's funny, I wouldn't even mind people knowing the truth; it's just, I'd hate to disappoint my fans. The best part of the job is making people happy. If that makes sense.'

'It does,' I say. 'You give them a little fantasy to spice up their everyday lives.'

'Exactly. And most of my fans, of course, are women.'

I nod.

'So what I'm trying to say is, if there's anything I can do to help you with what you're going through' – he leans even closer to me and whispers into my ear – 'then you must let me.'

I'm not sure which is stronger, the urge to hug him, or the urge to laugh. I focus instead on the fact that this can't seriously be happening. I mean – me? Dominic Kennedy? And yet, who am I to quell his altruistic urge to 'comfort' me? But as he lifts his hand to my cheek and tries to turn my head to kiss me, I know I have to stop.

'What the hell is going on?'

My heart slams against the hard edge of Luke Thornton's voice.

Dominic lets go of me and scrambles to his feet. 'Luke,' he says, his voice deep and professional. 'Lizzie here was just helping me rehearse.'

'Is that what you call it, Dom?' His lips flatten into a line. 'Because I don't remember anything in the script about comforting a grieving widow.' He turns to me, his eyes cold. 'Or a merry one.'

'How dare you?' I jump up from the bed and in two strides I'm standing in front of him. Before my mind can catch up to what I'm doing, I slap him hard across the face. 'You're a rude bastard, Luke Thornton, and I wish you'd never come here. Take your film and stick it up your arse.'

His mouth gapes open in surprise; he lifts a hand to his cheek. I'm shocked at what I've done, but there's no way I'm going to apologise – not now, or ever.

* * *

Shit, shit, shit. I grab the black dress and run out of the room. Down the stairs, through the main hall, not caring who sees me or thinks I've shagged the leading man, assaulted the director, or just plain looped the loop. I ditch the black dress in the closet by the door and go outside – I'm dying for some fresh air. This is my house, and it was my bed, and...

God, that man. Instead of smacking him, I wish I'd clawed those eyes out of his head. Cool and green, seeing everything, judging everything. Who the hell is he to judge me?

I avoid the gardens where Phillipa and Theo might be lurking and make a beeline for the front gate. I lean against the wall gasping for breath (a bad idea since the toilet block has been parked right outside). Across the drive I see Connie directing Danny the security guard, who's backing his SUV up to the caravan's hitch.

Connie frowns as I draw near. 'Take a breath, Lizzie – whatever it is can't be that bad.'

I bat my hand in irritation. 'These film people are getting on my nerves.'

'I won't say I told you so.' She shakes her head. 'A little to the left, Danny,' she calls out.

'What's going on?' I ask her.

'John J says the caravan's in the way. They need to get a lorry through later on with the cameras and electrics.'

I cross my arms. 'You're not to move an inch – do you hear? This is your home for as long as you and Simon want to be here.'

'Really, Lizzie, I'm not a shrinking violet. If I minded, I would have said.'

'Well *I* mind. I've bloody well had enough. They have no right to act like they own the place.'

'You're the one who signed the contract – I'm sure you know what they can and can't do. I was trying to be accommodating. But in truth, I'd rather not move. I like to be here where it's all happening.'

'Then don't.'

'Stand down, Danny,' she commands.

John J, the short one who's in charge of logistics, comes round the back of the garage. 'Everything OK?' He looks at Connie.

'She's not moving.' I cross my arms stubbornly.

'But John C said—'

'Read. My. Lips,' I say. 'She's not going anywhere.'

'But look—'

'John, what's going on? Is there a problem?'

A trickle of sweat beads down my neck at that voice – again! If I wasn't sure that the ill feelings were mutual, I'd almost say the jerk was following me.

'No, it's not OK!' I say, loud and undignified, turning to face Luke Thornton. 'Your people want Connie to move her caravan, and she's not doing it. So tell them to find another way to get your lorry through, or else—'

'Or else what? Stick it somewhere unpleasant? Along with the film?' For the first time since I've known Luke, he laughs. I stare at him, startled. Connie looks at him, then at me. 'Of course you don't have to move your caravan, Connie,' Luke says to her. 'I'm sorry if you've been inconvenienced in any way.' He turns to John J. 'Send John C to me if there's any issue. And if it's OK with Lizzie, you can take down the fence to get the lorry through.'

'It's OK with me,' I grumble, feeling a bit like a toddler, post-tantrum.

'Thanks.'

With a bemused look on his face, Luke turns around and walks to his car. He does a six-point turn to avoid the other cars parked higgledy-piggledy near the wall and drives off down the lane.

Connie, John J, and I stand there watching until the car disappears from sight.

'I'd better go get some of the lads to help with that fence,' John J says.

I feel like running after him, because I know my mother-in-law is not going to let me live down my little 'performance'.

Sure enough, Connie gives me a pained smile and shakes her head. 'I won't say I told you so,' she repeats.

34

With Luke off the premises, the fight has gone out of me. I apologise to John J and offer to make a pot of coffee. (There's coffee in the marquee, but the water is a little tepid, and the coffee is instant.) He takes me up on it, and I'm glad. I like the crew and I'm grateful that they're treating my house and me with respect.

In the kitchen, I find Phillipa King sitting at the table writing in a small notebook. I don't really want to disturb the muse at work, but she looks up at me and smiles.

'Lizzie,' she says. 'Sorry – do you mind my sitting here? I needed a quiet moment.'

'I don't mind. It's no trouble.' I'm relieved that although she set her book here, she's not acting like she owns the place. And if she's heard about my altercation with Luke, she's not letting on. 'If you need a private space, you can maybe use my son's room.' I surprise myself by making the offer. 'It's not being used for the filming.'

'Thank you, Lizzie, that's kind – and I may take you up on it. I'm used to working in peace and quiet. I haven't done a screenplay before, and I'm finding it a little tricky, to be honest.' Her eyes widen in mock distress. 'The leading man isn't happy with his bedroom dialogue. What *will* I do?'

I laugh. 'I'm sure Dominic would be happy to *rehearse* whatever you end up writing.'

Her laugh is merry but dignified. 'Ah, so the rumours are true. But I fear that I'm far too old for him.'

'I thought I was too!' I grin. Now that we're on our own, I'm warming to her. I go over to the coffee machine and start making a fresh pot.

'I'm so glad you're here, Lizzie,' she says. 'I was a little daunted by the idea of all the stars and the crew. I know it's my book, but I still feel like a bit of an outsider.'

'Really?' I say. 'That's how I feel too, but they've all been very nice so far. Everyone except—' I catch myself. The kiss, the smile... Luke and Pippa; Pippa and Luke.

She pauses like she's reading my mind. 'Don't tell me... Has Luke been giving you trouble? Shame on him.'

Something in the way she says it makes me bristle. The self-assurance, the possession. But I'm determined to take a charitable view of her. At the end of the day, the fact that her book is being filmed at my house is a godsend. Phillipa King is helping me save Tanglewild. For that alone, she deserves a chance.

'You and he are old friends?'

'Yes. We go way back.' She smiles wistfully. 'We knew each other when we were kids. I suppose you could say that he was my first real love.'

'Really?' I try to sound neutral. 'That's interesting.'

'It was donkey's years ago. He was, what? Fifteen maybe? So long ago. But it was' – she pauses, choosing her words – 'instrumental in my life. We've encountered each other off and on over the years since then. I was married; he was married. Never the twain shall meet, if you like.'

'Yeah.' I pour the coffee into the filter. 'I understand.'

'But who knows? Maybe this time the planets will finally be aligned.' She gives me a sad smile; I decide that I want to be happy for her – and Luke, goddamn him.

'That's... good.'

She scribbles something in her notebook before looking at me again. 'Theo told me how you came to own the house,' she says. 'I hope you don't mind, but I was interested.'

'I don't mind. But I'm ashamed to say that I know very little about Tanglewild's history. I did go to the museum though, and learned about the smugglers and the woman – Veronica Jones?'

'Yes,' Phillipa says. 'I used it for one of the subplots. They never did find her body, you know.'

The room suddenly feels chilly. 'What do you think happened to her?'

'Oh, I'm sure the husband probably did her in. The simplest explanation is usually the right one.'

'It's sad,' I say. 'But you're probably right.'

'Obviously, though, I had to change the ending. I couldn't have the hero as the murderer. People expect a happy ending – both on the page and in real life. In my genre, no one wants to know the truth.'

'What do you mean?'

'Romance novels are about escape,' she says. 'Escape from the mundane, from the pain – and the little annoyances – of everyday life. I'm like an abstract impressionist who tries to paint a beautiful view, embellishing reality until it no longer is reality. Catching a dream and putting it down on paper.'

I nod, thinking of how unwittingly involved in Victoria's story I've become. It's good to know that despite the twists and turns in the plot, she'll have a happy ending. Unlike real life, where there are no guarantees.

'Did you always want to be a writer?' I ask her.

'I suppose I did.' And as the coffee machine burbles in the background, she tells me more about herself and her inspirations – the romantic suspense novels she read when she was young, and how much she loved Tanglewild when she stayed here as a teenager. How she'd set some of her earlier novels in more usual places like Cornwall and the Scottish Highlands. But she always knew that one day, she'd set a book at Tanglewild.

As I finish making the coffee, she asks me about myself. At first, I feel a little daunted – like she couldn't possibly be interested. But I find myself telling her briefly about Dave and my struggle to get back on my feet after his death. I tell her how the film project has truly been a blessing, and even mention the idea of turning the house into a B&B.

'That would be wonderful!' she says. 'I'm sure it would be very successful. And such fun.'

'Yes.' I'm buoyed by her reaction. 'I think it would be.'

We talk some more and have another coffee. She tells me about her two marriages, and two divorces, and how she's struggled with depression. And whether her books are Booker Prize material or 3 for 2 at an airport WHSmith, I find myself empathising with the ups and downs that she's suffered. I'm also a little bit spellbound by her passion and drive to succeed. Part of me wants to hate her – for turning the men in the room into a pack of feral dogs, bringing a smile to the face of Luke Thornton, and making Theo hero-worship her. But I find myself genuinely taking pleasure in her company. She's charismatic and easy to talk to, but it's more than that. It's the sense I get that, for Phillipa King, finding a kindred spirit is just as important to her as it is to me.

* * *

Eventually, I tear myself away. John J's coffee is long cold and I've forgotten how he takes it. Worse, in between my encounter with Dominic Kennedy, smacking Luke in the face, and hobnobbing with a famous author, I've completely neglected the fact that, technically, I'm supposed to be working.

I have just enough time to go back to the guest room and check my emails (thirty-six new in the last two hours). I've got three missed calls from Harry, and one from Theo.

I decide to text Theo. Yes, he acted a little starstruck today around his mentor, but then again, so did all the others. I type in:

> Had a great time the other night. L.

As I press send, I wonder if I'm just going through the motions. Maybe I'm not ready for a relationship. Or maybe Theo's not the right one. Either way, I decide I'd better call Harry back. Because ultimately, when the film people leave, I'll be back to square one. Until I can get the B&B up and running, I need a job – and I have a job. *The Lady's Secret* is pure fantasy; none of it is real.

I spend several minutes assuring Harry that, under normal circumstances, I answer emails within the hour – usually under ten minutes. I tell him things have been a little crazy (and to my infinite shame, make up a phantom case of chickenpox for Jack that's taking my time and energy). I assure him that I'm *so* looking forward to The Lawyer Awards and am flattered to have a place at the table. By the time I hang up, I feel utterly sick from the lies and platitudes. With all the turmoil and excitement going on, real life can't compete.

Unfortunately, it's *real life* that pays the bills.

I spend the rest of the afternoon working, and when I finally go down to the main hall, I discover that the painting is finished and the room is dazzling. The dark panelling has been cleaned and smells of linseed oil, the fireplace has been laid with a huge bank of wood and twigs. I can picture the Lady of the Manor walking through the house on the day it was completed, 400 years ago.

The drawing room and the library have been similarly transformed. It's amazing, but also a little disconcerting. I feel a heightened sense of responsibility towards this new Tanglewild. If (when?) I do turn it into a B&B, this is the house that I want my guests to see. But I also want my children to be happy in their home. I don't have all the answers yet, but I'm seeing the place with new eyes. Two months ago, at the estate agents, I'd wanted Tanglewild to become a blank canvas for my future. And here it is, right before me. It's even better than I could have dreamed.

* * *

The house may look brilliant inside, but chaos has spread outside. When I go out to my car, there's a commotion as all three Johns are trying to help guide the lorry with the cameras and electronic equipment through the narrow lane past the garage and into the field behind. I feel a little pang of guilt – it would have been easier if Connie had moved the caravan, but luckily, just as I'm standing there debating whether to offer to move it, the lorry makes an almighty lurch, taking out a few bricks, but getting past.

John J comes over to me and assures me they will replace the bricks, and I assure him that it's fine. He also, however, recites a litany of other issues that have cropped up. A neighbour has complained about the traffic on the lane, someone let the dog out and she ate a plate of biscuits in the tent, the TV aerial is going to have to come down, they need to get a digger for the dock excavations...

I give him free rein to sort everything. My life already feels like it's been turned upside down, so a few issues more or less are just par for the course. I leave to get the children from school and to drop Katie's friend Flora off at home; now that I'm not doing it every day, the school run feels like a novelty, and I'm grateful for Connie's ongoing help.

Slightly more worrying, however, is what the kids are getting up to after school when I'm at work. Connie seems fairly strict on Katie's homework and Jack's potty training, but in the car, all Katie can talk about is how Chloe, one of the costume crew, allowed her into the trailer to see the costumes and even try some things on. As soon as we arrive home, she runs off to find her again. I call out after her that she's not supposed to disturb the film crew, but she's long gone.

I get Jack out of his car seat, determined to 'go with the flow' and stop worrying about everything. If the kids are in the way, I'm sure someone will tell me. Still, I wish I was here more often so that I could keep a closer eye on things.

The men are unloading the cables, dollies, and large black cases that I assume contain cameras, lights and sound equipment. All the hubbub seems to worry Jack, and as we get out of the car, he clings to my leg.

'It's OK,' I say, leading him by the hand. 'They're moving in cameras and stuff.'

'Why?'

'So they can catch Superman on film when he gets here.'

'Really?' His little face is so earnest that I regret lying. But at least it calms him down. I take him into the marquee to get him a snack from the food table, where we've been told we can help ourselves. More than a dozen people are about: typing out call sheets, setting up monitors, cleaning camera lenses. I spot two of the neighbours at the food table chatting to Annie and a few of the other assistants. I'm relieved that John J must have sorted them out with a bribe of tepid coffee and biscuits. As I'm about to go over to them, Jack pulls on my trouser leg.

'Where's Luke?' he says.

I look down at him, stunned. 'What's that?'

'He said we could kick a ball again.'

'Again?' My voice rises unnaturally. 'Are you saying that Luke—'

'Jack?'

At the sound of the voice from outside, Jack runs out the door of the tent.

'Sorry I'm late, fella. Where's your grandma?'

I detour to the door of the tent. Outside on the lawn, Luke Thornton is bent down level with Jack. He's holding a small soccer ball. He puts it down at Jack's feet and straightens up, raking back his unruly blond hair.

I stand there staring, racked by a pulsing wave of anxiety.

Luke catches sight of me, and for an instant he looks like a deer in the headlights. 'Oh. Lizzie. I thought Connie was here. Um, we were just—'

'Come on!' Jack picks up the ball and throws it at Luke.

'Hey, mate, no handball, remember?' Luke passes it to him gently with his foot. Jack kicks it back, hard and high, straight at Luke's face. The ball smacks him in the forehead.

I gasp.

'Great!' Luke says, a little shakily. 'But pass to the feet, OK?'

'OK!'

'Over here!' John C calls to Jack for the ball. My son makes a feeble attempt to kick it to him. A few of the other assistants come out of the tent to join the game.

Unwanted tears burble up inside of me as I watch my son running around on the lawn, laughing and happy.

35

Turbid and overwrought, I go inside to make the kids' tea. In only the short time since I've been away doing the school run, the great hall is no longer a pristine blank canvas. It's now filled with huge cases of electronics and crewmen running cables, and erecting large dollies made of metal pipes, and setting up huge umbrella-shaped lighting shades the size of kettle drums.

Something drops, and someone curses, but all my attention is focused on the lawn outside, where my son – my beloved Jack – is trying to run down a well-built, athletic, six-foot tall man, whom, for only the second time since I've known him, is smiling and laughing too. Luke trips over the ball and goes flying onto the lawn. Jack sticks his thumb in his mouth and laughs hysterically. A couple of the crew stop what they're doing, someone lets the dog out of her run, and in less than a minute, there's four of them kicking the tiny ball, teaching Jack to dribble and pass, with Jammie nipping at their heels like a young puppy.

'Your son is so lovely!'

I turn, startled, as Phillipa King comes up behind me at the sink. She gets a glass out of the cupboard and runs it under the tap.

'Thanks,' I say, 'but I just worry that the kids are getting in the way. I mean, it's so chaotic around here, it's impossible to keep track of them.'

She gives me a friendly pat on the shoulder. 'I wouldn't worry, Lizzie. As far as I know, everyone loves having the kids around, and your mother-in-law keeps them in line.' She winks. 'I've only just met her, but I think Connie could keep anyone in line.'

I laugh, feeling a bit brighter. 'You've got that right,' I say.

I look out the window again.

Next to me, Phillipa sighs. 'It's such a shame Luke and Tessa never had children. But I suppose that's what happens when you marry the wrong person.' She shakes her head. 'At least, that's what happened in my case.'

'You don't have children?'

'My second ex and I tried for a while,' she says. 'But it never happened.'

'Gosh, I'm...' I stop myself before 'sorry' can come out. Because, in fact, I don't really know what to say. All too often, I've taken my kids for granted when I was feeling defeated and low. But at the end of the day, they're everything to me. Phillipa has many things going for her – charisma, talent, international success – but the more I get to know her, the more I wouldn't trade places with her.

'That's OK, Lizzie. It was just one of those things.' She says it matter-of-factly, as if she's learned not to let the emotions touch her. 'I feel like I can tell you because you've been through the mill yourself. I don't usually find it easy to open up to people.'

'I know what you mean. I was practically a hermit before all this came along.' I gesture towards the goings-on outside. The football game pauses temporarily as a lorry driver comes through the gate and approaches Luke. Luke confers with John C and points and shrugs, clearly irritated with some problem that's come up. They follow the driver back out the gate. Jack carries on playing with the other men and two women who have joined the game.

Phillipa laughs. 'Well, there are worse places to be a hermit, surely. It's lovely to be so secluded – like a little nest where you can hide away. Unfortunately, I rarely have that luxury. The press are always looking to get hold of some titbit of gossip. Which, in my case, is bad for business.'

'Don't they say that all publicity is good publicity?'

'Yes, but unfortunately, that's wrong.' She leans back against the worktop and takes a sip of water. 'Most of my readers think that because I'm a romantic novelist, my life must be *so* romantic. They want it to be the case; need it. Because if my life is full of sex and romance, then it can be real for them too. Readers don't want their romances to be written by a plump old woman with fifty cats. Because that would make it all fantasy.'

'I guess I've never thought of it that way.'

'It makes it hard, when in reality, it couldn't be further from the truth.' For a brief second, her mask of self-possession slips and I see the bitterness underneath.

'I think I understand,' I say. 'People thought that about me too – living in this house with a man who seemed like the perfect husband. When underneath, things were rotten to the core.'

'Rotten – yes, that's a good word. When interviewers and readers ask me if I identify with Victoria Easterbrook, they want me to say yes. When in reality' – she shakes her head – 'I think she's a stupid little airhead. And don't even get me started on William Clarke – the arrogant arse.'

'Really?' I'm a little taken aback. 'I guess I assumed that most authors like the characters they create.'

'We do have to put up with them for a long time living in our heads.' She taps her temple. 'And of course I'm so grateful for the success the book's had. It was a long time coming, believe me. It's difficult being a struggling author. I'd published three books before *The Lady's Secret*. None of them were big sellers by publisher standards. And before that were the years of rejections and self-doubt. It's not as glamourous as people think.'

'But surely all that's changed now. Your book is being made into a film.'

'It's definitely my big break.' She smiles. 'It's just that sometimes, I have this uncontrollable urge to tell the truth – how life really is, not how people want it to be. In actual fact, it's all there in the book, but not in a way that anyone sees. Even Luke doesn't see it, and he knows me better than anyone.'

'Oh.' I feel an odd clawing sensation in my chest.

Just then, Katie comes through the gate. She's wearing a long white nightgown and a curly auburn wig. The nightgown is thin enough that I can see her purple and white polka dot pants.

'What's she up to?' I say under my breath.

'Is that your daughter?'

'Yes. Katie. She's nine.'

'What a beautiful girl!' Phillipa's eyes are filled with admiration. 'I'm sure she must be so excited about all this. The costumes, the cameras, the actresses and actors.'

'Yes,' I say. As a mother, I can't help but feel proud that Phillipa is so taken with my daughter. She didn't have to say those things. 'It's great to see her so excited after all she's been through. She kind of' – I pause to choose my words – 'shut down after her dad died. It's been really hard getting through to her. I just hope that I'm doing the right thing.'

'I'm sure it will be fine. You're so lucky, Lizzie.' Something in her voice catches. I turn worriedly. Phillipa King is a fascinating woman, but I'm a little uncomfortable with her revealing so many confidences. Although, everyone and their dog seems to know about *my* situation.

Jack is still playing ball with one of the crew women; Jammie has given up the game, lying down by the marquee, her long pink tongue lolling from her mouth. Katie walks towards the front door of the house and out of sight. As the great hall is an obstacle course of cords, trip hazards, and expensive kit, I excuse myself to Phillipa and go to meet her at the front door.

'Look, Mum,' Katie gushes as she comes into the house. 'Chloe let me try on some of the clothes that Natasha, the real actress, is going to wear. It's so fab. I'm going to be an actress when I'm older.'

'And I'm sure you'll be superb.' Once again, I'm startled by Phillipa – I thought she was still in the kitchen. 'Hi, Katie, I'm Phillipa,' she says. 'I wrote the story that the film is about.'

'Really?' Katie eyes are wide and impressed.

'Yes. I was just having a chat with your mum. You look lovely in that costume.'

'Yes, Katie,' I say. 'You do look great. But you know you're not supposed to bother the crew. Besides, it's time to come in and do your homework and your piano.' I hate the way I sound like a boring, strict, old mum, but with everything that's going on, I feel the need to cling to what little control I have.

'You're so *mean*, Mum,' Katie shouts. I brace myself for the 'I hate you' that's sure to be coming next.

'Hey, listen, Katie,' Phillipa says. 'I don't want to interfere, but if you do what your mum says, then maybe I could do something for you – a little surprise.'

'What?' Katie and I say at the same time.

I feel a pang of alarm that she's interfering between me and my daughter. She smiles vaguely, like she's read my mind. 'Sorry,' she says. 'I should have discussed it with you first. It's just an idea I had. Since Katie's clearly so keen to be an actress.'

'What's the surprise?' Katie says.

Once again, Phillipa looks at me. Maybe she is sorry, and she definitely should have discussed it with me first, but the cat is out of the bag.

'Go on,' I say coolly.

'Well, since I'm writing the script, I might be able to add an extra character – just a bit part, you understand – I wouldn't want to upset Luke.'

'You mean a part for me?' Katie's eyes shine like small moons.

'Only if your mum says it's OK.'

'Please, Mum…' Katie turns to me. 'I'll do anything you say – my homework, piano – I'll clean up my room. It would be so great.'

A thousand objections come to mind: Katie has enough on her plate, *The Lady's Secret* isn't appropriate for children, I'm not sure I could handle a budding starlet in the house. But despite them all, I feel a ripple of excitement. My daughter with a part in a film! I think back to how much I wanted and needed this project – not only for the money, but for the new lease of life. And so far, it's delivered on that. I've become a different person: more open to change, more comfortable outside my comfort zone. Maybe Katie needs this to move on too.

'I'll have to speak to her teacher to make sure it won't be too distracting,' I say to Phillipa. 'And really – Luke probably won't like it. But if that can be sorted' – I turn to Katie and smile at her, ruffling her hair – 'then yes – fine.'

'Oh, Mum!' Katie grins and throws her arms around me. 'Thank you! I love you so much.'

That smile and those words make it all worth it. 'Thank you,' I say to Phillipa. 'And really, you must say if it's too much bother.'

'It's no bother at all. And I'd better get working on it.' She winks at Katie. 'It's going to be so much fun.'

As she disappears up the stairs, I give Katie a kiss and tell her to go back out to the trailer and get changed. 'Yes, Mum,' she says, like the dutiful, obedient child of old. She skips out of the house. The game of football has fizzled, and I call out to Jack. He comes running to me, grass-stained and red-faced.

'Can I have a treat, Mum?' he says.

I scoop him up in my arms. 'It's teatime,' I say. He begins to struggle and I set him down. 'I want a treat *now*!'

I glance sideways at Luke, who's come back into the garden and is talking to one of his assistants next to the marquee. He looks over in my direction, frowning.

'Shh,' I say to Jack. 'People are working. It's time to come inside.'

'Luke!' he yells. 'Can we play some more?'

'Come on,' I say gruffly, pulling him inside the house. Because the last thing I want is for Luke Thornton – of all the bloody men in the world – to suddenly hold the key to the happiness of *both* my children.

PART IV

He rose upright in the stirrups. He scarce could reach her hand,
But she loosened her hair in the casement. His face burnt like a brand
As the black cascade of perfume came tumbling over his breast;
And he kissed its waves in the moonlight,
(O, sweet black waves in the moonlight!)
Then he tugged at his rein in the moonlight, and galloped away to the west.

— ALFRED NOYES, 'THE HIGHWAYMAN'

36

THE LADY'S SECRET BY PHILLIPA KING

'I didn't kill her. I swear that on my father's grave.' William stared up at the folds of the canopy bed above them, absently stroking the smooth silken white of her thigh. 'But I know who did.'

Victoria wished he would stop talking. She believed him; that was enough. But he seemed determined to continue.

'The truth is that my marriage was over long before Charity deserted me. Her leaving, though, wasn't enough. Not for those who had other designs.'

Victoria shivered, nestling herself closer to him. But he threw off the covers and rose from the bed, making to dress.

'Who?' she asked in a small voice.

'I shall not burden you with the secret,' he said. 'But you must be careful. There could be danger afoot. That is why I did not take you to my bed sooner. Though matters, it would seem, have moved on apace.' He turned to her and smiled, and his eyes shone with the light that comes after a storm.

She melted inside, no longer feeling the fear and turmoil that had so plagued her over the last weeks.

'But you must keep this a secret and tell no one.' He whispered close to her ear, 'Not everyone in the house would be pleased for us.'

'I shall tell no one, I assure you.' Little did he know how much that arrange-

ment suited her. She closed her eyes, languishing in the warmth and safety she felt in his presence.

But her calm was shattered by a knock at the door. 'Master,' she heard the servant, Sambrooke, whisper. 'We have been discovered. The soldiers are coming.'

37

APRIL

Late in the night, I finish *The Lady's Secret*. I'd planned on saving the ending, keeping myself in suspense, but somehow, I kept 'turning' the electronic pages until I got to those two little words: *The end*.

After the lovemaking scene, the book goes back to the 'jealousy and intrigue' plot. The master's smuggling activities are given away by a traitor, and he leaves again to go into hiding. The Watcher is free to make all sorts of mischief, and Victoria's life is in danger. It turns out not to be Tom at all, but rather Charity's sister, Belle, who was in love with William Clarke all along. She murdered her sister, and now has it in for Victoria too. She lures Victoria out onto the roof, and this time, there's no one to rescue her. They struggle. Belle falls to her death. Victoria is shaken and shattered, but ultimately, alive. And, in a lucky coincidence, she heard through the servant grapevine that Tom too has been killed – falling off his horse while drunk. William gets a lucky break when the traitor ends up dead, seemingly at his own hand. There are a few more tense moments when Victoria reveals her true identity to William, but in true 'love conquers all' fashion, her deception is forgiven and forgotten. An omniscient hand having removed all impediments, Victoria and William marry and live happily ever after.

I flip back to the beginning of the book; I'll reread it, I decide, and follow along as they film the various scenes. In spite of my literary snobbishness, I've enjoyed the twists and turns in Victoria's fortune. Even if the happy ending was neat and inevitable, I'm satisfied that she got it. What more can a romance novel hope to achieve?

I turn off the light, but once again sleep won't come. It's been a few days since my altercation with Luke and my first meeting with Phillipa. Since then, I've mostly been at work so I haven't seen much of either of them. And Theo – he responded briefly to my text saying that he'd had fun too, but notably not making any further plans. My exhausted mind jumbles with thoughts of Victoria and William; Phillipa and Luke. As much as I've sworn never again to expose my heart to another person, I can't help but envy them. As my eyelids start to droop, I spare a thought for the stalker and would-be-killer – Belle. She may be the villainess, but she's not a monster – just a woman who's been unlucky in love and feels jealous of the happiness of those around her. It may not be an admirable emotion, but it's an understandable one. In a house full of would-be lovers, it's lonely to be on the outside looking in.

***

The next morning, everything kicks off. The lion's share of the cast arrives, along with their trailers and entourage. (The one notable absence is Natasha Blythe, who, due to a scheduling conflict, won't be starting her scenes until the second week.) In addition to the cast, there are make-up artists, costumers, hairstylists, camera people, key grips, runners, best boys – titles I've seen before in film credits but whose function I can only guess at. Luke has about five different assistants, and apparently there are different screenplays for all the various technical and artistic functions. Each of the assistants has their own assistants – it's like a small medieval society where everyone has a title and a fiefdom.

A van containing two black horses and a piebald pony arrives, and I learn that Simon has secured himself a job helping to look after them. I'm sure that he and Connie will enjoy watching the filming of 'William Clarke gallops off at dawn' and the like. Especially since Dominic

Kennedy is clearly the kind of actor who will insist on doing his own stunts.

Katie pretends to be sick so she can stay home, but I persuade her that if she really wants a part in the film, she'd better not put a foot wrong at school. She agrees, reluctantly. I know how she feels – that extreme sense of missing something. Because unfortunately, I have to go to work.

I grab a coffee and a copy of the day's call sheet from the marquee on my way to get the train. As I'm walking out of the gate, there's a minor bit of commotion. Danny and two of the Johns are trying to shoo away a couple of paparazzi who have turned up uninvited, with huge cameras with oversized lenses slung around their necks. I'm a little shocked when one of the men steps forward and takes my photo, the flash temporarily blinding me before I can raise my hand to shield my eyes. 'Stop that!' I say, like I'm reprimanding one of my children.

'It's my job,' the man says. 'Can I get a quote from you?'

'No, Lizzie, don't,' John J says.

'I can't,' I say to the man. The contract I've signed has a strict confidentiality clause that forbids me talking to the media. The last thing I need is to breach it. 'Sorry.'

* * *

I try to work on the train, squeezed into a middle seat of three, but I can't even begin to concentrate. I unfold the call sheet, feeling oddly proud when the passenger next to me glances over at what I'm reading.

The call sheet has everything that the cast and crew need for the day's filming – from names and numbers to the weather, to where to park, to what time lunch will be served. The cast section is similarly detailed. I see that on the first day, the scenes only involve William Clarke, played by Dominic Kennedy, and Sambrooke, his servant, played by a young actor called Will Fairfax. The call sheet also gives the order of the day's filming, with scenes broken down into minutiae – 'William dismounts from his horse at the gate'; 'Sambrooke brings in supper on a tray'; 'the camera pans through the rooms to the library'; 'close-up of William taking off his boots in front of the fire.' The sheer detail makes me reluctantly impressed with the work that has gone into it by Luke and the various assistants. All those days when he was lurking around, he must have been visualising the film scene by scene, breaking down the screenplay into all of its component parts. The final product, whatever it is, will be very much through Luke's eyes.

I put the call sheet back in my bag. Though everything seems well-organised, there are a lot of moving parts, and it strikes me how much is riding on everything going well. There are hundreds of people involved, and millions of pounds. My role, or that of my house, is only a small part of the whole machine. But it's a critical part, and I want it to be a success.

Alas, though, duty calls. In addition to work, I also have The Lawyer Awards in the evening. My black dress is folded up in a bag, along with a pair of high heels. The day is long and tedious. My mind wanders back to the project going on without me. Will Phillipa have already added Katie to the script and cleared the whole thing with Luke? Or will I have to deal with more of his amateur dramatics and moodiness and then have the burden of telling my daughter that the whole thing is off?

My boss Harry is unusually chipper as he and I, and two other associates from our group, get into a taxi after work for the awards ceremony, where we're up for 'Best Project Finance Department'. Since the awkwardness in the conference room, Harry's kept his distance. But from the moment we arrive at the venue and are each handed a flute of champagne by a roving waitress, I sense that I need to be on my guard.

'You look lovely, Lizzie,' he says. His hand hovers over the small of my back. The dress is more low-cut than I remember it being, and his eyes drop to take in my cleavage.

'Thanks, Harry.' I make an effort not to cringe. 'I'm still trying to fend off chickenpox – Jack has a bad case and I've never had them.' I'm hoping he hasn't either and will keep his distance, but the hand stays where it is. Giving up on infectious diseases, I excuse myself to go to the loo.

I manage to blend into the crowd, keeping my distance from Harry, until the dinner starts. Unfortunately, however, I'm seated next to him. On his other side is the CEO of one of our big clients who will hopefully keep him occupied until my earliest opportunity to slip out and get the train home.

My wine glass is filled, and the emcee, a famous comedian I recognise from TV, comes out onto the stage and starts telling jokes. A crowd of lawyers, rapidly becoming lubricated by alcohol, makes a raucous audience. I'm halfway through my first glass of red wine when I feel the hand on my thigh. As the fingers snake up my tights, my skin shrinks with revulsion and disgust. I compare through a fog of drink the various outcomes. If I remove the hand, I may lose my job. If I let the hand stay, I'll have to quit. I check my watch. It's only half-seven.

'You look so hot tonight, Lizzie.' Harry's breath in my ear stinks of wine. 'Let's leave after the entrée. I'm staying in town tonight.'

The emcee tells a joke that has the whole room practically wetting themselves in laughter. But all I feel is a sense of outrage. In one fell swoop, I remove the hand and whisper in my boss's ear, 'Get your hands off me, Harry,' I say. 'Now.'

'You bitch,' he snarls in a low voice. 'I did you a favour, taking you back. Now it's time for you to show a little gratitude.'

'Gratitude?' I say aloud, standing up. 'Is that what you call it?' Ignoring the startled looks from the others at the table, I grab my things and leave the building, walking in the direction of the Tube station. As much as it might be nice to go out in a blaze of glory and spring for a taxi, I'll need to save every penny as I take a flying leap into the unknown.

38

By the time I stumble onto my home platform two hours later, I've lived a whole decade of emotions: jubilation, pride, fear, and regret. I owe it to myself and other women in a similar position to contact HR and get transferred to another group, but I wish the evening had never happened. I think about Victoria: forced to walk away from her life because of the power some man had over her. Things may have changed a lot since those times, but sadly, much has stayed the same.

It's dark by the time I reach the house, and a full moon has risen above the trees. I'm relieved to see that there are no paparazzi camped out by the gate. Most of the cars are gone, except for a dark blue Mercedes wedged between the wall and the toilet block and Danny's orange SUV. Danny is sitting in the passenger seat with the window rolled down, eating a bacon butty and listening to *Talk Sport*. I wave to him as I walk by.

Inside the marquee, tables are still stacked with fruit and biscuits, obviously left by a city person unused to the mice and squirrels that will make short work of it by morning. I cover the food with a cloth and close the doors out of habit, and then go into the house.

The great hall is now a jungle of cables, cameras, lights, reflectors and monitors. As the house electrics weren't up to scratch for their needs, a thick cable runs out a window to an electrical generator. In one corner, a dark wood coffer chest has been set up near the fireplace, next to a pair of old boots. The electrical equipment aside, the little corner looks straight out of the 1790s. It may be all 'smoke and mirrors', but I feel like I've gone back in time and am seeing the house through someone else's eyes – maybe the ill-fated Veronica Jones'. If there are ghosts in the house, they must be having a field day.

I go through to the kitchen and find Connie and Simon sitting at the table drinking coffee and watching something on Connie's computer. Connie takes one look at me and frowns. 'You're home early. You haven't done anything stupid, have you?'

I consider my answer as I go to the sink for a glass of water. 'If by stupid you mean I've told my arsehole of a boss that he can't feel me up under the table while listening to some comedian give out awards to a bunch of arrogant bastards, then I'm guilty as charged.'

'Good for you.' Simon gives me a thumbs up.

'I guess you know what you're doing,' Connie says doubtfully. 'I just know how important the job was to help you get back on your feet.'

'I'll stay on my feet, thank you. Because I'm not about to get down on my knees for any man – not again.' I down the water and set the glass aside. 'In fact, I've decided to take your advice and think outside the box. I will open a B&B at Tanglewild.' Though I hadn't planned to say them, the words sound right. 'Somehow I'll make it work.'

'I'm sure you will,' Simon says.

'Just don't get carried away by all this.' Connie sweeps her hand in the vague direction of the hall. 'It's not real life. Except maybe for them.' She gestures with her head in the direction of the lake, where I see two dark figures sitting in chairs at the edge of the terrace.

'Who?'

Connie shrugs. 'I'm not one to listen at keyholes. Now, I think you'd better go up. I don't think Katie's asleep. I was about to go check on her.'

'How is she?'

Connie raises an eyebrow. 'Excited, rebellious. Wilful. Star-struck. Dying for some bit part in the film that you apparently gave permission for.' She shakes her head. 'Are you sure you know what you're doing, Lizzie?'

'I wish you'd stop asking me that!' I snap. 'When you know full well what the answer is.'

*　*　*

I leave the kitchen with a mumbled 'sorry' for being rude and go up the back stairs to the guest rooms. Jack is asleep in his travel cot and Katie is in her bed reading a copy of *Hello!* magazine.

'Where did you get that?' I say.

'Chloe gave it to me,' she says proudly. 'Look, Mum.' She points her finger at the open page. 'There's an article about the film.'

I look down at the glossy page. There are photos of Dominic Kennedy wearing dark glasses in an open-top convertible, Natasha Blythe in a skimpy bikini on a beach somewhere, and on the second page, a large photo of Phillipa King and Luke Thornton sitting at a table in some kind of sunny tropical garden. Below the photo is the caption: 'Writer and director? Or romantic heroine and hero?'

Nausea ripples in my stomach. 'You shouldn't be reading that kind of rubbish, Katie. Don't you have reading for school?'

'I did it earlier. And I did my piano. I'm focusing on school, just like you said.'

'Good.' I debate taking the magazine, but then decide in the interests of mother-daughter harmony to leave it be. 'But give that back to Chloe tomorrow.'

'I will.'

I kiss her on the forehead and go through to the bathroom. I wash the make-up off my face, brush my teeth, and undress, throwing the tights – tainted by Harry's fingers – in the bin. I go to my room and without turning on the light, go over to the window. The two dark figures are still there, but one of them has stood up and is pacing back and forth. I recognise those long strides and arrogant profile. Luke Thornton.

I check my watch as anger simmers in my chest. The contract gives the crew the run of the place for the filming, including night scenes. But Luke and Phillipa have no right to sit in my back garden this late and socialise. If 'the planets are finally aligned' for them, they can damn well go into orbit somewhere else. I open the window to tell them to go. But I overhear Luke speaking in a loud voice.

'Goddamn it, Pippa. You know it's for the best.'

I hold my breath. Will there be a response – or a passionate embrace to follow?

'...blame you, Luke.' Her voice is almost too quiet for me to hear.

'Of course not, for God's sake. But I'm not going into it again.'

Another whisper – '...just a kid.'

I freeze. Could they be arguing about Katie and giving her a part in the film? Surely not.

The conversation continues, but in a quieter tone. I can only catch the odd snippet. Luke stops pacing. They're standing very close together.

'...I did it for you,' Luke says softly. 'You know that, Pippa, don't you?'

I don't hear Phillipa's reply, but a moment later, she reaches out and touches his face. I want to look away, but I can't. I wait for Luke to take her in his arms, kiss and make up...

Luke pulls away suddenly. 'I'll tell Richard tomorrow. It's for the good of the film.'

'So that's it then?' Phillipa's voice is sharp. 'You'd just walk away – again?'

He turns and stalks off without replying. I wince as the kitchen door slams. In the dim light, a match flairs as Phillipa lights a cigarette. She stares out across the lake, the smoke taking on a strange bluish cast. I watch her for a few minutes, until she stubs out the cigarette and walks back towards the house. Several minutes later, I hear the sound of a car in the distance.

I go back to Katie's room; she's sprawled out on the bed asleep, with the magazine fallen to the floor. I turn out the light and go back to my own dark room.

What were they arguing about? Something about the project? Something from the past? And Luke – was he threatening to walk off the project? Would he really do that? I think about the work he's put into visualising, planning, and mapping out the film in his mind. I think about how I've dreaded encountering him and done my best to avoid him. If he does walk away now, it should make me happy. Overjoyed. They'll bring in a new director with a new vision: someone who truly appreciates Tanglewild. Never again will Luke Thornton darken my door with his moody, unpleasant nature and those sharp, judgemental eyes.

Luke Thornton is off the project. I should be over the moon.

So why the hell don't I feel it?

39

THE LADY'S SECRET BY PHILLIPA KING

Victoria sat by the cold grate of the fire, staring at the words on the page of her book. But her mind was miles away. If only the master, her dearest William, were here, then her heart would be at ease. But he had been betrayed by a young accomplice, who had given in to the temptation of a bounty hunter's purse, and gone into hiding. Was he safe, or had he been captured? All she knew for certain was that he was alive – that her heart would know instantly the moment his ceased to beat. But when would she see him again?

'I met an interesting gentleman over Horsham way when I was visiting my cousin.' Belle's words roused Victoria from her thoughts. She glanced up at the girl, who was attacking her embroidery haphazardly. Underneath her gay yellow curls and cornflower blue eyes, Belle had a strange coldness about her that made Victoria ill at ease.

'His wife ran off, so it was said. He's seeking her whereabouts, and even laid on a reward.'

'Oh?' Victoria tried to sound disinterested.

Belle leaned in and lowered her voice. 'It seems the thing these days among certain women,' she says. 'I mean, look at my sister.'

'Was her marriage so cruel?'

Belle laughed. 'She and Will never had a hope together. It was me whom he'd chosen. Before my sister ever laid eyes on him.'

'I see.'

'But that's by the by.' Belle waved her dainty hand. 'Charity's gone, and eventually, the master shall marry again. And when he's ready, then it will be as if all the years have vanished. Then it shall be my turn to be a bride, walking down the aisle, to my rightful place at his side.'

Victoria felt a drop of sweat form between her breasts. 'How... nice for you.'

'Yes,' Belle said. 'It will be. And I shall never leave him. Not like this woman I mentioned. The harlot.'

Victoria didn't respond. She fought the urge to leave the room.

'But perhaps you know of the couple,' Belle said. 'Don't you come from over that way, Tilly? Apparently, her name is Victoria. Tall, with auburn hair and a pretty face.' The blue eyes never wavered in their seemingly innocent stare, but there was a kind of hidden laughter on her lips. 'And the poor husband's name is Tom.'

40

To their credit, Richard Silverman and the Johns do a good job of covering when Luke Thornton, big-shot Hollywood director, fails to turn up the next morning. I must confess I didn't think he'd do it – actually walk off the project. I may not like the man, but he's always seemed focused and professional.

Now there are upwards of forty people here at my house: actors, extras, make-up artists, costumers, runners, risk managers, assistant producers, horse handlers and stunt coordinators, all going about their business like the crew on a ship, seemingly unaware that it's hit a rock and is about to sink like a stone.

Behind closed doors, my kitchen becomes a battleground between Richard and his studio executives on the other end of a phone. The conversation grows heated as I'm making my morning coffee, and while I can only hear one side of it, I quickly get the gist. The studio has put a heck of a lot of money into the project, so someone needs to find Luke right away and get the cameras rolling.

When Richard gets off the call, I hand him a mug of coffee. It's only then that he seems to notice that I've been there all along. Before he can shout at me, I tell him about the argument I overheard between Luke and Phillipa.

'Oh for Christ's sake,' he says. 'So this is just some damn lovers' tiff?'

I rewind the conversation, wondering if this is true. The first time I saw them together, Luke was a changed man around Phillipa, whom I know is after her own 'happy ending' befitting a romance author. But is Luke on board with her plans? *I did it for you*, he'd said last night. Done what? Taken on the project? Returned to Tanglewild? Or something else entirely? The words screech in my head like fingernails on a blackboard.

'I don't know, Richard,' I say. 'But maybe if Phillipa takes a few days' leave from the set, he'll come back.'

'Jesus Christ.' He checks his watch. 'We're losing thousands as we speak. I'm going to find the bastard.'

He stalks out of the house and, a few minutes later, roars off on his motorbike. I go out to the marquee where I can sense tension around the food table; rumours are spreading that the ship might have sprung a leak. Annie revises the call sheet to reschedule the scenes already missed this morning. Dominic Kennedy, his hair wild for the 'master rides through the gates on his horse' scene, chain-smokes an entire packet of cigarettes just outside the tent, mumbling his lines.

Not long after Richard leaves, Connie comes through the gate like the vibe has disturbed whatever she's been getting up to in the caravan. Instead of coming up to me, she goes straight over to Dominic. They have a little tête-à-tête and I see her pass him something – a silver flask. He takes a sip. Catching my eye, Connie gives me a conspiratorial wink.

Knowing what I know, I too feel jumpy and on edge. How can Luke let everyone down like this? Can Richard sort it? What happens if he can't?

I'm still hovering in the tent when Phillipa arrives and asks Annie for the call sheet. Annie waffles, telling her that there's been 'a little blip'. Phillipa's smile doesn't waver as she makes herself a coffee and comes over to me. 'You all right, Lizzie?' She puts a companionable hand on my arm. 'Did you sleep well?'

'Yes, fine. But I'm not sure if you've heard. Luke didn't turn up today.'

A cloud darkens her face for less than a second. 'Really? How unlike him.'

Her nonchalant manner is starting to annoy me. The studio may have millions riding on this production, but I've got a stake in it too – a big one.

'Listen, Phillipa,' I say, keeping my voice low. 'I overheard you and Luke arguing. I heard him threaten to walk off. Which seems to have happened.'

She laughs, giving no sign that I've upset her. 'You're right, Lizzie, we did have a silly argument. About who the film should be dedicated to, of all things.' She rolls her eyes. 'I wrote the book in honour of an old friend. Someone, I fear, that Luke would rather forget.'

'That's it? He'd walk away for that?'

'Oh, I don't think so. But he is a man – arrogant, vulnerable, and dying to feel appreciated. He'll want Richard Silverman to beg a little. Grovel. And I guess I'll have to do a little grovelling too.'

'Is your "friend" the reason he hates this house?'

She pauses for a second too long. 'Yes, I suppose that's it.' Her eyes dart down to her watch. 'Give him a little time – he'll be back.' She takes a last sip of her coffee and throws the paper cup in the bin. 'Now, I really ought to be getting on. I've got piles of notes that need adding to the screenplay. And I'll work something in for Katie. It probably won't be a big part, mind you. Just a kitchen maid or something. But I'll give her a line or two. I'm sure she'll have a great time.'

'Really, Phillipa,' I say, 'with all this bother, don't feel you have to. I don't want to make things worse.'

She smiles. 'It might be best to wait a bit before telling Luke. Let me work out the details first. But it will be fine. Luke has bigger problems to contend with, I think.'

Before I can ask her what she means, there's a small commotion at the gate. Theo and Richard appear, frogmarching Luke Thornton back on set. A knot of tension inside me gives way to relief.

'See,' Phillipa says breezily. 'Nothing to worry about.'

Luke breaks away from the other men and comes into the tent. 'Sorry I'm late,' he says to the assembled crew, offering no excuse or explanation. He turns to his assistant director, Laura. 'We'll start with Scene 54 in ten minutes.' Several people hurry off to convey the order. Luke then comes over to Phillipa and me, his eyes looking glazed over. 'Sorry, Pippa.' He gives her a kiss that doesn't quite meet her cheek.

'Oh, go on with you.' She pats him playfully on the arm.

For a second he looks at me, and I catch a glimpse of something tortured in those eyes. Then he turns brusquely, barks an order at Annie to print him out the revised call sheet, and walks towards the house.

As soon as he's gone, Theo comes over to us. 'Whew,' he says. 'Crisis averted – I think. Can I get you ladies a coffee?'

'No thanks, Theo, I've had one,' Phillipa says. 'Now that everything's back on track, would you mind proofing some revisions this morning?'

'Not at all,' he says eagerly.

Phillipa turns to me. 'Is it still OK if we use Jack's room?'

'Yes, of course.'

'Good.' She turns to Theo. 'Get yourself a coffee and I'll go get set up.'

She walks across the lawn, leaving me with Theo. I feel suddenly awkward, and he too looks like a deer in the headlights. Which is a shame, because I really did like him.

'Coffee?' I offer, trying to put him at ease. 'You look like you need one.'

'I do, thanks. This business with Luke...' He shakes his head. 'Let's just say, he didn't come willingly.'

'Luke's a pain.' I spoon some instant coffee into a cup and fill it with hot water. 'But at least he's here. And anyway, it sounds like your job is going well.'

'It is. It's really interesting work – and I'm learning so much.'

'I'm glad for you,' I say, meaning it.

'And Lizzie,' he says, 'I'm sorry we haven't spoken. And I'm sorry if... well... I came on too strong.'

'Please don't apologise.' I hand him the coffee. 'I was just... a little overwhelmed.'

'I understand, and you were right. And with the project in full swing, it might be better to wait. You know, before taking things any further—'

'It's OK, Theo.' I take a step back, giving him space. 'You don't need to pretend. I get the idea that your feelings lie... elsewhere.'

He blushes to the roots of his ginger hair. 'Is it that obvious?'

'Now that I've met her, I completely understand. The rest of us can't possibly compete.'

'It's not that, Lizzie,' he says. 'I mean, Phillipa's wonderful. But I worry that *her* feelings lie elsewhere.'

'Maybe.' I feel an odd pang in my stomach. Phillipa seems so assured when it comes to Luke. Whatever this issue is over the 'friend' and the dedication, it doesn't sound like anything insurmountable. And it's just like Luke to blow hot and cold – one minute acting aloof, and the next giving her that rare smile that transforms his face...

Theo swirls the liquid around in his cup with a stirrer, looking unhappy that I've affirmed his suspicions.

'I really do like you a lot, Lizzie,' he says finally. 'You're beautiful and clever, and any man would be lucky to have you. But right now, I'm not sure I'm the man for the job.'

'I appreciate your being honest.'

'Good.' He takes a long swig of his coffee. 'I hope we can be friends.'

'Friends – of course.' It might not be what I'd hoped for originally, but anything is better than being awkward.

'And now, I'd better get on. Can't keep the lady waiting, can I?'

'Absolutely not.'

He leaves to join Phillipa at the house. Watching him go, I can't help but recall the scene in the book where Victoria Easterbrook is betrayed by Tom, her first love. She was driven to despair and even attempted suicide. But ultimately, she went on to bigger and better things, like Idyllwild Manor and the arms of William Clarke.

As I linger for a few minutes watching the film crew scurrying around to meet Luke's ten-minute call, I think about how much easier it would be if I, like Victoria, had my destiny written down in the pages of a book. But would it be a happy ending? Right now, I don't have the slightest clue.

41

It's not a happy ending forty-five minutes later when I get off the phone with Harry, who 'regretfully' thinks it might be best if we 'part company'. Struggling to remain professional in a conversation rife with corporate speak and air quotes, I force myself to listen to his reasoning: I've seemed unfocused and unsettled since I've rejoined the firm, and maybe I'm not quite ready to come back to work after my bereavement. I take copious notes during the call in case I need to bring a claim for wrongful dismissal. I ask if there have been any specific complaints (no) or any issues raised by clients (no). I calmly remind him that refusing to engage in sexual conduct is not a sackable offence – for me at least, and I 'suggest' that perhaps it's best if I'm transferred to a different group. I don't mention how much he disgusts me, and how I'm a hair's breath away from calling up his wife to tell her to get her head out of the sand. I don't mention my plans to leave the firm in the near future to open a B&B – let him sweat and squirm a little passing me in the corridor or at the coffee machine. I don't mention that until I put my new plans into effect, I need to keep working at the firm because I need the money.

In the end, he grudgingly says that he'll 'put the wheels in motion' to transfer me out of his group. Until then, I'm a free woman.

Unfortunately, I'm a bit like a prisoner in my own house. The scene they're filming – a conversation between William Clarke and his servant Sambrooke – takes place in the great hall, so that's off limits. I tidy up our temporary rooms and gather up laundry. The washing machine is in the cellar, accessible from a staircase in the kitchen. It's damp and cold down there, and the bare bulb flickers when I flip the switch. I shove the laundry in the washing machine and slam the door shut. The machine beeps when I press the button, the programme clicks on, and there's a whoosh of water.

'Cut!' a voice yells.

The door between the kitchen and the great hall flies open. Luke's assistant, Laura, comes in, her face stricken.

'Shh,' she says. 'We can't have any noise.'

'Sorry,' I whisper, feeling like a right tit. I glance behind her into the great hall. The two actors are standing over a table that's been set up in front of the fireplace, looking over what appears to be an old map. But I barely even notice them. All I can see are the wires, the cables, the lighting shades, the glass-eyes of the camera – making my hall look more like an alien spaceship than a seventeenth-century manor house. And at the centre of it all, sitting in a canvas director's chair, is Luke Thornton. If he was hostile before, he now looks positively murderous.

I draw my head back as he barks at the cameraman to move over by six inches. Then he calls for a close-up on Sambrooke's face. The technicians scramble to obey. One of the other assistants is holding up one of those old-fashioned black and white clapperboards – who knew they actually used those?

'Again,' Luke orders. 'And Dom, get closer – put your hand on his arm. Then point to the map. You've got to convince him that he can hide the boat in the cove.'

With a last glare at me, he gestures to his assistant. She slams the door in my face.

* * *

I'm embarrassed and livid and feel like an intruder in a club that will never have me as a member. I storm back up to my room, conscious that the wooden stairs creak as I walk, half-hoping, half-fearing that I'll cause another disruption to Luke and his precious scene. I throw the empty laundry basket across the room and collapse onto my bed. All the recent events – the date with Theo, meeting Phillipa, Luke's walking off the set, the harassment at work – are like demons swirling around in my head. I close my eyes, hoping I can just fall asleep; retreat into my own fantasy world with dark-eyed men whose faces I can't see, who will teleport me into my own happily ever after. But sleep won't come.

Eventually, I get up and go downstairs and out onto the terrace. The crew is on a break between scenes. I see Luke walking on the lawn near the plane tree with the young actor, Will, who's playing Sambrooke. They're deep in conversation; Luke gestures expansively as he speaks, and something he says makes Will laugh. I suppose Luke's 'championing a young actor' and working his magic to 'draw the emotion from the script'. All those things that people in the know seem to admire about him. Whereas all I've managed to do today is disrupt things with my laundry.

Avoiding them, I go round to the side garden where I come upon Dominic Kennedy pacing back and forth, mumbling his lines and stubbing his shoes – high-heeled with a brass buckle – into the stones on the path.

'Hi,' I say, walking towards him. 'Sorry about interrupting your scene.'

'Ah, Lizzie,' he says in a voice that makes me question whether or not he's in character. 'Don't you worry about a thing. It was unfortunate that we fell behind schedule. But thanks to my fantastic acting ability' – he raises a wry eyebrow – 'I believe we're just about back on track.' He leans in, whispering in my ear. 'Either that or Luke just accepts that the whole thing is rubbish.'

'Is that what you think?' I feel oddly defensive of *The Lady's Secret*. 'Then why did you take on the role?'

'Oh, I love the book and the script,' Dominic assures me. 'And, if I may say so, it's the perfect role for me.'

'I couldn't agree more,' I say, thinking of the botched 'rehearsal' in my bedroom.

'And I don't want to let Phillipa down. She's had enough of that in her life, I dare say.'

'She seems to be doing OK. She and Luke may have had a lovers' tiff, but everything seems back on track now.'

'A lovers' tiff?' His brow furrows. 'Is that what you think?'

'Of course. They're "old friends". Luke seems different around her. For one thing, he's not rude to her in public. And she... well...'

'She's smitten, yes, poor thing.' He nods. 'And who could blame her?'

'I don't know what you mean.'

Dominic laughs. 'Luke's a dark horse, isn't he? Maybe I ought to be worried for my job. He's clearly on the wrong side of the camera if he's convinced you – of all people – that he and Phillipa have a thing going.'

'Do they not?'

'Between you and me, he hates her guts.'

'No,' I say, frowning. 'That can't be right.'

The assistant director calls out from the drawing room window that 'Scene 62 is filming in three minutes.'

'Sorry, love.' Dominic leans in and kisses me on the cheek. 'That's me. I think I'm due to deflower a house maid – or something equally delicious.'

I stare out at the murky green water of the lake, mulling over what Dominic said, and why I feel less surprised than relieved. 'Don't let me keep you,' I say.

* * *

By the time I'm due to collect the children from school, I'm tired and annoyed at having to skulk around, trying not to make noise or otherwise be underfoot – difficult when almost my entire house has been assimilated into the alien collective. I've stayed closeted up in my room most of the day, ruminating over what happened at work and what the future will hold. My mind also keeps wandering back to Luke and Phillipa, Phillipa and Luke – what I've witnessed, what Dominic said, and why whatever they do or don't have going between them is so under my skin.

When it's time to go, I escape from the house through the back door. The obstacle course has extended out to the garden where giant lights taller than me are being used to shine in through the windows. Getting my car out of the garage requires getting John J to track down the owners of four cars and one motorbike that are blocking me, causing even more consternation on set. I back the car into a squelchy pile of horse poo. By the time I finally pull out of the drive, past the paparazzi that are hovering there again, I'm completely frazzled, not to mention late.

My mood improves as soon as I see Jack – there's nothing like a three-year-old bounding up and grabbing hold of your leg like a loving little koala to put things into perspective. We search around the cheerfully painted nursery until we find his Spiderman, and then I take him by the hand to go find Katie. She's waiting for us at the front gate, and instead of her usual glum self, she's bubbly and animated. As we walk to the car, she talks non-stop about the film, and about how her speech and drama teacher has agreed to give her extra coaching for the part Phillipa's writing for her.

'It is exciting.' I choose my words carefully. 'If it happens. Phillipa means well – she's a lovely lady, and very creative. But even so...'

Katie's mood descends like the blade of a guillotine. 'What do you mean "if it happens"? Phillipa's writing me a part. It's *going* to happen.'

'It's not really her decision though, is it? She's not the director.'

'It's *her* book.'

'Of course.'

I wait for the 'God, Mum, you're so mean's and the 'I hate you's that form her usual rejoinder at this point in our conversations. But for once they don't come. Instead, she pulls a face at Jack to make him laugh. As soon as we're home, she jumps out of the car and runs off behind the garage in the direction of the trailers that are parked in the field behind the garage like a travelling circus. Part of me feels upset that my daughter wants to run off and join them. But over the last year, she's been so withdrawn and depressed that I can't help but see this as a good thing. Sort of.

Jack too runs away when I take him out of his car seat. But he runs inside the gate, looking for Luke to 'kick the ball'.

'Luke's working,' I say, teeth clenched as I think about how he glared at me earlier. 'They're behind schedule, and we can't disturb them.'

Like an approaching police siren, Jack's howls spiral in waves, louder and louder. I tense up, shushing him and trying to pick him up, which only makes it worse. Several people come out of the marquee, grimacing as if I'm committing murder and mayhem. The door to the house, shut for the filming, opens suddenly.

Luke appears, his hands on his hips. The crew who have come out of the marquee stare at me, then at Luke. My stomach clenches like a vice.

'Take ten,' he barks in a tone to rival any drill sergeant's.

'Luke,' Jack yells. He pulls away from me and goes running over to him. An assistant makes a ball magically appear. Luke sets it at Jack's feet to kick. Two techs, a cameraman, and a key grip join in.

Jack doesn't so much kick the ball as trip over it, but his wails have turned to high-pitched shrieks of joy. As Luke lopes down the lawn trying to get Jack to pass him the ball, he catches my eye. He mouths a word: 'sorry' – I think.

My heart ticks jerkily, out of time. And I know that I can't put it off any longer. I need to talk to Luke – brave those haunted, judgemental eyes – and tell him to stay the hell away from my son.

* * *

That evening, the crew works overtime filming the sunset and night scenes. It's more money for me, but I can't escape the feeling that things are careering out of control. Around seven, Phillipa emerges from where she's been closeted away in Jack's room working on revisions. She cheerily invites me to come to dinner at a nice pub she knows in the area. For a second, I consider it – anything to avoid what I know I need to do. But when I see Theo, trailing her like a lapdog, I gracefully decline.

'I can't tonight,' I say, 'but maybe another time.'

'Sure.' Phillipa smiles wanly. It may be my imagination, but her face seems lined and a little haggard.

When they've gone and the kids are tucked up in the kitchen watching *Minions* with Simon on his computer, I steel myself to look for Luke. I spot him in the marquee with one of the techs, viewing the day's footage on a monitor, entirely focused on whatever he's seeing on the screen in front of him. I listen as they discuss and debate the details frame by frame – the lighting, the image capture – and he replays it time and time again, focusing on what seems like three words of dialogue. At one point, he jokes about something on the screen and gets the other man laughing too. The sound is totally incongruous with my opinion of him. An opinion that's based on what? His rejection of my house; a few off-colour comments? The fact that I've caught him looking at me a few times like he can't square my presence with the view of the set in his head? The thing I've seen flicker in those eyes that I can't square with his arrogant self-assurance?

I stand there for I don't know how long, staring at the two men from behind the tent flap. But then my phone rings in my pocket, and Luke turns. His eyes lock with mine, and I suddenly feel like I'm in one of those dreams where I'm running, but my legs are jelly and I can't move. The ringing continues.

'Sorry,' I say. I turn and stumble back to the safety of the house. Just inside the door, I answer the call; it's my new boss – a woman partner called Diana, who tells me in a short, matter-of-fact tone that she's sending me some work through and wants a draft on her desk first thing.

'Of course.' I'm relieved to have an excuse to closet myself away for the rest of the evening. But while we're still on the phone, I hear footsteps outside the front door.

'Lizzie?' It's Luke's voice. 'Can I talk to you? Please?'

My breath grows shallow and I fire away what I'm fairly sure are a few obvious questions on mundane points. I manage to keep Diana on the phone until I finally hear the footsteps retreat, my heart stops racing, and I know for sure that he's gone.

42

THE LADY'S SECRET BY PHILLIPA KING

Tom had found her — that much she knew. Belle's careless words had sickened her to the core. No longer would she be safe in the haven of anonymity. The master had not returned, and she could do nothing to protect herself.

Why then didn't Tom come to claim her?

She increased her vigilance, forgoing her early morning walks in the woods along the river and staying at all times close to the house. She went about her day's work in the company of the master's aged mother, glancing frequently over her shoulder as they made their way along the paths of the garden. Every bush and hedge seemed to hide a shadow, and her heart raced as if she'd been running for miles.

But there was no sign of Tom.

There were little things, though, that stoked her suspicion like a breath to a flame. First, there was her mother's locket. She'd found it at the top of the stairs leading to her room. The glass had been broken, and she'd cut her hand when she went to pick it up. The miniature painting inside had been ruined. A few days later, when she went to put on her dress for church, she discovered that it had a deep gash in the fabric, though she couldn't remember catching it on anything. It was as if someone had slashed it with a knife.

And then there was the poor little robin that nested in the tangled vines outside her window. She came in to discover the window open and the poor creature dead on top of her pillow, its wings bloodied and broken. Could one of the old lady's infernal cats have got at it? She wanted to believe it. But in her heart she knew it was a message. She was like a bird who had escaped its iron cage and had now been recaptured. It could not be Tom himself who had perpetrated the deeds, so it must be someone in his employ. But why go to such lengths? She was his rightful property – why not take her away and be done with it?

In a way, it would be a relief to throw off the cloak of deception. To love freely in her own name and her own body, and be accepted by the master for who she was. But Victoria knew that he would never accept her if he knew the truth. His own wife had been unfaithful and betrayed him for another man. Victoria had left her husband and therefore been unfaithful too. Even though she'd had a good reason – Tom's own infidelity – in the eyes of society, she was the fallen woman. She must never let the mask slip of her own accord. The only person she could trust was herself.

But eventually, she knew, others would force her day of reckoning.

43

The following day, I wake up early to the low rumbling sound of a machine. I open the window and crane my neck to see what's going on. There are several workmen standing by the lakeshore, about fifty metres from the house. One of the Johns is operating a small Bobcat digger, the shovel breaking ground in my back lawn.

I've given them permission to build a small dock for the smuggling boats, and to sink a pile for the camera zip wire. The pile will be removed when they're finished, but I'm considering whether or not to keep the dock. It might be useful for the B&B – I could buy a little canoe or a rowing boat for the guests to go out on the lake.

Jack is fast asleep when I go to wake him. I tell him that if he gets dressed quickly, we can go see the digger before he leaves for nursery. I also chivvy Katie (bribing her with a promise that she can watch the filming this afternoon *before* she does her homework). By the time the three of us get downstairs to the kitchen, the digger has excavated a man-sized hole.

Despite my efforts to hold him back, Jack breaks away from me and runs out to where the men are standing. One of them lifts him up on the digger, and he shrieks with delight as he's allowed to pull the lever back to move the shovel. Katie rolls her eyes like the whole thing is lame – well beneath the dignity of a budding young *actrice*.

I exchange pleasantries with John C, who tells me: 'By the time you get home tonight, you won't recognise the place.'

I laugh nervously. 'Is that a good thing?'

He laughs too – which is not particularly reassuring.

Jack 'helps' operate the digger for a few more minutes before it's time to go. Predictably, he kicks and screams when I try to make him come off. It takes three of us to extract him, by which time John J has acquired a toddler trainer-sized bruise just below his eye.

'Sorry,' I say. 'Thanks for letting him have a go.'

'No problem,' John J says. 'Tell him I'll see him later for the football.'

The mention of football is like a cloud passing over the sun. Why didn't I speak to Luke last night when I had the chance? Why am I such a great big chicken? I have a duty to protect my son from people who might be… nice to him. Because is there really any harm in my son kicking a football around with the film crew members? Why should I spoil the fun just because I have a problem with Luke?

As we pass the marquee, there's a distinct buzz. I get a call sheet from Annie and see that it's a big day. Natasha Blythe is on site and ready to start filming her scenes.

I've already been round to the costume trailer and seen the coterie of dresses and period undergarments she'll be wearing. A whole wall is devoted to wigs in different hairstyles – prim, windswept, wanton, posh – and I've seen on the call sheet that she's due to spend three hours in hair and make-up each day. Apparently on the agenda for the morning's shoot is: 'Victoria unpacks her trunk'; 'Victoria wheels Mrs Clarke in the rose garden'; 'Victoria cuts herself on the broken locket'; and 'Victoria meets Belle'.

I deposit Jack with Connie to be taken to school, but to my annoyance there's no sign of Katie. Connie tells me she'll handle it. But curiosity gets the better of me and I take a quick detour round the back of the garage to the field of trailers.

Except for the absence of barefoot children and vicious dogs, it could be a traveller's camp. My daughter is sitting in a plastic chair outside the costume trailer, next to Chloe, and a young, petite blonde woman wearing a tracksuit, her hair in a ponytail.

Natasha Blythe is shorter and thinner than her pictures in the glossy magazines make her out to be – and I wonder if I'd even recognise her if I passed her in the street. She laughs at something Chloe says and drinks from a sports water bottle. I must say, this young woman doesn't fit the image in my head of the sultry, auburn-haired Victoria. I wish I could be here in a few hours when she'll no doubt be transformed into a completely different person by movie magic. But, alas, I have a train to catch.

'Hi,' I say, going up to them. 'Katie. It's time for school.'

'Oh, Mum, can't I stay and watch?'

'No. Come on.'

Katie gets up from the chair, a petulant pout on her face. 'See you later,' she says to the other two women.

'Sorry about that,' I say.

'No problem,' Natasha says. I know from what I've read that she's English but has spent quite a bit of time in Hollywood, and I can just detect the trace of an American accent. For some reason, I find that a bit unsettling. Will Katie become like this woman when she grows up? Half herself, half Hollywood starlet?

'I love your house,' Natasha adds. 'It's good to be here.'

'Thanks,' I say. 'I hope everything goes well for you today.'

I shepherd Katie away and rush off to get the train. Outside the gate, four paparazzi swarm around me, asking if I can confirm that Natasha Blythe has arrived. John J and Danny run them off, maintaining their standoff against the outside world. But when one of them lifts his camera and takes my photo, I give him my best smile. If I'm going to be caught on camera, I may as well try and look the part.

* * *

Like Katie, I'm disappointed not to be there for the day's filming, and I feel a strong sense that I'm missing out. But as I sit on the train and crunch some numbers on the B&B, for now, I need to keep my job. Pray that nothing goes wrong to upset my precarious finances that are still teetering on the brink.

At work, I meet my new boss, Diana, in person. She's a born and bred Londoner with two kids, a stay-at-home husband *and* a full-time nanny. She already knows about Dave (I think everyone at the firm knows) but she skips the platitudes and gets straight to the *other* issue.

'When Harry hired you, we all assumed it was for your tits,' she says. 'But I've been through the document you sent me last night, and maybe there's a bit more to you.' She hands me the draft that I spent hours on after the kids were asleep. There are very few comments.

'Thanks,' I say with a nervous laugh. 'Though Harry must be pretty desperate.'

'Some men love a fresh widow. I should know. I lost my first husband in a boating accident.'

'Really?' I look at her with interest. I never would have guessed in a million years.

'It was a long time ago. And what they say is true – it does get better with time.' She suddenly has that same dreamy smile that I've seen before on Connie's face. 'Besides, the second time is twice as nice.'

'So I'm told.' I shrug, picking up the draft. Because she's happy with the work I've done so far, she's given me more to do. 'I'd better be getting on.'

'I can see you don't believe me, Lizzie. But take my word for it. Your time will come.'

Shaking my head, I go out the door. While I'm glad that I've found something in common with my new boss, on this one point at least, I'm sure she's wrong.

* * *

At lunchtime, I eat a sandwich at my desk and get on with planning the B&B. I phone the council to ask about change of use and permits, and a local builder to ask about getting the house compliant with fire and building regulations. I write everything down, trying to remain dispassionate and unfazed by how much things cost. I've already done some research on the kind of rates I could charge – all in all, the numbers are solid, but the first year looks daunting. I make a mental note to run it all past Connie, whom I can always count on to be brutally honest.

I close the notebook and put it away. All of it is exciting, but scary too. Am I really ready to take such a big risk? In my old life with Dave, I didn't take any risks. Maybe that's why things stagnated. Now, though, I've taken a risk with the film project and can envision a new dream. Step by step, I'm moving closer to the unknown.

I'm so busy all afternoon that I barely even have time to worry about the goings-on at Tanglewild – how Natasha gets on with her scenes, whether a part for Katie has been written in, or whether or not any football gets played. By the time I leave the office, it's after seven. It's a sunny evening, and crowds spill out of every pub I pass on my way to the station. I text Connie and ask her to put the children to bed, feeling grateful that I've survived the day, and glad that by the time I get home, the film crew will have left.

I don't get home until after nine. The cars are gone from the drive, and only Danny is there, watching a video on his phone. As I come through the gate, I'm hit by a sudden feeling of sadness. It's like I've come upon the remains of a circus, shuttered and empty, the joy and memories held only in the scattered popcorn and candy wrappers strewn on the ground. In this case, the rubbish is in bags waiting to be collected early the following morning, and there are trays of picked-over fruit on the table outside the marquee. The doors have been left open, as if waiting for people to return who have vanished into thin air.

There's a light on in the kitchen. Connie's there by herself doing the washing-up. There's a bottle of wine on the table that she must have got out for me. 'They're both asleep,' she says. 'So if you don't mind, I'm going to call it a night.'

'Sure.' I set down my bag on the kitchen table. 'Thanks so much.'

'See you tomorrow.' She goes out of the room without any of her usual chat.

I debate whether to go upstairs and give the kids a goodnight kiss. But as I look out at the dark outline of the trees across the lake, with the last pink of the setting sun behind them, I decide to take advantage of this rare moment to myself. I open the bottle of wine and take a glass from the cupboard. I'm about to sit down at the table to pour it when I notice that the back door to the terrace is ajar. I take the bottle and glass with me and go outside.

The silence is unusual. The birds are quiet, and I can hear the burble of the lake water emptying into the weir at the far end. In the opposite direction, the new dock hasn't progressed much since the morning. There's a large pile of dirt and a single pole sticking out of a hole. The digger is parked at a slanted angle next to the lake shore. Well beyond, where the lake bends in a curve, I see the edge of the dovecote, nestled dark and secluded in the copse of trees. The chairs and loungers, usually on the terrace, have been pushed towards the lake.

All of a sudden, I hear a creak of wood coming from one of the loungers. A dark figure rises up and turns towards me.

For a second, I stand there unable to move. A thousand incoherent emotions flood through me. Anxiety is the one that wins out. 'Sorry, I thought everyone was gone,' I say. 'I'll go back inside...'

'No.' Luke's face seems hazy in the twilight; only his eyes are in focus. 'Please... won't you stay?' He pulls one of the other loungers next to the one he's been sitting in.

I take a hesitant step forward. 'I was just going to have a glass of wine...'

I can feel the blood coursing through my body as I set the glass and bottle on a small wooden table between the loungers. I consider going back to the kitchen for a second glass, but something stops me. If I leave now, I won't be coming back. And there's something unbearable in that.

I sit down and pour the wine. It's almost black as it splashes into the glass. I gesture to him to take a sip. He lifts the glass and drinks.

'I'm sorry,' I try to begin, 'for slapping you, and acting rude, and—'

'Don't apologise.'

He holds the glass out to me and our fingers brush as I grab the stem, setting my senses on high alert. I take a sip and pass the glass back to him. Neither of us speaks as the strange communion continues. My mind races in the background about what the hell I'm doing, and why suddenly, everything I'd planned to say seems irrelevant. But I banish all thoughts, focusing on this one unlikely moment.

'It's me who's been a complete bastard,' he says finally. 'And I'm sorry for it, Lizzie.' He draws out my name as if it's an unfamiliar taste on his tongue.

The glass is nearly empty as I hand it to him to finish. 'Why don't you want to be here?' I'm certain I don't want to hear the answer, but know I have to. 'Why were you so set against Tanglewild from the start?'

He swings his long legs onto the lounger and puts his hands behind his head, elbows outstretched. He stares out at the darkness of the lake as the orange glow begins to fade from the sky behind the trees. I find that I'm unable to look away from him. I can sense that he's warring with something inside himself. I pour more wine in the glass and hand it to him. He takes it and turns the glass; I swear his lips touch the place where mine have been.

Somewhere deep inside of me, I feel a rippling like the waves of a pebble thrown into a pool of deep water. And I know that whatever I'm longing for – that precious and fragile thing I can feel awakening within me – will live or die by the next words that come out of his mouth.

'Let me tell you a story,' he says.

44

'Once upon a time, there were three teenagers. Two girls and a boy. A very stupid boy.'

I wait as he seems to falter. He's only a few feet away, but it's like he's slipped away into a different time.

'I was the boy, of course. I'm sure you figured that one out. I grew up on a housing estate in Hull. My dad was a car salesman. My mum was an accountant for a shipping company. We were normal people. Happy – or, at least, content.'

I nod.

'My mum had a cousin she was close to. My "Aunt" Roz. She was the posh one in our family. She got married to a London stockbroker with a big weekend place in Sussex.' He sighs. 'This house. We used to visit in the summers, sometimes for a week, sometimes two. They had a son named Max who was a few years older than me, and a daughter called Julie who was my age. When we were kids, Julie and I used to play together – build dens in the woods, climb trees, things like that. We made up secret clubs and could talk about anything. We were close, I guess.

'Anyway, Julie's dad died when she was twelve. A few years later, Aunt Roz announced that she was getting married again. The new husband had one child – a daughter.'

'Phillipa?' I whisper.

'Back then, everyone called her Pippa. She was two years older than me and went to an expensive boarding school in Kent. That summer, I'd just turned fifteen and Julie was sixteen. Roz and the new husband went off on an extended honeymoon, so my mum agreed to come down here to look after the lot of us. I didn't want to go. I didn't like Max, and I didn't want to meet some new stepsister of Julie's. All I wanted to do was make films with a new Sony video camera I'd got for my birthday. That was my dream, even then.'

He shifts uncomfortably in the lounger.

'I went, of course. And when I saw Pippa for the first time, everything changed. It was scorching hot that summer, and she and Julie were always out at the dovecote – on the terrace. Sunbathing in shorts and bikini tops with the ties undone. It didn't take long before I had a massive crush on her.'

'I'm not surprised.' I sigh inwardly.

'Julie started acting weird,' he continues. 'With Pippa around, she changed. She tried to act cool – worldly. It really pissed me off because I knew she wasn't like that. And what's worse, I had this idea that she felt... different about me that summer. I mean, we were cousins. It was weird.'

'But you were all so young.' I try to sound neutral. 'Surely that sort of thing is normal.'

'Everything felt *wrong* that summer. It was like there was a stain creeping over the days. Things were weird with Julie; Pippa started running the show. The dynamic was completely off.

'Then, in August, Max came down for the weekend with his girlfriend and his mates. They planned to party out in the dovecote and they'd brought loads of cider and vodka with them. Mum couldn't stop him – he was almost twenty. I had the idea that the three of us – me, Julie, and Pippa – could sneak out at midnight and go to the party. But when the time came, it was just me and Julie. Pippa had already gone.'

He sighs. 'I remember that night so clearly. It was hot, and the music was so loud. They'd lit votive candles and put them in all the pigeonholes. The older kids were drunk when we got there – maybe on drugs too, I don't know. They were doing cannonballs into the lake from the balcony, trying to see who could make the biggest splash. They were throwing beer bottles in too. Basically just screwing around.

'As soon as I came inside, I saw Pippa and Max. They were arguing, and Max's girlfriend wasn't there. It was pretty clear they were "together", and that made me feel jealous and angry. Max was a total prick and I couldn't believe Pippa would go for someone like him. I'd never drunk alcohol before, but I started downing can after can of Strongbow. I was off my face pretty quick.

'Pippa acted like everything was normal. But Julie was upset too – horrified that her brother and Pippa were having a thing. By then, things were pretty vague and I passed out.

'When I woke up, Julie wasn't there, but Pippa was next to me. The others had gone back to the house – it was just her and me. She said she knew how I felt about her, and that I was the only one of them who really cared. We started kissing – and things moved on from there.'

It's like a sudden chill has risen up from the lake. I pour the last of the wine from the bottle into the glass and take a sip, hoping it will warm me, but it doesn't.

He turns to me, sensing my discomfort. 'I'm telling you this, Lizzie, because I want you to know the whole story. The truth, as awful as it may be. It was no fairy tale and there's no happy ending.'

'You were fifteen.' The words taste like cardboard in my mouth.

'To make a long story short, Julie came back and found us like that. She totally freaked out. She started shouting at Pippa and ran upstairs to the upper level. I wanted to go after her, but Pippa said to leave her – that she'd get over it.'

He picks up the empty wine bottle and flings it hard towards the lake. It bounces and comes to rest in the tall grass at the water's edge. 'I should have gone after Julie. Told her I was sorry – that I wouldn't fool around with Pippa if it made her upset. Instead, I left them both there. I heard a splash as I was going down the path, but I kept going back to the house. Later, Pippa said that she called up to Julie, who told her to go away – she was going for a swim to clear her head.'

He shakes his head back and forth, his eyes wide and haunted.

'They say Julie hit her head on the edge of the balcony when she dove into the water. That she wouldn't have felt anything when she went under. When she... drowned.' His voice catches. 'But I don't know.' He stands up and walks a few steps towards the lake shore. I have the urge to go after him, but the story has knocked me like a physical blow. The awful truth that haunts this house, this man...

He rakes his fingers through his hair, making it stick up. 'So, to answer your original question, that's the reason I didn't want to be here. Every day I live with it. Julie's death, and the fact that I'm responsible – at least in part. It was my idea to go to the party. Julie was upset because of me. None of it ever should have happened.'

'But surely it was just a terrible accident.' I want to go to him, shake him. I grip the sides of the lounger, making myself stay put.

'Yes, you're right. But even so, it ruined everything. Broke the family apart. Mum and I stayed after the funeral, and then we went home. Aunt Roz split from Pippa's dad. Mum felt terrible but she tried to get back to normal. I tried to do the same – get on with my projects and my studies. I went through the motions, did well, got a scholarship. I went away to film school and I got to live my dream.' He bows his head, staring down at the dark water. 'But sometimes I feel like the stain from that summer managed to spread over my whole life. Like everything that's gone wrong over the years – my marriage, the divorce – was all due to what happened that night. That one stupid night when everything fell apart.'

'But that's...' I pause, unsure what to say. Arrogant? Defeatist? A perfectly human response to a terrible tragedy? All those things, surely. I stand up, unsteady on my feet.

'That's no way to live your life,' I say. 'These things happen. They shape us but they don't define us. That's what I believe, anyway.' I feel desperate to argue some sense into him. 'And in your case, whatever battles you've fought, you've forged a brilliant career. So many people look up to you and count on you. Even *revere* you.'

I look out across the black water. I can feel him watching me, listening to what I'm saying. I'm ultra aware of how close we are, but I don't move away.

'And take it from me, you can't control everything,' I continue. 'I know that as well as anyone. So many nights I've lain awake wondering what I could have done differently. I wanted to believe I had that power.' I sigh. 'But I didn't – and neither do you.'

Luke turns to me and leans his forehead against mine. My breath catches and I feel overwhelmed; caught in a whirlpool of conflicting emotions. Anger edged with pity, to be sure, but also a deep, primeval longing that I'm afraid to acknowledge.

'You have a right to hate me.' He steps back, his eyes cast downwards. 'Me going on like this after what you've suffered. I've heard about your husband.'

'Dave had a weak heart. It was all very sudden and unexpected. Afterwards, I found out the truth. Who he was, what he did…' I shake my head. 'Worst of all was not knowing who *I* was during and after. It's been hard – and painful. But I'm coming through it; I'm finding out. Slowly.'

He nods. 'I know what you mean about not knowing yourself. When I was going through the divorce, I wanted to kill something. I *became* my anger – I needed it to fill up the hole that was left. Without it, I felt so useless and empty.'

'The anger is hard to deal with,' I say. 'I tried to bottle mine up for the sake of the kids. I'm not sure it's worked very well.'

'I think it has.' His sudden smile lights up the darkness. 'Your kids are brilliant. Whatever you're doing, it must be the right thing. I'm sorry if I've made it harder…'

He falls silent, and I sense that he's already aware of what I had planned to say – to stay away, leave my family alone – leave me alone. I won't be saying those things now.

'Don't apologise,' I whisper back.

And when he turns to me again, I can make out the contours of his face as if his skin is glowing from within. He takes a breath, then another.

'I built up a picture in my mind of what it would be like to come back here,' he says. 'I lived every moment of the agony just like the frames of a film. I tried to control it that way, enough to do my job and get on with the project. But from the moment I arrived, things were different than I'd imagined.'

'Different how?'

'I walked in and saw you.' He moves closer. 'Dropping that damn laundry all over the floor. In that single moment, I felt something that I couldn't account for. Something that I didn't want to feel.'

'What was it?'

'Hope.'

I inhale swiftly as he continues. 'Your face – it betrays your emotions. Do you know that? You seemed so strong, and beautiful, and yet vulnerable all at the same time. I almost wished you were starring in my film.'

I laugh at that, but seismic waves are radiating through my body.

'I couldn't square the past and the present,' he says. 'I didn't know how to act around you, and everything I did was wrong. I felt like I was glimpsing the world through a camera. Something that isn't real, something... that I can never have.' His voice catches, and I glimpse the wild creature in his eyes. A day ago – an hour ago, even – I would have retreated. Run away from this man and his belief that some wounds can't be healed.

'Why not?' I whisper. 'Why can't you have those things?'

Without answering, he moves behind me. He lifts the hair from the back of my neck and twines it in his fingers. I shudder as his lips touch my skin, slow and deliberate. I sink back into the solidity of him, the rightness in that touch, the feeling like my legs might melt from underneath me. He turns me round to face him, his lips finally reaching mine, savouring them, his tongue slipping into my mouth. And a powerful shockwave of longing sweeps through every cell of my body, and I try to reach out to him but he holds my arms at my side...

Then, just as suddenly as it began, his mouth breaks from mine. I stare at him questioningly as he brushes my cheek with his finger one last desperate time. In the dim light, the path of a tear glitters on his cheek.

'I can't, Lizzie,' he says. 'I'm sorry.'

He turns away, and in a moment, he's gone.

45

The night and all the next day is agony. I ruminate over what happened between Luke and me. The turmoil he created in me has now been untangled, revealing a deep desire that I admit has been there all along. I replay his story over and over in my mind, trying to think of a way to make it better. But I can't. For twenty-five years he's suffered from survivor's guilt, internalising it until it became self-hatred. My natural instinct is to try to fix it, and even if I can't, then do my best to provide comfort and healing. But it would be wrong to try – there's too much at stake. I can't risk my family on a prayer and a broken wing. Luke was right to stop things before they went any further. Even if I wish he hadn't.

And then there's Phillipa King. Now that I know the truth of what happened, she's the one I can't work out. Why did she set a novel at the house where she experienced tragedy? Why did she champion using Tanglewild for the film when Luke was so against it?

Did she do it to atone? To try to come to terms with the past? Or as some kind of a tribute to Julie? I remember her vague comment about the 'friend' and the 'dedication'. Clearly, she and Luke were arguing about Julie. Dedication or not, the whole thing seems very strange.

I open my e-reader and flip through *The Lady's Secret*, as if the romantic dross might hold some clue to unlock its author. I come to the scene where Victoria Easterbrook tries to drown herself in the river, sinking down, the dark green water closing over her head...

I slam the case shut; everything feels wrong. A young girl lived in this house and died in the lake outside. Her whole life and future gone in one tragic moment. Luke and Phillipa both have to live with that. And now, I do too. As Luke said, everything seems... stained.

* * *

I don't see Luke the next day or the day after that. I catch glimpses of him from afar: directing the placement of cameras and props, reviewing the images on the monitors, walking up and down in the garden with Natasha, patiently coaching her on the emotions she's supposed to be feeling as she says her lines. There are whispers on the set that Natasha is having trouble getting into character as Victoria Easterbrook, and despite all the historically accurate costumes and fancy hairstyles, her scenes are running over time and budget. When I see Luke with her, I feel an aching stab of jealousy. Natasha is young and beautiful – a rising star. But as far as I can tell, he's treating her with the same professionalism as the others: offering guidance, but ultimately, demanding perfection.

I manage to watch a few of the scenes being filmed, standing in the background amongst the technicians and assistants. The scene where Victoria discovers that someone broke the locket with the miniature of her mother and cuts her hand on the glass requires over a dozen takes. It's only when poor Natasha breaks down in real tears of frustration that they get any usable footage. It's obvious that tempers are running high. In between takes, Richard Silverman seems to be constantly on his phone, talking to the powers that be. Whether he's there to check up on Natasha's progress or Luke's whereabouts, I'm not quite sure.

Luke doesn't seem to notice me. Clearly he's busy and stressed, but even so, I start to wonder if what we shared was a trick of the light – smoke and mirrors – nothing more than Hollywood movie magic.

I almost want to tell Connie what happened and get her advice. But she seems unusually snappish and focused on whatever she's getting up to on her laptop in the caravan, emerging only to have a cigarette with Dominic and help him run his lines. Besides, I feel too shaken and embarrassed by this hopeless, futile thing that I've allowed myself to feel. I have the strong urge to retreat back to the safety of my own loneliness – that I never should have left in the first place.

On my next home-working day, I spend most of the time in my room, and by lunchtime, I feel like a caged animal. They're filming inside the house, so I sneak out the back door and go out to the lake.

Behind the house, the loungers have been moved, and the empty wine bottle is gone. It's like Luke and I were never here and none of it ever happened. But the memory of the kiss, the feel of his body against mine, is imbedded inside me; and the sharp pain I feel whenever I catch sight of him is testament to the fact that it did.

At the lake shore, the men are sinking the main supports for the dock. I wander past them and continue walking through the lakeside garden that was designed in the 1920s by Gertrude Jekyll. Almost overnight, the garden has exploded with colour – pink and mauve rhododendrons and azaleas, primulas in deep burgundy, a crab apple tree with delicate white blossoms. I walk along, pulling a few weeds aside the path. I'm tempted to go back and get Jammie – I feel like I've barely seen her since the filming started. But she's happy in her dog run by the marquee where there are bound to be people, and I don't want to see anyone just now.

On the other side of the lakeside garden, the forest path has been lined with rubber matting, and a long metal track for the camera has been installed. I continue on to where the track grows wild and untamed near the copse and the dovecote. Huge rhododendron and laurel branches arch over the path, their skeletal trunks dark and twisted. I think about Phillipa and Julie walking down this path all those years ago. Julie – who saw Luke 'differently' that summer. And Pippa – the object of his teenage crush.

The path ends at the front of the dovecote. The ivy is thick and cloying, growing up the bricks and even over some of the windows. Behind the little structure, the lake glitters like a dark green jewel. I've brought the keys with me, but on closer inspection, the door is already open a crack. Above the knob, one of the panes of glass has been smashed.

My hand trembles as I push open the door. I now understand what I've sensed out here – a darkness, a feeling of wrongness. And now, someone has come here and violated this place where a girl once died. Was it Luke? Phillipa? A curious cast member, or a paparazzi who cut through the woods from the rail line?

Inside are several sets of footprints in the dust both on the ground floor and going up the stairs that wind around to the floor above. Someone's clearly been upstairs, and above my head, a few of the planks they walked on have splintered and cracked. It's a miracle they didn't fall through.

I go up the stairs to check out the state of the floor. Beside me, the brick wall is damp, with green algae growing up the side and into the little pigeonholes. The first-floor joists are visibly sagging, and for a second I have a terrible vision of Jack or Katie coming out here, going up the stairs and crossing the rickety floor to the balcony, leaning over the railing to look down into the water, the rusty iron giving way... and then nothing but air and deep water below.

Fear rushes through me, along with the knowing – that if another tragedy happens here, I'll have to live with it for the rest of my life the way Luke does. I'm teetering on a knife-edge. On one side lies happiness; on the other, a bottomless pit.

The balcony door is wide open, as if the intruder left it that way to lure me into danger. I have no choice but to try and close it. Keeping as close as I can to the outer edge, I walk gingerly from joist to joist, praying they hold my weight. As I'm nearly at the door, two crows land on the balcony, sizing me up with their shifty eyes. One of them flies inside, straight at me in a flurry of inky black wings. With a cry, I leap back and go sprawling towards the centre of the floor, the boards shifting under me. The crow panics, flying around in terror, battering itself against the tiny windows.

I get to my knees and try to shoo it out the open door. Instead, it streaks upward towards the ceiling, hits one of the bare oak beams, and flutters broken and injured to the floor. It lies there dazed, staring at me through one frightened white eye. It seems to have lost its spirit, its will to live. I try to push it with my foot out onto the balcony, but I trip over another loose board and fall to the floor, my ankle twisting under me. The bird suddenly revives enough to fly at me again, its sharp beak aimed straight at my eye.

Pain shoots down my ankle as I struggle to my feet. I manage to fend the bird off with my arms and, at the last moment, it flies out the balcony door. I close the door and stumble back across the dangerous floor, desperate to be away from there and back to civilisation.

***

They're filming a scene in the great hall when I return, panting for breath, my ankle throbbing. A confused and dishevelled Victoria Easterbrook is supposed to come down the stairs and run out of the house to clear her head.

Which is why I practically run headlong into her at the front door, and she lets out a little scream.

'Cut!' Luke yells from behind. The entourage of assistants surge forward, as if to escort me from the premises like a prisoner.

'I'm sorry,' I say to Natasha. I focus in on Luke. 'I need to talk to you.'

Everyone seems to be holding their breath as he moves out from behind a camera monitor.

'Everybody, take five,' he says.

Two make-up artists, a costumer, and a dialogue coach descend on Natasha Blythe and for a second she looks like a deer in the headlights. Luke gestures for me to go out the door. We go round the side of the house to the garden, out of sight and earshot of the others.

'What is it?' His face reveals nothing.

'Someone broke into the dovecote.' I feel as panicked in his presence as I did with the crow. 'They smashed a pane of glass on the door and went upstairs. They left the balcony door open, and some loose boards have cracked.' I gulp in a breath. 'It's dangerous.'

'Damn it!' For a second, I think he's upset because I interrupted his precious scene.

'Maybe I should have told one of the Johns,' I blurt. 'But I thought...' I hang my head, feeling embarrassed. I want to tell him about the crows; about the uneasy feeling I've had every time I've been out there. I want to tell him how sorry – that stupid word again – I am for what happened to Julie. But I can't say any of it because he's busy, and I'm interrupting, and I've got no claim whatsoever on him, despite what passed between us – which I can't stop thinking about.

'What about Jack and Katie?' he says. 'They weren't in danger, were they?'

'No, they're fine. Jack doesn't go anywhere by himself, and Katie – I don't think she'd go there either.'

'OK. That's a relief.'

'Yes, I mean... it is.' The fact that Luke cares about my kids gives me a new stab of longing that I don't want to acknowledge. I take a step backwards, wincing at the shooting pain in my ankle.

He frowns. 'You're hurt, Lizzie.'

'It's nothing, I just turned my ankle.'

'May I see?'

He crouches down and lifts up the leg of my trousers, feeling my ankle over my sock. His touch sends lightning bolts through every nerve of my body. It feels so intimate, and yet I know he's only acting out of concern, as he would for anyone else. In our last encounter, the finality was very clear.

'I think it's just a sprain,' he says. 'Go to the first aid trailer and get them to bandage it. Then you should take it easy.'

'I can't. I need to go back out there and put something over the broken glass.'

He rises to his feet and puts his hands on my arms. For a second, I shudder with anticipation and wanting, but just like before, he removes his hands and steps back.

'Leave it with me,' he says. 'I'll tell John C to get it fixed right away – this afternoon – and we'll make sure everyone knows the place is off limits.'

'Thanks,' I say. 'But who do you think—'

'I don't know.' He cuts me off with a shake of his head. 'Please, just leave it with me.'

* * *

I return to my room, avoiding the cameras and the people. I want to curl up in a ball and forget about everything that's happened – or not happened. Only days ago, I was content in my dislike of Luke Thornton; content in my resolution to be alone. But in a sprinkling of movie magic, he dangled hope in front of my face like a rabbit pulled from a hat.

And yanked it away.

The rabbit was stuffed, and the hat had a false bottom. The magic was nothing more than a charlatan's sleight of hand.

He'd explained it away – with the story of Julie's death and the creeping stain over his life. A story that lives inside the walls of my house along with all the other stories of people who have lived, loved, been born and died here. A stain that is now affecting my life too.

Was Luke the person who broke into the dovecote? Of all people, he had both motive and opportunity. I try to excise the thought from my mind, but it only grows in size.

I find a bandage in the kitchen junk drawer and wrap my ankle, taking two ibuprofen for the inflammation. Before going up to my room, I detour to the cellar to collect a load of clothes from the washer-dryer that I put on early in the morning to avoid any unfortunate noise during scenes.

Wincing with every step, I descend the stairs to the cellar. But when I reach the bottom step, there's a splash. I jerk my foot back. The entire cellar is filled with almost a foot of water! It's almost up to the bottom of the washer-dryer – it's lucky I wasn't electrocuted.

Leaving the laundry marooned in the machine, I go back outside to find one of the Johns. I find John J inside the marquee tucking into a plate of Eton Mess and chatting about Watford's chances of relegation with one of the assistant something-or-others.

'Sorry to bother you,' I say, 'but my cellar is flooded.'

John J cocks an eyebrow like it's not his problem. 'Oh?'

'Yes, it's never happened before. Could it have something to do with the digging by the lake? That's the only thing I can think of.'

'I don't see how,' he says. 'We hit stone and had to divert the pile, but I don't see why that would have flooded your cellar. Sounds like you'd better call a drain specialist.'

'Fine.' I turn away, fighting tears. How much is a drain specialist going to cost, let alone any necessary repairs? The film project has been a blessing on many levels, but right now, I'm feeling cursed.

Returning to the house, I phone three different drain companies, all of which want to charge a hefty call out fee. While I'm on hold with a fourth, I check the cellar again and discover that the water has risen higher.

When the dispatcher comes back on the phone, I don't bother trying to negotiate the call-out charge. 'You need to send someone right away,' I say. 'The water's rising. And there are electrics down there.'

'This afternoon? Three o'clock?'

'Fine.'

I return to the top of the stairs. Luke's assistant, Laura, whom I've clashed with previously, is standing there ready to shush me.

'Look,' I say, 'I'm dealing with an emergency here. You'll have to film outside this afternoon.'

'We can't do that,' she says. 'We've got a schedule. And you need to keep your voice down.'

'And *you* need to understand that this is serious,' I say. 'There's water down there – and electrics.'

'We can't just—'

'What's going on?' Luke appears behind the woman, his face carved with a deep frown that's meant for me. If only I could just go on hating him like I did before...

Swallowing hard, I point down the cellar stairs. He goes down partway.

'She wants us to change the schedule,' his assistant says. 'Again.'

'Well of course we'll have to change the bloody schedule, Laura,' Luke snaps. 'Go sort it now.' He looks out the window. 'It's clouding over. So we can do a retake of 63 in the forest.'

Clearly annoyed, Laura goes off, leaving me there with Luke. I take a deep breath, ready to shout at him. Instead, I burst into tears.

'It's just that sometimes,' I say, sobbing, 'everything – every *bloody* little thing – seems so difficult.' I cover my face with my hands.

'I've known the feeling,' he says. 'In fact, until quite recently.'

He removes my hands from my face, running his finger down the lines of my tears. The touch vibrates through me like ripples in an underground pool, bringing back memories of that night. The feel of his lips, the warmth of his body... I close my eyes, willing it to happen again, and this time for him not to stop...

Then Phillipa King walks into the room.

46

I don't know who's the most embarrassed or who hides it best. Luke steps away from me, his trademark frown unwavering. Phillipa smiles blandly, and Theo, just behind her, raises his eyebrows. A flush creeps down my neck.

'Hi,' I say, wiping my eyes. 'Just dealing with a little disaster.' I point down to the cellar.

'Sorry to interrupt,' Phillipa says to me. 'We were hoping to make some proper coffee before starting work.'

She seems nonplussed, as if seeing Luke standing so close to me – touching my face – is normal and of no concern to her. Now that I know the truth of her connection to my house, I can't make out whether she's as cold as an iceberg or a very good actress.

'Please, help yourself.' I gesture towards the coffee maker; Theo goes over and starts making a new pot. 'I'm just waiting for the drain men.'

'We need to change the schedule,' Luke says to Phillipa. 'Do you have those revisions to 63 that we talked about?' Seeing them together in the same room, I can't help being teleported once again back into Luke's story. A hot summer's night. Three teenagers getting drunk. Two of them fooling around. One of them dying...

'Of course, Luke,' she says matter-of-factly.

'OK, we'll do it this afternoon.' Turning, he strides out of the room.

I'm left there with Phillipa and Theo, wishing I could crawl under a rock. Damn Luke for just walking off. I hobble off towards the back stairs, hoping to make my own quick exit.

But Phillipa stops me. 'I'm so sorry, Lizzie,' she says, her smile unfaltering. 'But I'm going to have to let your daughter down. There are so many revisions – we're having trouble keeping up with them all. I just can't seem to work in a new part, I'm afraid.'

'Oh, but...'

I know I should say it's fine; that I never expected Katie to be given a part. But when I think about how excited she's been lately – how utterly different from the sullen, depressed child crushed by the loss of her father – and how the film project has been the catalyst for that change, I feel a simmering anger. Phillipa *offered* to write Katie a small part. She dangled it like a carrot in front of her nose. And now she's snatching it away. Is it because of what she just saw?

'Katie will be disappointed,' I say. Without meeting her eyes, I swiftly leave the room.

* * *

Waiting for the drain men, I feel completely overwrought. I go out to the drive and knock on the door of Connie's caravan. She opens up with one of her usual 'you look like shit' greetings. Her laptop is open on the table, and I can tell she was in the middle of something, but I don't care. I come inside and collapse on the two-seater sofa, lamenting about the rising water and the damage to the dovecote.

'You were right,' I say. 'This film has been a disaster from start to finish. I don't know how much more I can take.'

'Come on, Lizzie.' She puts her hands on her hips. 'Far as I can tell, everything's going great. Best decision you've ever made.'

'Really? How can you think that?'

'I don't know, you daft girl. Maybe it's because you seem to be blossoming. I take it you talked to *him*?'

'Him?' I cringe. 'Who are you talking about?'

She rolls her eyes. 'Gee, I wonder.'

I loll my head back, breathing in the odour of stale cigarette smoke. My eye snags on Connie's screen: a double-spaced document with a chapter heading on top. An odd idea goes through my head. Is Connie writing a book?

She sees me looking and closes the laptop.

I shrug, like I haven't noticed anything, and respond to her irritating insinuation. 'If you're referring to Luke Thornton, then you're the daft one. I mean, he's a famous Hollywood director. I'm a widow with two kids. *The Lady's Secret* may be addling brains right and left around here, but not mine.'

'Don't sell yourself short, Lizzie. You're an intelligent, attractive woman. Not necessarily in that order.'

I shake my head. 'Thanks, I think. And in actual fact, I did have a chat with him the other night.' I give her a pointed look. 'As I'm sure you knew, he was outside by the lake.'

She shrugs, giving nothing away. 'I had an idea he might have been out there. He said he needed to clear his head.'

'Well, he may have a clear head, but I'm afraid he doesn't have a clear conscience.' I outline very briefly the story Luke told me about the 'love triangle' between him, Julie, and Phillipa, and how it all ended in tragedy.

'So that's why he didn't want to use Tanglewild,' she muses. 'I asked him, of course, early on. He gave me some song and dance about the creative vision and practical logistics. I could tell immediately that it was tosh. He may be a talented director, but he's not much of a liar. This new version makes more sense.' She frowns. 'But what I don't understand is why Phillipa wanted to come back? Set a book here, for God's sake?'

'I overheard her and Luke arguing about the dedication. I think she sees it as some kind of memorial to Julie.'

'Odd,' Connie says. 'But then, she strikes me that way.'

'Really? To me, she seems perfect and polished.'

'That's always a sure sign. From the moment I met her, I've known that something's a little off.'

'Connie,' I say, levelling with her, 'are you just talking rubbish to cheer me up, or is there something you're not telling me?'

But I don't get an answer, because a white van pulls up into the drive and is detained by the security guard. The drain men.

I jump up from the sofa. 'Gotta go,' I say. 'Thanks for listening.'

'Sure thing. But Lizzie...'

'Yeah?' I turn back briefly. Connie's brow is wrinkled in concern.

'Be careful.'

47

THE LADY'S SECRET BY PHILLIPA KING

Victoria awoke in the night and sat bolt upright. Her heart was beating wildly in fear. The Watcher – he must be out there. She ran to the window and looked out, searching for the eyes that crawled over her from beneath the black hood night after night. Whether it was male or female, spirit or corporeal, she didn't know. All she knew was the chill she felt at its presence, its malevolence. Drawing her every night to look out the window, knowing she could not hide.

But on the lawn outside, there was no one there. She leaned out the window until the sound that awakened her repeated itself. A low sob – a woman crying. It seemed to be coming from somewhere... above her?

Victoria put on a dressing gown over her thin white nightgown. The narrow staircase outside her door led up to the eaves, but why would someone be out there? Other than the servants, the only woman in the house was the master's mother, and she wouldn't be able to climb the stairs.

And yet, there it was again – the sound of plaintive sobbing punctuated by a moan of distress.

She took the heavy brass candlestick from beside her bed and unbolted her door. The moonlight penetrated the shadows as she mounted the stairs that narrowed the higher she climbed and eventually twisted into a small attic room. The long casement window was wide open. The sobs grew into a long wail.

'Who's there?' *she said, going to the window and leaning out.* 'Do you need help?'

All suddenly went quiet. Directly outside the window was a gently sloping roof that led to the steeper gables, and before her, a twisted brick chimney rose up. There was no sign of anyone. Her heart in her throat, she stepped out onto the cool clay tiles.

'Go away,' *a female voice cried.*

'You shouldn't be out here,' *Victoria said.* 'If you slipped, you'd fall to your death.'

'Let me fall.'

The voice came from around the other side of the chimney; Victoria stepped forward into the gloom. The moon was swallowed by the tall bulk of the chimney. As she advanced around the corner, she heard a breath directly behind her.

And felt the sharp nick of a blade pressing into her back.

48

As I escort the drain men inside the gate, once again I'm nearly flattened by Natasha Blythe, her auburn wig loose and wild as she runs off in the direction of her trailer in tears. I take it that Scene 273, 'Victoria discovers that the Watcher has slashed her clothing', did not go well.

'Can I help?' I say as she goes past.

She slows down for a moment, her eyes round and wide. 'Thanks, but I'll be fine.'

I feel a little sorry for her – it can't be easy starring in a film, especially one that Luke is directing. He seems to demand perfection in every aspect of his work. Which begs the question: what, if anything, does he see in me?

'You're doing great,' I say, hoping to reassure us both.

She shakes her head and goes off as Luke's voice rises in the marquee. 'Look, Richard, I'll talk to her. It's going to be fine. Just be patient.'

'You know how patient I've been!' is the reply.

'I think it's me who needs to talk to her,' Dominic Kennedy says, weighing in. 'Will you let me have a go, Luke?'

I don't hear the response, but a second later, Dominic strides out of the tent in his cloak and tricorn hat, looking like a swaggering Puss in Boots who's just swallowed a canary.

The two drain men exchange a glance like they've landed on Mars or something. I've already explained to them about the filming, but knowing and seeing are two different things. I lead them into the house, warning them not to trip over the cables, cameras, lights, and all the other hazards about, and show them down to the cellar.

The water level has risen even further. The washer-dryer, boxes of baby stuff, chair cushions for the loungers, electric tools, old paint cans – it all looks to be a dead loss. And only a few feet above the rising waterline is the electric box. I try to stop my racing thoughts and frantic calculations and stay calm now that help has arrived, but it's too overwhelming. Like a sandcastle on a beach, I'd begun building up dreams about the future. But now, a tide of water has risen – literally – leaving nothing in its wake but furrows in the sand.

The men put on waders and slosh through the water. I listen to snippets of their conversation from the top of the stairs: 'Nothing obvious...' 'Broken well cap...?' 'Water coming in from the lake...?' 'Just waiting to happen...' None of it sounds good. I go upstairs and check the insurance documents: as I suspected, there's an exclusion for flooding and water damage caused by a natural source. I cry more tears. This time, there's no one to wipe them away.

When I finally pull myself together, the drain men have brought in a portable pump. It rumbles and glugs, sucking at least some of the water out the washing machine drain. I steel my courage and ask the boss what they've discovered.

'Nothing yet,' he says. 'When we've cleared the water, we'll have to dig up the floor.'

'Dig up the floor?' I say in horror.

'Well, you need it sorted, don't you?'

'Yes,' I croak. 'I do.'

* * *

Everyone on the film set seems on edge. Whether it's due to the flooding, the schedule, or the problems with Natasha Blythe, I don't know. I can only focus on my own problems, which are multiplying fast. The drain men leave to fetch more equipment, returning with two large jackhammers. I feel sick with worry – surely the floor must have been keeping water *out*, so I don't know how digging it up will improve things. But all I can do is trust the professionals.

When the jackhammering begins, it can be heard not only all through the house, but also in most areas of the garden. When I catch a glimpse of Luke from afar, he looks apoplectic. I can hardly blame him. The noise is doing my head in and I'm not the one responsible for keeping sixty people and a multimillion-pound film on track. Eventually, they give up, abandoning yet another day's schedule. I'm particularly worried when I see Michelle, the head of locations, on the lawn talking to Luke and Richard. Could they possibly be thinking of abandoning Tanglewild and moving somewhere else? I want to run out to them and tell them that it will all be fine – I'll call off the jackhammers, let the house flood – anything to keep them here, filming their movie. But even if I would really do such a thing, I'm too late. Luke drives off with Michelle in her car, and the assistants close down the set for the day. Phillipa and Theo, who were working in the marquee (I 'accidentally' locked the door to Jack's room and 'can't find' the key), also leave earlier than usual.

The relentless noise makes my ears ring – and it takes me a few seconds to notice that the jackhammers have stopped. In the kitchen, the waterlogged washer-dryer has been brought up the stairs, along with a toolbox and a few soggy cushions. All are clearly bound for the skip. At least the low hum of the pump is reassuring, almost soothing compared to the awful din that's been going on most of the afternoon.

One of the drain men comes up carrying a bucket of broken tiles, the reddish clay at the bottom damp and dripping like congealed blood. 'Hi, Mrs Greene,' he says, almost gleefully. 'I'm afraid there's good news and bad news.'

I like to fix things, which is why I'm normally a 'bad news first' type of person. But in this case, I just can't bear it. 'The good news,' I prompt.

'The good news is that the temporary pump is taking care of most of the problem for now. We found a large hole in the bottom of your cellar underneath the tiles. It's probably an old well.'

'A well? I didn't know.'

'It goes down about thirty feet. Normally, there's only a few feet of water in the bottom. But obviously, the level has been rising.'

'Obviously.' I sense we've reached the bad news. 'So what caused it to rise?'

'Search me.' He goes out the open door to the terrace and chucks the bucketful of broken tiles into a wheelbarrow. 'It could just be one of those things.'

One of those things. The words I'd been dreading. One of those normal wear-and-tear kind of things – like needing a new roof or a new boiler – that *just happen*. Just happen to set you back thousands of quid you don't have, that is.

'So what now?'

'We need to drain the hole completely and see what's down there. Check the wellhead and see if there's something we can fix. Because if not...' He shrugs.

'If not, what?' Irritation injects itself into the mix of panic and worry churning around in my stomach.

'Then we'll have to install an industrial-sized permanent pump.' His smile is not reassuring. 'Which would be expensive.'

As opposed to all the rest of it. 'And how long will this all take? When are you going to know if this "expensive" solution is going to be required?'

'It may take a few days before we can get down the well.'

A few days. The project... Luke...

'OK, but what about now?'

'As long as the electrics are on, the pump should keep running.'

The man goes back down for another load of debris. His boss presents me with a clipboard and some paperwork to sign. The estimate is three times what I was expecting, even in the worst-case scenario. My fragile dream of opening a B&B floats away down the river like the body of an ancient warrior, and over a waterfall to its death.

PART V

But I, being poor, have only my dreams;
I have spread my dreams under your feet;
Tread softly because you tread on my dreams.

— WILLIAM BUTLER YEATS

PART V

But I, being poor, have only my dreams;
I have spread my dreams under your feet;
Tread softly because you tread on my dreams.

—WILLIAM BUTLER YEATS

49

'You said something to Phillipa, didn't you?' Katie flings her piano book across the room. It's a day since the discovery of the water in the cellar. I was going to tell her yesterday that she's not going to be in the film, but honestly, I couldn't face it. 'You didn't want me to do it from the start!' she yells. 'I know you, Mum, you just want to ruin my life!'

I'm resigned to Katie's rage, though it still hurts. She picks up her maths homework from the desk, crumples it into a ball, and throws that at me too. Then she runs out of the room.

I let her go. What else can I do?

On cue, Jack starts to scream. Him I do manage to comfort, eventually. We curl up on my bed and read a few of his favourite books: *The Busy Bug Book*, *Aliens Love Underpants* and *Potty Time with Elmo*. I feel a little better, but there's still a nagging Katie-shaped hole inside me. I carry Jack downstairs and out of the house to find her.

Outside, things are worryingly quiet. The flood waters have thrown the schedule into complete disarray. I know they filmed some outside shots earlier this morning, but John C informed me that, for health and safety reasons, filming in the house will have to be curtailed until it's confirmed the electrics are safe. Though the temporary pump appears to be working, there's been no sign of the drain men. As I walk past the marquee, carrying my son, only a fraction of the usual crew is on site. The ones inside are milling rather than scurrying, which is a very bad sign. I haven't seen Luke all day, and no one seems able or willing to tell me what exactly is going on.

The front gate is open, which might be a clue to the direction Katie's gone (though just about everyone involved in the film seems incapable of closing it). On my way out, I set Jack down and let Jammie out of her run.

'Find Katie,' I say, sending her off. She's not trained to sniff people out but I feel a little better when she ambles out the gate, her nose to the ground. Leading Jack by the hand, I follow the dog, stopping on the way to knock at the door of the caravan. Neither Connie nor Simon have seen Katie, but Connie scoops up Jack and takes him inside to have some fresh-baked biscuits while Simon and I go and look.

We check the shed, then walk through the field of trailers and vans. I don't feel panicked – Katie has lots of hiding places and, undoubtedly, she's in one of them, sulking and not wanting to be found. As we walk, I pour out everything to Simon. I tell him that Phillipa saw something between Luke and me that she misinterpreted, and now Phillipa's pulled the plug on the film role. Katie now blames me. The more I go on, the angrier I get. For all Phillipa's so-called empathy, she must not *get* how hard it's been – not just for me but for my kids. If Phillipa had done something petty and hurtful to me, I could live with it. But the fact that she's involved my daughter...

In the apple orchard, Simon stops walking. 'I don't know if anyone's told you lately, Lizzie,' he says, 'but you're doing a terrific job with the kids. I really admire that.'

'Really?'

'My dad died when I was little,' he says. 'He was a horse trainer in Ireland, and he got kicked in the head by a stallion. Mum had five kids, and she kind of fell apart. Drinking, going down the pub every night and that sort. Whereas you've had a rotten time, and you're just getting on with things. The kids see that – they see you're strong. And in time, they'll be better for it. You'll see.'

I feel like a leaky water fountain as once again my eyes fill with tears. 'I'm sorry about what happened to you,' I say.

'It was one of those things,' he says. 'I survived. Had a bad patch or two when I was a young man, but now' – he smiles – 'I'm happy.'

'That's great.'

'And it may be annoying to hear people say this, but you'll be happy again too, Lizzie. Your new bloke, Luke, he's an all right sort. I may not be smart or educated, but I know people.'

'He's not my bloke, Simon,' I say. 'But thanks anyway.'

We continue walking, calling out Katie's name. I feel a creeping uneasiness as we reach the forest path that leads to the dovecote.

'She wouldn't go there, would she?' I worry aloud. Even if Luke kept his promise to speak to John C about the door, there won't have been time to fix it properly.

'I don't know,' he says. We both walk a little faster.

As we come into the clearing, Jammie bounds up to us, her hackles raised. The dovecote is in shadow. Behind it, the surface of the lake is still and inky like a dark mirror. Above our heads, clouds have gathered in the sky and it looks like a storm is coming. The air seems too thick to breathe. From somewhere near the lake, I hear voices speaking low in conversation.

Jammie goes to the door, growling. A piece of cardboard had been taped over the broken window, but it's been pulled away. I try the knob, but the door is locked. I reach through the jagged glass and unlatch it from inside.

'Katie!' I cry out. The dog lunges past me and up the stairs.

'Wait, Lizzie,' Simon says, 'let me go first.'

Ignoring him, I barge in. The lower floor is empty, so I rush up the stairs to the upper level.

Katie is sitting out on the balcony, her back to me, legs dangling over the edge. Beside her, almost a head taller, is Phillipa King. The dog, continuing to growl, picks her way across the rickety floor.

'You shouldn't be here!' I yell, looking at Katie, but directing my anger at Phillipa. 'This place isn't safe. No one's allowed out here.'

Katie kicks her legs and doesn't turn round to look at me. Phillipa, however, gets to her feet as the dog comes onto the balcony.

'Jammie, come here,' I command.

The dog ignores me, planting herself firmly between Phillipa and Katie.

With a strained half-smile, Phillipa bends down to pat the dog. I can tell that Jammie is wary, but she's no longer growling.

'I saw Katie running this way, so I followed her,' Phillipa says. 'I've spoken to her. She knows it's dangerous and has agreed not to come here again. We were just about to head back.'

'Katie.' I ignore Phillipa. 'Come here, please.'

'Let me go get her,' Simon says. He steps out onto the floor, testing each step to make sure the boards will hold his weight. 'Come here, Katie. I've got you.'

At the sound of Simon's soothing voice, Katie gets to her feet. She buries her hand in Jammie's fur, and I hold my breath as Simon takes her hand and the three of them navigate the dangerous floor. When they get to the safety of the stairs, I grab Katie and smother her with a hug. She squirms, but not too much. She even hugs me back a little.

'Sorry, Mum,' she says.

'It's fine.' I run my hands through her hair. 'As long as you're OK.'

'Yeah,' she says, the stroppiness returning. 'I'm fine. I come here lots.'

'Lots?' I look at Simon.

'I'll have a look tomorrow at the floor,' Simon says. 'I think the joists need replacing, but we need to make sure it's safe.'

'If you wouldn't mind,' I say. 'Thanks.'

I ask Simon if he'll take Katie and the dog back to the house. 'Sure.' He looks doubtful. 'But...'

'I need a word with Phillipa – alone.'

'OK...' He puts his arm companionably around Katie's shoulder. 'Let's go home.'

* * *

When they're gone, I go back upstairs. Phillipa is sitting down again on the balcony, staring out at the water. There are a thousand things I want to ask her – confront her – about. The floor creaks as I take a tentative step on the boards. Is she telling the truth that she came out here after Katie? Or did she lure her here?

'How do you live with the ghosts?' Phillipa's voice, low and quiet, startles me, and I stumble over a loose board. My injured ankle twinges through the bandage.

'What?' I reach the other side of the floor and grip the edge of the door frame.

'All the people who have lived here – and gone?' She shakes her head. 'I couldn't do it. I live in a new-build house. I guess you could say it lacks character, but that's why I like it. There are no memories, no stories, nothing to spoil it.'

She looks down at her hand. Her fist is clenched tightly around something. The rings on her fingers look heavy and dull.

'Why did you come back here?' I say. 'After what happened to Julie.'

'Ah, so you have been talking to Luke.' Her laugh is strange, and high-pitched. 'You think he's going to give up his glamourous career to come and run a B&B with you?'

'No,' I say hoarsely. 'I don't think that. Whatever I do next, it will be entirely on my own. Though, it's probably safest not to make plans at all. Life has a way of scuppering them.'

'I suppose it does,' she says. 'And death too. I once learned that lesson. Some people live, and some people die. It sounds simple, but it defines everything.'

She opens her hand then. Her palm is covered with blood from where she's been clutching a shard of broken glass. I gasp, instinctively feeling in my pocket for a tissue.

'They found a shard of glass in Julie's skull – did Luke mention that?'

I shake my head. I'm desperate to leave. Go back to the house; pretend I was never here. But I'm unable to move.

'Brown glass, from a bottle. At the inquest, the coroner explained it away. He said it was mostly likely a piece of broken glass from the bed of the lake when she sank to the bottom. But I don't think anyone believed that.' She closes her hand again. 'I loved Julie so much. She was like the sister I'd always wanted. She was a troubled girl, but even now, I still miss her sometimes.'

'It was a terrible accident.' The words sound impotent as they leave my mouth.

'Was it?' She turns sideways to look at me. 'Maybe Luke ought to be the novelist, not me. He can tell a good story, even after all these years.'

I clench my fists by my side. 'What are you saying, Phillipa?'

'Did he tell you how he followed us that summer – sneaking around with his camera? Constantly watching us. And how jealous he got when he saw me and Max together? Max locked the door to piss him off, and he smashed the glass to get inside. Did he tell you that? Did he tell you we played truth or dare?' She lowers her eyelids. 'You won't need much imagination to figure out what he wanted me to do.'

'You were kids,' I say weakly. 'That's what kids do.'

'Is that what you're going to say when Katie's old enough to be out alone with a boy?'

'Leave my daughter out of this.'

'Oh, but she's not out of it, is she? Or dear little Jack – a real footballer in the making. Don't you think you owe it to them? To know these things about the man you want to welcome into their home and their lives?'

'Look, Phillipa, I know you're angry with me, and to be honest, I don't know why. As you say, Luke and I have no possible future together, so let's just leave it, OK?'

'Do you want to leave it, Lizzie? Or do you want to know the truth of what happened all those years ago? Because if you're interested, it's all there in the book. Not in a way that's straightforward or easy, but it's there nonetheless.'

'The book?'

'Starting with the opening scene.'

She stands up then, her sharp chin raised defiantly. I'm forced to move aside as she walks back in the door, crosses the sagging floor without a care for any possible danger, and disappears down the stairs.

I stand there staring down at the piece of bloody glass she's left on the balcony, an icy chill coursing through my veins.

50

Phillipa's right – I've let these people into my home and my life; I've staked everything on this project. For months now I've been collecting the fragments of my heart like the shards of a broken vase, gluing them together with fortitude and hope, and creating something stronger and more beautiful. And then, in a single moment of madness, I'd come close to handing it over to someone else: someone I wanted to trust to hold it and keep it safe. Not dash it to pieces.

I pick up the shard of broken glass, still slick with Phillipa's blood. I rewind the conversation in my mind – the things she said, and didn't say. What was she implying about Luke? That he raped her like Victoria is 'seduced' by Tom in the opening scene? That he was the Watcher, stalking her like Belle stalked Victoria? That somehow, Julie's death was something more than just a terrible accident? My stomach lurches as I recall his words to Phillipa that night by the lake. *I did it for you.*

I don't have a tissue to put around the glass. Standing on tiptoes, I reach up to the highest pigeonhole and shove the piece of glass inside. My hand touches something furry and soft. I draw it back quickly. A dead mouse or rat? No – not an animal. I put my toe into one of the lower pigeonholes and boost myself up to take a look. It's too dark to see anything so I reach in again.

I draw out a small rectangular-shaped object covered in dust and cobwebs. It's a small book with a cover of moth-eaten pink fur. I shake the dust off and try to open it. There's a little vinyl strap holding the pages together, and a tiny clasp with a keyhole, but no key. I use the piece of glass to cut through the vinyl strap and try to open the book. Many of the pages are water-damaged and stuck together. But I am able to read the inscription inside the cover:

Diary of Julie W – DO NOT READ!

Outside the balcony window, a flash of lightning arcs across the sky, followed, only a second later, by a clap of thunder. My body jolts from the close impact. I take the book and go downstairs to wait out the worst of the storm. The air hums with electricity and the voices from beyond the grave that are closing in around me.

* * *

I hate Mum.

She's beyond horrible. I can't believe I'm even related to her. I mean, the look on her face when she told me the 'wonderful news' – that I'm going to have a new dad, and a new sister, and I'm going to be a bridesmaid at the wedding, and we're going to be one big happy family. Seriously?! She's such an idiot. Sometimes I think I should run away, or kill myself – anything to get out of here. I miss Dad. This summer is going to be the worst ever – I just know it.

Rain batters the roof. Carefully, I separate the pages as best I can. Most of the entries are short and written in purple or green pen. The ones I'm able to read have the same theme – Julie hates school, Julie hates her mum, Julie misses her dad who died. As I read, I keep hearing Katie's voice. It's as if she could have written the words that spill across the page in big, loopy writing.

I pull apart a section of pages further on. These entries have a different tone.

I'm going to have the coolest sister ever. P is UBER cool, and so perfect, and we're going to be best friends. I know I'll never be half as pretty as her, but maybe she'll help me. I've never felt like this before about anyone. I can't tell Lisa, because if I do, she'll know she's not my best friend any more. Lisa is such a child compared to P. I can't wait until she comes here – for the whole summer! I'm counting down the days.

Apparently, Julie got used to the idea of her new sister. The next few entries are all about how cool 'P' is, and how she's so grown-up and pretty. Julie writes down copious details about her clothing, her make-up, the way she does her hair, even what brand of deodorant she uses. Everything seems to be going well.

Then, her aunt and cousin arrived.

When L came in and saw her, I totally wanted to laugh. His mouth looked like a big 'o' – it was so silly. I didn't like the way she smiled at him though, and I told her so later. She told me not to be such a drama queen. Then she said he was cute. P can be so mean and awful sometimes.

The next few pages are stuck together and I can't read them. However, it seems that there is trouble brewing in paradise.

...just can't believe that she would let him do that. It's sickening. She said she was sorry – he got her drunk, and that it was all a mistake. I said that everything would be better once we had the money from the drawer and could get away. I'm going to do it tonight.

I feel a strange, crawling sensation on my skin and close the book. Julie is dead, but I have no right to be reading her all-important adolescent thoughts. Maybe I should put the book back, or throw it in the lake. One thing's for sure – I don't want Phillipa to find it. Or Luke.

Outside, the torrential rain has trickled off to a drizzle. I don't have a pocket big enough for the diary, so I tuck it under my arm to protect it from the wet. I leave the dovecote, not bothering to tack the cardboard up over the broken pane of glass. The place is in need of proper repairs to make it less hazardous. Especially if Katie has adopted it as one of her secret places.

The ground is muddy and the dripping branches overhanging the path soak my clothing. But my spirits revive a little when I catch sight of the peaked roofs and lofty chimneys of Tanglewild. I cross the field and enter the garden. The lights are on in the kitchen, and I can hear the sound of children's voices. But in the distance there's another rumbling of thunder. The ghosts are still here, lurking just out of sight.

***

Inside, I hide the fuzzy pink diary underneath my mattress, then go down to the kitchen where Simon and Connie are making spaghetti for the kids. Jack's at the table scribbling with a crayon in his superhero colouring book and Katie is frowning over her maths homework.

'Sorry, Mum,' she mutters as I come inside.

'I'm just glad you're OK.'

Connie looks like she's about to say something, but I shake my head. She and Simon stay for dinner, then go back to the caravan. I take Jack upstairs, read him a story and put him to bed. Katie's still in the kitchen reading a book when I return.

'Do you want some hot chocolate?' I say.

She looks up and nods. Her almond-brown eyes hold an ocean of expression. I think about what Luke said about my own face, and feel a painful tug of longing in my abdomen. I banish all thoughts of him, focusing instead on making the hot chocolates with a sprinkling of cinnamon on top.

'We don't have to talk about what happened,' I say as I bring the mugs to the table and sit down opposite her. 'But just so you know, I didn't ask Phillipa to stop writing you a part. Quite the opposite, in fact. Once I got used to the idea, I was excited for you.'

She closes the book. 'I thought you stopped it because I went to see

Chloe and Natasha and made you late for work. But she said it wasn't because of that.' She takes a sip of hot chocolate.

'Did she give a reason?'

'She said that Luke wouldn't like it.'

'Luke?'

'He's such a bastard.'

'Katie! Don't use that word. Ever, OK?'

'Whatever.' She licks the cinnamon from her lips. 'Phillipa told me what happened to her sister. The one that drowned in the lake.'

'What?' My anger bubbles to the surface. How could Phillipa tell Katie such a macabre story, especially when Katie was already in a fragile state? And now, it seems she's trying to turn Katie against Luke too. I've no idea if Luke even knew about the bit part she promised Katie.

I take a sip from my own mug, the hot liquid burning my tongue. None of it matters anyway. Because at the end of the day, Phillipa's right about one thing. Whatever happened that summer at the lake, Luke isn't the man we need in our lives. There are too many question marks... too much darkness.

'It was her stepsister,' I say. 'More of a friend, really. They shouldn't have been out there, and then something bad happened – an accident. That's why I don't want you going out there either. It isn't safe.'

'Phillipa said she was trying to protect me. Make sure I didn't get hurt. She said it was better if I wasn't in the film, and that she'd talk to another director friend and get me a part in something for kids.'

'I'm not sure you should get your hopes up, Katie. Phillipa is busy and has a lot on her mind, though I'm sure she means well.' The words sound as insincere as they are. 'And just for the record, I wouldn't interfere with your dreams of being an actress just because you made me late for work. I might get mad at you sometimes, but I want you to be happy – and safe too. You know that, right? I only want the best for you.'

'OK, Mum.' Katie finishes her cocoa. 'I really *do* want to be an actress. So maybe I can take some acting lessons or something.'

'That sounds like a brilliant idea.' The knot of tension inside me begins to loosen a little. I may be facing an enormous bill for the cellar, and who knows how much to repair the dovecote, but right now, I'd do anything to get Katie those lessons.

'Thanks, Mum.' She picks up her book and goes back to reading it. I have the strong urge to smother her in a hug, but I resist it. One step at a time. Because there's nothing more important in my life than my relationship with my children and being the best mother I can.

Especially now there's no hope of anything else.

51

It's a relief to go to work the next day. As I'm leaving to get the train, only a handful of crew members have turned up, and I skip my usual coffee in the marquee. I'm distraught that the film project seems to have derailed, along with my plans for the B&B. Then there's the issue with Katie and Phillipa... But I'm not kidding anyone. The real reason I'm upset is that I haven't seen or heard anything from Luke since I saw him go off with Michelle in her car two days ago. And while I know it's for the best, there's still a hole inside my chest where my heart has been ripped out.

Before leaving the house, I'd checked the water level in the cellar. The pump appeared to be confining the water to the hole underneath. I'd stood at the edge and looked down into the dark chasm that had been underneath my house all along, with no one knowing it was there. And I'd wondered what other secrets lie buried within the walls of the house I've made my home. The events of the last few days have reinforced the fact that my life is just one more pageant unfolding within its walls. Tanglewild was here long before I was born. It will be here long after I'm gone.

Around midday, I get a call from Connie. I answer with a stab of trepidation. Has something else gone wrong?

'Lizzie.' Connie's voice sounds distant. 'You'll never guess what's happened.'

'What? Is it the children? The film? Is someone injured?'

'Well' – she hesitates – 'not exactly. In fact, someone's dead.'

'Dead?' The word screams through my body.

'Sorry, maybe I shouldn't have put it in those terms. They found a skeleton, down in the tunnel.'

'The tunnel? What tunnel? What are you talking about, Connie?' My hand starts to tremble as I switch off my computer and shove some papers in my bag. 'I can be home in' – I check my watch – 'an hour and fifty minutes. If I leave now.'

'Come home if you like, but there's really no need. Nothing to be done for the poor chap. He's been down there for about 200 years.'

* * *

I do leave, right there and then. I tell Diana's PA that I'm going home to deal with an emergency, and catch the next train. When I arrive home, two police cars are double-parked next to the Portaloos. I break into a run.

The marquee is empty as I go past the entrance. I catch sight of John J and John C over near the dock, having a heated argument with a drain man. Luke is nowhere to be seen, nor Phillipa, nor any of the cast. I feel nauseous as I approach the giant hole in my back lawn, about halfway between the dock and the house. Connie and Simon are both there, standing behind a cordon of yellow tape. A tent has been erected over the opening and a ladder has been put down the hole. Two more drain men are sitting on the lawn under the big plane tree eating their lunch.

'What the hell is going on!' I say, grabbing Connie's arm. 'You didn't mention police.'

'They aren't police,' she says calmly. 'They're forensic archaeologists. I told you, the skeleton's been down there for a long time.'

'But how did they find him?'

'Your drain chaps. At the bottom of the well they found the entrance to a tunnel that led to the shores of the lake. It had been sealed up for years with rubble, but when the set crew started digging down to make that dock, they broke through. That's what caused the flood – the water rushing in and filling up the tunnel. The pump cleared enough of the water for the drain men to go into the tunnel. That's when they found the skeleton. And a lot of other stuff too, apparently.'

'What stuff?'

She raises an eyebrow. 'It's not clear yet. Some barrels, I think.'

'The smugglers? They were really here?'

'Seems so,' Simon confirms. 'This find could be really something.'

I shake my head back and forth. 'I'm not sure I can handle any more surprises.'

Connie sniffs and takes out a small silver object from the back pocket of her jeans. 'Here,' she says, 'I think you need this.'

I unscrew the lid of the flask and put it to my lips. Right now, I wouldn't even dream of saying no.

* * *

Whatever the forensic archaeologists are doing down in the hole, they aren't letting on. Thankfully, Connie had the foresight to ask Hannah to take the kids after school, so I don't need to tell them what's going on. Not that I know myself. I hang about for half an hour pacing back and forth, having, admittedly, more than one nip from Connie's flask. I've just handed it back to her for the third time when John C comes over to me.

'We aren't admitting liability, just so you know,' he says.

'Of course not.' I roll my eyes. 'As the police are involved now, I suppose they'll say what's what.'

'They aren't police,' he replies. 'They're—'

'Yes,' I cut him off. 'I know.'

Just then, a woman in a white plastic boiler suit pops her head out of the hole. 'We're bringing her up,' she says.

'Her?' I exchange a glance with Connie.

'The skeleton is female.'

'Female? Two hundred years old?' I step forward, stretching the tape at the edge of the cordon.

'Give or take,' the woman says. 'I'm afraid we're unlikely to find out much more than that. Like who she was, or how she died. Or if the body was dumped there after death. There just won't be that kind of evidence left.'

'I think I know who she is,' I say. 'Veronica Jones.'

'Who?' Simon asks.

'A woman who disappeared back in 1790. Her story is in the museum. Her husband, Zachary Jones, was a smuggler. It was rumoured that he murdered her.'

'Oh.' Simon bows his head.

I stand there in silence, thinking about poor Veronica and what she must have gone through. We may never know the details, but her ending must have been brutal and terrifying.

Later on, the forensic archaeologists hoist a black vinyl bag up through the hole and carry the remains to their van. The rest of us follow solemnly behind. When they're gone, I go into the marquee and collapse in a chair, my head in my hands.

A while later, someone puts a hand on my shoulder.

'Lizzie, are you OK?'

I look up and see Theo, his eyes full of sympathy and concern.

'Yes, fine.'

'Good.' He removes his hand. 'Because I'm told this is all only temporary.'

'Temporary?' I repeat. 'Veronica's been dead for hundreds of years. That seems pretty permanent to me.'

'Veronica?' He looks puzzled. 'Sorry, I was talking about the main set location. They've found another place down the road to use as Idyllwild Hall – at least until things get sorted here. The production company is all over Luke and Richard. They won't tolerate any more delays.'

I stare at him dumbly. 'They found a skeleton in a tunnel underneath my house,' I say. 'I don't know about any other film location.'

'A skeleton?' His interest suddenly perks up.

'Yes,' I say, feeling a numbness spread through me. 'I think it's Veronica Jones.'

'Wow, I can't wait to tell Phillipa,' he says. 'She researched that story at the local museum. You know about it, right?' Without allowing me to answer, he launches into a recap. 'Back in the late eighteenth century, the house was owned by a nobleman called Zachary Jones. He lost his fortune in America and made ends meet by doing a little smuggling on the side. His wife, Veronica, disappeared – some people said she ran off with another man, but others said he did her in. After seven years, he married another woman. A woman who had been a servant in his house. It was quite scandalous back in the day.'

'It must have been,' I say.

'So now we know he did her in after all.' He makes it sound like this newly revealed slice of history is all part of a fiction novel – which, of course, it is. I wonder if he knows about the other 'story' that Phillipa claims is part of her novel. The story about Julie, and her, and Luke – all in the past, but the much more recent past. Somehow, I get the feeling that he doesn't. All along, Phillipa has been the puppet master, pulling strings for her own purposes. Theo, at least, seems more than willing to dance to her tune.

'A husband murdering his wife is not very romantic, if you ask me.'

'I agree,' Theo says. 'So it's a good thing Phillipa rewrote history and gave it a happy ending.'

'It's a good thing her audience isn't looking for truth. Because there are no happy endings in real life, are there?'

Without waiting for him to answer, I get up and walk off to the house.

* * *

I do the washing-up and then sit down at the table with a cup of tea, unable to drink it. I'm grieving again, I realise. For a woman who died alone in a tunnel under my house. For the film project that brought me such a mixture of joy and despair, and will now, from the sound of it, be finished elsewhere. For the friend I thought I'd made in a charismatic yet unfathomable woman who wrote a bestselling novel. For the young girl who died in a tragic accident and never had the chance to grow up, live her own life, have her own successes and failures. For something I shared with a most unlikely man – a moment, sparkling with possibilities, that will never be realised.

I'm aware of people speaking outside the door – the drain men, the two Johns. Life going on around me. The tea stops steaming and then grows cold.

'Lizzie,' Simon says softly from the door. 'They found some things down in the tunnel.'

'What?' I say through a tide of despair. 'More bodies?'

'No. If you're up to it, you should come have a look.'

I pour the cold tea down the sink, trying not to think or feel anything. I follow Simon over to the hole in my lawn that's still covered by the tent.

'It's quite wet down there,' he says. 'But it's safe to go down the ladder. Do you want me to go first?'

'I'll go.' With a last breath of clean spring air, I climb down the ladder. The tunnel is deeper than I expected – at least twenty feet down to the bottom. Some large portable lights have been set up, making it look like a subterranean film set. Even so, it takes a minute before my eyes adjust to the damp, cloying darkness.

One of the drain men is down at the far end of the tunnel, just beyond the light. His shadow flickers large on the algae-covered wall.

'What am I looking for?' I ask as Simon comes down the ladder. The ceiling is low so we both have to stoop.

'This way.' He flicks on a torch and leads me away from the big lights towards the house. The tunnel seems to be blocked up by stacks of debris and rubble. As Simon shines the torch, I make out geometric shapes. Casks and barrels, and large wooden crates. Several of the boxes have been pried open.

'What is this stuff?'

One of the forensic archaeologists working down at the other end of the hole comes to join us. 'We're not sure yet,' he says. 'But it looks a little bit like buried treasure.'

I wait for the laugh – for any indication that he's joking. When none comes, I frown at him. 'You can't be serious.'

'I don't mean coins and jewels or that sort of thing,' he says. 'But rather treasure of a historical nature.'

He goes over to one of the open boxes as Simon shines the torch in his direction. He takes out something soggy – a large piece of fabric. 'Pure

Chinese silk,' he says. 'Sadly, I don't think the fabric is going to be salvageable. But some of the rest might. Have a look in there.' He gestures over at the other open crate. I go to it and take the lid off. Inside, it's full of wet sawdust and cotton. But peeking out from the packing material is a large piece of ceramic. He comes over and stands beside me as I grab onto it and gingerly lift it out.

It's an exquisitely painted blue and white vase.

'I'm not an expert, but I'd say that's a Qing dynasty vase from the late seventeenth century,' he says. 'Maybe even earlier.'

'Oh!' I set it back down in the packing material, afraid that I might break it.

'There's plenty more here, as you can see,' the man says. 'Of course, it may well not all be porcelain. There may be rum, or other spirits, plus the fabrics – whatever the smugglers could get their hands on.'

I feel like I've stepped into an episode of *Time Team* as I stare at the crates and barrels crammed into the tunnel.

'What do I do now?' I ask the man, praying that he'll know the answer.

'I can give you some names,' he says. 'A couple of experts who will be very interested in documenting this find. They can get a museum on board, or whatever you want to do.'

'But it isn't mine. Surely someone must have a claim on it.'

'After all these years, that might be unlikely. And I'm afraid that since it's been found on your land, you're going to have to take some responsibility for dealing with it. There are laws on the ownership of treasure once the find has been documented. But that aside, if I were you, I'd let in one or two of those reporters who are camped out at the gate.' He looks at Simon, who nods. 'Your mother-in-law told us that you were thinking of opening a B&B. Whether or not you get to keep the treasure, I'll bet you get some great publicity from this.'

'Yes,' I say, barely able to register what he's saying. The B&B, the film, publicity... real life. I'm still in shock, but I need to pull myself together. 'But what about the skeleton?' I say.

'The experts can look at that too. It's a great find for local history.'

I feel the sudden urge to get out of that tunnel. I'll call in the experts and get them to document the artefacts and donate them to a museum. As for the reporters – publicity is the last thing I want right now. Veronica's remains should be treated with respect and dignity, not like a three-ring circus, and I want to make sure she receives a proper burial. And if, someday, her true story can be told, then so be it. That, however, I'll leave to other people.

I walk back to the ladder, light-headed. I feel like I've dived into deep water and am struggling to swim up to the light. Simon's hand on my back steadies me as I grasp the sides of the ladder. I put one foot over the other and slowly climb upwards.

PART VI

Gentle, soft dream, nestling in my arms now, you will fly, too, as your sisters have all fled before you: but kiss me before you go...

— CHARLOTTE BRONTË, *JANE EYRE*

52

My resolve to keep out of the limelight and away from the press backfires. The paparazzi photo of me at the gate is published online, along with details about the film. The story is picked up by the local newspaper, and then a regional one. Two days later, *Smuggler's Treasure Found Underneath Sussex Home* makes the *Telegraph*. My phone begins to ring off the hook. I take a few days off from work to deal with the publicity, and to supervise the ever-larger growing trench in my back garden required to bring up the 'loot'.

To his credit, the expert – a professor of English archaeology and anthropology from Brighton – arrives promptly to supervise the removal of the artefacts. It takes three days for them to photograph and catalogue the find in situ, then move each crate, barrel, and casket up to the surface.

The 'Law of Treasure' requires us to present everything to the local coroner for a determination of ownership – which, according to my research, is not a straightforward process. Though I'm not expecting to be able to retain anything that's found, I do feel a genuine excitement as each container is opened.

But the excitement is tempered by a strong sense of loss. While the film company still has a skeleton crew at the house – mostly security people and some technical staff – the main set has moved to the 'other'

Idyllwild. I see nothing of Luke, Phillipa, or Theo, nor any of the rest of the cast. To my chagrin, I do get a call from a risk manager at the production company who's trying to get to the bottom of the media interest that's in violation of the confidentiality provisions of the contract. I have a few tense moments worrying that they might try to wiggle out of paying me. I summon all of my lawyerly negotiating skills and make it clear that I've done nothing wrong and expect the location fee to be paid in full. The woman is unable to confirm when – or if – filming will resume at Tanglewild.

At night, I cry. Quietly enough to not wake the children, but steadily, and for what seems like hours on end. I cry for Dave and the fact that I've moved beyond him for good. I cry for 'Veronica' found buried in the tunnel. I cry for Julie, another ghost who haunts Tanglewild. I cry for the end of the film project – stupid, I know, as it was always going to end. The one thing I won't allow myself to cry for, but that underlies every tear that soaks my pillow, is Luke.

* * *

On Friday, a week after the find, I return to work. I plan to put everything behind me and start afresh. My plans for the B&B are on hold until everything is sorted with the drains and the dovecote, but I've still got my job, and I need to keep moving forward.

As I'm heading to the train station, I see two cameramen and the actress who's playing Belle, stalker sister-in-law, go into the marquee. Several cars are parked behind the garage, and when I reach the top of the road, I find that two extra security guards have been posted there. I feel a surge of hope – could the hiatus finally be coming to an end? I cross my fingers tightly.

All day long I have trouble concentrating, as if I've become a different person to when I was last in the office. My mind keeps wandering back to the house and what might – or might not – be going on there. In the late afternoon, Connie texts me saying that she and Simon want to take the kids and Jammie to the seaside for the weekend in the caravan, and would that be OK? I text back that it's fine, wondering if I should offer to go along. But I'm exhausted from not sleeping, and things are cramped in the caravan with two people let alone five plus a dog. I decide that they'll be better off without me.

Knowing that the kids will be gone when I get back, I stay late at the office to catch up on some work from the days I missed. I don't get back to the house until after eight, at which time I'm surprised to see the lights ablaze inside. I whisper a silent thanks to the powers that be. The crew has definitely returned!

As it turns out, the shoot finished hours earlier, but the lights were left on because no one bothered to turn them off. A few of the tech people are still in the marquee when I return. I pop in to say a quick hello, but then I catch sight of Luke, reviewing footage on the monitor with two other people. I make a quick retreat to the house, feeling a raw pain deep inside.

I've had a lot of time to think things through, and I've come to the conclusion that I don't believe Luke harmed anyone. Phillipa was jealous and angry and tried to upset me by planting seeds of doubt in my mind. But all that aside, I can't shake a feeling of betrayal. Luke left without saying goodbye. I haven't received a single call or text from him. I suppose that to him, I was nothing more than a toy to be played with, broken and discarded on a whim. Is that what he did to Phillipa when they were teenagers? To Julie?

I let the anger flow through me. It just about masks the joy I feel at seeing him again, even from afar.

Inside the house, I turn off lights as I go: in the downstairs toilet, the hall, the stairwell. I reach the kitchen and put the kettle on. It's strange not seeing Jack and Katie, and I feel lonely. I should have gone to the seaside, especially now that everyone – now that Luke – is back.

I could go upstairs and pack a bag. Jump in my car and drive to the coast – I could be there in under an hour. I could find a B&B for the night and expense it as research for my own business prospects. Spend an exhausting day in the sun dealing with drippy ice creams, strops over sun cream, and eating greasy fish and chips.

No.

As soon as I hear the footsteps coming into the room towards me, I know that tonight, come what may, I'll be staying right here.

* * *

'Lizzie,' he says from the door.

The way my name sounds coming from those lips... But *no* – I can't think about that. That road has come to a dead end. Things have to stop right here.

'It's after hours,' I say. 'You should knock.'

Bemused, he knocks on the door frame and comes inside. I sit down at the table, the mug of tea placed protectively in front of me. I don't offer him any. He sits down opposite and stares at me.

I try to ignore the sensation those eyes evoke in me. I look at the mug, the table, the steam rising into the air. He doesn't speak; is he expecting me to break the silence? I don't want to do it, but anger wins out.

'Filming going well?' I say with an edge of sarcasm. 'I'm surprised you came back.'

He leans back in the chair. 'Why surprised? We're behind schedule. The water was a health and safety issue and then the press coverage became a problem. We moved to our second and third location a few weeks earlier than planned. We'll need to tack on an extra week here at the end of the shoot, most likely. Assuming it's OK with you, of course.'

'Second and third location?'

'Yes. We filmed all the early scenes. Victoria at the vicarage, in the church, and at the farmhouse. We also did some filming in the kitchens at Petworth House.' He gives me the familiar frown. 'But surely someone told you. You knew.'

'Theo said you'd found another house to be Idyllwild. That's all I know. And it's not like you bothered to call and tell me yourself.'

'No.' The word hangs in the air between us. 'I didn't.'

I feel my heart begin to shrivel up and die.

'I needed time to think,' he says. 'I thought maybe we both did.'

I shrug noncommittally. 'As you can imagine, things have been busy enough here. What with the treasure, the skeleton, and trying to convince your production people that I had nothing to do with a leak to the press. And before all that kicked off, I also managed to fit in an interesting little chat with Phillipa.'

'Did you?'

'We spoke briefly about what happened all those years back. Her account differed somewhat from yours.'

'Oh?' He shifts in the chair.

'Yes. There was something about a smashed window, and a game of truth or dare. Though I suppose it's your word against hers.'

'No.' He looks steadily at me. 'She's right. Those things happened.'

Having expected a denial, I pause, unsure what to think. 'She also said they found fragments of glass in Julie's skull. From a bottle.'

'Yes. That's right too.'

'Funny, your omitting that in your "story".'

He stands up, and I'm sure he's going to walk off. Instead, he goes over to the window, staring out at the black water of the lake.

I take a sip of tea to steel myself. Having started, I have to continue. That night by the lake, Luke wanted me to know the truth – his version of it, anyway. What was it he'd said? *It's no fairy tale and there's no happy ending.*

'Phillipa also told me that "the truth of what happened is in the book". Starting with the opening scene. What do you suppose she means by that?'

'The opening scene?' He frowns. 'Scene 254? Tom seduces Victoria by the lake shore. Some people call it the rape scene. Are you saying that really happened?'

'I don't know – you tell me.'

'What? Are you saying that... she said that I...' His eyes flare with panic and injustice. 'No.' His voice is heavy. 'That's not what happened.'

As much as I want him to suffer, I can't bear to witness it. He may have omitted some details, but ultimately, I believe he's told me the truth.

'She wanted me to think the worst of you,' I concede. 'But I don't believe you did... that... if it helps.'

He bangs his hand on the window frame. 'I can't believe she would say that. Things between us *never* went that far.'

'She was jealous of what she saw that day in the kitchen. She thought there was something between us. But she was mistaken.' I can't keep the bitterness from my voice.

'Jesus Christ.' He shakes his head. 'This is exactly what I was worried about all along. That she might twist around what happened back then. It is her word against mine.'

'Maybe.'

He rubs his forehead like it's giving him a headache. 'God, Lizzie. I'm sorry – so sorry that I dragged you into this. I need you to know – need you to believe – that I never hurt Phillipa or Julie. I certainly never did… that, for Christ's sake.' He starts walking to the door. 'But you have no reason to trust me. I shouldn't have come back here tonight.'

'Wait, Luke.' Suddenly, I'm desperate to stop him going. 'I said I believe you. But I still have a lot of unanswered questions. Like why you agreed to take on this project. I mean, it was clear from the start that you didn't want to. It was Phillipa's book, but surely *you* didn't have to be involved.'

'That damned book.' He clenches his fist like he wants to hit something. 'Fine – I'll tell you. I'll tell you everything – anything you want to know. Not that it's going to help.' His words are quick and full of venom. 'It started when Phillipa contacted me around the time of my divorce. She always knew when to choose her moments. I was feeling sorry for myself, and hating everyone, and hearing her voice brought that summer back again – the good bits, as well as the bad.'

I nod, saying nothing.

'I was feeling so low that I agreed to see her. We met for brunch at the Beverly Hills Hotel. At first, I didn't recognise her. I mean, it had been over twenty years since I'd seen her at the funeral. She'd suffered ups and downs in her career and her personal life – just like I had. I guess that made me warm to her a little. She told me about her struggle to make a living as a writer, and then her big break, and how thrilled she was that *The Lady's Secret* was being optioned for a film. Of all the people out there, she just *had* to have me as the director. Would I do it – for old times' sake?

'I gave her a flat-out no. For obvious reasons. Seeing her for lunch was one thing. Directing the film of her novel was quite another. I hadn't read the book, but I knew it wasn't my kind of thing. The one thing I've done in my life that I'm proud of is built up my career. I'm proud of the films I've made, the work I've done. Though a few of my efforts around that time weren't the commercial successes that were expected.' He paces a few steps.

'But the main reason I didn't want to do it was because seeing her brought everything back, like it happened yesterday. All the years had made no difference. I gave her the names of a few people I thought would do a better job, and made my excuses that I was tied up with other projects.' He laughs bitterly. 'But she'd already sweet-talked her way into the studio and got them on board, telling them that she absolutely *had* to have me as the director. She can be very persuasive when she wants to be.'

'Yes, I'm sure.'

'So there was pressure on me from that front. And that day at lunch, she told me that she wrote the book "for Julie", and that we both owed it to her to see it through.

'I got angry and was going to walk out. But then I noticed a camera in a bush – the paparazzi filming us together. I knew that if I took on the project, that meeting wouldn't raise any eyebrows. But if I didn't, someone might go looking for a connection between us, and they might find it. If the story came out, I thought it might destroy my career. Either way, I just couldn't face any more stress or publicity.' He sighs deeply. 'So I took the path of least resistance. I said I'd direct the film as long as she wasn't involved. The location needed to be my choice – certainly not Tanglewild – and when it was all over, we'd never see each other again.'

'But she went back on those things too?'

He spreads his hands. 'I'm here, aren't I? And so is she.'

I think of the argument I overheard between him and Richard, and later on, with Phillipa. I can understand Luke's reluctance to return, but Phillipa's motives still baffle me. 'I just don't understand why on earth she'd want to come back to Tanglewild, of all places,' I say.

'I asked her that when she rejected the first location,' he says. 'She gave me some song and dance about how setting her book at Tanglewild helped her come to terms with what happened to Julie. About how she used to dream about Tanglewild when she was at boarding school. Phillipa never returned here after that summer either. Aunt Roz split up with Phillipa's dad and sold the house. Probably to the people you bought it from, I don't know. She died a few years back.'

'Oh.' I struggle to process this history I've known nothing about.

'I could have walked away at that point. I probably should have. I saw the photos that Theo took – photos of the house, and the dovecote – and it made me sick to think of coming here again. But a part of me wanted to believe that Phillipa was right. That by coming back here, I could come to terms with my memories.'

I think about Julie, struggling under the water, trying to rise to the surface. Her strength gradually giving out as the head wound swept away all consciousness. And Luke... and Phillipa. I try to cast out the image of them together. Along with my own memories of that very first day when I met Phillipa in the kitchen; Luke smiling at her, kissing her cheeks. My conclusion was correct – there was something between them. Just not what I expected. Only Dominic Kennedy saw the truth behind the act. Telling me that Luke was on the wrong side of the camera if he'd convinced everyone that he and Phillipa were an item.

'And do you know the worst thing?' His voice rises in anger. 'I can't tell you how many times I've wished that if one of them had to die that day it... hadn't been Julie. Does that sound horrible?'

'It sounds understandable.'

He slumps against the window frame, looking tired and broken. 'When I started to have feelings for you, I didn't want to acknowledge them. When that became impossible, I thought it was right to get everything out in the open. But that made me realise another awful truth – that I have too much to answer for.'

I long to go to him. Comfort him. But I remain where I am. He's suffered a lot – but so have I. And a major cause of my suffering right now is *him*.

We stay like that in silence. Eventually, I get up and put the kettle on again and make him a cup of tea. I set it at the far end of the table and sit back down.

'Thanks,' he says. But he ignores the tea and instead comes over to where I'm sitting. My entire body goes limp as he gets down on his knees and rests his head in my lap.

For a second, I can't move. His head is warm and I'm aware of his every breath, his pulse resonating with mine. My fingertips sense him even before my hand moves with a will of its own to tangle in his hair and trace the contours of his face, his eyes, his cheekbones, the lines etched by pain and regret. I touch his lips, indenting the soft flesh and putting my finger into his mouth where he twines it with his tongue. It's intimate and full of intent, my body awakening despite my mind warning me to be wary.

'I did change the schedule and the location,' he says finally. 'I couldn't bear to see you; I couldn't bear to want you. Sorry – but I thought you should know.' He raises his head from my lap and turns to look at me. And at that moment, my anger returns in a flood, redirected into something raw and primeval.

I stand up, holding out my hand to draw him to his feet. He rises, and I can sense he's about to pull away. But I tighten my grip on his hand so hard that he winces.

'Here's the thing, Luke Thornton,' I say. 'I never want to hear the word "sorry" again. I spent years of my life trying to be a good wife and a good mother. I let my husband control me and our marriage. And in return, he betrayed me, and then he died. And you know what? Everybody was "sorry". The lawyer, the bank manager, my boss – all of them "sorry", and all of them controlling my life in different ways. And then there was the project, and your schedule, and your memories. You awakened something inside me, and then you bloody well walked away, leaving me with nothing more than an "I'm sorry". You decided whether your past mistakes were too much to answer for, and you decided when you needed time to think, and you decided whether or not I could trust you. And then you decided when – and if – you came back.

'And now...' I take a step closer so that we're only inches apart. 'Just so you know – I'm *done* letting other people call the shots. I'm done letting other people decide what's best for me. If I choose to love again – if I choose... you – it's going to be on my terms.'

His face softens; the wild, haunted look passes from his eyes and is replaced by something else. Surprise... and – amusement.

'And what are your terms?' His low voice close to my ear makes me shiver inside.

'Come with me.' I lead him out of the kitchen and through the forest of electronic equipment in the hall, to the bottom of the main staircase. There, I stop and turn to him. 'And for your information,' I say, 'I don't give a damn if my bed is part of the set.'

His face is transformed by a smile, one that's only for me. 'Do you mind if I add one directorial flourish?'

'What?'

I let out a little cry of surprise and then laughter as he suddenly lifts me into his arms and carries me up the stairs to the bedroom.

53

I didn't believe them – all the people who told me things could be better the second time around. That eroded by grief and shame and worn down by life, I could ever find a spark within myself to share with another person – or that I could even be bothered to try. But making love to Luke is a revelation. Not to mention pure joy.

The huge canopy bed is surrounded by wires, cables, and dark, silent cameras, but in the light of a single candle taken from the props table, it becomes a cocoon of two. Luke is a passionate lover, but also unexpectedly giving. For many hours of the night, we lie together, kissing tenderly. We drift into sleep, then make love again, and as the sun rises, we talk. About where we come from and about the good parts of our past. And I don't need dreamcatchers or romance novels because I have all that and so much more. With his solid presence next to me, his body moulded to mine, I no longer feel afraid. Because I've had this moment that's restored my belief in love. Being here with him, there's no room for the memories, or the dark places. No room for anything but him.

'You're a very special woman, Lizzie,' Luke says to me. I lay my head on his chest, listening to his heartbeat. 'You're so grounded and real. I never thought I'd meet anyone like you. Or feel like this.'

'You mean I'm ordinary,' I say, bemused. 'I'm not a film star or a creative genius. I'm not famous or rich, and sometimes, I'm not a very good person.'

He laughs and lifts my face to his. 'OK, well, if you say so. In that case, I'm happy that you're ordinary. I'm happy that you're you.'

'I'm just happy,' I say. 'In a way that I never thought I'd be again.'

* * *

When it's fully light, I hear the sounds of the cars in the drive – the film crew arriving. Luke stretches out and yawns. 'That time already?'

'I'm afraid so.'

I start to swing out of bed, but he stops me. First with a kiss, but then, with hesitation.

'I want this, Lizzie. More than anything. I know it's early days, but I want you to know that. It's just…'

Two words and a pause – they slam into me like a cement wall.

'Yes?'

'I think it would be better if we kept this to ourselves for now.'

'Of course. I don't want to put you in an awkward position on set.'

'It's not so much that as, well… Phillipa.'

I picture the last time I saw her, a piece of jagged glass pressed into her hand. I expect she's been at the other location all this time, as I haven't seen or heard from her. But now that the crew is back, I'll have to see her again. What will she be thinking? I don't feel guilty over Luke and me, but I also don't have a clue what to say to her.

'I won't tell Phillipa – or anyone else,' I say. 'But please, Luke, tell me that there's nothing else. Nothing that I should be worried about, for now at least.'

He reaches over and takes my hand. 'I don't want to have any secrets from you, Lizzie. That's why I told you about my past. Believe it or not, I never told my ex-wife the story. I guess at first it seemed irrelevant to our fake, glamorous existence. And then, the longer I waited, it became too late. I hope I've made the right decision this time. Because I don't want to ruin what we could have.' He brushes a finger against my cheek and over my lips.

I suddenly want to hold him, crawl back into bed and pull the covers over us. Breathe in the smell of his skin and feel his body against mine. Because last night, he made me feel safe; like together, we might be invincible. But that's not reality. If I've learned one thing, it's that life is about coping with whatever happens, not trying to shut it out.

'Then don't ruin it.' I pull him close and stand on tiptoes to kiss him on the mouth, my fingers tangling in his hair. 'Now, you'd better get in the shower or you'll be late for work.' I trace a smile on his lips.

'Fine,' he says. 'Join me?'

'In a minute,' I say. 'First I'd better get on with fixing up your precious film set.' I cock my head towards the messy bed. 'Which, you'll agree, really needs a change of sheets.'

54

As soon as Luke is gone, a wave of anxiety sweeps through me. What does he see in me? I feel so ordinary. He's given me no reason to doubt him – I'm no longer convinced that he's after the likes of Phillipa, or even Natasha Blythe. Even so, he could have his pick of women on set if he chose. I suppose it will take time for my new reality to sink in, and being insecure won't help anything.

At least three people spot me as I'm going downstairs from the bedroom. Luke's assistant, Laura, one of the cameramen, and... Dominic Kennedy.

He's clearly dressed for some 'ladykilling' – his white shirt billowing open, showing a well-muscled (and, I imagine, shaved) chest; his breeches tight in all the right places.

'Oh my, Elizabeth,' he says, giving me the full treatment of his long-lashed 'bedroom eyes'. 'Wasn't Luke looking a whole new man this morning? Well done you.' He takes an imaginary hat off his head and bows with a mock flourish.

'I don't know what you're talking about.' A flush creeps down my neck.

'We've been placing bets, you know. About how long it would take that domino to fall.' His laugh is so over the top that I laugh too. In truth, hearing him validate what's happened – even if he can't possibly know anything about it – makes me feel a lot better. Like I can do anything.'

'And how did you do?' I say. 'In the betting pool?'

'Oh, you two – both tough nuts to crack. So proud and downright pig-headed. Weak-minded fools like myself can only draw upon our own experiences. I'm afraid I've lost pots of money, it's taken so long. But no hard feelings. I just hope he hasn't caught it on film. Might put me out of a job. I'm afraid my darling Natasha is having a few problems getting into character.'

'Sorry to hear that.'

'Yes, well' – he rubs the five o'clock shadow on his jaw – 'Luke's good at what he does, but I'm not sure he'll be able to pull a rabbit out of that hat. But we'll give it a go. Today's the big day.'

'The love scene? That's *today*?' I choke back a laugh.

'Yes.' He frowns. 'Though the dialogue is still a bit rubbish. I'll just have to pretend it's you in that big bed of yours. Or maybe, the three of us.'

'Which three?' I joke.

'Ah…' This time, I've surprised him. 'Good question.'

I reach out and punch him playfully on the arm. 'You're incorrigible,' I say.

'Yes, well, I've got a reputation to keep up – so to speak.'

'That's it,' I say, laughing, 'I'm leaving.'

'I understand, love.' He pulls me to him and gives me an over-egged kiss on the cheek. 'And I'm sure that's absolutely for the best.'

* * *

When I go outside to the marquee, I get the feeling that everyone knows about Luke and me. For one thing, people who have never even said hello to me before are suddenly friendly, and asking me, 'Hi, Lizzie, you OK?' One of them asks me about the kids and the seaside, and it's then I realise that Connie might well have been in on the plot.

But nothing deflates the good mood I'm in. Little things remind me of last night – Luke's name on the call sheet, the props table full of candles like the one we lit – and with each flash of memory, I feel like I'm sparkling all over. It doesn't even bother me that the entire morning session consists of filming Dominic and Natasha Blythe pretending to make love in my bed. In fact, it feels oddly... liberating.

As the morning progresses, I gather that things aren't going particularly well: forty-five takes and still no 'rabbit from a hat'. But when Luke comes downstairs during the mid-morning break, I get the distinct feeling that he's not overly bothered by it. He's busy, and we don't speak, but when he looks at me, I'm overcome by a shiver of desire. I watch as he scribbles notes on a copy of one of the scripts. He writes something at the bottom, tears it off, folds it over, and hands it to an assistant who hands it off to another assistant. Though I'm less than ten meters away, it gets delivered to me. I unfold it, feeling like everyone's watching us, though most people are at least pretending to be about their business.

Dinner? the note says.

I nod once in his direction and walk out of the tent.

***

Without the children around, I spend some time working on the business plan for the B&B. I keep careful notes of all the start-up costs that I'll be incurring. Though in the end, it was determined that the likely cause of the flooding was the excavation near the lake, and John C reluctantly agreed to contact his insurers to cover the costs of the drain men, the whole incident was a sobering wake-up call as to how fragile my finances are going to be for the first year, maybe longer. Nonetheless, with the flood waters having receded, I get on with ordering towels and bed sheets, and a set of dishes to use for the breakfasts. It's the first time I've done any real shopping since my splurge at M&S, the date with Theo now a distant memory. I wish I had time to buy something new to wear to dinner with Luke, but I don't feel like braving the crowds and fitting room queues. Besides, I already feel that Luke accepts me for who I am, and the rest can come later.

I make myself coffee and take it upstairs. It feels odd to be in the guest room again after a night in the big canopy bed. The room is untidy with toys and clothing on the floor, the bed unmade. As I'm tucking in the sheets, I find Julie's diary under the mattress. I still don't know what to do with it, and I probably should have mentioned it to Luke last night. But understandably, my mind was on... other things.

I sit down on the bed and open the book. Now that it's been inside the house for over a week, the damp pages have dried out further and a few more towards the back come unstuck when I pull on them.

I read the first new entry:

...stupid camera. Following us around all the time. I'm pretty sure he's noticed. Before, it was just annoying, but now, I'm starting to feel really...

...is worried too. I wish he wasn't here at all – that it was just us. And soon it will be.

I feel a tiny stab of alarm reading the words, but the next two pages are stuck together, and I can't read on. On the third page, however, I can make out more of Julie's writing in her favourite purple pen.

Mum discovered that the money was missing from the desk drawer. I've never seen her so angry. But angry I can handle. Because she'll never find it, and soon we'll be gone. I'm soooo happy. I can't wait to get away from here for good.

Stolen money, running away? Normally I'd just chalk up what I've read to the shenanigans of a teenage girl. But Julie died that summer – she got away for good, but not in the way she'd planned. And there's another thing niggling at me that I can't quite put my finger on.

Gingerly, I pull apart the next page and read on.

...says she doesn't want to any more. It's just so unfair. I hate her – she makes me sick. He's ruined everything. But I'm not going to let them...

A picture is building in my mind – one that I'd rather erase. Things went on that summer that no one's talking about – certainly not Luke, and certainly not to me.

I make out one last entry:

...got me feeling really scared...

I close the diary, my stomach queasy and unsettled. It all happened so long ago – does it even matter any more? Is this little book, that I failed to mention to Luke when I had the chance, going to be the thing that spoils everything? I think of what Phillipa said about the glass in Julie's skull; about Luke following them, watching them. Her words had planted a seed of doubt in my head. But he told me he didn't hurt either of them, and I've said that I believe him...

Did he do it? Victoria's thoughts from *The Lady's Secret* pop into my mind. And I think of the way Luke's lips feel against mine, the way my skin glows when he touches me. I think of the look in those green eyes, no longer haunted but full of warmth and passion. And just like Victoria, I begin to question everything – especially my own values, and my own role in the story that is still haunting the walls of this house.

Did he do it?

Do I care?

55

THE LADY'S SECRET BY PHILLIPA KING

'You,' the voice hissed. 'You think you can come here and ruin everything, Tilly? Or should I say... Victoria?'

'So you've discovered who I am, Belle.'

'You had a husband and you threw him away. You came here, charmed your way into my lover's bed.'

'He's not your lover if he's so easily won over.' Victoria felt oddly calm, even as the knife pressed harder into her flesh.

'William and I were meant to be wed, but my sister got in a bad way with a local boy. She told my father it was William's, though he had never laid a hand on her. My father persuaded him to marry her – he was a magistrate and could turn a blind eye to certain "activities" of William's.'

'So that's why they married. He did it out of honour.'

She laughs. 'Is that what you call it? But anyway, Charity lost the baby so it was all for naught. I hated her for that.'

'You killed her. Your own sister.' Victoria made to turn, but the knife was suddenly at her throat.

'I killed her,' Belle said. 'And now, you filthy little whore, it's your turn.'

As the blade pierced her skin, Victoria acted. She grabbed Belle's hand holding the knife and with her other hand brought the brass candlestick up hard into her jaw. The woman's eyes widened in shock for a brief second, before she lost her footing. Victoria tried to grab her clawing hands and stop the fall, but it was too late. With a scream of terror, Belle slid down the steep slates in front of the chimney.

Victoria mouthed a silent prayer as she was suddenly alone on the roof.

56

Late in the afternoon, the marquee is buzzing. Apparently, after spending the entire day trying, they finally got a useable take of Victoria Easterbrook and William Clarke making love in my bed. Dominic Kennedy comes out of the house, looking exhausted and gorgeously dishevelled. He gives me a grin like the cat that caught the canary.

'Got there in the end, did you?' I say.

'Natasha's quite something!' he says. 'Just between you and me, I think she liked having to do it over and over again.'

'I'm sure that's it.' I roll my eyes.

'Now that we've rehearsed it, I'm hoping to do it for real – too bad the cameras won't be rolling.'

'You'd better have your evil way with her somewhere else besides my bed.'

'Of course.' He winks. 'I'm fully aware that *votre chambre à coucher est occupé*. But I've found a nice little country hotel over the way. Natasha's agreed to have tea with me there.' He reaches into his waistband and pulls out a silver flask of the same vintage as Connie's – or maybe it is Connie's – and unscrews the top. 'So, bottom's up!' He takes a long swig. 'Quite literally.'

He holds the flask out to me, but I wave it away. 'Have fun,' I say. 'Hope it's not too exhausting.'

'Well, if it isn't, there's a nice young waiter there who's been eyeing me up. So either way, I'm glad Luke's given us tomorrow off.'

'Has he?' I flush in surprise.

'Yes. Didn't you know?' He lowers his eyelashes. 'That's why he and I get on so well – great minds think alike and all that.'

* * *

When Dominic is gone, I return to the house. Luke's still tied up with the technical people, but I've heard rumours of an early finish so I decide I should dress for dinner. Dinner with Luke, and then a whole night and a whole Sunday free. This morning, it all seemed like a dream come true.

I put on a light cotton summer dress, then brush my hair and put on make-up and earrings. When I study myself in the mirror, I look young and happy, and carefree.

Too bad looks can be deceiving.

I flop down on the bed, cursing myself. Why did I decide to read the diary, and why didn't I tell Luke about it as soon as I found it? Now I feel it hanging over my head like Macbeth's dagger: incorporeal and invisible, but a sinister presence nonetheless. I'll bring it to the restaurant, I decide. It may ruin the meal, but I've got to get it out in the open. My relationship with Dave was riddled with secrets and lies. I don't want that for me and Luke.

My mobile phone rings on the nightstand, startling me from my thoughts. I'm expecting it to be Connie – though she's already texted me some pictures of the kids having a great time at the seaside. Instead, Theo's name flashes on screen. I haven't seen him since the day 'Veronica' was brought up from the tunnel. I debate for several rings whether to answer it, and finally decide that I'd better do so.

'Hi, Theo,' I say, 'you OK?'

'I'm fine. But I was wondering if you've spoken to Phillipa. I'm worried about her. She was supposed to be on set today, but Richard said she never turned up. And lately she's seemed... I don't know. Different.'

'Sorry, Theo, I haven't seen her or spoken to her since before the hiatus.'

'It's OK, Lizzie. I shouldn't have asked. Sorry to bother you.'

The call ends.

Odd, I think as I put the phone aside. There's a knock at the door, and I instantly forget all about the call.

'Lizzie, it's me.' My body reacts to Luke's voice even before my mind has processed that it's him.

'Hi.' I fling open the door. He looks tired, but his face lights up when he sees me. His shirt is damp with sweat as he pulls me to him. We kiss each other long and deeply, and my earlier doubts and worries flee to a dark corner of my subconscious. All I'm aware of is the sheer unlikely joy of Luke and me.

'Hold that thought, tiger,' he says as we eventually come up for air. 'I've booked us a table for eight o'clock, so we'd better get on the train.'

'The train?'

'It's a little place I know in London near my flat in Primrose Hill. I hope you don't mind.'

I smile. 'You gave the cast the day off tomorrow. That's out of character for you, isn't it?'

'A little bird – OK, a rather largish bird – phoned me to say she'd be out all Sunday with a couple of lovely children, and not returning until the evening.'

'So Connie has been in on this all along!'

'In my job, you quickly learn that the most important part of the creative process is the logistics behind the scenes. You learn to accept what help is offered. Connie and I have had, shall we say, an exchange of favours.'

I punch him playfully in the chest. 'I should have known.'

'Right now,' he says, sweeping me up again in his arms, 'I'd say we both have quite a lot to thank your ex-mother-in-law for.'

* * *

We don't make the train, or the restaurant. We stay in bed until well after eight, when finally, I'm satiated but starving.

'Pub?' He teases my ear with his lips.

'Sure,' I say, 'though if you keep that up, we may never get out of here and we might starve.'

He laughs and points to the light above the bed. 'By the way, is that your dreamcatcher?'

The feathers move ever so slightly from his breath, the beads catching the light. I realise that ever since that night by the lake, I haven't dreamed of my mysterious stranger. I run my fingers over Luke's face, memorising it, imprinting it into my subconscious. 'Yes,' I say as he pulls me to him again. 'Connie and Simon gave it to me. I'm happy to say that it works very well.'

We don't leave the bedroom for another hour. By that time, neither of us are in the mood for going out at all, and he offers to make dinner instead. 'I'm not much of a cook though,' he admits.

'Good, because all I've got is pasta.'

'Pasta I can do.'

I put on a pair of jeans and a T-shirt and we go downstairs together to the kitchen.

As he's getting out the pan, I go down to the cellar to find a bottle of wine. The water has receded but there's a cloying atmosphere of damp. The chasm at the bottom of the stairs has been covered over with a large metal plate, the kind they use for roadworks. The new washing machine and separate tumble dryer are on top of it. I can still hear the faint sound of dripping water and the occasional swoosh of the pump. I have an odd sensation of being underwater, struggling to breathe. I grab a bottle from the rack, eager to be out of the cellar. But the phantom water has reminded me once again of something I'd rather forget. Julie's diary. As much as I don't want to ruin the evening – and everything else – I know what I have to do.

I hand Luke the bottle and tell him I'll be back in a minute. I run upstairs and get the little book from underneath the mattress. I feel a strong reluctance to show it to him. The lovely evening – the pasta cooking on the stove, the nice bottle of wine, the man I'm falling in love with – will they be spoiled by my finding the diary? Stained?

When I return to the kitchen, Luke is standing with his back to me, watching the water bubbling in the pan. 'Luke,' I say, 'I found this.'

I hold up the little book.

'What's that?' The water in the pan begins to boil over; he turns down the heat.

I set the diary on the table and walk over to the window, staring out at the lake. From that angle, I can't see the dovecote, though a part of me can sense its dark, looming presence. Steeling myself, I take a breath.

'It's Julie's diary.'

'Her diary?' He turns towards me, his eyes suddenly hooded and unreadable.

'I found it in the dovecote,' I say. 'Up in one of the pigeonholes.'

'When was this?'

'The day when Katie and Phillipa were out there.'

'That was over a week ago.' There's an edge to his voice.

'Well, you weren't here, were you?'

He turns back to the stove to stir the pasta in the pan. I want to go to him, tell him that I don't want a row over this. But I stay rooted to the spot, waiting for him.

'What does it say?' he asks absently.

'A lot of the pages are stuck together with damp. I managed to pull a few of them apart. There were some things in there though – about some money that got stolen, and some talk of running away. I couldn't make heads or tails of it, to be honest.'

'I don't really want to read it, or dredge up those memories. Back then, everything seemed so important. So urgent. But I'd thought – hoped – we were done with it.'

'I think Julie was scared, Luke. Was she was scared of you?'

I hold my breath as he sets down the spoon and comes over to me. I can tell that he's angry and trying to hold it in.

'Why would you think that?' he says. 'I told you the truth – I was a boy with a crush on a girl. That summer it was Pippa. I loved Julie too, but more like a sister. We were good friends, and I didn't understand why everything changed between us. And yeah, I did make a nuisance of myself: following her and Pippa around, filming them. I saw a few things I shouldn't have. I told Julie I was going to tell Aunt Roz. But I never did. Maybe I should have.'

'What did you see?' The words come out haltingly, as I don't really want to hear the answer.

He turns and looks out the window at the waning light. 'Grab a torch,' he says, 'and I'll show you.'

57

He drains the pasta into the colander and I get a torch from the drawer. My feet feel leaden as I follow him out the back door and onto the lawn. He stops underneath the huge plane tree by the shore of the lake near where the dock is being constructed.

'This tree has seen a lot.' He shines the torch over the bark, searching. About three feet up from the bottom of the trunk, there's a bald patch where the bark has been peeled away. He crouches down and runs his fingers over the blond surface of the wood.

'Here,' he says.

I kneel down beside him. There are some scratches in the wood, deep and deliberate. Initials in a wonky heart. I can make out what might be a 'P' at one end, with a '+' sign next to it. The other initial, however, is harder to make out. A straight vertical line.

'Is it an "L"?' I say, my heart tightening. Luke and Phillipa, Phillipa and Luke.

'No.' He runs his fingers over a fainter line that I can barely make out jutting out from the bottom. 'It's a "J".'

'"P" for Phillipa, "J" for Julie?'

'Yes.'

The truth slams into place.

'You mean they were... together?'

'Does that shock you?' He traces the outline of the heart.

I think back to the entries I read in the diary – Julie's initial reluctance to accept Phillipa, followed by her ever-growing infatuation with her new stepsister. 'I don't know,' I say. 'Maybe that was true on Julie's side. But you said that you and Phillipa – you know...' I can't bring myself to say it.

'Phillipa toyed with people,' he says. 'She wanted all of us to love her. Worship her, even. And I guess we all did. She also liked to hurt people. She played me off against Julie.'

I nod silently as another piece of the puzzle clicks into place in my head. The tree, the initials. I've never looked closely at the tree, and I had no idea something was carved into the trunk. Not consciously, at least. But there's a part of my brain that did know.

The part that's read *The Lady's Secret*.

'The opening scene,' I say. 'Victoria is on a blanket by the river with Tom. He cuts an apple with a knife, then uses the knife to carve their initials in the tree.'

'Yes,' Luke says. 'We filmed it two weeks ago.'

I swallow hard. 'And then Victoria is "seduced" by Tom. I suppose that could have been Julie. Or maybe Max. I don't know – it's ambiguous.'

'It also could have been me, Lizzie. You only have my word that it didn't happen.'

'Which is enough,' I assert. 'I said I believed you, and I do.'

He rips at a piece of loose bark. 'You've already asked me the million-dollar question. Why Phillipa wanted to come back, and why she wanted me here with her. I told you what she said – about catharsis and returning to the scene so that we can move on. But the truth is, I have no idea. She's manipulative. I suppose she wants to control me, or maybe she genuinely thought that after all these years, we might have a future.' He shakes his head. 'And now that things are completely different, and I actually *want* to be here – I don't want this to spoil everything.'

I step closer to him and put my hands to his face. Tears are sparkling in his eyes, making them even more vivid in the darkness. 'It won't spoil things if you don't let it. You have to let the past go, Luke.' I wipe away his tears like he once did for me. 'If we're going to have a future together, then you have to move on. Can you do that?'

He folds me in his arms and I rest my head on his chest, listening to the beating of his heart.

'And as for Phillipa – she's hurt and angry, and jealous,' I say. 'I understand all those emotions. And finally, she's not getting her way with people. With you. I feel sorry for her.'

Nodding, he strokes my hair. 'I suppose she identifies with Victoria. A woman seeking her happy ending. Only, she didn't find it. Not here, anyway.'

'Does such a thing even exist in real life?'

'I don't know, Lizzie, and I don't care.' He lifts my face to his. 'I'm not looking for a happy ending.' He kisses me gently. 'Because I don't want this to end at all.'

* * *

I put Julie's diary back upstairs and we don't speak of it again. Instead, we eat the pasta and drink the wine, talking of other things. Our jobs, our favourite films; books, art, places we've travelled to. The more I get to know him, the more I find we have quite a bit in common. I tell him about my family: how my father died when I was nineteen, and how I wish I'd been more supportive of my mum and grown closer to her rather than further apart.

I tell him in detail about what happened with Dave, resulting in so many ugly emotions and the loss of my self-esteem. I tell him all my secrets, shining a light into the shadows. Confronting them; banishing them. He takes me in his arms and I cry a little. He whispers in my ear that I'm beautiful and that I deserve to be happy and loved. And in the moment, I feel all of those things. I dry my tears and tell him more stories about the kids. He laughs, and tells me stories of film set antics that make me laugh. Eventually, however, the conversation works around to the one thing that still terrifies me.

The future.

'I'm not going to lie to you, Lizzie,' Luke says. 'I'm not the easiest person to be with. My job is very demanding. It can be very draining physically and emotionally. I have to travel a lot, be away a lot. It will be hard for you, and I worry how it would be on the kids.'

The kids. Never for a second has he disregarded them or tried to ignore that they are a critical part of the equation. To me, that means everything. 'But you'd... come back?' I say. 'Right?'

'I know it's early days, Lizzie, but I feel like you're my sanctuary. You, this place – a family. I'd love to be a part of it. Jack and Katie are such great kids. I mean, I know I'm not seeing the whole picture, and that it must be the hardest job in the world to be a parent. I've got two younger brothers so I know a little bit about it. And I guess I always thought...' He hesitates. 'Well, anyway. Not having a family is the biggest regret of my life – and that's saying a lot.'

'You don't want children of your own?'

I watch him closely as he considers the question.

'For me, that's not the most important thing.' His smile melts away my fears. 'I want... you... us.'

Our hands entwine across the table, and I find myself talking about my own dream of opening the B&B. A dream that I'm already making a reality. 'It would be a lot of work, of course,' I say, 'and without my job in London, money will be tight. But I'm used to that now.'

'I could—'

'No.' I put a finger to his lips. 'Absolutely not. This is something I have to do on my own.'

'I get it,' he says. 'And it's a great idea. Maybe you could get a proper bar installed – I've always wanted to serve up hand-pulled pints.' He grins.

'You have not!' I laugh.

'OK, maybe not.'

Laughing too, he stands up, clearing away the dishes. I come and join him at the sink to do the washing-up, our fingers touching in the sudsy water and sending little electric sparks down my body. Then he leans over and nuzzles my hair.

'Hey,' I say, dabbing a sudsy finger on his nose. 'Stop that or we'll never finish.'

'Stop what?' His wet hand travels down my front and inside the waistband of my jeans.

'Nothing,' I whisper, succumbing to the new-found realisation that with the right man, even the little things can be twice as nice the second time round.

58

I lie in bed, my body twined with Luke's, feeling happy and content. His breathing grows even, and I listen to his heart beating next to mine. No matter what the future may bring, right now, I feel open and willing to face it. Inside me, there's a deep and growing sense of hope.

I close my eyes, but sleep doesn't come. My mind drifts to Victoria Easterbrook and *The Lady's Secret*. Since finishing the book the first time, I've read most of it again, generally out of sequence in accordance with the call sheet. Women of Victoria's time and situation would have been at the mercy of others – of men – and been largely powerless over their own lives. How odd that we find their stories so romantic. I remember the picture on the cover of the book: the twisted gateposts of the manor house, the wild auburn hair of the heroine. I'd judged the book by its cover. Dismissed it as an enjoyably titillating, but ultimately unremarkable, story.

It's all there in in the book.

Phillipa once told me that part of the fantasy of a romance novel is convincing the reader that the author has found that elusive secret to everlasting love that she or he can impart to the rest of us. When often, the truth is something quite different. I think of everything I've learned about her and Julie – and Luke. For some reason, her words are like a tick in an old vinyl record, keeping me awake when I'd rather be asleep. A part of the equation is still missing; there's something I'm not quite seeing. As much as I want to put the past behind us, and for Luke to do the same, I worry about the undiscovered truths that are still festering below the surface.

Gently, so as not to wake him, I disentangle myself from Luke. I find my e-reader and Julie's diary and go down to the kitchen. I pour myself a cup of yesterday's coffee, take a notebook and pencil from the drawer, and sit down at the table.

When I open up the diary, I find that a few more pages near the end have come unstuck. But Julie used a felt-tip pen to write and most of the words are smudged. I manage to decipher a few more passages. The first one seems to be about Luke:

He's always following us around and watching us. It's totally creepy. I think he saw us under the tree that day when I gave her the daisy...

...she doesn't seem to mind. She even flirts with him sometimes. I swear, I'm going to show her that she can't just...

The Watcher? Luke? I make a column on the paper and jot down the reference, followed by 'initials', and 'daisy ring'.

...can't believe she lost the money. I mean, I only did it to help her. But she said that he took it. I think the two of them might be planning...

I transcribe the words, but I'm not sure what to make of them. In a previous entry, Julie spoke of stealing some money. Just as Victoria did early on in the novel, prying her father's desk drawer open with a lizard-shaped paperknife.

She just doesn't get it. I mean, she's part of the family now. She started crying when I ripped up the photo of her mum, but doesn't she see I did it for her own good?

I jot down the reference. In the book, the Watcher destroys Victoria's locket with a miniature painting of her mother. But in the diary version – Julie, not Luke, destroyed the photo.

> *...I mean, I'm the one who loves her. But she just laughed and said I was totally...*
> *I hate it when she laughs like that.*

Phillipa and Julie – two girls with more between them than just a teenage crush. They stole money to run away, and then Phillipa lost it – or it was taken. Luke saw them together and threatened to let the cat out of the bag. Another question mark...

The rest of the diary is unreadable; the pages flake to dust when I try to pull them apart. I push it aside and then tackle *The Lady's Secret*.

To be honest, a lot of the plot details in between the love scenes went over my head on the first read. But this time, I focus on the little things that I missed before. The opening chapters that reveal the initials on the tree, the broken locket, the daisy ring, the stolen money. I reread the Watcher scenes: the malevolent figure, the dead bird, the shredded gown. There are many missing pieces, and it seems that Phillipa's chopped and changed the characters and their various roles. But as the hours go by and the moon rises over the lake and then dips again below the horizon, ever so slowly, a new story begins to emerge.

* * *

It's almost dawn when I crumple up the piece of paper with my musings. I leave the diary and the e-reader behind on the table and go back upstairs to crawl into bed with Luke. I'm exhausted, but also frustrated with myself. There's something there – I'm sure of it – but there are so many red herrings and misdirections that I can't put my finger on it.

Luke wakes up briefly, and I fall asleep in his arms, my body cocooned in his. We stay in bed late, until eventually he gets up and goes downstairs to make breakfast for me. In the light of day, whatever it is I was looking for last night and didn't find seems like pure fantasy.

I shower and get dressed and check my phone to see if Connie has texted any more photos from the seaside. She hasn't but there are three missed calls from last night – all from Theo.

I go downstairs and show the phone to Luke.

'You're not two-timing me, are you?' he jokes. His smile fades when I don't laugh.

'He rang me yesterday evening. He sounded a bit off. He's worried about Phillipa. Asked me if I'd seen her. I'm afraid I wasn't terribly keen to discuss whatever the issue is.'

'Can't imagine why.'

I stare at the pitcher of orange juice and the plates set out on the kitchen table. There are also two coffee cups – Luke's and one that's half-full of coffee pushed to one side. I'd put my cup from last night in the dishwasher before going to bed. The cup on the table has a smear of pink lipstick on the rim.

'Where's the diary?' I say.

'The diary?' Luke frowns. 'I don't know. Why?'

'I came down in the night and I had it with me. I left it on the table.'

'I haven't seen it.' He stares at me. 'Why were you looking at it again?'

Before I can think of an answer, the phone rings in my hand. Theo's name comes up as before.

Luke raises an eyebrow. I answer the phone.

'Lizzie!' Theo sounds breathless. 'Thank God I got you.'

'I'm sorry I couldn't talk yesterday. What's the matter?'

'Phillipa's disappeared. I mean... well, I hope this doesn't upset you, but we've kind of started seeing each other.' He pauses awkwardly.

'OK,' I coax.

'But she's been acting so strange lately, and last night we had plans but she didn't turn up. Now she's not answering her phone. It's been almost twenty-four hours.'

'She's a grown woman, Theo. But I haven't heard from her. Have you tried the hotel?'

'She's not there. It's just, the way she's been lately, I'm worried that she might do something... I don't know. Maybe I'm totally wrong.'

He's speaking so loud that Luke overhears. 'Can I talk to him?' he mouths.

I hold out the phone.

'Theo,' he says, 'Luke here. What's going on?'

But as I stare again at the cup with the smear of lipstick, I stop listening to the conversation. I rush out of the room and put on my shoes.

Leaving through the main door, I run round the side of the house and race along the borders towards the far gate to the paddock.

'Lizzie, wait!' I hear Luke calling out behind me, but I ignore him. Because this isn't about him – not any more. The last piece of the puzzle has finally clicked into place.

59

In only a few days' time, stingers have grown up on either side of the forest path. I can feel them lashing against my ankles as I run, but I don't stop. By the time I get to the dovecote, I'm panting for breath and flushed with fear. The last thing I want is another tragedy.

'Phillipa!' I yell out.

Since I was here last, Simon has clearly been at work. Outside, there's a pile of rotten boards that he's taken up from the floor. The broken pane of glass has been repaired and a plank nailed across the door with a sign on it that says 'Danger Keep Out'. But behind the plank and the sign, the door is wide open. Phillipa must have taken the key from the kitchen.

There's no response. I run up the stairs.

Phillipa is sitting on the balcony just like the last time, her legs dangling over the edge. The water below is dark and murky. The pink diary is on her lap, and beside her is a small pile of shredded paper, a book of matches, and a small silver letter opener with a lizard on the handle. I recognise it from the props table.

The upper floor now consists of a lattice of joists, some of which are clearly rotting away. All but a few boards on top have been removed. Holding my breath, I carefully tiptoe from joist to joist, trying not to look down at the ten-foot drop onto the stone floor below. I reach the other side and exhale. My heart, though, is thundering in my chest.

'Phillipa,' I say. 'People are worried. Let's go back.'

'Lizzie?' Luke's voice comes from below.

Laughing, Phillipa takes a match and lights the pile of shredded paper. The words of Julie from beyond the grave go up in a small whorl of grey smoke.

'You'll never be able to prove anything, Lizzie,' she says.

'Maybe not. But I think you want to tell the truth, don't you? Otherwise, you wouldn't have come back here.'

'Lizzie?' Luke reaches the top of the steps.

'Keep him away,' Phillipa says, picking up the letter opener.

I turn to Luke. He nods warily, but remains at the top of the stairs. An ocean of empty space separates us now.

'Don't do anything you'll regret, Phillipa,' I say.

As soon as the words are out, I know it's the wrong thing to say.

'I regret everything.'

'All this time,' I say, 'I've been asking myself why you came back here. But now I think I know. You wanted to atone, didn't you? *The Lady's Secret* isn't a romance. It's a confession.'

'A confession.' She mulls over the word. 'Interesting theory.'

I take a second to gather my thoughts. 'You were Victoria all along. Most of it – the romance bits – were pure fantasy. But you scattered little clues along the way that told the true story.'

She crosses her arms. 'Maybe you should be the fiction writer, not me.'

'Maybe. But at the beginning of that summer, everything was perfect, wasn't it? Everyone loved and admired you. Luke and Julie both had a crush on you. And then there was Max, Julie's older brother. He liked you too. But that's when things started to go wrong. You and he were an item, but then he dropped you.'

'You make it sound so poetic,' she says, pressing the tip of the knife into her palm. 'It was Max's birthday. He got me drunk and wanted sex. Just like in the opening chapter. And have you guessed what happened next? Because even Luke – who's studied the book cover to cover – hasn't figured out the truth. But then again, he's a man.'

'What Max did was despicable,' I say. 'And worst of all, I think you got pregnant. You were stuck, just like Victoria was.'

'You have no idea what it was like. I felt so alone. The only one I could tell – the only person who understood me – was Julie.'

'You used Julie and the feelings she had for you. You led her on – gave her a daisy ring and carved your initials on the tree. Then you asked her to steal money from her mum. You told her that it was to run away together.'

'I did what I had to do. I needed money to have an abortion. It was utterly ridiculous, but she chose to go along with it. At first, anyway.'

'At first, yes,' I say. 'But then things started to go sour. It was fine when it was you and her against the world. Sunbathing and sharing make-up tips. But then Luke came. You toyed with him too, and that made Julie angry. She started acting weird, didn't she?'

'Weird?' She laughs. 'Julie started stalking me. She destroyed the one photo I had of my mum. Then she cut up my clothes with scissors and left a dead bird on my pillow. She was crackers.'

'She was the Watcher, right? It wasn't Luke at all.'

'Luke.' She smirks. 'Mr Innocent. Following us around, taking his videos. Among other things.'

'The stolen money.' I glance at Luke. 'You took that, right?'

'I did it for your own good,' he growls at Phillipa. 'At least, that's what I told myself at the time. I didn't want you and Julie to get in trouble.'

'And got a nice lens for your camera out of it too, didn't you?'

'Yes.' He nods. 'I'm not proud of that, obviously.'

Phillipa laughs. 'Julie was livid that I'd lost the money. She thought I had a thing going with Luke – that it was us against her. In the end, I couldn't stand it any more. I went out to the party that night to find Max. I'd decided to tell him the truth and get him to help me. It was his fault after all. But he just laughed at me. I was so upset; I just wanted someone to hold me. But Luke wanted more than that. So I gave it to him.' She gives me a satisfied look, knowing full well that I don't want to hear about it.

'Yes,' I say, trying not to show any emotion. 'Your game of truth or dare. In the middle of the dare, Julie walked in on you.'

'In a way,' she says, 'I was glad. I thought she'd finally get the hint. But Luke chickened out. He walked away and left the two of us alone. I thought she'd want to have it out, but she ran upstairs.' She presses her lips together and for a moment, I worry that she won't continue.

'What happened?'

'I went upstairs after her. She screamed at me – I'd never seen her so angry. But I never thought for a second that she might be dangerous.' She turns and looks at Luke. I take a step backwards but there's nowhere to go.

Luke's eyes are wide, his face panic-stricken. 'Wait a second. You told me that Julie went up to the balcony but that you didn't follow her. I asked you about it – more than once. You said you stayed downstairs to "give her time to cool her head". You told me that she jumped off the balcony to have a swim like the others had been doing. That's' – he lowers his voice – 'what you told me to say at the inquest. What I did say...'

Phillipa gives him a pained look. 'Sadly, Luke, in the end, you were the only one I could count on. If I've never said it before – thank you.'

'Tell me what happened.' He takes a step forward onto the rickety joists.

'No. Don't,' I say sharply. To my relief, he steps back.

'The truth is, I went out to the balcony,' Phillipa continues. 'Julie was raving – going on about how much she loved me – and hated me.' She takes a breath. 'I'm afraid I laughed in her face. So she picked up an empty bottle and came at me. She tried to hit me, but I managed to grab another one.'

She stops speaking again and turns away. But not before I've seen the haunted look darkening her eyes.

'The bottle shattered, and the force of the blow knocked her into the lake,' I say.

'Is that true, Phillipa?' Luke's voice is low and icy. 'You hit Julie on the head with a bottle?'

'You didn't mean to kill her, did you?' I interject. 'It all just happened so quickly. Just like in the book. Victoria is lured onto the roof by the Watcher – Belle. There's a struggle, and the heroine – that's you – defends herself and survives. Julie fell to her death. That's your secret – *The Lady's Secret* – such as it is.'

'The lady's secret,' Phillipa says, looking down at the dark water. 'In real life, it's more like a worm living inside you. It slowly eats away at your insides, wanting to be let out.'

'You killed her,' Luke says. Once again, he starts across the floor. I can see the joists bow under his weight. 'My God, Phillipa. You *killed* Julie. Why didn't you try to save her? Did you hate her so much?'

'Don't, Luke,' I say.

'You have no proof of anything,' Phillipa repeats. The last tendrils of smoke rise up from the little pile of ashes. 'And for your information, Luke, I didn't jump in and save her because I'm afraid of the water. I never learned to swim.'

From below there's another shout. Phillipa's name – and mine. It's Theo. I know he means well – like a knight in shining armour who bumbles in to slay the dragon and save the princess... and ends up making a complete hash of everything.

'Don't let him up here,' I say to Luke.

Luke starts making his way back to the stairs, but it's too late. Theo is already at the top. 'Phillipa!' he shouts. He runs out onto the floor. Under the combined weight of the two men, the rotten joists finally give way, collapsing like a house made of matchsticks. There's a cry as they both crash down to the floor below.

'Oh God!' I cover my hands with my mouth. All I can see is a cloud of dust and debris. 'Luke? Theo? Are you OK?'

There's no immediate answer, but after a few seconds, someone coughs.

'Luke?' I'm frantic to go to him, but I'm trapped too. The entire floor is gone, and I'm stuck out on the balcony with Phillipa.

'Help!' Theo cries out. 'My leg – it's stuck.'

'Hold on!' I say. 'I'll try to climb down. Luke – are you there too?'

But there's no answer.

'Is there a way to climb down from here?' I say to Phillipa. I go to the balcony railing and lean over, staring downwards to see if there're any foot or handholds. A tangle of wisteria vines snakes up the stones at one side, but it looks too fragile to bear the weight of an adult. My heart is in my throat; I have to get down.

'I'm not going anywhere.' Phillipa sweeps the ashes and debris into the lake.

'They need help down there.'

She shakes her head. 'You remember what I told you – that romance novels always need to have a happy ending. That's what readers expect. But real life isn't like that. Look what happened to poor Veronica Jones.'

'I'm going to try to climb down.'

She grabs me then, swift and hard by the wrist. 'No,' she says. 'You're staying right here.' She picks up the little silver knife. 'I know that you, and Luke too, think my book is soppy, fairy tale rubbish. And you're right – it is. I sold a lot of books, but now, I want to aim higher. You were right – I *do* want to tell the truth. There's no such thing as a happy ending...'

'Phillipa, stop it! We need to get help. Luke!' I yell out again. 'Theo, can you see Luke?'

'No,' he croaks. 'But I've got my phone. I just dialled 999.'

'OK, good.'

'Move back against the wall.' Phillipa brandishes the thin silver blade.

I take a step backwards, raising my hands, until my back is against the brickwork. My throat is so constricted that I can barely breathe, but I know my only chance of escape lies in not letting her see that I'm panicking.

'Don't be stupid, Phillipa,' I say. 'You don't want to make things worse. As you've said, there's no proof of what happened back then.'

'True.' Her laugh is wicked and sinister. 'But you and I have unfinished business, don't we? Do you know, I was stupid enough to think that coming back here with Luke might make all the difference? That we might finally be able to put it all behind us. He was the only one who stood by me all those years ago. I thought that maybe, we could finally have our moment. But you've taken that away, Lizzie.'

'Stop it, Phillipa.' I try to step forward but my knees are shaking too hard. 'Back off and let me go.'

There's a rustling and snapping sound coming from the woody tangle of wisteria vines and ivy below the balcony. A few seconds later, behind

Phillipa, Luke's head appears just above the floor of the balcony. He puts a finger to his lips and grabs the railing. There's an almighty screeching sound as the metal bends under his weight. I gasp, unable to move. Phillipa whirls around. Luke grabs the vine, clinging onto it.

'Don't come up here,' she hisses.

Luke tries to pull himself up, but Phillipa goes to the railing and jiggles it, until it's attached only by a single rusty bolt.

'Let Lizzie go,' Luke says. 'It's me you want. We're in this together, Pippa – we always will be. I see that now.'

Phillipa laughs. '"Together forever" – is that the best you can do, Luke? I think you'll find that you're in no position to be calling the shots.'

'No,' I say. 'But neither are you.'

I lunge forward and try to grab the blade in her hand. But she pulls her arm away and I go sprawling onto the fragile stone. I wait for her to advance on me, to feel the cold steel penetrate my skin. I'm aware of Luke crawling onto the balcony, and for a second I feel a blinding fear that he's the one she'll turn against.

He reaches out to grab her leg, but she steps back against the railing. Her eyes are upon me as she drops the blade. And then, she goes over the edge. For an agonising moment, she seems to hang in the air. Then a huge splash erupts as she hits the water and disappears beneath the surface.

My body reacts before my mind. I rush to the edge and dive off into the void.

'Lizzie!' Luke cries out.

I pierce the surface of the cold, dark water, sinking down to the black and airless depths. The hazy green light above seems so far away. I open my eyes, desperately searching for Phillipa. Her answer to Luke's question shrieks into my mind. *I never learned to swim.*

I spy a dark shape a few metres in front of me. The water is murky and the visibility is poor, but I swim towards it. It turns out to be a log. I can't hold my breath any longer; frantically, I kick upwards towards the light.

When I break through the surface, Luke is in the water too.

'Has she come up yet?' I gasp.

'No.' He dives back under. Taking a giant breath, I do the same. But I can't go very deep. Hope begins to slip away. Another tragedy in the making... This time, my making.

I glimpse something else – another shape, moving, flailing frantically. Using every last ounce of strength, I propel myself towards it. It's Phillipa, her eyes huge as her limbs twitch and then fall still. I try desperately to get beneath her and put my shoulder under her arm. I kick wildly, but even in the water she's heavy. The green blur above me gets brighter, and I kick harder. And then, together, we break through.

Luke comes back to the surface. I draw a breath and shout, but Phillipa's weight pulls me back under. In a flurry of arms and splashing, he swims over to me. We drag her head back up above the water; I will her to take a breath.

'Is she...' he says.

'I don't know.'

We haul her limp body to the side of the lake and onto the bank. I hear distant voices; I pray that it's the emergency services.

'Over here!' I yell. I try to remember what I learned in a long-ago first aid course, but my brain feels murky and slow. 'I think we're supposed to turn her on her side, is that right?'

'OK. Let's do it.'

Together, we do just that. A trickle of water comes out of her mouth, but there's no breath. Ignoring my own panic, I ease her down onto her back. 'We'll need to try CPR,' I say. 'Do you know how?'

'Pump her chest and breathe,' Luke says.

Kneeling beside her, he pumps her sternum with the palms of his hand. I take a deep breath and blow into her mouth.

'Come on, Phillipa!' I yell, gasping between breaths. 'Breathe!'

We switch places – I pump and he breathes. I pray frantically for some sign of life, but she's taken in a lot of water. We switch places again.

'Come on, Phillipa!' I repeat. I take her by the shoulders and shake her.

There's a gurgling sound in her chest; a stream of water comes out of her mouth. I take another deep breath and breathe into her mouth. I keep going, breathing in and out, until she starts to cough and sputter. She's alive!

'Hello!' a man's voice calls out.

'Over here!' I cry.

Three emergency service workers break through the thicket. I've never been so happy to see anyone in my life. They're carrying a stretcher, and I can hear more voices behind them.

One of the men comes forward to my side.

'She was in the lake,' I stammer. 'We pulled her out and tried to give her CPR. I just hope…'

He bends over her, feeling her neck for a pulse. 'We'll take over from here,' he says.

'There's another man too.' Luke points to the dovecote. 'The floor collapsed under him. I think his leg might be broken.'

'We'll go have a look,' one of the other paramedics says.

All of a sudden, the world seems to dip and sway. I'm clawing through the water, desperately trying to reach the light, with a great weight dragging me down…

'I think I'm going to be sick,' I say, gasping. The ground comes up hard beneath me.

60

I wake up in an ambulance, lying on a stretcher with a blanket over me. When I open my eyes, my vision is blurry and unfocused and once again I feel like I'm fighting my way to the surface of the green water, trying to reach the light. But then someone squeezes my hand. I force myself back upwards. Luke... Safety.

'What happened?' I say breathlessly.

'You blacked out,' he says. 'You're suffering from shock. But it's going to be OK, I promise.' He relaxes his hand, and when I study his face, the years have melted away. I can picture the boy he must have been – shy, vulnerable, full of ambition and hope.

'And the others?'

'A bit worse for wear. Theo's leg is broken. And Phillipa...'

'She was breathing – she'll be OK, right?'

'She was under the water for a long time. But she is breathing on her own. Whether or not she'll be OK, I don't know.'

We lapse into silence as the ambulance speeds along. I replay the events in my head like a film on fast forward. *The Lady's Secret*... Phillipa. Julie...

'I didn't know the truth, Lizzie,' Luke says. 'I didn't know Phillipa went onto that balcony with Julie. I heard the splash, but I didn't go back, and I believed Phillipa's account that Julie had dived in for a swim. I was in shock after it happened. I couldn't believe that Julie was gone.' He gives a bitter laugh. 'And what a vain prick I was to think that Julie was jealous of Pippa for getting together with me that night. When all along, she was jealous of me.' He shakes his head. 'God, I feel sorry for Julie – and for Pippa. When, back then, I only felt sorry for myself.'

'You were all so young,' I say solemnly. 'What happened was a tragedy. I'm not sure if knowing the truth will help put things in perspective, but maybe it will put your mind at rest. You aren't responsible for Julie's death.'

'No, I suppose not. But at the inquest, I gave them Pippa's version of the story. That was wrong.'

'Maybe so.' I recall the argument I overheard between Luke and Phillipa: *I did it for you.* 'But it's all in the past now.'

'Except for the film,' Luke says. 'It all makes sense. Pippa wanted me to see the parallels – I was the only one who could untangle what she'd written. But I didn't. I must be the worst director in the world.'

'You saw what was on the page. It was all done so cleverly. I never would have guessed any of it if I hadn't found Julie's diary.'

'But I was the one who lived through it. It's my story too.' He shakes his head. 'I knew Pippa and Julie were close. And I knew Julie could get very jealous. I remember the ripped-up photograph and the daisy ring from that time. All those things are in the film. But I didn't see the connection.'

'It's different when you're on the inside looking out,' I say. 'Theo once told me that Phillipa had "many inspirations". The story of the smuggler and his wife, Veronica Jones, for one. She added a lot of red herrings – such as the main love story. That's the part that most people focus on, and it's the most fictional part.'

'I'm glad I've got you.' He grins. 'You see beyond words on a page or scenes in a film. You found the story behind the story. Something I used to be good at, but I've got rusty. I need someone like you who can get my head out of – well, you know.'

I laugh. 'I hope that's not the only reason you're glad.'

***

The ambulance arrives at the hospital; I resign myself to being rolled in through the fluorescent-lit hallways. I feel dizzy and anxious, and pray that I'll be discharged and home before Jack and Katie are back from the seaside. More than anything, I just want to hold them in my arms.

A nurse comes to escort Luke to X-ray and to get his cuts and bruises bandaged up. He kisses me, and then goes off. Without him there, I can sense the panic swirling in my chest like an underground cataract.

'Put her here,' a voice says. I turn my head as another stretcher is wheeled into the bay next to me. The person is covered in a blanket and there are tubes and wires everywhere. The nurse sees me looking and draws the curtain between the two bays.

'Name?' The nurse gestures at the new patient.

'Phillipa King,' the paramedic says.

'Phillipa King the author?' The woman sounds excited to have such an illustrious patient.

The paramedic shrugs. 'No idea – never heard of her.'

'Well, I'm a big fan,' the nurse says. 'I hope she'll be OK.'

***

I lie there for what seems like hours. No one comes to so much as take my blood pressure, but an army of nurses and attendants bustle in and out of Phillipa's bay. From the snippets of conversation I overhear, apparently, several of them are 'big fans'.

'They're making a film of her book, *The Lady's Secret*,' one of them says. 'In fact, she got hurt on location.'

'Really?' another replies.

I purse my lips, hoping Tanglewild doesn't become 'that place where Phillipa King got hurt'. I feel like pulling the curtain back and setting them straight. Tell them that in fact, Phillipa King is responsible for putting three other people in hospital – and that's just today's tally. But instead, I lay still, fighting my own dizziness and the vision of dark green water that I can still see when I close my eyes.

Phillipa coughs a lot, and I gather she's been given a sedative to make her sleep. Eventually, however, I hear her voice: 'Take this tube out of my nose – I'm fine.'

There's a flurry as several nurses hovering near her bay all respond at once.

'Now, my dear, you have to keep it in,' one of them says. 'We want to take good care of you.'

She coughs so violently that I want to cover my ears. But when she finally stops, the next thing she says surprises me.

'Is Lizzie Greene here?'

'Yes!' the nurse says. Without so much as a by-your-leave, the curtain between the bays is pulled back in a screech of metal hangers. So much for patient confidentiality. 'In fact, she's right next to you.'

'Um, I don't think...' I start to say.

'We'll leave the two of you to chat.' Ignoring me, the nurse smiles at Phillipa. 'What an ordeal you must have suffered.'

The other two nurses follow her outside the door, still well within earshot. For a while, Phillipa is silent. I can hear the rhythmic sound of her breathing through the tube in her nose. It takes me back underwater again.

'Why did you do it?' she says finally, her voice throaty and hoarse.

'Do what?' I feel trapped by the close proximity.

'Why did you pull me out? It would be better if you... hadn't.' She takes a gulp of air, as if the effort of talking is too much. But she's not struggling to breathe. She's crying.

I pause, choosing my words. 'I pulled you out because it was the right thing to do.'

'Just like that? It was that easy?'

'Yes. That was the easy part. The hard part comes now – the part you'll have to do alone. Putting the past behind you, coming to terms with it, moving on. I don't envy you having to do it. It's not easy to make yourself swim up to the light.'

'I understand why he chose you.'

'Pardon?'

'Luke. You were both wounded – deeply and fundamentally – and yet both of you are strong underneath. I don't think I am, though.' She sighs. 'I'm just so tired.'

She's quiet for a minute. I force myself not to fill the silence with platitudes and words of comfort. There's no doubt in my mind that Phillipa's in for an uphill struggle. I've done what I can and saved her life – but it's her life.

'I told you the truth before,' she says. 'I did love Julie – she was my best friend. It was wrong of me to let her think it could have been more than that. But at the time, I was just so grateful for her helping me. For loving me.' She shakes her head. 'After she died, I had a miscarriage. Then I tried to kill myself – it was a terrible time.'

'Sounds like it.'

'About a year after it happened, Luke wrote to me. I guess you could say that he saved my life. We never had a romantic attachment and I didn't see him again for years. But I never stopped hoping...' She smiles faintly. 'Anyway, I just wanted you to know that that's the kind of man he is. He's loyal, and good – not what I tried to make you think before.'

'Thank you,' I say. 'I appreciate your honesty.'

Another coughing fit overtakes her. When the spasm subsides, she speaks again, lowering her voice to a whisper. 'Are you going to tell the police about what I did? To Julie – and to you? I won't blame you if you do, Lizzie. At this point, I deserve what I get.'

I sink into the pillow, staring up at the florescent ceiling panels. I don't know how I'm going to answer her, but somehow, the words come out.

'Julie died,' I say. 'And nothing is going to bring her back. She loved you and hurt you and you loved and hurt her. Then you kept it secret for all those years. You had your successes and your failures. You had a future – something she was never able to have because you took that away. But you suffered too. The guilt rotted inside you until you had to get it out. And in a very subtle way, you confessed to millions without them knowing it.'

'But you know the truth. You were the only one who figured it out.'

'I'm no judge and jury, Phillipa. I don't know if you've suffered enough, or got away with too much. All I know is that I want to get on with my life.

I want to enjoy the happiness I've found – a happy beginning, not an ending. I suggest you do the same.'

I'm expecting her to laugh in my face, but instead, she turns to me and nods.

'I've treated Theo abominably,' she says. 'I was angry at you and Luke, and myself. I wanted to hurt him too. That seems to be the story of my life – making people love me and then hurting them.'

'Then rewrite it,' I say. 'Time and time again until you get it right. I think Theo will stick by you no matter what. He's a good person – and he's smitten with you. He won't be frightened by what's lurking in the dark corners. But you have to tell him the whole truth. Don't let what you could have be stained by secrets.'

'I didn't think there was any hope before. But now... maybe.'

'"Maybe" is better than "no",' I say. '"Maybe" is a door to a whole new world. And you know what they say: "The second time is twice as nice." Though in your place, you might need to change "second" to "third".'

This time, her laugh sounds almost normal. When I look at her, I catch a glimpse of the woman who came into my kitchen and charmed every person in the room. The woman who can make people love her, sell millions of books, and give her readers the special magic that they're unlikely to find in real life.

'Thanks,' she says. 'Now that it looks like I'm still alive, I'll give that some thought.'

'You do that,' I say.

* * *

A while later, I get out of bed and call for the nurse, determined to be discharged so I can go home. Following our conversation and another coughing fit, Phillipa was given more medication and is now asleep. While I'm waiting, the curtain draws back and Luke comes into the bay. His right arm is in a sling and he's got a plaster over his forehead. Wincing a little, he kneels down in front of me. I wrap my arms around his neck and give him a long kiss on the mouth.

'How are you feeling?' he says when we finally separate.

'Fine. But if I don't get out of here soon, I can't be held responsible for my actions.'

'I understand.' He smiles. 'Let's go.'

I get to my feet unsteadily. When I've gathered my things, I move the curtain that separates my bay from Phillipa's to check she's breathing.

'Is she going to be OK?' Luke says.

'I think that's up to her, don't you?'

'You're right. And despite all that's happened, I really do wish her well.'

'Me too.' I pull the curtain back.

'Come on then,' he says. 'We've spent enough time here. Connie texted me that the kids will be home soon. I may look a bit of a wreck, but I think a round of football is just the ticket.'

I laugh. 'And when you're done with that, maybe you can help Katie with her piano. She might actually listen if you're the one giving her performance tips.'

'OK,' he says, 'it's a deal. And actually, I've been thinking. In the original screenplay, Phillipa had a dream sequence that was a flashback to Victoria's childhood. Picking flowers in a field, running up to hug her mother. All hard daylight and soft focus. It got cut – but maybe we ought to reinstate it.'

'So...?'

'I'll need to find an actress. Nine, ten years old. Got any idea where I can find one at short notice?'

'Might do.' I picture the happiness, the delight, on Katie's face. A whole new chapter in all our lives is beginning.

'Great.' He takes my hand, gripping it tightly. He's right – there's no time to lose. More than anything in the whole world, I'm looking forward to spending an ordinary Sunday afternoon with my beloved children and this most extraordinary man.

And that's just what I do.

PART VII

If we shadows have offended,
Think but this, and all is mended,
That you have but slumbered here,
While these visions did appear.
And this weak and idle theme,
No more yielding but a dream...

— WILLIAM SHAKESPEARE, *A MIDSUMMER NIGHT'S DREAM*

PART VII

> If we shadows have offended,
> Think but this, and all is mended,
> That you have but slumbered here,
> While these visions did appear.
> And this weak and idle theme,
> No more yielding but a dream...
>
> —WILLIAM SHAKESPEARE, *A MIDSUMMER NIGHT'S DREAM*

61

THE LADY'S SECRET BY PHILLIPA KING

As she stood at the back of the church, Victoria said a prayer for the dead. In her mind's eye, she saw the broken body of a woman lying on the paving stones, still clutching the knife in her cold, dead hand. She saw the twisted body of Tom – the man she had loved a lifetime ago – dead after a fall from his horse just outside the gates of Idyllwild Hall. She thought of poor, misguided Charity, trapped by an unwanted marriage and killed by her own sister.

And then, she put all of them from her mind forever.

For, in front of her, she saw him – tall and strong, dressed in a black velvet coat and tall black boots. His dark hair pulled back from his face, and the clean white ruffles of his shirt billowing at his throat. He quite literally took her breath away.

The music started to play. Before she began the walk up the aisle, she gave silent thanks. That she had had the courage to tell him the truth, and he had put aside his pride and accepted her love despite the stain upon her. That, at last, there were no secrets between them.

Her steps were light and brisk as she walked over the scattered rose petals. His eyes never left her – intense and wanting. She reached the altar, and before the priest could even begin to speak, he pulled her close and kissed her until she was breathless. And when the words were finally spoken and the ring was placed on her finger, he took her by the hand and kissed her again.

62

JUNE

On a glorious afternoon at the beginning of summer, Connie and I stand on the lawn in front of the house watching the crew strike the marquee on the front lawn.

'You OK, kid?' she asks me with a sharpish elbow to the arm.

'I don't know.' I want to tell her how I feel, but the words stick in my throat. I think about the person I was before I got the letter in my post box about the film. Angry, directionless, wallowing in self-pity. How this project was a risk I needed to take – to either kick-start my life or go down in flames. 'I just feel a little sad, that's all.'

'I get it,' she says. 'We were part of something, weren't we? In a small way.'

'Yeah. Though most of the time I felt like I was in the way – tiptoeing round my own house to avoid making noise or breaking some expensive piece of kit.'

The last month has been one of the best, and most stressful, of my life. The film crew worked round the clock to get back on schedule, and even Richard and his bosses were satisfied. For me, the high point was the sunny day in late-May when the bluebells were out in the orchard and the light was right to film scene 547(A) – 'young Victoria runs to her mother'.

I felt like I'd swallowed an entire family of butterflies as I tripped out to the field with Connie, Simon, Jack, Hannah, and two of the mums from school who came to watch the filming. I'd seen the cameras, the cables, the giant lighting umbrellas and sunshades, and the host of people in attendance – costumers, make-up artists, hair stylists, camera and sound people, assistants, and assistants of assistants many times during the filming of various scenes, but this was so much different.

Katie came out of the garden, walking slowly next to Luke, who was leaning down, talking to her in a low voice, gesturing with his hands.

The woman playing Victoria's mother, a friendly-faced woman called Joyce, patted me on the arm. 'She'll be brilliant, mark my words.'

'Thanks.' I felt like I might be sick.

Katie gave me a shy smile as she walked past. She was wearing a rose-pink muslin dress with a white apron and a lace cap on her head. Her hair was done in a long, dishevelled plait down her back. She looked beautiful and otherworldly, and I felt like I might burst with pride and nerves. Connie nudged me in the ribs. As soon as Katie walked by, I took the flask and put it to my lips.

Luke and Joyce walked her through the scene four times, and she practised saying her line, 'Oh, Mother, do I have to come in now?' at least seven more times.

The camera and lighting people made her pause at various points to make adjustments to the giant sunshades and reflectors. Jack got a bit overexcited at the whole thing and wet himself, and Simon took him back to the house. Connie filmed the whole thing on her phone so he didn't miss out.

Finally, the cameras were ready to roll. The assistant director clacked the clapperboard and the shoot began. It was only when it was over and everyone started to clap that I realised how hard I was gripping Connie's hand. I let go to wipe away a tear, and blew Katie a kiss.

Afterwards, some of the crew members came up and got Katie to sign their autograph books. I knew they were just being nice, but she was so happy and proud, and I was glad she had her moment. (OK, I was also a little scared that after this, she might really decide to pursue this acting thing – but I'll leave that for another day.)

Now, though, as we stand in the garden watching the marquee come down and the men loading the vans with props and equipment, my tears rise close to the surface again.

Connie puts her hand on my arm and gives it a painful squeeze. 'You were right all along, Lizzie. The film was just the thing you needed – what we all needed.'

'Thanks,' I say. 'But I couldn't have got through it without you and Simon. I know I don't say it enough, but I appreciate your being here.'

'Oh, none of that now.' She gives me a judgemental smile, and I can tell she's chuffed to be acknowledged. I make a mental note to do it more often now that things are coming to an end.

An end...

My vision blurs into a murky green haze, as it's done occasionally ever since the day I dragged Phillipa up from the depths of the lake. I blink hard and the memory goes back into hiding. Instead, I catch sight of Luke coming through the garden gate towards us.

'Hello, ladies,' he says. 'I'll bet you'll be glad to see the back of this lot.' He gestures towards the open door of the house and the trail of people carrying out furniture and props like busy ants.

'I will be,' Connie says. 'But right now, I'm going to get another croissant before they disappear too. I'm going to miss those food tables.'

'Me too,' I say.

Luke laughs. 'Well, sorry about that.' He turns to Connie. 'But it might cheer you up to know that I got a response to my message. They want to set up a meeting.'

'Really?' For the first time ever, Connie seems almost at a loss for words.

'Yes. Next week, if possible. It's perfect for their Christmas list, apparently.'

'Oh God, I must tell Simon. Thank you!'

Before he can even react, she pulls Luke to her in an embrace and gives him a kiss on the cheek. He squirms like a kid trying to escape an over-affectionate maiden aunt. Letting him go abruptly, she rushes across the lawn, leaving us standing there.

'What was that about?' I say.

'Connie's project.' He wipes his cheek. 'I think it's OK to tell you now that there's been good news – she was too embarrassed before. Swore me to secrecy.'

'Embarrassed? Connie?' I raise an eyebrow. 'Is this something to do with the book she's been writing? And your "exchange of favours"?'

'What? You know about the book?' He looks at me in surprise. 'She said you didn't have a clue – her words.'

'No, but I suspected it was something like that. All those hours holed up in that caravan. And once I caught a glimpse of her screen.'

'Right. Well, she told me about it a month or so ago. I was sceptical, of course. But since she's been so instrumental in helping me out, I wanted to thank her. I gave her the name of an e-book publisher friend, on a no-guarantees basis. My friend read it and loved it. You could have a budding author on your hands.'

'Great... I think. I'm happy to support her. And I'll need something – a new project, now that this is over.' I quickly wipe away a stray tear, but he's already noticed.

'Lizzie? Are you OK?'

'I just feel a little sad, that's all. Don't you ever feel that way when you finish a film, Luke?'

He lifts his hand and traces the line of the tear on my cheek, his eyes deep and thoughtful.

'I'm not sure sad is the right word. Every project is special in some way. Each cast and crew feels like a family. And there are little stories to tell, little things to laugh about and remember afterwards. This project, though...' He shakes his head.

'You're lucky you survived it.'

'Something like that.' He strokes my hair. 'Besides,' he adds, 'it's not over for me – not by a long way. I'll be involved in the post-production work; then there's the publicity, the premieres – the interviews and the travel.' I can feel him tense up as he speaks. 'I know I should be grateful. I mean, most people would look at me and think I have the best job in the world.'

'That's true.' His words give me zero comfort.

'But once the creative bit is over, I find the rest of it quite tedious. Does that sound awful?'

'A little.'

Smiling, he puts his arms around my waist. 'And normally at the end of a project, I don't have anything to look forward to. Just returning to my empty little flat in Primrose Hill.'

'Maybe you should get a cat,' I joke.

He manoeuvres me into the hedge just out of sight of the others. Sparks shoot down my spine like fireworks as he presses his body against mine. 'That's not quite what I had in mind.'

His kiss overwhelms me, filling me up until I'm overflowing. And there's no room for the past, no room for the future, no room for anything beyond this moment – no room for anything but him.

63

SEPTEMBER

The grand opening of *Tanglewild Inn and B&B* takes place on a sunny day with a trace of autumn nip in the air. The gardens are blooming with monkshood, chrysanthemums, goldenrod, and Michaelmas daisies, and the trees across the lake are starting to turn. The yellows, oranges, ochres and greens are perfectly reflected in the dark emerald waters of the lake, like a bright patchwork quilt. A little rowboat bobs up and down at the dock – it's one of the actual boats used for the smugglers in the film, and John C let me keep it as a souvenir.

I host a small champagne reception on the back terrace for the first guests – a couple from Yorkshire on their fortieth anniversary, and a couple from Somerset who are staying in the area while their daughter settles in at uni. There are grapes on the vine growing down from the back chimney, and Connie has baked fresh scones and teacakes. She and Simon are no longer living in my drive, but have rented a cottage nearby. It's a temporary arrangement while Simon converts the dovecote into a little flat for them to live in when they aren't travelling the world (which they're keen to set off and do again). For now, though, Connie's helping me out with the B&B, cooking the breakfasts and helping entertain the guests. She's also busy going through the editing process on her book.

For today's event, I even tried my hand at baking a cake – chocolate sponge with buttercream icing and raspberry jam between the layers. It looks good, and I'm crossing my fingers that I won't send anyone off with a belly ache.

Luke is there, and Connie and Simon. A few people come from the film crew – John J, John C, and a few of the assistant something-or-others I'd become friendly with during the shoot. I've also invited Hannah, Parker, Mary, and most of the other mums from school. My mum is also flying over – she'll arrive tomorrow. Finally, I called and told her everything – took the first step to bridge the gap. Now that I've got so much closer to Connie and Simon, I realise how important it is to connect with all the people I love, even when, sometimes, it doesn't come easily. But as far as guests go, I'm especially delighted when someone who didn't respond to the invite turns up – Dominic Kennedy.

'I didn't think you were coming,' I say as he bows down and kisses my hand with a flourish. 'As there are no bright young things to deflower now.'

'Oh – and what about them?' He gives Mary and Parker a bedroom pout that makes them practically collapse in giggles.

'Keep your hands off the mums, Dom.' Luke comes up and pats Dominic on the back, smiling like a schoolboy.

'I'll leave that to you, old chap,' Dominic says. 'And in fact, I think you'll find my chaperone has just arrived.'

A tall, drop-dead handsome Asian man comes into the garden. 'Meet Raj, my new agent,' Dominic says.

Luke smiles wryly as introductions are made.

'Lovely place,' Raj says. He picks a grape off the vine and eats it.

'Wait until I show you the main bedroom,' Dom says, leading him off.

'Hey, I think you'll find that's now private,' Luke calls after them.

Dominic beams us his dazzling smile. 'Raj just wants a quick peek in – a bit of "professional curiosity" – I'm sure you understand.'

'I understand.' I laugh, turning to Luke. 'This is what I get for opening up my house to film people.'

One of the guests, a Mrs Charles, of the anniversary couple, comes over with her glass of champagne. 'The filming sounds very exciting,' she says. 'And we've heard all about the tunnel and the treasure. Just imagine!'

'I know,' I say. 'It was very bizarre to think that all this time I've been doing laundry above a hoard of priceless artefacts.' And the skeleton of a 200-year-old woman, I don't add.

Luke takes my arm. 'It was a bit stressful at the time, for all of us – especially Lizzie.'

'Yes,' I say, 'but it just goes to show how we're only passing through. The house was here long before we were, and I hope it will be here long after. Tanglewild has given up some of its secrets, but it's seen a lot more than we will ever know.'

'Well, I wish you many years of happiness here together,' Mrs Charles says. She turns to Luke. 'You remind me a bit of my Henry – back when he still had hair.'

Luke laughs awkwardly. 'Actually, I'm not here all the time. I... uh... still have a flat in London.'

'Whatever for?' Mrs Charles looks horrified. 'I'm sorry, I hope I haven't spoken out of turn.'

'Not at all,' Luke says. 'And in fact, I've offered to "make things official", but Lizzie won't have me.'

'That's not quite true,' I say, a little flushed. 'It's just that I needed to do this on my own. Get the B&B up and running, find my feet after the film crew left.'

'I understand,' Mrs Charles says. 'But take it from me, when you find love, it's better not to waste a single day.'

'I agree, and—'

'Dad! Can we play football?' Jack runs into the garden sleepy-eyed from his nap, with Jammie following at his heels. Katie comes after them, looking bored. She's being paid to babysit her brother – basically keep him occupied and out of trouble – but I know she'd rather be out here with the adults. So far, she's managed to keep her school work on track despite the weekend acting classes that she's now taking.

'He's not your dad, silly,' she says. 'When he and mum get married he'll be your stepdad.'

Jack ignores her. 'Can we play football?' He tugs on Luke's trouser leg.

'Maybe later.' I bend down to scoop him up, but he clings to Luke. I smile, happy that the pair of them are so content together.

'Well now,' Mr Charles says. 'I wouldn't mind a bit of a kick-about.' He turns to the dad in the girl-at-uni couple. 'You fancy it?'

'Sure. It will be just like the good ol' days.'

'Is that OK, Lizzie?' Luke asks me.

'Fine. The ball's in the closet by the door.'

Luke, the two guests, Simon and Jack all go off into the front garden. Katie stays, and one of the waitresses hands her a champagne flute of orange juice. In only a few months, she seems so grown-up. Although she's very clear on the relationship Luke has to our lives, so far she's accepted it. In fact, I'd say she hero-worships him a bit – as long as no one's around to see it. She seems less stroppy, and sometimes she even comes to me for a hug, the way she used to. Small steps, but she's young, and resilient. And I've learned that loving someone is not so much about the destination as the journey.

'Looks like the decision's been taken out of your hands,' Mrs Charles says.

'So it would seem.' I smile.

The other guest, Mrs Anderson, comes up to join us. 'I read that Phillipa King was here during the filming,' she says. 'I just adore her books. It must have been exciting to meet her.'

'That's one word for it.' I gesture to a hovering waitress to refill our champagne. 'She's a very, umm... interesting person.'

I glance out at the lake and for a second, my eyes swim with murky darkness. I haven't heard from Phillipa since the conversation we had in hospital, nor am I expecting to. She never returned to set, and the screenplay was finished by others. I know that Luke spoke to her, and while I don't know what was said, he told me that she won't be contacting us, nor will she be a part of our lives.

In a way, I feel sad about that. I did like her (at least in the beginning) and respected her efforts to vanquish the darkness lurking inside her. And while some nights I've lain awake and wondered if, for Julie's sake, I should have contacted the police, I've come to terms with my decision to keep 'the lady's secret'. I told Phillipa that I was no judge; no jury. And yet, I suppose that by deciding that her guilt is punishment enough, I've become exactly that.

'I read that she moved to America,' Hannah says. 'She's bought a house somewhere in the south – Georgia or New Orleans – and is going to turn her hand at writing an American Gothic series. Civil War belles, dashing Confederate captains – that sort of thing.'

'Really?' This is news to me. A month or so after the film crew left, Theo contacted me to close out the contract. His leg was healing well, and now that I think about it, his phone number did have an American prefix. I hope for both their sakes that he and Phillipa are still together creating a 'happy beginning' to something lasting and fulfilling.

'Well, I can't wait until her next book comes out,' Mrs Anderson says. 'And the film of *The Lady's Secret*.'

'It won't be long now,' I say, smiling. 'And if you're interested, we've actually got a new budding author here at Tanglewild.' I wave my hand in Connie's direction. 'My ex-mother-in-law has just sold her first novel to a publisher. It's a romantic thriller about a woman in a police squad who becomes entangled with an Irish gypsy. Totally fictional, of course. And frankly, it's a bit racy for my tastes.'

'Is it?' Mrs Charles winks at me. 'I'll definitely have to check it out. It's all such fun!'

'Yes,' I say. We raise our glasses and clink them together. 'Such fun.'

EPILOGUE
LONDON – SIX MONTHS LATER

The world explodes in a blaze of flashing lights. As I step out of the car, I pray that my very high-heeled sandal doesn't snag my very long dress – silver lace covered with pewter sequins. This afternoon at the hairdressers, I sat there flipping through fashion magazines full of glamorous celebrities looking chic and confident on innumerable red carpets. How many of them, I wonder, were secretly terrified of a costume malfunction in front of all those cameras?

Luke takes my hand and positions me next to him for a photo. Standing beside him, I'm able to breathe again. I resist the urge to tug at the plunging cowl neckline of my dress or worry about the fact that Luke looks more like a film star than the director – whereas I look like a suburban mum in Jimmy Choo's and a couture gown by a fashion graduate student at Chelsea. 'You look incredible,' he whispers as the photographer snaps away.

'I'm incredibly nervous,' I whisper back, wishing I could bury my face in the crook of his neck. Or better yet, go to that special little restaurant in London that we've still never managed to get to, where Luke knows the owner and no one ever recognises him. A bottle of wine, a candle-lit table at the back...

'You're Lizzie Greene, is that right?'

I turn to face a gangly reporter holding a fuzzy microphone. Her teeth are so white that they almost hurt my eyes. I grip Luke's hand. Photographs I've psyched myself up for. But an interview...?

'Yes, that's right.' I do my best to smile without grimacing.

'So how does it feel to be engaged to a famous director?'

'Well, I mean... it feels' – I hesitate, knowing that I'm on the cusp of blathering like an idiot – 'like a dream I didn't know I had.'

The woman nods, seeming satisfied with my response. She turns to Luke and asks him a string of questions. I twist the ring on my finger. A gold band with a small, dark-green emerald set with seed pearls. I finally gave in and said 'yes' in part due to Katie's demands to be a bridesmaid, and in part because I revealed to Luke my own secret – our secret – one that I won't be able to keep for much longer. I lay an unconscious hand on my stomach, taking comfort in the life that's inside, and the look of amazement and joy on Luke's face when I told him. The main reason, though, that I said 'yes' to Luke is because I'm completely and utterly in love with him.

I lose myself in the lights and the noise of the crowd standing behind barriers waiting to get into the theatre. I feel like I'm swimming out of my depths once again, but this time, I burst through the surface of the water and begin to fly. I'm happy. Scared, but happy. That's how things are with me and Luke. He challenges me – leads me out of my comfort zone. But I'm a better person for it. And I like to think he's a better person with me at his side, an anchor to the real world. A testament to the fact that while the past may shape us, it's the future that defines us.

'And how was it having a film crew in your home? I'll bet it must have been quite the disruption.'

I startle as the huge fuzzy microphone is once again waved under my nose.

'Other than the buried treasure, the skeleton, and coming to terms with a tragedy, it was fine.' I smile. 'Just fine.'

The woman looks bewildered. 'Does all that happen in the film?'

'No,' I say. 'But sometimes, truth is stranger than fiction.'

We continue our way down the red carpet. It's such a bizarre experience that I decide that just this once, I'm going to enjoy it. A few more reporters come up for a sound bite or a quote from Luke, but luckily by then, they've got bigger fish to fry. Natasha Blythe is beautiful and sexy in a backless cherry-red silk gown with a thigh-high slit, and she and her up-and-coming actor boyfriend naturally soak up most of the attention. Dominic Kennedy does himself all manner of favours by arriving in a designer Italian suit with the shirt half unbuttoned, and, more importantly, no date (of either sex) to interfere with the fantasies of his fans.

When he catches up to us, he greets me with a well-placed hand on my bottom and double air kisses. 'Elizabeth, darling... what an exciting night.'

'It is,' I say. 'But where's Raj? Or is there now a Raja?'

He waves his hand expansively. 'I've saved him a seat, but right now he's getting me a bottle of Scotch and some Gaviscon. I usually spend these premieres camped out in the loo. I get damned nervous.' He shakes his head. 'Ridiculous, I know. But seeing myself up on that screen... it makes me feel like a right twat.'

I laugh. 'I might join you. Seeing my house up on the screen, and certain goings-on in my own bed, I might feel rather the same way.'

'I'll save you a nip from the bottle, Lizzie, never fear.'

He gives me another kiss on the cheek, then turns to go off. His well-polished heel snags the hem of my dress, and there's an almighty ripping sound. My legs suddenly feel well and truly ventilated.

I grab Luke's arm. 'Come on, let's go inside. It will be dark, right?'

He looks down at my ripped dress. 'I agree. Let's get inside. Because the way you look, I might just have to find a dark little corner somewhere to finish what Dom has started.'

'Look, mister,' I say, 'some of us are actually here to watch the film.'

'Seen it.' He grabs my hand and leads me inside the theatre. 'And yeah – it's OK.'

* * *

The lights go out and the theatre is black. Gradually, the screen morphs into an oozing greenish brown colour, grainy like leather. The green comes into focus as a music box begins to play. Trees, a lake. The weave of a wicker basket. A hand touching a daisy woven into auburn hair. The bark of a tree splitting apart under a knife as something is carved into the trunk... Initials, a heart.

The Lady's Secret...

As the images unfold on the screen – some beautiful, some heartbreaking, some downright soppy, I feel for a woman who should be here now but tonight is thousands of miles away. I feel for a character – a little stupid and naïve maybe – who is betrayed by her first love. I feel for an actress that needed hundreds of takes to finally get it right, but has somehow managed to find within herself the one perfect moment to be captured on screen, time and time again.

And as the film continues, I feel for a man, wild and ruined, and for the secret he carries with him, eating away at his dignity and humanity. And I feel for the love they both find, unlikely and unexpected.

Most of all, I feel a deep stab of love for the man next to me who created this, and for the family that he's become part of as if he always belonged there.

I watch the film, laughing, crying, and wanting to shout in outrage; cheering as the characters on the screen navigate their way to a happy ending. I fight the urge to close my eyes when the image comes on screen of a field of bluebells, soft and blurred in the summer sun, and a little girl rising up to hug her 'mother'. But she's perfect and I nearly erupt with pride.

And as Luke's hand grips mine, I know he needs me because he's nervous too, and I feel overwhelmed by the joy, and the sorrows, the loss and the incredible treasures that I've found inside myself and with another person.

As the credits begin to roll and the crowd stands up applauding and cheering, I stay in my seat unable to move. Unable to do anything but stare at the words on the screen that seem to hang there, suspended in time and place.

This film is dedicated to Julie – the past. And to Lizzie – my future.

A LETTER FROM LAUREN

Thank you for reading *The House of Love and Dreams*. If you enjoyed this book, please can I ask you to leave a review. It really helps other readers find my books and might help someone discover their perfect next read. If you want to keep up to date on my new releases, or are interested in becoming a beta reader for my books, please sign up at the following link. Your email address will never be shared and you can unsubscribe at any time.

https://www.laurenwestwoodwriter.com

This book was a lot of fun for me to write, as it was based in part on a real-life event when a film crew came to my house to do a photo shoot for an American version of *Howard's End*. For a whole week we lived the excitement and chaos of Hollywood movie magic. (Though, alas, all depictions of on-set romance, as well as the characters and events in my book, are strictly fictional.)

A big thank you to Francesca Best and the team at Boldwood Books for giving this book a second chance to find a new readership. Thanks also to Kiya Evans, Ronan Winters, and Alison Smith. I'd also like to thank my family for their love and support, with a special thanks to my mom for her support over the years and also my partner, Ian. I'd also like to thank my daughters for being my true inspiration in life.

Most of all, I'd like to thank my readers. Being a successful author is my dream, and it's thanks to you that I'm able to realise it.

Best wishes,

L—

Surrey, 2024

ABOUT THE AUTHOR

Lauren Westwood writes about old houses and quirky historical mysteries. She is also an award-winning children's author (Laurel Remington), a mother of three, and works as a lawyer in renewable energy. Lauren is originally from California, and now lives in the UK, in an old house built in 1604.

Sign up to Lauren Westwood's mailing list for news, competitions and updates on future books.

Visit Lauren's website: www.laurenwestwoodwriter.com

Follow Lauren on social media here:

- facebook.com/Lwestwoodbooks
- instagram.com/lwestwoodwriter
- goodreads.com/laurenwestwood

ALSO BY LAUREN WESTWOOD

Secrets and Love Series

The House of Second Chances

The House of Hidden Secrets

The House of Love and Dreams

Letters from
the past

Discover page-turning historical novels from your favourite authors and be transported back in time

Join our book club Facebook group

https://bit.ly/SixpenceGroup

Sign up to our newsletter

https://bit.ly/LettersFromPastNews

Boldwood

Boldwood Books is an award-winning fiction publishing company seeking out the best stories from around the world.

Find out more at www.boldwoodbooks.com

Join our reader community for brilliant books, competitions and offers!

Follow us
@BoldwoodBooks
@TheBoldBookClub

Sign up to our weekly deals newsletter

https://bit.ly/BoldwoodBNewsletter